DEMONIC AWAKENING

DEVIL HUNTER ISAWA

Volume 1

DEMONIC AWAKENING

K.P. Merriweather

MAJESTIK MULTIMEDIA • ST. LOUIS

Demonic Awakening (Volume 1)
Devil Hunter Isawa Chronicles: Book 1
Published by Majestik Multimedia
A subsidiary of Create Space Independent Publishing Platform
Copyright © 2005 Kimberly Merriweather

First Edition

This book is set in Georgia Type Text with some portions set in Georgia Ref, Gentium Book Basic, Gentium Basic, Book Antiqua, Calisto MT and Palatino Linotype.

Printed in the United States of America
First Edition: November 2014
First Printing: November 2014

ISBN-13: 978-0692326510

ISBN-10: 0692326510

For more awesomeness, visit *Majestik Multimedia*!

www.majestikmultimedia.com

PART ONE

THE JOURNEY

ONE

Chaka Isawa awakened in a medical tent, with a bandaged chest and arm. Feeling his long sandy hair gracing his shoulders, he glanced over and saw his brown-laced breastplate and helmet with bandana lay beside him near the cot and his two trusted blades, an ivory-handled golden tachi named Kagesureiyo and his slender blue-steeled blade, an uchigatana named Hitokiri leaned against the armor.

Chaka tried to speak, but could only form voiceless words. Outside the encampment, he heard the roar of battle in the distance, of swords clashing and of horses thundering across the plains. The moderately humid air was thick with the scent of death and Chaka felt ill at ease when he sensed something *else*, an alien otherness that made his skin hairs stand on end.

He wondered if his side was winning the battle against the invaders, a group of devils formerly in control of the Hakukishinoheiya area. His brigade, in charge of holding them back while Clan Champions closed the gate, had many losses yet continued pushing forward, clearing the fields of the demonic threat. Chaka passed on being Clan Champion, instead becoming an officer to fulfill his dreams of directing a unit.

In the era of the court nobles, mainly commoners set foot on a battlefield and just a handful ever survived. The House in which Chaka belonged produced only Champions trained in the art of destroying demons. Wanting nothing to do with such barbaric practice, Chaka disregarded his former duties and proved he could force unruly foot soldiers into proper fighting men capable of destroying any aggressor that set foot on the Emerald Island, Midorishima.

Originally groomed to become a Clan Champion for his House, Chaka learned the art of the sword and using *kamui* to defeat demons. This holy power was inherent to all people of Midorishima as the gods blessed them; however, those with exceptional skill honed these powers further and fought in the name of the Empress, keeping the devils that threatened the isle at bay.

During his strict training, Chaka kept his personal opinions to himself despite being told that he and others like him were ordained in keeping the delicate balance between the Material World and Oblivion. He was told in no uncertain terms that the honors of battle were few and far between, as demons made swift work of even the best skilled master sword fighters.

Chaka knew demons killed innocents and stole souls from the living - that he understood, yet he always wondered if demons simply committed such atrocities as a way to live. As far as he was concerned, the devils came from the Void, born of hatred from the hearts of men. Punishing the living was part of their mode of operation since the gods were not able to do so.

Chaka preferred fighting other swordsmen, taking any chance he could to improve his technique. He at times fought other armies in the trenches and sometimes faced the occasional harquebus or field cannon, yet fighting demons seemed never ending. He hoped at least the war would end one day, some day, though it was not any time soon. Watching his companions falling by the dozens, Chaka thought killing others would be small comfort instead of watching devils or disease take people he knew away.

Having no worries about revenge for taking the life of some innocent and having to deal with a vengeful family member starting a new recurrence of violence, he felt some solace that the enemy he faced was someone he did not know. Destroying devils wasn't quite the same as killing humans, but Chaka knew he had to keep fighting on through every battle while his sword arm was still working.

Working for the Imperial Army had better prospects than living in a farming or fishing village. It was either die of disease or hunger - and thousands of people did every cycle in Midorishima - or died trying to stop others from going across the river. The army had some benefit - two meals a day and never without action fighting some new enemy. Campaigns were frequent, as the various demonic gates that littered the islands were difficult to close and soldiers fought the remaining devils that weren't destroyed.

Imperial officers made frequent appearances in various townships, encouraging able-bodied men and women to join the fight and that going to war was the right thing to do, as a fighter's place in society was to die for the honor of the Empress. There was no real point in applying and there was no choice in wanting to go to war or not, since conscription was mandatory and escaping enlistment meant death when caught.

Convinced that his chance arrived when a gold-emblazoned banner stating an army mobilization order was posted in his village's magistrate's office, Chaka yearned to enter the fray and prove his mettle, wanting desperately to demonstrate he was a force to be reckoned with. He even looked forward to decapitating an enemy general, quickly rising in rank and command his own squadron.

Chaka hated the Imperial officers who found death amusing, watching others below them dying on their account. It hardly affected them, since they were descended from nobility and never really had to dirty their hands with death. They dictated battle from the rear lines safely in their tents, gaining notice of formations and the tide of battle from scouts who kept track of the current conflict. At times, the information came late and the generals made errors, which amounted to more needless loss of lives in the very domain they had sworn to protect.

At the same time, Chaka envied the Imperial officers, who were ignorant fools so rich that they could afford to throw money away by wasting on entertainment, fine wine and delicacies such as sushi that he never had access to. The Imperial officers learned useless arts from Imperial instructors, which such forms would never survive on the battlefield. Chaka swore to his protector god that if he rose in high enough grade, to grant him a place in the Imperial instructional schools, defeating the masters with his martial power honed by constant deadly combat against soul-hungry devils.

Twenty cycles ago, strong *mahoutsukai*, sorcerers skilled in controlling demons, successfully closed the gates. Yet demonic remnants still combed the lands, struggling to remove the seals and reopen the portals between realms.

Chaka secretly wished the land-plaguing devils would take down those useless officers and let the battle-hardened men and women who knew exactly what went on in the fields take control and put an end to the fighting. For over two-hundred and fifty cycles, the islands were constantly at war.

"Isawa," a voice called to Chaka, breaking him out of his thoughts.

Chaka immediately stepped out of his cot and stood at attention as an army captain with a cut over her eye and wearing dented crimson armor entered the tent. "Ho, *Bansho* Kurebayashi," he greeted.

Kurebayashi nodded and Chaka relaxed slightly. "You probably won't survive the next campaign," Kurebayashi said grimly. "*Taichou* Kazunao, Shimukita, and Narikore have fallen and we haven't received word yet of the fates of *Taishou* Uchitsune and Hisamasa."

"What of their units?"

"They've blown like leaves in the wind." Kurebayashi gestured with her chin toward the outdoors. "If I get injured tomorrow, you'll have to move on to the next battle. We barely have one brigade left and I need you to hold out until we gain more reinforcements."

Chaka nodded and Kurebayashi exited the tent. He then proceeded to pull into his breastplate and tie on his pair of swords. After placing on his bandana and tying on his helmet, Chaka exited the tent, catching sight of the battle below the steppes: a wave of soldiers and their tattered battle flags clashing against a horde of warriors in black and navy armor.

Charging forward from the front line in heavy soaked armor, Chaka sliced into approaching enemy soldiers who kept coming as a wave. Never once shrinking away, he focused his attention to his lightweight one-handed sword Hitokiri, hacking off limbs easily with each swift blow from the slender sharp blade. Above him, low dark clouds shifted ominously across the sky, throwing a torrent of blinding rain that drenched the plains of Chinokaigan.

Chaka's uchigatana clashed with another soldier's katana and he quickly deflected a fast succession of fatal strikes with the seasoned fighter before finally taking off the man's head. Surging forward, Chaka continued fighting and around him, soldiers fell by the dozens, their corpses littering the muddy ground beneath his feet. He felt as if he was the only one fighting and the other allied soldiers from the two regiments that merged with his unit was just dolls holding back the invasion.

The encounter's tide soon turned and battle flags from his allies were everywhere. Others in crimson armor, azure armor, and emerald armor cluttered the blood-soaked grasslands. The battle stretched on late into the night as the enemy kept coming with renewed strength, as if animated by a sinister force.

Chaka found his blade that at first made considerable damage now no longer cut into the flesh of his opponents. It merely passed through without spraying blood and soldiers in his unit reversed their positions, the offensive now turning for the defense.

The roar of shouting men and clashing swords were suddenly cut by the sharp sound of a blowing conch shell, signaling a rout. Chaka grew enraged at the sound of retreat, continuing his fight despite how numb his body became from the cold hard rains.

Withdrawing his secondary blade, his golden field sword Kagesureiyo cut easily into the revived soldiers and Chaka knew these men were no longer among the living. He had no qualms about sending them across the river to spend eternity in Hell contemplating on their mistake of coming across his path.

A flash of steel cut across Chaka's head, throwing off his helmet. He turned with a whirlwind slash, cutting down more enemy soldiers armed with thick heavy blades that easily busted iron and steel headgear with a strong enough blow.

Sharp pain slammed into Chaka's side and fiery agony ripped into his shoulder. A fierce strike rammed into the back of his head and Chaka fell forward on his face as his world darkened around him immediately.

Awakening some time later, Chaka found himself lying among the thousands of lifeless corpses that surrounded him.

The harsh frigid rains tapered into a heavy drizzle, pattering against the mud and slain bodies their dented armor contained as the wan skies slowly darkened once another evening approached. Chaka noticed one nearby corpse moving and he clenched his teeth, stunned.

"*Please let not that soldier be possessed,*" he prayed. "*I don't have enough <u>kamui</u> to defeat them...*"

Chaka struggled to turn over onto his side and his body refused to respond. When he tried raising his head, his world spun crazily from the minute movement. Lying back, Chaka blew a hard sigh, begrudgingly accepting the cloudy dementia that filled his numbed mind.

"Isawa," a voice barely groaned over the patter of rain. "Are you still here?"

"Yes, I am!" Chaka answered weakly. "Is that you, Kurebayashi?"

"You'd better not die out here, Isawa, or I'll haunt you for the rest of your days!"

"I don't plan to, *Bansho*!" Chaka heard the clatter of armor and strained to move his head. He spotted Kurebayashi crawling over with difficulty on her elbows, dragging her legs stiffly behind her. "Are you the only survivor?"

"It seems we're the only ones left here," Kurebayashi hissed. "Either the *kamisama* favor you or you're really lucky..."

"Don't speak so soon," Chaka muttered. "Obviously we weren't strong enough against the *akuma* that still haunt the area."

"We can still get rid of them! Get up and grab your *Amahagane* blades!"

Chaka blew a hard sigh. "I'll try, *Bansho*..."

Struggling to sit up, Chaka groaned and fell back, unable to stand. Kurebayashi grunted and withdrew her sword sheath, jamming it into the ground. Leaning against it, she got up on her knees, and then stood unsteadily to her feet. Lending Chaka a hand, Chaka took it, being pulled upright.

Suddenly the ground beneath them began to rumble and Chaka turned, stunned at the sight of lines of cobalt and sable-armored cavalry hurtling in their direction. Kurebayashi tensed and withdrew her sword, a large heavy oversized katana.

"Those bastards returned with devil horses!" the captain exclaimed. "We need to defend this gate, Isawa!"

"What happened to our reinforcements?" Chaka inquired as he quickly searched the ground nearby where he fell, finding nothing that resembled his blades. "*Taishou* Setsuna should've been here by now!" He snatched up a nearby katana and stood at ready beside Kurebayashi as the approaching whirlwind closed in on them.

"They seemed to have fallen by those hell spawn charging toward us." Kurebayashi turned to the horde. "Cover my back," she ordered. "We'll have to give everything we got!"

"Our souls even, *Bansho*?" Chaka cracked.

"With this *Zanbatou*, I'll handle the horses. You handle the soldiers."

"Then it's a good day to die!"

Kurebayashi grunted and glared ahead at the devilish equestrians and their corrupted steeds that soon drew around them, riding roughshod over the fallen soldiers in the fields. Letting out a battle cry, Kurebayashi attacked violently, hacking at the horses and riders alike that flew past them, arresting any attack from the soldiers.

With weapons clanging, Kurebayashi immediately dispatched all fighters who neared her, dodging the lethal muddy hooves that nearly trampled her. Chaka treated the devilish riders with fierce wild abandon, taking off heads and arms with swift strokes.

The devils kept coming, seemingly at the hundreds as the evening light dimmed and turned to night. Chaka found it increasingly harder to breathe and his sword arm hurt tremendously. He switched hands, only to have that side sear in pain as well.

After beheading another soldier, the head dropped near Chaka and its helmet crashed against him, slamming against the chest. Chaka staggered back and glanced down, realizing the helmet belonged to the former officer of his unit.

"*Bansho*, these are our men!" Chaka cried. "They've been turned into *akuma heishi*!"

Kurebayashi turned toward Chaka, only to get a soldier's spear piercing her through the back with its end protruding from her chest. Chaka watched in horror as the captain fell without a sound. Growing incensed, Chaka's energy flared, cackling around the sword he held as the spear fighter circled, coming after him.

"*Yaketsuku Yunahikari!*" Chaka screamed and slammed his blade into the coming lancer aiming at him. A blast of light charged through the soldier and the others that rushed onward to where he was. The demonic fighters immediately turned to ash, ending the onslaught.

Chaka jammed the katana he held into the mud and fell to bended knee, gasping hard for breath. Once the drizzling rains subsided, an eerie quiet surrounded him in the looming darkness.

Chaka looked around the battlefield, noticing the last of the rains washed away the ash and blood, revealing skeletal remains in busted armor. Glancing skyward, Chaka found the clouds breaking and only stars dotting the heavens.

"Lady Shidzuki won't shine my way this night," he mused. *"It'll be dangerous on the road tonight, with patrolling akuma looking for stragglers."*

Blowing a heavy sigh, Chaka rose shakily to his feet and slowly made his way across the drenched steppes, heading for the wooded hills in the distance.

TWO

For two days, Chaka walked in the woods, barely putting one foot ahead of the other and pressed onward with a single mission in mind – return to his station and report the battle results. He found it odd that he heard no scouts or any more soldiers in the area and wondered if the generals gave up, declaring a loss and moving on.

"Maybe the *mahoutsukai* finally closed that gate," Chaka muttered to himself. "They probably think I've died out there as well!" Unable to take another step at the mere thought, his legs gave out from under him and he collapsed to the ground on his face. The sword he carried struck a nearby stone, snapping in half.

Chaka shut his eyes, too tired to open them. His mind wandered in a haze, somewhere between dreaming and hallucinating from exhaustion. He grew tense when he thought he heard voices after some time, unable to discern whether they were friendly or adversarial.

"I'm too weak to fall on my blade," Chaka thought in disdain, *"however at this point; I'd rather be captured than trying to keep moving on."*

The voices drew closer, followed by snapping branches and ruffled vegetation as someone came through the forest. Chaka realized he didn't understand what the voices said, unsure if it was merely his hearing going bad or if they were foreign. The voices, louder now, spoke in alarmed tones and became shrill. Footsteps rushed over and Chaka grunted when poked in the side.

"Are you alive?" a voice asked in stilted Teikoku dialect.

"Put me out my misery," Chaka groaned.

"Do you want to rest?" asked a second voice.

"Just send me to Oblivion," Chaka grumbled. "I'm not sinful enough to go to Hell."

"Who cares about how sinful you are?" inquired the first voice. "Is living a sinful life a decent way to live?"

"Can you make it on your feet?" questioned the second.

"I'm all right," answered Chaka weakly. Then darkness enveloped him.

Chaka's eyes snapped open and he found himself carried on the back of a stout young man who wore a chain mail shirt and riding trousers. Following beside him was a lean athletic older woman wearing a short jacket over a loose tunic, short trousers and a pale blue bandana over her head, carrying a bundle of broken swords. On her arms, she wore scale-plate bracers.

Looking around, Chaka saw they were walking down a worn dirt road and the skies overhead were cloudy as cool winds blew lightly around them.

"Ho, where are we?" Chaka grumbled. When he received no answer, he pulled the man's short hair, only to be immediately dumped on the ground. Chaka yowled in pain.

"I heard you," the young man snapped over him. "If you're all right to talk, then you can walk the rest of the way!"

"Don't mind him," the woman replied. "He's just cranky from not eating for a couple of bells."

Chaka grunted when the young man lent a hand and easily pulled him to his feet. Turning about face, he noticed they stood on the edge of a small plain surrounded by a sea of rice paddies and reeds battered and broken from the storm.

Ahead, smoldering burnt houses and numerous corpses littered the grounds around the fields and along the roads, lying where they fell having been hacked to pieces.

The young man cried out in horror and took off running down the track, yelling intelligibly in the dialect Chaka didn't understand.

"Did *akuma* do this?" Chaka asked the older woman who looked ahead with a grim expression on her face.

"I wish," she muttered after several moments of silence. She stormed onward and Chaka followed her, taking in his surroundings.

He frowned at a nearby head that lay in tall grass and several paces away was its body in a bundle of limbs. Chaka passed the body of the local magistrate entangled with his equally dead horse, the bodies of farmers armed with simple weapons and bodies of women and children strewn along the wayside - all cut down grotesquely in such a brutal manner.

"I never thought *akuma* were this brutal," Chaka murmured.

"They're not," answered the woman.

"You mean to say—!"

"Not even a man possessed would do such carnage."

"Well...!"

As they entered the village square, they encountered a pile of lifeless bodies of the local defense division slain and torched. Chaka's eyes glazed over at the sight of gore, while the woman took in the scene with unsympathetic indifference.

Abruptly a clanking sound cut into the air and Chaka shrank back, bracing himself for a dangerous encounter while searching the corpses for signs of movement. "Is it the ghosts of the dead?" he tentatively inquired. "I don't have the skill to get rid of that!"

"I don't see anything," the woman replied. "Let's move on to the next village."

"But it'll rain soon!"

"You seem well-rested to me."

"Where are we going?"

The woman pointed ahead and Chaka looked in the direction she indicated - a large hill surrounded by marshland.

Chaka grunted and followed the woman without further protest.

The darkening clouds later burst with steady moderate rains and Chaka blew a disconcerted sigh, overcome with dread. He grew increasingly worried while walking silently behind the woman, stomping through swamps, climbing steep hills, and covering several miles of muddy tracks.

Chaka glanced behind himself at times, anticipating the young man she traveled with earlier to be behind them, only finding nothing but more corpses of soldiers, horses, and farmers along the way.

Once they climbed another hill, the basin below revealed a small farmhouse stationed near the marshes and behind it led to a forest of umbrella pines. Taking the only path that led there, Chaka pushed aside the old wooden gate that was in disrepair aside from the road.

"It seems no one's been here in ages," Chaka noted.

The woman gave no reply, only walking toward the worn door. She rapped lightly and after a moment when no one inside answered, she left the bundle of broken swords on the steps and pushed past Chaka, going elsewhere.

Chaka watched her leave and then sat on the steps, at a loss on what to do next. The woman gave no indication to follow her and she never once turned back, returning to the road in the rain.

"Is anyone out there?" a voice suddenly called.

Chaka cried out and leapt to his feet, putting up his hands on the defensive. The door slowly creaked open and a middle-aged man with leathery weathered sunburnt skin and short sandy hair flecked with silver poked out his head, squinting at Chaka.

"*Shitsurei Shimasu*," Chaka said. The man blinked, staring blankly back. Chaka grew slightly irritated by the lack of response. "Who are you?" he demanded, relaxing his stance.

"Who are you?" the man parroted. When Chaka didn't answer the man grunted and shut the door.

"Wait," Chaka called. "This woman left a package for you."

"Oh?" The door came open and the man glanced around, then down at the ground, noticing the bundle. "Ah, you're right. Say, bring that in for me; I threw out my back."

"Yes, Honored Uncle," Chaka replied and collected the swords on the stoop.

"My, how polite!" the middle-aged man cracked. "*Kengo* these days are always so rude!" He shuffled indoors and Chaka shouldered the door, stepping inside a small shop that had metalworking tools hanging along the walls and strewn across several tables. The man held a hand to his back, stooping forward as he headed for the rear of the workstation and Chaka noticed he favored his left leg more so than his right.

"Where would Uncle like these?" Chaka inquired.

"Oh, just drop them with that pile there," the man replied and left to another room.

"I'm sorry to bother you with my presence, Uncle," Chaka said, placing the blades aside on a table that held many other snapped swords, split sheaths and a variety of handles. Glancing around, Chaka noted large crates lined the walls and inside some of them were all manner of claws, feathers, or hides of various kinds.

"At least it's not the dead of night," the man called back. "It's only a little after the eighth hour."

"I won't stay here long, Uncle - I just need some rest; I've been walking for a very long time."

"Don't just stand there, take off that armor and come inside. You will have to draw the bath yourself however; I put the fire on."

Chaka sighed in relief and entered the rear room, a small area with a stone floor that consisted of a futon, a fire pit with a cooking pot hanging above it and several chests. The man sat on one of the heavy crates, leaning forward against his knees toward the fire. He grabbed a nearby blackened iron prod and stoked the dying flames.

Chaka silently pulled out of his armor, setting it near the door.

"Would you like some tea?" the man asked after Chaka stripped down to his loincloth. "I'll have it ready after you soak." He gestured behind him with his head. "Bath is in the back. I already drew from the well and..." The man chuckled. "I'm not getting any younger."

"Do you have family?"

"Go, soak and we'll have plenty of time to talk," the man said instead, waving away Chaka.

Chaka passed him, opening the rear door that led to a small washing tub situated on old planks covering a dirt floor. A bucket of water rest beside it and nearby was a washboard leaning against the wall. Another door led outside and Chaka walked over, opening it. Across the way, he spotted a well and a woodshed that had cords of cut bamboo and pine stacked into a pile.

"I'm sure you're tough and all," the man suddenly called, "but if you want hot water, get it now before we drink it all!"

Chaka shut the door and returned to the cramped living quarters, taking the cooking pot off the hook. He poured its steaming contents into the tub then followed with the other bucket of water. Afterwards, Chaka exited outdoors, drawing more water and returned, refilling the cooking pot. Once he placed the pot back on the hook over the fire, the man handed Chaka a towel and Chaka took it, returning to the rear room.

Dropping the towel into the warm water, Chaka pulled out of his loincloth and stepped in. Grabbing the nearby bucket, he dipped it into the water and poured its contents over his head. Setting the bucket aside, he scooped up the rag floating in the water and sat down, putting the towel over his face as he leaned back, sighing contently. His sore muscles slowly loosened as he relaxed and then he drifted off into sleep.

THREE

"*Tadaima*, Atsu!" a loud voice shouted, violently waking Chaka from deep sleep. Chaka cried out and swung at the air, expecting an assassin and splashed cold water everywhere.

"*Okaeri nasai*," the middle-aged man's voice replied. "Don't be so loud, Taiji; we have a guest here! He's sleeping in the back."

Chaka sighed in relief once he realized where he was and then grunted at the realization of his towel on the dirt floor. Picking it up, he shook it out and dumped it in the tub. "Can't be more dirtier than I," he muttered and scrubbed at his arms.

"Oh, so that pile of junk near the door wasn't found by Akeno and Suzuko?" Taiji said incredulously.

"He's possibly a soldier from Chinokaigan," Atsu answered.

"If the Imperial patrols find him here, we'll be in trouble!"

"Bah," Atsu spat. "I've a bad back and rocks are smarter than you. Nothing will happen to us."

The door suddenly banged open and Chaka quickly rose to his feet, clutching the towel. On the other side stood a slender young man with long dark hair oiled and held up in an elaborate bouffant with ivory hairpins, wearing a bright blue kimono with rounded sleeves and a wide dark blue obi with intricate white lilies stitched into the fabric around his waist. His narrow face was painted white, his lips red and dark charcoal shadow lined his eyes.

"So, *Kengo* Chinokaigan, are you fleeing from a crime?" Taiji accused. "You're far from home, obviously!"

"I committed no crime," Chaka replied. "I hail from House Suzume of Shinkunotani, fighting under the banner of House Suzaku, allied with House Kuren. We were fighting the devils around Hakukishinoheiya and they destroyed the entire battalion."

"I guess those *akuma* won't waste their time on *heishi* that hadn't bothered dying gloriously!" Taiji snorted. "Very well, you can stay here, but you're sleeping in the shed tonight." Taiji stormed out and Chaka blew a heavy sigh.

"What is his problem?" Chaka muttered and finished washing.

"Why are you being so rude?" Atsu complained from the next room. "He'll catch Death out there!"

"Then you feed your new cat," Taiji retorted. "Certainly he's got another life or two left."

"Give him that old kimono there and be nice! If you keep up that squawking, I'll give him your *ochazuke*!"

Taiji returned moments later with a bundle of clothes in his arms and Chaka dropped what he held, tense at the other man's presence. "Are you going to stand there and shrivel like a prune," Taiji snapped, "or are you coming out?"

"Forgive me," Chaka murmured and stepped out the tub. Taiji suddenly dropped the clothes to the floor and stalked out.

Growing annoyed, Chaka shook them out and pulled into a loose-fitting quilted robe and trousers, then drained the tub.

On return to the small living quarters, Chaka smelled scallions and radishes cooking. Peering into the doorway, he spotted Atsu ladling a bowl of rice and vegetable soup from his place on the trunk and Taiji sat across from him near the futon on a cushioned pillow. Taiji glared at Chaka then huffed and turned away, folding his arms across his chest.

"Have a seat over there," Atsu said. "Don't worry, these trunks will hold up your weight."

"Thank you, Uncle," Chaka murmured and stepped around Taiji, taking a seat on the other trunk beside the middle-aged man.

"Taiji, stop being rude and serve the tea!" Atsu commanded. Taiji said nothing, rising rigidly to his feet and stomped out the room. "So what's your story?" Atsu questioned, handing Chaka the bowl and a pair of lacquered eating sticks. Chaka nodded and took them both.

Before Chaka answered, Taiji returned with a tray that held three cups and a small table. He slammed the table to the floor before Atsu and dropped the tray with a clang. Chaka bit his eating sticks and captured one of the cups that rolled off before it crashed to the stone floor with his free hand.

Atsu grunted and ladled another bowl of soup, saying nothing as Taiji took the kettle. Chaka set the cup on the tray and Taiji poured the tea, splashing Chaka's hand. Chaka growled and grasped Taiji's wrist, twisting hard. Taiji cried out, slipping to his knees.

"Please handle your wife," Chaka said through gritted teeth, "or I'll beat her for you."

Atsu chuckled and waved a dismissive hand at Chaka. "That's enough," he said. "Now calm down and enjoy dinner, eh?"

Chaka let go and Taiji set the kettle on the table with shaking hands. He drew away, cradling his arm close to his body.

"I can't serve this brute!" Taiji whimpered. "I'll skip my meal then!"

Atsu shrugged his shoulders. "Your loss then," he muttered.

Chaka glared at Taiji while he ate his meal and Taiji withered under his intense gaze, looking away elsewhere.

Over the next several days, Chaka sat with Atsu by the recessed floor hearth, eating meals with him and telling stories about his adventures in the various campaigns he fought. Taiji constantly avoided him, secluding himself to the corner. In addition, every evening Taiji put on face powder, fixed his hair and changed into increasingly elaborate kimono and obi then leaving once he washed the dishes for the night.

After another evening of the same results, Chaka's curiosity was aroused and he asked Atsu about Taiji's whereabouts.

"I could care less about what he does," Atsu replied. "During the day, I fix those old blades and armor Suzuko and Akeno bring me and I resell them in town once a month."

"Would you like any help?"

Atsu smiled and pat Chaka on the knee. "I'm enjoying my time off from working," he said brightly. "That's probably why my back is so bad. All I do is work, work, work."

"I see," Chaka said smugly. "I would work myself to death as well if I had that screeching harpy for a wife!"

Atsu burst out laughing and Chaka snorted, cracking a smile.

When the next evening came and Taiji took the dinnerware, Chaka grew increasingly annoyed and marched after Taiji for the rear room where he prepared a bucket for washing.

"I have been nothing but kind to you," Chaka said in a controlled voice. "Your rudeness makes you a very ugly person, did you know that?" Taiji stiffened, saying silent as he scrubbed plates. "If your Atsu wasn't a mere craftsman, he'd take off your head for such infractions!"

"You're in no hurry to return home, are you?" Taiji suddenly said.

"Eh?" Chaka ran a hand through his ashen hair. "Are you saying I'm imposing on you?"

"Yes, I'm saying you're putting me in so much trouble!" Taiji rinsed the dinnerware and set them aside on a nearby tray.

Chaka grunted and folded his arms across his chest. "You act as if I'm a troublesome pest!" he snapped. "I'll leave when Uncle Atsu tells me so. Obviously he enjoys my company."

"I'll have you know, *akuma* have been keeping close watch in this area and roads are crawling with hellspawned troops!"

Chaka laughed and waved Taiji away. "I haven't heard anything like that," he said. "As far as I know, *Taisho* Uchitsune and Hisamasa haven't been killed yet."

"Then go outside and check, neh?"

"Oh stop pestering the man," Atsu called irritably from outside the door. Chaka turned, finding the middle-aged man standing there. "You're acting as if we'd get arrested for keeping him here."

Taiji narrowed his eyes at Chaka. "If those demons follow him here, we'll die!" he complained. "You're only a metalworker and I'm an entertainer. We have no chance, not even in the seven levels of Hell defending ourselves!"

"I'll protect you," Chaka said seriously.

"Don't bother yourself with that," Atsu grumbled. "Go, rest and let me worry about things."

Chaka shrugged his shoulders and left through the rear door, returning for the woodshed.

He later found sleeping difficult, with a cool hard wind blowing outside. Chaka constantly tossed and turned over on the pallet of bamboo he stacked in the corner. Unable to enter the dreaming world, he grunted and sat up, puffing a heavy sigh. Leaning back against the wall, Chaka mindlessly listened to the sounds of crickets chirping and frogs croaking when the winds calmed.

After several long moments, a minor rapping on the woodshed door startled Chaka and he immediately stood.

"It's me," Taiji's voice called back softly before Chaka could demand who it was.

"What do you want?" Chaka grumbled.

"Well, Osanojin is finishing his stay here and Shinatsuhiko is taking his place, preparing for their sister Yukinogami. She's due to arrive in a few days."

Chaka opened the door, revealing Taiji holding a paper lantern in one hand and a heavy blanket draped over his arm.

"And to think your heart is made of stone," Chaka cracked, taking the blanket.

"How are you feeling this week?"

"Much better, thanks to you and your husband."

"Do you like sleeping out here?"

"It's cozy," Chaka replied dryly and returned to his pallet. Draping the blanket over his body, he settled back against the wall. "Good night and I'll see you in the morning."

"Well..." Taiji seemed uncomfortable and shifted nervously on his feet. "Would you mind drinking with me for a while?"

"What brought this on?" Chaka waved Taiji away. "At first you fuss at me for imposing on you and now you want to serve me drinks? You're extreme!"

"The roads to nearby Hanamura and Kaedemachi are blocked by *Banshi*," Taiji murmured.

"I don't have a *tegata*, if that's what you're asking," Chaka said sourly. "Now if you have finished your business with me, please let me sleep."

"I can't use your travel pass anyway!" Taiji complained. "I just need to get through the *sekisho*."

Chaka growled under his breath and threw the blanket over his head. "Why are you so persistent in getting through the checkpoint anyway?" he griped. "Can it not wait until the morning, or later?"

"I don't want you staying here after the snow comes," Taiji said firmly and slammed shut the door.

Chaka still had his reservations about Taiji, pacing in the woodshed worrying about what machinations could be brewing in that man's oiled head when sleep was fleeting. Atsu constantly offered Chaka his futon to be more comfortable while he healed from his injuries and Chaka politely declined, citing Taiji's discomfiture with him.

After another night, once Chaka finished with dinner, he rose to his feet, ready to head for the woodshed and dreading the heavy drizzle he heard pattering against the roof's tiles.

"Don't go out there!" Atsu protested, waving at Chaka. "I don't want you cooped up in that drafty box getting soaked by freezing rain." He pat the trunk he sat on. "Say, let's grab some *saké* and keep warm by the fire, eh? What say you?"

Chaka grinned. "I can never turn down *saké*," he replied.

"Taiji, serve our guest some of that *shochu* we have in the cellar, neh?"

Taiji huffed and left his place in the corner, going into another room.

"There's another reason why you're not quick to let me go," Chaka said as he took a seat beside Atsu who stoked the fire.

"I enjoy your company," Atsu replied. "Is that a bad thing?"

"I'm quick to recover from most ailments and injuries, even the occasional sword cut or two." Chaka pulled out of the sleeve of his robe, holding up his arm as he leaned sideways. "See, even that cut to my side's sealed up fine!"

Atsu chortled as Chaka readjusted his clothes. "Yes, you're quite hardy," he murmured. "But still…"

"You're acting as if I am being incarcerated," Chaka spat and rolled his eyes. "I've been in worse places campaigning – even that shed is decent compared to all I've slept on or in."

"You're still young," Atsu insisted. "I've got a good twenty-five cycles on you, possibly thirty and I've been through much, much worse."

"Oh?" When Atsu failed to elaborate, Chaka leaned forward on his elbows against his knees, looking at the flickering flames. "Why hadn't you told me much about yourself, Honored Uncle?" he murmured.

"Oh, there isn't much to tell."

"If you have a few drinks, you'll probably loosen those lips!"

Atsu grinned, but said nothing in reply.

Later Taiji returned with a tray and three serving cups balanced in one hand while grasping a large bottle of strong rice liquor in the other. He sat on the floor at the low table between them and set aside the tray. Withdrawing the bottle's cork, Taiji poured Chaka's cup first, then Atsu's and then poured for himself last.

"To our honored guest," Atsu said, raising his cup.

"*Kanpai!*" Taiji and Chaka said in unison and drank their servings as Atsu gulped his down.

"Any stories to tell us, Taiji?" Atsu asked. "I'm sure *Kengo* Chinokaigan's told all the stories he could possibly tell, being a young grasshopper and all."

"Hey!" Chaka snapped and Taiji giggled. "You don't get this tough living a charmed life!"

"There's a difference between suffering willingly and suffering needlessly," Atsu noted.

"Oh, what would you know about suffering?" Chaka said incredulously. "You're a mere metalworker!"

"Heh, looks can be deceiving."

The drinking went on late into the night, with Chaka trying to pry personal information from Atsu, only to get rebuffed with vague answers instead.

"We're down to half a bottle," Taiji said after another round of drinks. "Maybe we should call it a night?"

"The rain hasn't let up," Chaka complained and stood unsteadily to his feet. "You must be mad to think I will go out there!"

"You don't have to go out there," Atsu said gently. "You can have my futon for the night."

"No, I want Taiji's," Chaka slurred and grabbed Taiji roughly by the arm. Taiji let out a surprised yelp when pulled to his feet. "Let me warm you tonight, eh? Maybe you'll be less chilly!"

Taiji swatted Chaka's free hand away when reached for. "Don't fondle me!" he shrilled, giving Chaka a hard slap across the face.

Chaka narrowed his eyes. "Tuh! Why are you always so cold to me?" He shook Taiji forcibly. "What have I ever done to you?" Chaka bellowed.

"Now, don't get boisterous," Atsu said gently. "Go easy on my wife there, will you? If you break him, then who will massage my back?"

"I have feelings too," Chaka complained and ran the back of his hand down Taiji's cheek. "Warm lovely ones!"

Taiji immediately became indignant. "Don't do that!" he protested, pushing his hand away. "Let me go!" Chaka huffed and snapped loose his hold, then shoved Taiji aside. Taiji cried out once he hit the floor and cringed under Chaka who stood over him with clenched hands. "That hurt!" Taiji cried. "I'd rather get mauled by a tiger than the likes of you!"

"I don't see how you can even love that ugly crowing raven," Chaka muttered and dropped back on the chest beside Atsu. He scooped up his cup as Atsu grabbed the bottle of wine, pouring some for him.

"People like what they like," Atsu said as he poured more wine for himself. "I like Taiji because he reminds me of my sister."

Chaka's eyes widened, at first unsure what he just heard. After throwing back his drink, it finally clicked and he suddenly found it hilarious. Chaka doubled up in laughter, holding his sides as he let out a rolling laugh.

Taiji crawled over near Atsu's side and curled up at his feet. "I don't see why you keep that animal here," Taiji complained. "You're a cruel man! How can you embarrass me so?"

Chaka snorted and set down his cup on the table with a firm bang. "You?" he said, skeptical. "Embarrassed?" Chaka scoffed, waving a dismissive hand. "I don't believe you!"

"I'm mortified!" Taiji wailed.

Atsu chortled at the exchange. "Well, *Kengo* Chinokaigan here reminds me a lot of my younger self," he explained. "Say, you wanted a story, eh? I feel like telling one tonight."

"About time," Chaka muttered and sat back, crossing his leg at the knee as he leaned against the wall with his hands clasped behind his head. "I'm listening."

Atsu held his cup of wine in his hands, staring intently into the fire. "I used to be a hunter," he said softly. "Of men, of beasts, of devils, all kinds... No manner of jaws or claws or hooves or talons or spikes or venomous stings could ever stop me - if it had blood pumping in its veins, it went across the river to Oblivion."

"What made you become a hunter?" Chaka inquired.

"My whole life had been the stalk and the hunt and the battle and the kill," Atsu continued, ignoring Chaka's query. "Pitting myself against the most dangerous and cunning beasts was the ultimate meaning of life for me and I could not imagine living any other way."

"Do you still do that now?" Chaka pressed. "I'm sure you know if you tried again, you'd surely perish!"

"My wish then was that whatever beast brought me my last breath did so while dying by my hand; however, fate decided something else for me." Atsu set aside his cup of wine and pulled out of his kimono, revealing numerous old scars crisscrossing his chest, upper back, and arms. "There had been many close calls throughout the cycles - I have even more on my legs and a nasty one across my hip - that's why I walk slower now than I used to." Atsu drew a line from near the middle of his lower back, tracing down his right thigh.

Chaka gasped and he unfolded from his position, leaning forward with his hands on his knees. "Such a blow would've incapacitated a lesser man," he said in shock, "even killing him!"

"Oh, I've always been quite healthy," Atsu replied. "It laid me up for months." The older man shrugged. "If you saw the aftermath, even strong men like you would've gone sick at the sight. But it's nothing now."

"You sleep less comfortably on that side now than you used to," Taiji murmured.

"Oh, I know my comfort and happiness mean a lot to you," Atsu said and took up his wine, gulping it down.

"How long have you been together," Chaka cut in, "if I may so ask?"

"Eight cycles now," Taiji answered and picked up the wine bottle, pouring more for Atsu when he set aside his cup. "He's not cruel or evil and never struck me in frustration or anger."

"I always preferred to get to the point as efficiently as possible," Atsu added, "and when I give instructions, it's always with a quiet, calm yet firm word."

"How can you manage that despite that unruly and disobedient creature you've taken a liking to?" Chaka quipped and Taiji's face reddened in anger.

"No more *saké* for you then!" Taiji said sharply.

"Now these days, I craft what I can from the remains of war," Atsu said instead. "I can craft all manner of armor or weapons – no matter how light or heavy, long or short, design in such a way from the Eastern Provinces or the West, I can craft it all."

"How did you have time to learn smithing if you were a hunter all this time?"

Atsu laughed and wagged a finger in Chaka's direction. "My secret," he teased.

"So does it have anything to do with all those animal parts?"

"Decoration of course," Atsu said and handed Chaka his glass of wine. "What else you thought it for?"

Chaka shrugged and took his drink, gulping it down. Setting down his cup, he stifled a yawn and rubbed at his eyes. Glancing back at the door that led to the rear room, he frowned when he heard the rain continue pelting the roof.

"Taiji, bring out the cards," Atsu said, nudging Taiji with his knee. "It's still early yet to retire, *Kengo* Chinokaigan."

"I'm not ready to sleep yet," Chaka mumbled as Taiji stood and went across the room, sorting through another trunk. "This strong drink is starting to catch up to me."

"Then let's keep your mind active over a game of Mah Jong, eh?"

Chaka suddenly straightened up and gave a devious grin. "I'll have you know I'm the best card player around," he admitted. "I've never lost a hand!"

"Oh? Even the best players have bad days."

"We'll see!"

Taiji returned with a tall leather box and set it on the table between Chaka and Atsu.

"Let's play eight hands to start and work our way up to thirteen," Atsu said as Taiji opened the box and withdrew the ivory tiles. "Sounds good?"

"I'll beat you so quickly; you'll have to cut yourself open in shame."

Atsu burst out laughing, slapping his thigh. Chaka smiled, his spirits lifted.

FOUR

Light rapping took Chaka out of the realm of dreamless sleep. The knocking became louder and he groaned in pain once he opened his eyes, trying to remember where he had been. Looking around, Chaka found himself sitting in the washtub, naked and his clothing gone.

"How did I get here?" he grumbled and staggered to his feet.

The persistent thumps continued and Chaka shuffled for the next room, yawning loudly and rubbing at his eyes. He came to a pause when he saw the cooking fires were out and Atsu gone from his usual place on his crate. Chaka then glanced to the other side of the room where Taiji usually occupied, also finding the area void as well. The knocking brought Chaka back to attention and he stormed through the shop, heading for the front door.

"I'm sorry," replied Chaka once he opened the entranceway, "Uncle Atsu's not home."

"Oh!"

Chaka stared blankly at the woman on the other side, who wore a dark gray uniform underneath a simple bronze breastplate, copper bracers and bearskin boots. "Well, are you going to leave a message for him or what?" Chaka grumbled. "I need to sleep this off."

"Don't you have any clothes to wear?" the woman said.

Chaka's ears burned and he immediately stepped behind the door once he realized his nakedness. "I'll find them when I remember where they are," he called from the other side. "Please leave if you have no business."

"I came to pick up my sword today," the woman answered. "I sent my blade for repairs."

"He hasn't worked on anything for nearly eight days," Chaka said. "I'll let him know you came by." He immediately shut the door before she could say anything else and held his head in his hands, groaning. "What happened last night?" he muttered, running his hands through his hair. "That man must drink like a fish... I hardly kept up!"

Chaka peeled away from the door and went about starting another fire in the pit, then later drawing water from the well for the tub.

After bathing, Chaka did callisthenic exercises, trying to regain some limberness to his sore muscles after sleeping uncomfortably for nearly a week. He heard voices outside and tensed, waiting. When the voices grew closer and the door opened, Chaka relaxed slightly in relief when he recognized them to be Atsu and Taiji.

"I'm sorry to have left you like that, *Kengo* Chinokaigan," Atsu said as he entered the room with a basket of groceries cradled on his arm. Taiji came to a stop at the sight of Chaka and turned around, marching back outside. "You got a little too rowdy and started tearing off clothes, so I had to throw you in the tub."

Chaka shrugged his shoulders. "I'm sorry," he answered, "I don't recall anything."

"Oh?" Atsu suddenly burst out laughing and waved Chaka away. "Then disregard what I said!" he said brightly. "It's nothing important." Atsu walked past Chaka, heading for the cellar steps. Chaka looked after him, even more puzzled than before.

"Honored Uncle," Chaka called after him, "were you expecting anyone?"

"No," Atsu called back, "why?"

"A woman stopped by, stating she was awaiting an order of blade repair."

"Which kind?"

"She didn't specify." Chaka took a seat on the nearby crate, waiting for Atsu to return.

"Then that means someone must be looking for you." Atsu came up the stairs, holding the now empty basket. "That regiment you were waiting on finally arrived."

"I'm in no hurry to return to war," Chaka admitted, "but it is my duty for my House and for the Empress."

"Don't forget you still have a soul, neh?" Atsu murmured. "You're a man, with feelings, thoughts, and desires. Don't ever forget you still have a voice, because once they take it away, you can't complain."

"Maybe you're right," Chaka murmured. "I'll keep that in mind, Honored Uncle."

"That's the best way to handle things." Atsu nodded. "So, what do you feel like eating tonight?" he inquired, changing the conversation.

"Whatever you feel like tonight."

"I ought to cook my best. I have a feeling the winds of war will be blowing this way again."

"I'll go draw water for you then."

"Bring in the laundry then and check on my wife for me, will you?"

Chaka nodded and left his trunk, heading for the rear entrance.

Exiting outdoors, Chaka found Taiji pulling down clean articles from the clothesline, with a basket next to him that had folded sheets. Nearby in the grass lay the padded kimono.

"Don't leave that on the ground!" Chaka scolded. "It's still wet!"

"So do your own washing," Taiji retorted.

"Why are you in a foul mood today?" Chaka demanded and picked up the robe, pulling into it. "Don't tell me you are offended by my nakedness."

"I'm cross because you're still here," Taiji snapped, "like a stain that refuses to be rubbed out!"

"Something happened last night obviously," noted Chaka, "but I can harbor a guess."

Taiji paused in folding clothes and glared at Chaka, his face etched with an expression of alarm. "Get that thought out of your head!" he shrieked. "I don't know what it is about you, but you're a beast when you drink too much!"

"You hoped it'd put me to sleep, is that so?" Chaka flashed a smile. "Did you have other plans for me then?"

Taiji dropped what he held, clearly horrified. "You are mistaken, *Kengo* Chinokaigan!" he yelped. "Your manner may sway demons not to gainsay you, but you cannot influence me!"

"I can no longer pretend that my thoughts about you are driving me so," Chaka protested. "I'm trying not to be rude here – please, just listen to my thoughts."

"Control yourself," Taiji retorted and snatched up the basket of linens. "If you even dare try taking the opportunity to show your feelings to me again, I swear you will not walk in this lifetime and in the next!"

"Rather you take advantage of me then?" Chaka jibed.

Taiji's face flushed beet red and he pushed past him, storming indoors.

Chaka blew a sigh and went to the well, drawing water. On return to the main room, he saw Taiji putting away sheets in a trunk across the room. Placing the bucket near the cooking fires, he followed Taiji, staying close behind him as the man hurried to put away the laundry.

"What do you take me for?" Chaka complained. "If you think I'm just another wastrel of low estate, living for the thrill of adventure, then surely you know nothing at all!"

"Obviously I'm unmoved by your pleas," Taiji replied icily as he placed clothing in another trunk.

"Your utter rudeness you keep imposing on me is foolish."

"Then nothing should surprise you, even such disorderly emotions you're displaying in response."

"What an obstinate and insensitive wretch!" Chaka thundered. "How can another man love you is mysterious indeed!"

"Then this conversation is dismissed, I suppose?"

Chaka growled and clamped a firm hand around Taiji's arm, forcing the man to drop what he held. He whirled Taiji around, leaning in close nearly nose to nose. Taiji narrowed his eyes in return and set his jaw.

"Why all this unfriendliness toward me?" Chaka demanded. "Whatever have I done to make you dislike me so?"

"You know altogether little of the world, *Kengo* Chinokaigan," Taiji said firmly. "There is nothing to be gained by trying to interest me."

Unable to reason with him further, Chaka let go then headed for the woodshed, too upset to bear being in the same room as Taiji.

Light knocking roused Chaka out of sleep and he grunted, sitting up.

"Did you sleep well?" Atsu's voice called from outside. "Dinner is ready."

"I don't feel like eating," Chaka groused.

"What's making you so unhappy?"

"I have no excuses."

"Oh, come out and enjoy some time with me, eh?" Atsu persisted. "Your company is appreciated."

"Go on without me," Chaka moaned. "I don't want to be in the way."

"I insist."

"Please, no."

"Therefore, I'll come in there then."

Chaka growled under his breath and got up from the pallet, making his way for the door. Throwing it open, he saw the middle-aged man on the other side, dressed in a loose-fitting cotton kimono and trousers with the legs rolled about his knees. He held a paper lantern in hand, lighting his brightly smiling face in the darkness of the evening.

"Why do you pester me so?" Chaka grumbled.

"Don't look so bad, eh!" Atsu said cheerfully. "There's more to life than silly perfumed women!"

Chaka snorted. "Some woman!" Exiting the woodshed, Chaka crossed the yard to the house and paused when he saw Atsu not following. "Is something the matter, Uncle?" he inquired.

"I sense something unpleasant," Atsu murmured, frowning. "Go around front and check for me, neh?"

"Surely," Chaka responded and tied his robe shut.

Atsu handed Chaka the lantern and he headed around the side of the farmhouse. Ahead on the road atop the hill, he spotted an approaching heavily armed soldier, taking long strides. Looking towards the grove, Chaka noticed the woman he saw earlier standing on post.

"Was she spying for that man?" he wondered as the soldier came closer.

"Isawa!" the soldier barked once she approached. Chaka froze, stunned that the woman knew him. "Is that you?"

"Depends," Chaka called back hesitantly. "Who's asking?"

"There aren't many fair-haired giants who tower over the Empress's elite guards matching your description," the soldier responded. "So you've been hiding here for the past eight nights, I've heard."

"Who is making such accusations?" Chaka demanded.

"*Taishou* Uchitsune Kaya of House Ryusen."

Chaka stiffened and cold sweat broke out over his forehead and neck. "The same captain-general of *Daigo Rentai*?" he asked weakly.

"Yes, that same fifth regiment sent to support *Taichou* Kurebayashi's troops in Chinokaigan."

Chaka dropped the lantern he held and bowed stiffly as the soldier stood before him. "*Taishou* Uchitsune," he said weakly. "I did not recognize you in that armor..."

"I also hardly recognize you without your armor," Uchitsune spat.

"It's not what you think!" Chaka protested and stood at attention. "*Bansho* Kurebayashi and I were the only survivors..." He explained the events that led him to where he now stood and Uchitsune snorted, unmoved.

"You refused to die in valiantly in battle, simply put," she snapped. "Scouts never reported anything about devils resurrecting armies of freshly fallen men."

"Any word from *Taishou* Hisamasa?" Chaka asked, disregarding her comment.

"He's busy chasing *akuma* that are invading nearby villages," Uchitsune answered, "but what concern is that to you?"

"But I was separated from my regiment!" Chaka insisted. "Because I survived by the grace of the *kamisama*, *Bansho* Kurebayashi went on without me across the river!"

Uchitsune raised a hand, silencing Chaka. "Our numbers were badly depleted in the neighboring villages that were being cleared of demonic activity," she explained. "We had to resort setting fire to military supplies and spreading false rumors, routing the devils into a more favorable location." Uchitsune gestured toward the modest house Chaka stood in front of. "Scouts tracked down this metalworker from a nearby camp so we can get the troops outfitted before moving on."

"I'll tell him right away." Chaka turned to leave and Uchitsune grabbed Chaka by the arm, arresting him.

"Call him here and I shall tell him myself."

"Honored Uncle," Chaka called. "Your services are requested."

"Come back in the morning," Atsu called back. "My shop is closed for the night."

"How convenient," Uchitsune snarled and forcibly let Chaka go. Taking up the lantern at Chaka's feet, she pushed past him, forcing open the door behind him.

Entering the shop, Uchitsune looked around and Chaka stood at the door, unable to move from his place as the general went over tables and kicked at discarded weaponry on the ground.

"What is the meaning of this?" she thundered. "This table alone here has armaments from our allied regiments!" Uchitsune turned to Chaka. "I'll have to order this place burnt to the ground. He's a freebooter and we won't allow a thief who willingly steals from the Imperial army to keep in business!"

"He's a simple craftsman," Chaka persisted. "He gains these things from his couriers who pick up around the area."

"It's true," Atsu called from another part of the room. "How am I to know what my servants bring in are Imperial arms? I merely make a simple living to support my wife."

"Let me see you," Uchitsune commanded. "I don't have time dealing with shadowy men."

Atsu returned from the rear room and stood at the door, arms folded across his chest. "Do you fault me for trying to live a modest life?" Atsu said in an even tone, glaring at the general. "After my village grew less in number due to famine, disease, war, and demons, I had to make do with my skills."

"Fine, I'll spare your life," Uchitsune grumbled, "that is if you agree to rearm my men."

Atsu shook his head. "I refuse," he snapped. "Unless you get me a promissory note from the lord of your estate in which you hail."

Uchitsune withdrew her golden-handled broadsword and pointed the tip at Atsu's throat. He continued to glare back unflinchingly. "You rearm my men and live," she snarled.

"I'll have the lord of my House pay for the work, Honored Uncle," Chaka suddenly said, "to return the kindness of your hospitality you've shown me."

"I'll agree to that," Atsu said.

"Fine then," Uchitsune grumbled and sheathed her sword. "Be ready to return at dawn." Chaka grunted when shoved past and he watched the general stalk out, taking the lantern with her. "Either die in battle or cut your stomach open," she called over her shoulder, "your choice."

Watching Uchitsune depart for the woods, Chaka blew a heavy sigh and sagged against a nearby table. "Honored Uncle..." he started.

"Let's not discuss this now," Atsu replied as he relaxed his stance. Turning toward the room, he called for Taiji. "Get out my best weapons and gear from the hiding place."

"You're not preparing to die, are you?" Taiji cried out in horror.

Atsu let out a short bark of a laugh. "No, it's not for me," he said and turned to Chaka. "Let's enjoy our last evening together."

Chaka shook his head, appearing despondent. "I doubt I will be able to," he muttered.

"Why are you moping so?" Atsu gave a slight smile. "I'll bring out my best wine, how's that?"

"If to cloud my troubles, then I'll surely partake!"

"Let's not leave a drop undrunk!" Atsu waved at Chaka. "Come, relax, and play another round of Mah Jong with me, eh?"

Chaka grunted and peeled away from the table, following the middle-aged man into the next room.

FIVE

For most of the night, after a large meal of brown rice and vegetables, and going through two bottles of wine, Chaka and Atsu sat at the hearth hunched over the table, deeply engrossed in a game of cards. A third, larger bottle of wine rest near Atsu's foot and his cup set offside on the table next to the discard pile.

Taiji leaned against Atsu, having loosened his robe and trousers, and fondled the older man. Atsu kept pushing his hands away while trying to hold his hand of tiles.

"I'm trying to concentrate," Atsu fussed as he set down one stack of cards and picked up another.

"I can't walk," Taiji cooed drunkenly. "Lie down with me, please?"

"Sleep over there by yourself."

"Ooh, you're so mean!"

"You're clearly drunk and it's very late," Atsu said. "I'll play with you tomorrow."

"But I want to play now!"

Chaka cracked a devious smile. "I'll play with you any time," he insisted.

"No!" Taiji wailed, burying his face into Atsu's side. "He'll kill me!"

Atsu snorted in response. "No need to do that," he said and drew a tile then set one into the discard pile. "Your turn," Atsu announced, setting his hand face down on the table. "Let me put my wife to bed and I'll return to the game. No cheating!"

"I don't have to cheat," Chaka said, grinning. He picked up his cup of wine, nodding towards it. "I'm too drunk anyway..."

Atsu rolled his eyes then hoisted Taiji into his arms, grunting with effort. Taiji sighed contently, looping his arms around the older man's neck and leaned his head heavily against his shoulder.

"Off to bed with you," Atsu murmured, carrying Taiji to his pallet. Setting him down, he drew the covers over to his shoulders and kissed him gently on the cheek. "Sleep well."

"I won't!" Taiji complained, pouting. "Lie with me, please?"

"After this last hand, neh?"

Chaka leaned back in his seat, crossing one leg at the knee and studied his stack of ivory tiles he held cupped in one hand with the other held his serving of wine. "With the way you're stalling," he jeered, "you must have a bad hand."

Atsu held up his pants with his free hand and sauntered over to the table, plopping back on the crate. "Now, where were we?" he said. After tucking his robe's sleeves about his waist and cuffing up his trouser legs around his knee, he took up two sets of cards, one in each hand, and frowned deep in thought as he contemplated his next move.

"You can't beat my last hand," Chaka said, rolling the cup between his fingers. "I had all Four Winds, Seasons, Flowers and three Dragons over your full numbered set and Four Seasons!"

"I figured you were holding," Atsu grumbled. "Now hurry and lay your hand, so I can beat you!"

"Getting hot, old man?" Chaka retorted, grinning. He set aside his cup and scooped up one tile from the table, setting it in his hand, and then discarded another. "Your turn."

Atsu glanced at the discard pile, then again at his hand and the furrow of his brow deepened. "I pass."

"Let's see it."

Atsu laid out his hand and Chaka groaned, striking the table with his fist. "There's no way you can beat this hand, *Kengo* Chinokaigan!" Atsu crowed. "I have a Full Flush!"

"You're a cheat!" Chaka complained.

"What do you have?"

"Seven pair..." Chaka laid out his hand on the table. "That's the best I could come up with."

Atsu laughed and poured Chaka another drink. "Loser takes another," he said brightly.

Chaka gulped down the drink and set his cup on the table. "Let's call it a night," he said. "We have a lot to do in the morning."

"It's already early morning," Atsu said as he collected the cards and shuffled them across the table. "We've been drinking and playing all night."

Chaka stood unsteadily to his feet. "I can't go fight in this condition!" he thundered. "Are you trying to kill me?"

"I have no intention of doing that," Atsu said calmly. "Sit down, try to relax. That soldier won't be in until later."

"She'll be here at dawn," Chaka shouted, "or have you forgotten?"

"If you're so insistent, go draw a bath."

"You're in no hurry to work on anything!"

"I didn't agree on her behalf," Atsu said plainly. "I just agreed to get payment from you in return for my kind generosity."

Chaka opened his mouth to protest, and then shut it, realizing he backed himself into the proverbial corner. Blowing a hard sigh, he left for the rear room and paused when he saw a pile of lacquered onyx scale armor near the washtub.

Leaning against the wood was a dark navy cedar scabbard, holding a simple broadsword tied in ebony sharkskin. Taking out the sword, he admired the beauty of the blade, a perfect piece of art and destruction. Chaka noted the black steel held an inscription on the flat of the blade in a language he couldn't read. Turning it over, he read the blacksmith's name stamp, called 'Massai'.

Squeezing the handle, Chaka sensed the proportion of the straight blade to its length and held the hilt on the tip of his finger, noting its stability.

"*This* _chokuto_ *feels unusually lightweight for accompanying such a heavy sheath,*" he thought as he gripped the sword and swung it in the air. Feeling it unbalanced in one hand, Chaka set aside the covering and used both hands, making cutting exercises. After a few swings, pale blue light emitted from the dark steel, glowing softly. "*Is this enchanted to feel lighter than normal?*"

Shrugging his shoulders, Chaka grabbed the sword's case and sheathed it. Suddenly nicking his thumb, he cried out stuck his finger in his mouth. Chaka grew worried when the pale blue light surrounding the sword turned dimly in red.

"Oh, you like blood, eh?" he muttered and set the sword aside near the door. "There'll be plenty for you soon!"

"I see you found *Onikage*," Atsu said as he came near the entranceway. "How keen you are, *Kengo* Chinokaigan... it does like blood, a lot in fact."

"Is it cursed?"

"In a way, it is."

Chaka folded his arms across his chest. "What are you trying to tell me?" he demanded.

"This old man has only a single selfish request," Atsu murmured and looked away. "I'd like for you to protect this shop."

"You know I can't do that, Honored Uncle," Chaka said softly. "I'd love to, but if I neglect my duties..." He waved the man away. Atsu nodded, blowing a short sigh.

"I understand, but an old man can be hopeful, eh?"

A loud bang came from the front door and both Atsu and Chaka turned toward the sound.

"Wah!" Taiji suddenly cried from the next room as the banging continued. "They're coming to kill us!"

"Go on and answer the door!" Atsu called back. "I'm busy with other pressing matters!"

"What if I do decide to break rank and keep post here?" Chaka inquired instead.

Atsu shrugged his shoulders. "It's all dependent on what the *kamisama* feel like that day," he answered.

"Well, if I am to pay you I need to be alive."

52

"That doesn't mean anything if you fall in battle, *Kengo* Chinokaigan."

"Well, if I take that *Onikage*, it might keep my head on a little longer."

Atsu gave a tight smile. "Oh, so I assume you accept my offer?"

Chaka nodded. "I'll do my best, Honored Uncle."

"Go get ready and I'll handle that unsavory woman outside," Atsu replied.

Chaka snorted. "At first I found it strange with you two living alone here in the mounts," he said. "I'd never thought you to be *onna-girai*!"

"At the time I was young and ignorant and knew no better then," Atsu said seriously. "Now that I am wiser in the ways of the world, I no longer find them to my liking."

"Why is that you have such dislike against women?"

Atsu waved a dismissive hand. "They bleed," he said simply, with a small hint of disdain in his voice.

Chaka scoffed. "And so do men."

Taiji later returned, sobbing into his hands. "That horrid beast returned with two bodyguards," he wailed. "She said she has a hundred men coming along the way and you must give them your best at once they arrive!" Atsu appeared withdrawn as he placed an arm around Taiji's waist, pulling him close.

"Go, draw a bath and I'll prepare everything before you leave," Atsu said to Chaka. Chaka nodded and left the for the rear exit, taking the bucket at the door along the way.

SIX

Chaka washed in the tub, wiping down his arms while Taiji knelt behind him, scrubbing at his back.

"Yes, I grew up with such expensive tastes and had such beautiful things," Taiji chattered on. "Father was a skilled herbalist and made moxa. We lived in a large manse in a township called Kakushitani, with many servants. Mother never had to work at all if she chose not to."

Chaka scoffed. "There's no way a mere medicine worker could make that kind of coin!" he said and lifted a leg, wiping it down. "I'm sure your mother had to supplement income somehow. Seibushima is notoriously expensive to live in after all."

"She was a dancer, a famous one at that," Taiji replied. He grabbed a nearby bucket and dipped it into the water. "The public theaters were always sold out when she was scheduled to perform!"

"You said you were also an entertainer," Chaka noted as he wiped down his other leg. "Do you dance as well?"

"I do in fact," Taiji answered and dumped the water over Chaka's head. "I can't say I'm the best, because I'm forever in my mother's shadow... but I try my hardest." Setting the bucket aside, Taiji rose upright. "There, you're clean. Now get out."

Chaka grunted and stood, glaring down at Taiji who backed away from his imposing presence. "I've dealt with your rudeness long enough," he snapped. "Don't make me cut you down!"

"I'm not afraid of you!" Taiji snarled.

Chaka stepped out the tub and stormed over to the pile of armor near the door, snatching up the sword laying across the top. He swiftly turned around, pointing the end of the scabbard at Taiji's throat while meeting a closed metal fan branded in his direction. Taiji leaned back, glaring hatefully at Chaka in return.

"I see I have been misinformed," Chaka murmured.

"I'm not just any weak artisan," Taiji said evenly.

"A sword dancer, heh!" Chaka spat and lowered his sword sheath. "Despite your sniveling and terrible attitude, I'm surprised you have any fighting skill!"

"I can handle maybe a half-dozen men at best," Taiji admitted, "but if I must defend my home, I will give it my all." He withdrew his fan and tucked it into the wide sash at his back.

"Are you willing to follow your husband in death?"

Taiji said nothing, storming out the room.

Chaka shrugged his shoulders and set aside the sword, then started the process of putting on the armor. Moving the breastplate aside, he came across a pair of clean trousers, socks, a loose-fitting shirt and loincloth.

After dressing in the undergarments and arming himself in the breastplate, thigh protectors, gauntlets with bracers, shin guards and boots, Chaka picked up the black broadsword and entered the main room, pausing at the sight of Atsu sitting at the door, wearing a full plate of midnight-blue armor while holding a heavy ornately decorated glaive. On his head he wore a navy bandanna with gold leaves as the running pattern and beside him at his feet was a matching dark blue bucket helmet with gold leaves painted on the edges.

"Such exquisite armor...!" Chaka said in awe.

"I have a confession to make," Atsu murmured. "We both know my candle's flame is nearing its end, probably sooner than either of us suspect. That thought alone annoys me, even though I know it is inevitable."

"But you will live a long life," Chaka protested.

Atsu put up a hand to silence him. "Your words bring no comfort, *Kengo* Chinokaigan. You must understand, I am a hunter – it is my life, what I do and what I am. There are vicious beasts in the world that other men cannot kill and I have always been the one to track it down, stalk it, and find a way to end its life."

"Such fine armaments can't be afforded on such meager trophies, Honored Uncle!" Chaka interrupted.

"In my younger days, I traveled the countryside and lived in the wilds, by my wits and the grace of the *kamisama*," Atsu went on. "Whenever a beast threatened a village or town and the regular hunting parties couldn't destroy the creature, I was called upon to dispatch it." Atsu blew a heavy sigh. "I'm getting older, though not in the cycles of men. As a hunter, every chase, every encounter, every new injury slows me more and more. Very soon the day will come when I will not be fast enough and the beast will get the best of me."

"Why choose this battle?" Chaka wondered. "There is no beast for you to slay this time."

"Man is such a beast," Atsu answered, "however, and truth be told..." He hung his head, blowing a long heavy sigh. "I'm not a mere blacksmith. I am a former *Onmyoji*, of Izumimori Temple."

"I see what you mean by being a hunter," Chaka murmured. "I don't understand what made a highly-skilled exorcist like you hide out here!"

"My last major battle had been against several troops of *akuma* plaguing the southern marshes," Atsu explained. "That's how I gained that ugly scar." He waved a dismissive hand at Chaka. "So I retired here, perfecting my work in *Renkinjutsu*, hoping this would be a peaceful end to a tumultuous life."

"Alchemy, you say!" Chaka exclaimed, surprised. "So were you the one who crafted that blood-thirsty blade?"

"Do you think you can handle a hundred men?" Atsu asked pointedly instead.

"If they do show up," Chaka answered, "I'll personally greet them."

"Worry not; you won't be going at it alone."

Chaka bowed deeply to Atsu. "I'm very grateful to you, Honored Uncle. I will never forget how kind you've been for taking me in and all."

Atsu nodded and picked up the helmet. "Check outside for me."

Chaka righted himself and left for the front door. Opening it wide, he saw the dawn's light had ascended on the marshes and all was still. Exiting out onto the path, Chaka faced the old farmhouse, noticing the small smoke trail from the cooking fire creeping along the top, fading into the pale sky.

Taiji appeared at the door moments later, wearing a bright crimson kimono with narrow sleeves, a gold brocade sash and crimson slippers. His face, painted the usual white and lips red, appeared serious, as the dark charcoal around the eyes he wore was now deep cinnabar.

"Are you serious about defending us?" Taiji demanded sternly. Something in his voice, intense and resolute disturbed Chaka and he turned away, unsure how to answer. "Never had you to encounter such a formidable adversary, the Imperial Army. They're the best of the best, especially by the high ranks you've obviously entered."

"How could you tell?" Chaka asked weakly.

"That armor you came in with doesn't belong to mere *Ashigaru*."

"I just earned my rank a season ago..." Chaka blew a heavy sigh. "That last battle, I lost both my blades, the *Hitokiri* which was given to me once I became *Fukutaichou*, and the *Kagesureiyo*, which I earned after becoming *Ichizoku Eiyu* for House Suzume."

"Young and foolish, that's all you are," Taiji snapped. "Clan Champion or not, you lost your soul on that battlefield; you should've cut your losses and leave this world."

"I survived for a reason; also I made a promise to Kurebayashi…"

"What promise was that?"

Chaka shook his head, refusing to answer.

"Ho!" Uchitsune's voice abruptly called from afar. Chaka turned, watching the woman making her way through the woods with seven retainers at her side. "Has the old man everything for me?"

"What are you talking about?" Taiji spat back in irritation.

"Are you deaf?" Uchitsune retorted. "Has he readied my order for me?"

"Honored Uncle was unable to work last night," Chaka replied, feinting aloofness. "His back has failed him again and he requests that you come tomorrow."

Uchitsune stormed up to Taiji and the accompanying men trailed behind her, standing ill at ease. "You lie to me," she growled, "and I will take off your head!" Pushing Taiji aside, Uchitsune stormed the modest home. "Men, take whatever you see fit. This place is going directly to Hell." The guards followed her in and began rifling through the various crates, in drawers and across tables.

Taiji stood beside Chaka, steaming with hatred and glaring contemptuously as they hauled all manner of weapons and armor, setting it outside. Uchitsune stood in the center of the room, watching the men systematically ransack the shop, overturning everything that wasn't nailed down.

"Wouldn't you prefer to have the whole regiment here so they too can have free reign?" Atsu called after several moments. "How about something to drink, eh? I can give you that as well."

Uchitsune whirled around, growling under her breath as she held a hand to the hilt of her blade. "Come out here, old man," she barked, "so I can punish you!"

"Don't push me," Atsu snarled menacingly. "I've enough of you officers who feel they can do as they please all because you fight under the Imperial banner!"

"You're partly to blame," Uchitsune spat back. "Your coldhearted stubbornness put you in this position, so don't be that way."

"If you came nicely, I would've poured you a drink and we would've discussed reasonable rates."

Uchitsune scoffed. "Me? Nice to you?" She let out a short laugh. "You crazy old man," she suddenly exploded, "there is a war going on or have you forgotten in that addled head of yours?"

"I know there is war going on," Atsu said in a controlled voice.

"So come out here and defend yourself."

"I'll think it over for a while."

"I'll be happy to help you across the river!" Uchitsune withdrew her weapon, a heavy broadsword with a gilded golden handle.

"I'm overcome by your kindness," Atsu replied venomously and stepped into the room, holding his lance over his shoulder and his helmet in his free hand. "If you do me a favor, I will return a greater favor to you, but if you hurt me, I will not turn away. If you insult me, I will strike you. If you strike me, I will break you. If you break me, I will take away your blade and if you take away my blade I will send you to Hell!"

"You hate me, eh?" Uchitsune replied, unmoved. "I admit, I am not that likeable."

"Just answer me this: who destroyed my village?" Atsu leaned his naginata against the doorframe and tied on his helmet. "I suppose you expect me to believe that *akuma* have done such a thing, but even they're not that cruel."

"If you expect me to take revenge on the devils, then I am already doing what I can in my power."

"No, it was officers like you who killed the people of my village," Atsu said sharply. "You recruited them, promising them honor, glory, and the like, and they've all returned in coffins, one after another!"

"Bleeding needlessly isn't good for your health, old man," Uchitsune said smugly. "You really shouldn't say ugly things like that." She turned to the bodyguards who were still clearing out the shop. "That's enough," she called. "Go get the others and have them get ready immediately!"

"Do you think I'll simply let you go like that?" Atsu shouted and Chaka immediately blocked the exit, hand to the hilt of his broadsword. The retainers paused, hands hovering near their swords.

"Just as I suspected," Uchitsune snarled, glaring at Chaka. "You're a traitor all along!"

Chaka swallowed hard before answering. "He did no wrong to you," he said, struggling to find his voice. "You show up here in all manner of rudeness and tear into his shop like a wild boar, destroying his hard work!"

"So that's how it is, eh?" Uchitsune spat. "Come outside and get your punishment, Isawa!"

"*Ganbare!*" Atsu called and picked up his naginata, lunging at Uchitsune.

Uchitsune brought down her sword with both hands, but the older man proved too fast and the blow glanced off the spine of the partisan. He pushed back and Uchitsune whirled around him, aiming at his back.

Atsu sidestepped the attack, swinging the naginata around his body. The blade struck nothing but air as Uchitsune jumped in time, avoiding the glaive. She slammed down her broadsword and Atsu sidestepped her again, checking her hard in the chest with the butt of his lance.

The force of the blow threw Uchitsune across the room, slamming her to the floor. She bowled head over heels and Chaka jumped back as she spiraled out the door.

Atsu charged forward and made swift strokes at Uchitsune, who swiftly blocked with equal speed, then slashed back, forcing Atsu staggering rearward. Atsu recovered immediately and swung his blade, coming down on her head. Uchitsune immediately blocked with an overhead strike and booted Atsu in the groin, forcing him to cough and crumple against the doorframe. Uchitsune rolled over and sprang to her feet then fled, racing back to the woods. Atsu caught his second wind and quickly gave chase.

Chaka backed away and Taiji stepped aside near the door as the bodyguards converged out into the yard, all withdrawing their swords. Chaka withdrew his broadsword, tossing his scabbard aside on the ground and held his blade high, ready to bring it down on the first neck that ventured within striking distance.

One man to Chaka's right stepped forward and Chaka brought down his sword, taking off his head with a single stroke. Taiji withdrew his bladed fan and struck another soldier in the back, felling him instantly.

"I'll take care of it here," Taiji called. "Go and get rid of the others!"

Chaka nodded and kicked up his scabbard, then took off running once Taiji engaged the remaining bodyguards.

SEVEN

Racing through the forest and determined to not let Uchitsune escape, Chaka made up his mind to kill her thoroughly, making certain that not a breath of life was left – even destroying her soul so she wouldn't be able to reincarnate.

He strongly disliked Uchitsune's extreme, almost primitive wild nature – she came off as very negative and uncouth and it irritated Chaka to no end. He tried to withstand her harshness, taking her ferociously severe punishments during training, but the constant caning and deprivation made him hate the roughneck all the more.

At first, Chaka was intimidated, but even after learning the meaning of self-discipline and gaining the rank of Lieutenant, she still lorded over him, sending him out constantly on almost-suicidal missions that had slim chances of survival.

Barely taking the bloody catastrophe in stride, Chaka thought her detestable attitude would have gotten her killed, only to find to his dismay she was just too evil, unable to die even by the hands of a mid-ranked devil.

"Stand and fight, you coward!" Atsu's voice hollered.

"Men, destroy that monk and his retainer!" Uchitsune called back.

Chaka came onto a clearing where a small encampment lay, with several tents posted and across the way was a small stream and several cooking pots lined near the embankment. He spotted Atsu several paces ahead, backing away as several soldiers advanced and Chaka immediately tied on his sword.

"*Celestial soldiers, I call you! Fighters from the stars, I call you!*" Atsu shouted. "*All of you, descend from Heaven and arrange yourselves in front of me!*" The naginata he held began glowing brightly in golden light. "*Proceed forward and destroy this evil before me!*" Jamming the blade into the ground, Atsu released a powerful force that blew back the cluster of advancing soldiers, throwing them wayward into the fields.

"Get that *oni* Uchitsune," Chaka called as he withdrew his broadsword. "I'll keep them busy here!" Jumping the fray, Chaka engaged in battle at once, hacking off limbs with brutal velocity, forcing bloodcurdling screams piercing the quiet early morning.

Atsu pushed forward, running toward the embankment where Uchitsune waded across the water, proceeding toward the marshlands.

Chaka slammed his sword into one soldier's back and blood spurted everywhere as he withdrew his weapon with a swift stroke, then kicked aside the hulking frame before taking on the next challenger.

Smashing the blade into the head of another soldier, he sliced it in half like a melon, then delivered a swift swipe, snapping it off at the neck. The next soldier he jammed the broadsword into the heart cavity, breaking ribs as he ripped the blade upwards before kicking off the body by the face, smashing it into the ground.

The cursed blade Chaka held glowed brighter in vermilion light as he continued spilling blood and guts and the men kept coming, hoping to take down the frenzied soldier who tore into them with feral vigor. Chaka felt free, with no remorse, sending every last of those misguided souls with a straight trip to Hell, never to return.

After downing the last three soldiers, Chaka fell to one knee, panting hard for breath. He raised his arm, wiping rivers of sweat and blood from his brow. Glancing at his bloodied chokuto, he noticed the steel was no longer black, but bright ruby and soaked in blood, stained even right down to the braiding on the hilt.

"Look at you, stained with gore!" Atsu's voice called to Chaka.

Chaka looked up, watching the middle-aged man make his way across the clearing, panting hard for breath as he leaned against his bloodstained naginata.

"Those weaklings were no fighters!" Chaka said proudly. "They have no guts!"

"Can only stand up to corpses, eh? That'd be a real even match!"

Chaka chuckled then also stood once Atsu approached. "Are you satisfied now, Uncle?" he asked. "We worked hard today."

Atsu shook his head. "I'll have to move on," he said softly. "That scout was much too fast for me – she got away before I could take her head."

"You can't keep running all your life!" Chaka objected, aghast.

"I enjoyed my time as long as it had lasted, but it's near my end."

"What of your wife?"

"Taiji knew what will happen and understands as such."

"What shall I do?"

"It's your choice."

Chaka watched Atsu make his way onward to the farmhouse in the distance. Overwhelmed with guilt, Chaka walked in the opposite direction, heading for the brook.

Chaka crossed the water and followed the path of downed grass, finally approaching where Uchitsune met her end. He found the discarded sword first, and then happened on her hacked body.

A gaping hole bored through Uchitsune's chest where the partisan tore through her armor, her fighting arm removed and her head - severed from the neck and split in half - lay in the grass several meters away, with a single note written in blood pinned to her damaged steel helmet.

Chaka bent down, examining the note more closely, only to find he couldn't read the language. Glancing at his bloodied sword, he noticed its inscription and the note were written in the same script. Taking off her scabbard, he tucked it into his belt, then retrieved her golden-handled broadsword and made his way back for the stream.

Crouching down beside the water, Chaka rinsed off the blades then splashed water on his face, doused his hair and washed his hands. He suddenly felt unsettled when the sensation of some foreign strangeness bothered him.

Chaka nervously glanced around, finding nothing and hoped it wasn't the spirits of the soldiers he killed. Getting to his feet, Chaka collected the swords and headed for a nearby willow tree, taking a seat under it. After a long while of staring out at the creek as the sun rose higher in the sky, he nodded off into slumber.

A loud snort awakened Chaka and he immediately sat up, crying out in alarm. Glancing around, he faced a pale horse with red eyes looking at him with a blank stare. It wore simple bronze plate barding on its head and sides, with a lacquered saddle that had carvings of ivies ornately decorated with gold, silver and mother-of-pearl inlay.

"Bah!" Chaka spat and gave the animal's nose a sharp smack, forcing it to jerk its head and back away. Chaka yawned and stretched, noticing the skies were dark and the moon was out in full view, its luminance revealing the entire marshland and the woods around him.

Moved by the beauty of the moment, he suddenly composed a poem. *"Gazing at the stars, searching for signs of life, I question, 'will my creator pass me by?' Quietly I wonder with so much sorrow inside. The Universe, so vast and endless! I cry, wanting to know why as I await the Goddess and her return."*

The stray horse whinnied and Chaka glared sharply at the animal.

"You don't like my poetry, eh?" he retorted. The horse snorted in response. "You must belong to Uchitsune. Unlucky for you, for she's dead."

Picking up his swords, Chaka tucked them under his arm and made his way across the stream. The horse trotted behind him and Chaka grunted, coming to a halt.

"Go away!" he shouted. The horse gave Chaka a vapid look and Chaka blew a frustrated sigh. Continuing for the farmhouse at the bottom of the hill, the beast followed behind Chaka several paces away.

Once Chaka approached the modest home, he saw the discarded arms and weaponry had been taken back indoors. He tied the horse's reigns to a nearby post and knocked on the door.

After several moments, the door opened, revealing Taiji who appeared sleepy wearing an elaborate green silk kimono that had dragonflies as the running pattern. About his waist he wore a small green belt with white ferns stitched along its length. Chaka noticed Taiji's hair was down, free of oil and hairpins, gracing his shoulders and reaching the middle of his back. His face, devoid of face powder, lip stain and eye shadow, revealed his plain looks with a single long scar starting across his cheek and nose, ending at his jaw.

"Oh, it's you, *Kengo* Chinokaigan," Taiji murmured. "What are you doing here?"

"You look like as if you're in mourning!" Chaka exclaimed. "You actually look like a man and not some ugly old hag!" Taiji narrowed his eyes and Chaka blocked the door with his foot before it slammed shut. "Forgive me for being rude," Chaka said gently. "Seriously however, what's the matter? Atsu got his revenge and I did pretty well for myself, giving her forces a beating they'll never forget!"

Taiji appeared uneasy and turned away, returning indoors. Chaka nudged the entryway open with his shoulder and made his way inside, setting his swords near the frame. Closing the door shut, he approached the hearth and found Taiji sitting dejectedly by the fire. Beside him at the low table was a teapot and two cups.

"Are you going to have your blades polished before you leave?" Taiji asked softly.

"Maybe I should, eh?"

"Bring them here, I'll do it for you."

Chaka grunted and returned for the shop, taking up his collection of swords. Once he returned, he saw Taiji had brought out several accessories: a bottle of olive oil, a small satchel of sand, and several squares of cloth.

"You're the most difficult person in the world to please!" Chaka snapped once he entered the room. "What gratitude!" He set the blades aside on the table and squat down on his haunches next to Taiji. Reaching over, he grabbed the pot of tea and a cup.

"You don't understand," Taiji grumbled, taking up a sword. "You don't understand who he is."

"Of course I do!" Chaka said, rolling his eyes. He poured himself a serving of tea while Taiji busied himself with polishing the blades. "Uncle Atsu handled himself fine today, but it was I who had to work the hardest - a hundred men! Can you believe that?"

"You don't understand," Taiji repeated. "You thickheaded fool!"

"What is there to understand?" Chaka set aside the pot and sipped the tea, wincing at its bitter contents. "He's an *Onmyoji*... much higher ranking than I could ever be as *Ichizoku Eiyu*! A skilled fighter and defender, and with the knowledge of *Renkinjutsu* on top of it all! It would take me lifetimes to even learn the art, let alone master it."

"That cursed blade you carry," Taiji said softly, "it will end your life."

"Oh really now?" Chaka snorted. "That very blade saved my neck today!"

"You should be afraid of the path you're now taking, *Kengo* Chinokaigan. Your youthful foolishness is going to kill you!"

"Stop being so vague and just tell me!"

Taiji looked down at the floor. "That blade was created for a devil general with hundreds of followers," he murmured. "That demon swore to return for that blade when the stars aligned and his master was freed from his thousand-cycle curse."

"Why would he agree to create such a horrific thing?" Chaka asked, stunned. "*Onmyoji* fear no demons; they kill them as easily as we breathe!"

"It's hard to kill such *akuma* when he captured your sister's soul."

Chaka gasped, taken aback. "How along ago was this?"

"About fifty-one cycles ago..."

"So he's been waiting all this time?" Chaka cried. "What's taking so long?"

"Every fifty-two cycles, the stars align and the gates between *Busshitsukai* and *Makai* are opened," Taiji explained. "Also, that's when the binds of the great devil god weaken."

"So you mean to tell me this *onichuui* took Uncle Atsu's sister, forcing him to make this blade capable of slaying demonic gods?" Taiji grew silent, unable to say anything else and Chaka looked down at his tea, overcome with a sensation he felt unfamiliar with. He mulled over Taiji's words, overwhelmed and disbelieving all at once. "Well," Chaka said, after several moments of silence. "I'm afraid of no *akuma*. If I can kill him and save his sister, then his heart wouldn't suffer anymore."

"No," Taiji said firmly. Chaka put away his cup and Taiji grabbed him by the wrist, squeezing tight. "No," Taiji said again. "This is his burden, not yours."

"I owe him--!"

"You owe him nothing!"

Chaka shook loose Taiji's grip and rose upright. "Who are you to halt me?" he thundered. "I'll destroy those devils, no matter how many: a whole regiment, a whole battalion - I have even fought a whole army before, so what makes this any different? It was fate that I was spared this last battle and led to this place and to hear your story!"

"You're a fool!" Taiji screeched. "You're a childish fool! That fiend is the leader of *Akuma Jougi*'s elite army! You have no chance!"

Chaka stood there as Taiji went on, trying to persuade him from going after this particular demon, telling him about his large band of devilish soldiers under his command and his ability to resurrect the bodies of dead men and women, using them as pawns to overwhelm even the strongest armies of battle monks and exorcists.

This particular devil was an expert swordsman and adept at catching people off their guard, taking something precious to them without their knowledge and using it against them. The demon somehow knew Atsu's skilled alchemic abilities, even making his way through the gates to seek out his services for constructing that cursed blade. Obviously, Atsu refused and lost his sister in response.

"*He doesn't hate women at all,*" Chaka mused, now understanding Atsu's indifference. "*He's still in mourning after all these cycles!*"

"There's nothing you can do but turn your back and walk away," Taiji concluded. "This isn't your battle."

"I gave Uncle Atsu my word," Chaka declared. "I won't abandon him. He's getting older and he may die restless if he doesn't complete this mission."

"Stubborn idiot!" Taiji spat in disgust.

"Tell me where he is so that I may talk it over with him."

"Most likely at the nearby Tsukiakri Temple."

"How far is it from here?"

"About half-day's walk to the East." Taiji sheathed Chaka's blades in their respective scabbards. "I pray for your safety."

"Don't waste your breath," Chaka snapped and took the swords, tying them about his waist. Leaving Taiji's side, he headed outdoors and approached the horse, releasing him from the post. Getting in the saddle, Chaka slapped the reigns, forcing the horse taking off thundering the foothills, leaving a thick trail of dust in his wake.

Coming up the hill, Chaka spotted two figures walking the path and slowed to a gallop. As he approached closer, he recognized the taller older woman named Suzuko and the stout young man named Akeno.

"Ho," Chaka called, waving. "What brings you by?"

"We came to warn Atsuji an Imperial Officer was seeking him out," Akeno answered.

"He's gone to the nearby temple," Chaka replied. "Do you know where that is?"

"We'll lead you there, if you like."

"It's half of a day's walk, I'm told." Chaka patted the horse's head. "We'll get there faster with this fine steed."

"I'll come along," Suzuko offered.

"What of your companion?"

"I'll catch up," Akeno said. "I run fast."

Chaka stopped the horse and the woman got on the saddle behind him.

"Go toward the forest and follow the ridge line along the hills," Suzuko directed.

Chaka nodded and Suzuko held firmly to his waist as he directed the horse toward their destination.

EIGHT

Chaka rode far into the night, covering marshlands and rocky hillsides, eventually happening on a large temple dedicated to the moon goddess Shidzuki during early daybreak with Suzuko's directions.

The shrine, constructed of pale limestone, had large thick doors, small slotted windows and spires on its roof that seemed to rend the wan skies, creating long deep gashes in the gray clouds above. At the bottom of the staircase rest an adult-sized jade statue of the moon goddess wearing a necklace of onyx magatama, posed with arms outstretched toward the heavens.

A light drizzle fell around them as Chaka stopped the horse and he and Suzuko dismounted. He tied the steed to a nearby tree and approached the statue, pressing his palms together and raised them in front of his head. Giving a slight bow in deference, Chaka then entered through the door of the wooden gate that surrounded the temple, making his way up the stone steps with Suzuko at his heels.

Chaka's unease worsened when he sensed a pulse of a faint, yet powerful dark energy emanating from the shrine as he ascended the staircase. Reaching the doors, he looked around, searching for monks and found it unusual that the temple grounds were silent. Yanking the pull cord near the front entrance, he heard the gong inside the shrine quarters dong.

"They may be out saying prayers for the fallen soldiers from the last several battles," Suzuko noted.

"There has to be at least one *souryo* here," Chaka protested. "They'd never leave such a holy place unguarded, especially with all these *akuma* on the attack!"

"I'll go around back and see if they're meditating in the garden."

Chaka nodded and the woman left his side, going around the building's rear. After several more moments and gaining no response, he pushed open the door.

A sudden shadow shot forward at him and Chaka leapt back from the frame, unleashing the black broadsword from his side. The cursed blade glimmered brightly in crimson light as he swung at the wraith that swiped at him, destroying it on contact and three more appeared, swirling around him.

"You're not taking me next, *Shinigami*!" Chaka shouted, parrying the attack of one wraith closest to him. Twisting out with a diagonal slash, he instantly turned it into ash and turned to the third, sidestepping another attack. Hacking it into shreds, Chaka blocked a savage swipe from the fourth, then made an underhanded thrust, impaling it instantly.

Hurrying indoors, Chaka found the monks inside decimated, littered in piles of ash, blood and bone, with their holy enchanted weapons broken where their bodies lay. Following the trail of blood, he entered a large corridor lit by torches and surrounded by statues of the various gods and goddesses that protected the island. Ahead was a large golden door that had been smashed open.

"Honored Uncle," Chaka called. "Are you here?" Hearing no acknowledgment, he ran toward the exit, making his way down a steep staircase.

Entering the dark catacombs, Chaka encountered more dead monks and priest-soldiers, their polearms and hammers shattered near their decomposed bodies. Approaching the last door barred by a heavy gate, he encountered a switch, a dial, and a counter-sink weighing board next to the entranceway.

"I don't have time for this," Chaka growled in response and drew up his leg with his knee bent to his chest. Giving the barred door a powerful kick, the old metal bent and slowly creaked under the weight. He stomped again and the heavy steel door groaned open, crashing to the ground with a loud bang.

Stepping inside a room washed in eerie blue-green light; Chaka saw a single marble pedestal in the center of the room, with a glowing blue orb precariously balanced on a small pyramid of violet steel.

"What's this?" he muttered and approached the glimmering crystal, reaching for it. Suddenly a low rumble shook the temple and the light bathing the room turned dark. Chaka whirled around, facing a monstrous figure towering near the doorway. "Are you here to stop me?" he demanded.

"*I shall tell you only once,*" a disembodied voice hissed. "*Leave this place and never return!*"

Chaka held his broadsword at ready when the shadowy form near the door slowly fleshed out with black partial scale armor, wearing a conical helmet with horns on the top of its head. A large hooked axe strapped to the harness around his waist cackled with green energy.

"I'm not afraid of you!" Chaka snapped. "If this crystal is so important, maybe I'll borrow it."

"*Life comes at you!*" The devil unleashed its axe and released a burst of lightning with its other hand, hurtling the discharge toward Chaka.

"*Hanshaga Shokan!*" Chaka cried and slashed back. Cutting through the bolt, the energy sphere split, striking the wall behind him and shattered the stone as if it were paper. Its resulting force sent Chaka flying forward on the floor and plunging to the ground while his opponent vanished out of sight. Rolling to his feet, Chaka turned out of a concentrated killing charge from the shadowy fiend who abruptly appeared with his cackling blade. "*Yaketsuku Yunahikari!*" Chaka bellowed, unleashing a powerful thrust at the devil's side.

The demon easily turned away the energy attack with his own driving savage blow, slamming his axe deep into Chaka's chest. Chaka parried at the last moment, the daunting force sending him back several feet. He fell against the wall, stunned and the devil held his axe high, ready to unleash its obliterating maneuver.

"*What fearsome strength!*" Chaka thought as he staggered upright. "*Despite having <u>Onikage</u>, if I keep on, I'll be rent limb from limb!*"

"*Know this, <u>Satsugaisha</u>,*" snarled the shadowy fiend, "*my power is far beyond yours. Clearly you are indefensible!*"

"So you leave me no choice..." Chaka said through gritted teeth. "You think I will be desperate enough to attempt striking against impossible odds!"

"*You are no match against my formidable power!*" The demon savagely swung his axe and Chaka barely countered the attack in time, narrowly escaping being cut in half.

Chaka kicked the fiend rearwards and fought on the defensive, backing away as his shadowy opponent pressed forward with furiously fierce and fast strokes, creating a web of steel and energy that encircled Chaka's quickly tiring form.

"*Hageshii Arashi!*" Chaka screamed as the devil aimed for his head. A stunning bursting wave of golden flames released around Chaka and the following blast of explosive power sent both Chaka and the devil flying in opposite directions, crashing into the temple walls.

Chaka grunted when his body struck stone and slumped forward, gasping weakly for breath. The fiend vanished when he struck the opposite wall and a deep reverberation rumbled around Chaka, causing bricks crashing around him.

"*You may be extraordinarily gifted,*" growled the devil, "*but the kamisama cannot protect you forever.*" The shadowy fiend appeared over Chaka with charged hands. "*Remain silent and suffer alone forever in the shadows of Oblivion!*"

"*Inshotekina Sutoraiki!*" Chaka roared as he dashed out of a crushing strike from the electrified axe and struck back with his glowing broadsword, shattering the weapon into dust with a massive powerful hit.

Offside, Chaka heard shouts and sounds of blades clashing from another part of the room. He raced for the source and entered the inner sanctum, finding by chance Atsu battling a tall and agile warrior in a horned helmet and carmine lamellar armor who wielded a large thick vermilion dual-edged katana.

The crimson warrior wore a facemask depicting a demonic visage and gauntlets that had talons over the knuckles. Once Chaka took a step forward, the red knight suddenly halted his attack and Atsu fell to one knee, panting hard for breath as he leaned against his naginata.

"*You have what belongs to me,*" the warrior snarled. "*That weapon you wield... give it to me!*"

Chaka cringed, intimidated by the gravelly voice echoing off the temple walls. "Fight me for it," he said nervously and held the broadsword at ready. "I can take you!"

"Devil, begone with you!" Atsu called. "Return to Hell where you belong!"

"*We had a contract,*" the demon snarled, never once taking his eyes off Chaka. Behind the facemask blazed glowing green eyes. "*You give me what I want and I give you what you desire.*"

Chaka swallowed his fear and tightened his grip, standing straighter. "Release his sister's soul this instant," he demanded, finding his voice. "Then I'll give you this wicked blade."

"Don't!" Atsu cried.

"*I will destroy you to get it back!*"

"Try your best - in Hell!" Atsu shouted and charged the devil, making a mad lash with his partisan. The scarlet knight vanished and reappeared behind Atsu, holding out his clawed hand.

"*You wish for me to return your sister's wretched soul, eh?*" the demon replied, generating a sphere of frosty light that glimmered dimly in pale violet. *"Here, her soulstone I hold. Let's make an exchange."*

Atsu whirled around, gripping tightly to his glaive. "You're lying!" he snarled, narrowing his eyes. "Whatever you do, *Kengo* Chinokaigan, don't give it to him!"

"Silence, bothersome priest!" The devil growled, crushing the light in his hands.

Chaka charged forward, sword held high before the devil retaliated in response. The warrior flashed out of sight once Chaka brought down his broadsword and spun around on his heel, making a clearing slash.

"Weakling!" Chaka spat, sheathing his blade.

"What are you doing here?" Atsu demanded.

Chaka turned to Atsu. "I came to help," he replied.

Suddenly the earth beneath them trembled and a thunderous roar reverberated off the walls around them. Chaka let out a cry and ducked while Atsu held fast to his partisan and pierced it to the floor, holding onto it.

The floor cracked from the force and portions of the ceiling fell apart, dropping heavy stones around them. Part of the ground caved in, crashing into the lower rooms below.

"Atsuji!" Suzuko's voice called from afar. Once the quake quelled, Chaka and Atsu stood as the woman came running through the door with Akeno at her side, panting hard for breath.

"What are you doing here?" Atsu shouted. "Leave here before this place is rendered apart!"

"You need to leave here at once," Suzuko said urgently. "Troops on the march under House Sasori's banner are making their way here!"

"That must be *Taishou* Hisamasa," Chaka said, disturbed. "Why is he on the attack?"

"How many men?" Atsu demanded.

"At least two *lu* or maybe one *shih*," answered Akeno.

"Over a thousand men?" Chaka cried. "We can't possibly defeat them!"

"If a mere ant can defeat a lion," Atsu retorted, "then we can defeat a regiment together!"

"Commit *jisatsu* on your own!" Chaka complained. "I refuse to die like that with those odds!"

"They fear you, *Kengo* Chinokaigan," Atsu said and hoisted his naginata over his shoulder. "They also have to close this gate that leads to *Makai* as well, and we can't let them raze this temple."

"I had no idea..."

"Let's go." Atsu dashed out the door and Chaka glanced back at Akeno and Suzuko who appeared ill at ease.

"Either help us fight or die here," Chaka said.

"We'll catch up," Akeno answered.

Chaka turned away and hurried after Atsu.

NINE

Stepping out the temple's front door, Chaka clenched his teeth at the sight of a cluster of soldiers - male and female, swordfighters and lancers all - surrounding a tall bearded muscular man with tanned skin and narrow hazel eyes.

The imposing dragoon wore gleaming black and gold lacquered leather armor accentuated by oversized shoulder plates, and a horned helmet covered his flaming sandy-red hair. Over his shoulders, he wore a bright yellow cloak with his house's insignia on the back and saddled an orange-eyed midnight-black horse.

"Isawa Chaka!" bellowed the horseman.

"I'm here, *Taishou* Hisamasa," Chaka called back. "Returned from Hell to punish me, eh? I'll send you back so quickly before you can even take a breath!"

"Your list of crimes is extensive," Hisamasa shouted, "from deserting your unit to slaying an officer and killing a hundred men of the Imperial Army!"

"I hadn't much of a choice." Chaka put a hand to the hilt of the golden broadsword he wore. "I can't let you kill me. I made several promises and to carry them out, I need to live."

"Take up your sword and accept your fate, criminal!" Hisamasa thundered. "The same goes for you, Massai Atsuji! Death comes at you both!"

"I refuse to leave here," Atsu called. "Come up and take me down if you wish. My fight isn't with you, but with these *akuma* that continually plague us. However, if you get in my way, I will send you to Hell!"

The soldiers let out war cries as they advanced, three to four at a time, hoping to outmaneuver and take down Chaka who showed no signs of backing down.

Chaka withdrew his broadsword and taking a firm grip, he charged down the stairs as the lancers raced up them, spears held high. He swung with complete abandon at the first lance thrust at him, snapping the blade off the end.

Ducking under another pike aimed for his throat, Chaka hacked into the soldier, cutting him in half by the torso and lopped off the arm of another. Staying low, Chaka swung with wild abandon, hitting anyone who came near as he carved a path through the wave, making his way for Hisamasa. Behind him, Atsu stood guard at the door, naginata at ready.

Chaka turned out of a thrust from a spearman and leaned back from a step of another who came up on his side. Blocking with a backhanded strike, Chaka grunted when a third lancer sliced his wrist, aiming for his shoulder. Dispatching the solider before him, Chaka took off her head and kicked the other spearman aside, sending him bowling down the steps into others that crowded the area.

Chaka swiftly cut a spear in half aimed for his neck and smashed his broadsword into the head of the fighter beside him. Staggering back, Chaka panted hard for breath as the group below him charged again, working their way up the stairs.

Sudden pain surged from his mid-back, causing him to let out an agonized yelp. Turning, Chaka faced another lancer, surprised that the fighter slipped behind him unnoticed.

"They're too good," he thought as jammed his sword into the solider's chest, immediately felling her. Wrenching the blade free, he dodged the other spears from the remaining soldiers and quickly backed away up the stairs. *"Fighting with ease on uneven terrain, even cutting me despite my clear advantage! A hundred kenshi I can take, but a hundred yarikihei...!"*

Holding his broadsword at ready, Chaka ducked down when the spearfighters made their way up, throwing a clearing sweep that forced them back. Stepping forward with an underhanded strike, he took off the head of the solider in front of him and thrust the broadsword into the chest of another, stomping her down the steps.

Chaka screamed in pain when another spearfighter penetrated his guard, slicing into his shoulder. Unleashing the cursed broadsword from his holster with his other hand, Chaka immediately took off the fighter's arm and slashed across, slicing open her neck.

Suddenly a hail of arrows rained around them, piercing the remaining spearfighters in the head, arms, shoulders, chest, and legs, felling the group before Chaka.

Turning, Chaka looked up, spotting a stout muscular warrior in olive chain mail armor, wielding a great bow crafted of silver with numerous gemstones embedded into the outer shaft and shouldering a quiver of ebony arrows. On the archer's head, he wore an elaborate bucket helmet with bright feathers running down middle and a face mask of a fanged devil.

"*We can't let you close the gate,*" the mysterious archer called. "*We've been monitoring your movements and you need to be stopped.*"

"Is that you, Akeno?" Chaka called, disturbed.

"*Nay,*" answered the archer, "*I am called Akanasutsune.*"

"Your meager reinforcements will not save you," Hisamasa roared. "Try as you might, but you're only signing your death warrant!"

"Bring your best!" Chaka screamed, glaring back at the soldiers who climbed over the dead bodies, making their way up the steps again. "I'll send every last one of you to Hell!"

Letting out a war cry, Chaka charged, swinging wildly as another torrent of arrows pelted down from above. Pulling back as the spearfighters converged on him, a flash of steel beheaded the warriors.

Chaka fell down on his rear as a lithe warrior in azure scale armor jumped down before him, wielding a dual-bladed glaive. On her head she wore a heavy helmet with black spiral horns on the sides and her face was covered by a smiling devil mask with wild golden eyes.

"*Get up and kill!*" the azure warrior declared. "*Stab, slash, destroy! Make them burn in Hell!*"

"Is that you, Suzuko?" Chaka cried.

"*Nay,*" answered the lancer, "*I am called Shiranosuke.*"

Chaka jumped to his feet and swung his blade as he ran headlong into the armed crowd. Taking down men and women by the dozens, he jumped, twisted and turned out the way of swords, spears and daggers, overcome by a bloodthirsty frenzy the more blood he shed. Blocking low, Chaka made a sweep, taking legs off fighters and whipped the sword around, slicing off heads and arms.

Barreling through another group, Chaka kept up the pace, taking limbs and cutting through bodies until no more surrounded him. Covered in blood and gore as he held the dripping glowing broadsword at his side, Chaka sweat profusely from the brightness of the hot torturing midday sun, surrounded by dead bodies and wounded warriors. He panted hard for breath, exhausted and the muscles in his body hurt, abused from the fight.

"This is a long way from the end," Chaka thought, glaring at Hisamasa who sat on his horse, hand to the hilt of his heavy oversized field sword. It lay in a deep cobalt scabbard and had an onyx handle shaped as a dragon's head. "You're the only one left, *Taishou* Hisamasa," Chaka thundered. "Make it easy on yourself and just swallow your sword!"

"I have orders to kill you here," Hisamasa retorted, "no matter what, even if the Imperial Army could not."

"Ha!" Chaka barked. "You failed!"

"I don't care how many men you destroy - a hundred, a thousand, a hundred-thousand!" Hisamasa withdrew his violet-steeled field sword and kneed his horse, charging for Chaka. "Contemplate your sins in Oblivion!"

Chaka drew his blade with both hands, blocking the direct blow to his head and turned out, slashing his sword into Hisamasa's back. The cursed broadsword bounced back and Hisamasa made a tight turn around, charging again.

"Enchanted armor!" Chaka thought in horror and whirled around, leaning back as he thrust the sword behind him.

Chaka suddenly stopped as fierce fiery pain stabbed him through the chest. His grip around the black chokuto loosened and he looked down, catching a faint gleam underneath him. Protruding through his breastplate was the violet shiratachi and Chaka suddenly found it hard to breathe as red fluid shot out from his wound.

"No!" Chaka wailed. "Don't do this to me... I didn't come all this way to end like this!" The general wrenched his blade free and grabbed Chaka by his hair, hurling him to the ground. Chaka smashed into the steps and the blade he held slipped from his grip, clattering nearby beside him. "I'm not afraid to die," Chaka moaned as he struggled to his hands and knees, gasping, "but I didn't come here to be killed by you!"

"Arrogant fool!" Hisamasa growled. "Reflect on your disrespect in Hell!"

Atsu clutched tight to his naginata as Hisamasa raised his sword. *"Thunder from Heaven, ignite!"* he called and made a running leap, vaulting above with his glaive to Hisamasa standing over Chaka's downed form.

The general turned and Atsu drove his gleaming partisan into the lacquered, hardened leather armor with an underhanded stroke. A charge of electric aquamarine light burst forth, throwing Hisamasa off his horse.

The dragoon commander staggered to his feet as a large gaping vertical cut split through his armor, starting at the waist and widening as it went up, tipping off at the breastplate. Blood sheeted over his destroyed armor plate, flowing freely. Atsu landed on his feet and panted hard for breath, standing before him with the naginata held low.

Hisamasa laughed darkly in response. "Is this the best you have?" he crowed.

"*Wrath of Heaven, ignite!*" Atsu shouted and turned on his heel, flicking the partisan with a broad sweep at the general's feet. Hisamasa dashed offside and Atsu turned with an overhead swing, smashing the glaive into the general as he slammed his sword into his side from behind, connecting into the thick plating and shattering what was left of the breastplate. The force of the blow rent Hisamasa across the ground, smashing into the gate below. "*By the celestial laws I command you now: burn by the flames of purity!*" Atsu hurled down his naginata, releasing a blast of golden flame.

The torrential fires chased toward the general, striking him and his horse head on. Hisamasa screamed when caught fire, howling in terror and agony. The fires changed from brilliant gold to blazing blue then faded away, leaving behind charred armor.

Atsu turned to Chaka's downed body, kneeling by his side.

"I'm sorry you got mixed up in this, *Kengo* Chinokaigan," Atsu murmured. "I thought I could undo the chaos that *akuma* and his minions brought to our lands and I only caused more needless deaths..."

"You didn't have to save me," Chaka wheezed. "Now you're responsible for me..."

The warrior in azure armor walked up to Atsu, pointing her naginata at his throat. "*By saving his life, you inflicted his* continued existence on this world," she snarled. "*You're an impediment to our lord's plans... We can't let you live!*"

"What's the meaning of this?" Atsu demanded, glaring up. "Were you guarding the gate near this temple?"

"*Yes,*" the verdant-armored archer replied from offside. "*That's where the <u>akuma</u> have been escaping from, also that's why it's been difficult to combat those forces that have been fighting nonstop.*"

"I can't let you monsters live!" Atsu pushed away the azure demoness and rose to his feet, holding his glaive at ready.

"That's enough!" Chaka rasped as he struggled to his feet. Kicking up the crimson-stained broadsword, he held it in his right hand, pointing it in the general direction of the demonic pair. "Uncle Atsu, let me fight them. You've done enough for me!"

"This is my battle," Atsu protested. "*Kengo* Chinokaigan, whatever you do from now on, be it good or evil, is my responsibility. You're too weak to keep fighting!"

"I beg of you!" Chaka snapped. "I made a promise to *Taichou* Kurebayashi to avenge her soul against these devils. As long as they exist, she will never rest!"

"You'll be battling forever!"

"So be it!"

Chaka held up his sword broadside, standing with his feet apart and knees slightly bent and turned inward. "*My chances are slim,*" he thought as the demon in blue scale held her partisan at ready and her companion in green chain withdrew three arrows, drawing back on his bow. "*I won't have time to dodge the arrows and block her attack. If I take another strike, I'm dead!*" Chaka tightened his grip. "*Lord*

Shinkunikkou, help me!" Chaka dashed ahead, dodging arrows the olive devil unleashed from behind and let loose a horizontal strike as the azure demon countered with a whirlwind slash.

"*Inshotekina Sutoraiki!*" Chaka bellowed, blocking the swift blow with a reverse thrust. The naginata's end shattered and Chaka turned around, barely escaping another rain of arrows that whistled past him, following with an overhead swing as the demon overturned her blade.

Crashing the broadsword into the devil's skull, Chaka grunted once sliced through his other shoulder. He staggered back as the azure warrior fell to his feet then stumbled forward when struck in the back by another pelting of arrows.

Circling around, Chaka knocked away more projectiles and rushed to the archer, ducking down as he swung wildly. "*Ataushinai Okyoda!*" Chaka thundered, thrusting the sword into the archer's thigh. He ripped the steel upward and cut him in half by the torso.

Blood released in a spray, drenching Chaka as he jammed the broadsword into the ground once he fell, struggling to stay up. The archer fell in pieces, smashing into the ground as the ebony arrows disappeared and the jeweled bow tarnished, immediately turning to dust.

"*Kengo* Chinokaigan!" Atsu cried when Chaka suddenly loosened his grip and fell face first into the dirt. "*Kengo* Chinokaigan...?" Atsu rushed over to Chaka's side, touching his shoulder.

"*Good, that nuisance is finally out the way,*" a dark voice hissed. Atsu stood at once as the warrior in the crimson lamellar and horned helmet reappeared before him, unleashing his dual-edged vermilion katana. Violet electricity cackled around the sword as he pointed it at Atsu. "*Ha, so much for honor - you nearly killed him! Now dying will just be so much easier for you...*"

"The *kamisama* blessed him with a rare ability," Atsu said weakly. "Why they chose him, I have no idea..."

"*Liar and you know it!*" The devil vanished and reappeared behind Atsu, kicking up the fallen sword at Chaka's side. "*I shall thank you for returning my blade to me by sending you to suffer for eternity in Hell!*"

"You--!" Atsu stepped out of a cross slash and hacked off the demon's arm before he had a chance to raise it, ridding the hand that held the cursed sword. "*Swords from the fires of Heaven, ignite!*" Several bolts of flame unleashed from Atsu's forward pierce and the devil quickly sidestepped the attack.

With his other hand, the demon slashed at Atsu with the electrified katana, unleashing a force that shattered Atsu's naginata. "*Shisseki!*" the devil shouted and jammed his sword into the ground, unleashing fissures that broke apart the stone steps, throwing Atsu head over heels.

Atsu rolled to his feet and charged, picking up the cursed katana before the fiend could reach for it. "*Guardians from Heaven, protect me!*" he called. "*Let nothing pierce this mortal shell!*" Making a savage swipe at the warrior, the crimson knight flashed out of sight, reappearing from behind. Atsu dodged a heavy slash, sidestepping the swift strokes aimed at him.

"*Tachisaru!*" the demon thundered and rushed Atsu with a lunging thrust. Atsu countered at the same time, struggling against the warrior's strength.

"*I call down the perfection of wisdom!*" Atsu growled. "*The power of the Goddess compels you!*" The once sunny skies suddenly darkened and became illuminated with scarlet light as thunderous surges of energy cackled with force. A volt of purple lightning struck the demon, blasting him back into the ground and unleashed silver threads that bound around his arms and legs. The devil screamed as he crashed into the earth, breaking the stone steps beneath him. Atsu rushed over, sword held high. "*Power of Heaven, ignite!*" Atsu hollered. "*Be no more as you were formed!*"

"*Gensho Satsu!*" the demonic knight snarled and the energy surrounding his cackling red-steeled katana enveloped his body, shattering the threads that bound him. "*Join the afterlife without mercy, you worm!*"

"You first!"

Rolling out of Atsu's rushing attack, the devil stepped into his guard as Atsu struck down. "*Konzetsu Suru!*" the vermilion knight roared, countering the glowing sword with a forceful slash of Atsu's charged blade.

Turning out, the fiend struck at Atsu's chest who returned with an underhanded diagonal slash, piercing his breastplate and ripping upwards. The electric sword shattered in response and the demon's body became charged with bright lavender light, shattering his armor and charred his body into ash instantly.

Atsu struck the ground on his knees as the cursed black broadsword fell from his slacked grip, clattering away.

TEN

Chaka groaned weakly as he came to and opened his eyes, finding he lay in a pitch-dark world. Struggling to support himself, he sat up with great effort, only to fall back, gasping hard for breath.

"*You finally awaken,*" a strange ethereal voice said to him.

"Where am I?" Chaka commanded.

"*You are my captive, Satsugaisha,*" the mysterious voice answered. "*I overestimated your skill perhaps, but not that weak, fragile body.*"

"I will destroy you!" Chaka shouted into the darkness.

"*You detest me for capturing you, is that so?*" A sinister chortle pierced the shadows. "*Would you rather have died with such dishonor at the feet of Hisamasa?*" Chaka sat up with clenched hands and ground his teeth as his face burned. "*I'm giving you another chance, for such pure blood runs through you.*"

"Enough of your empty words," Chaka said through gritted teeth. "Who are you? You're no *Kamisama*, I can tell!"

"*You're on the brink of death, Satsugaisha. You only have one choice.*" Chaka gripped his hair, overwhelmed. "*You wish to keep your word to your dear comrades, true? For if you let go of this life now,*" *no one will avenge you, for you brought dishonor to your name and to your House!"*

"*He's right!*" Chaka thought in horror. "*I can't die now... If I stay in <u>Yomi</u> too long, I'll rot forever! But who is it am I giving my soul away to?*"

"*So what is your answer?*"

Chaka blew a heavy sigh and lowered his hands in his lap. "What are the conditions?" he muttered and shuddered, consumed by the sense of dread that made the hairs on his skin stand at end.

Looking up, Chaka noticed glowing green eyes staring hard down at him. He scrambled to his feet as a wan aquamarine light brightened the room. Before him stood the tall demonic-masked vermilion knight with his large thick crimson dual-edged katana in hand. Beside him appeared the horned athletic lancer in cobalt scale armor and the green chain-armored archer.

"You two - why are you here?" Chaka demanded. "What do you want with me?"

"*We follow our commander wherever he goes,*" answered the lancer.

"*We swore to fight for him for eternity,*" replied the archer.

"*You have a great skill I need,*" said the crimson knight. "*I aspire to use you to advance my plans.*"

"Know this," Chaka snarled, "I have no intentions of trusting you."

The demon snorted. "*Who said anything about this being a matter of trust?*"

"Why pick me?" Chaka demanded. "What is it about me that you need so badly? I'm nothing special."

"You are most impressive... You are the only one I've seen who can control himself under the bloodlust curse while handling Onikage." The demon pointed his sword at Chaka and Chaka drew back, only to pause when he realized he had no armaments.

"Why is that blade so important to you?" Chaka spat, putting up his hands in guard.

"You are a threat to these lands."

"Either I let you destroy me or I join your side and live, is that it?" Chaka hollered, growing enraged. "I'd rather go to Hell!" He lurched forward and the two other devils grabbed Chaka by the arms, holding him back.

"Listen!" the red knight bellowed, jamming his sword into Chaka's heart cavity. Chaka groaned as his chest burned and coughed. He looked down, expecting blood, but found none. *"You swear vengeance against me for all that you had lost, is that so?"* the demon teased. *"You're too weak!"* Yanking his sword free, the lancer and archer let go of their hold. The crimson devil kicked Chaka back, sending him hurtling rearward into the darkness. *"You cannot escape here and neither can I,"* the demon hissed and appeared over Chaka. *"We both have a need to return to Busshitsukai and finish what we started."*

"Why do you keep attacking innocents then?" Chaka sat up, glaring at the red fiend. "If it's to take over *Ningenkai* then you'll only have an uphill battle - the *Kamisama* protect that realm!"

"It's to prevent Majin Tensei..."

"Majin Tensei...?" Chaka shook his head. "How is it related to crafting that wicked blade and holding Uncle Atsu's sister's soul hostage?"

The crimson knight stomped on Chaka's chest, pinning him as he clutched the electrified sword in his taloned hand. *"It will take too long to explain and I need your body to finish my objective..."*

"What?" Chaka grabbed the demon by the foot, throwing him back. The devil riposted and Chaka grabbed the sword, only to get lashed at the wrist with the clawed gauntlets, forming deep gashes. *"Inshotekina Sutoraiki!"* Chaka shouted and golden light charged around his hand. The sword shattered, its resulting force knocking the crimson knight back into the shadows.

"Kengo Chinokaigan!" Atsu's voice called faintly. "Don't leave this world! You made a promise, remember?"

"I refuse to help you," Chaka snarled. "I'd rather rot here than deal with the likes of you."

"You can't go to the White Jade Pavilion," said the demon pointedly, *"especially with the bad <u>kharma</u> you've generated!"*

Chaka ground his teeth in response. *"I've got make up the <u>dharma</u> for it before I can even pass on!"* he thought in annoyance. *"He could be lying to me and have some ulterior motive in mind!"*

"What say you?"

"My power is too weak to eradicate such a high-ranking <u>akuma</u> and his followers!" Chaka blew a heavy sigh. *"I need to train more..."*

The crimson knight reappeared before Chaka with his attendants flanking him. "*Let me borrow your body until I finish my objective,*" he said. "*That is all I want.*"

"Until I know what this *Majin Tensei* is," Chaka spat, "I refuse."

"*But you already agreed!*"

"Fulfill that condition, then I will!"

The shadowy world suddenly grew dim around them and in the distance, a faint pulsing light appeared from afar.

"*Kengo* Chinokaigan!" Atsu called, his voice much louder now. "Please return! I'm too weak to hold on much longer!"

"I'm coming!" Chaka called back. He took off toward the steadily dimming light and the devils rushed after him.

"*You made a contract!*" the crimson knight roared. "*You will honor your word!*"

"I refuse!"

The demons tackled Chaka and they hurtled off the edge of space, falling into the light.

Atsu knelt at Chaka's side, pressing his faintly glowing hands on the young man's chest. Chaka's bloodied skin was cold to the touch, its warmth rapidly drawing away and his skin turning white.

"*Oh energy of the goddess, oh all attractive goddess, oh supreme giver of life and death, please engage me in your service,*" Atsu prayed. "*Renew this soul and may his life serve as a sign of your transformative power. Use him as your instrument for the renewal of society. Bring your mighty life-giving energy and lead him back to this world so that he will be a faithful follower of your power. Be the resurrection and the life for all and what you have created, for anyone anywhere who knows suffering and death in any form, and for Creation itself!"*

Soft violet light surrounded Chaka's body and a blast of lightning cracked from the heavens, striking Chaka's downed form. The force of the shock threw Atsu on his rear and Chaka's body suddenly seized, his limbs jerking involuntarily.

The lightning storm worsened and Atsu cried out when three sets of smoldering armor - crimson lamellar, green chain mail, and azure scale suddenly appeared from the sky, crashing on Chaka. They shattered on contact, becoming dust and Chaka immediately sat up, screaming, clutching his head in agony.

"No!" he wailed and swung at invisible forces. "Let me go!"

"*Kengo* Chinokaigan!" Atsu scrambled to his feet and rushed over to Chaka, only to get socked in the groin, downing him. Atsu staggered to his feet and Chaka grew silent, hunching forward as he heaved for breath. "Are you well?"

"I..." Chaka shuddered and gripped his wrist that oozed blood from three deep cuts. "I–!" His demeanor suddenly changed and he immediately stood, storming over to Atsu.

Atsu backed away, tense and Chaka let out a shout, rushing forward with a glowing fist. Atsu slapped away his attack and leaned out of another punch then whirled around him, kicking him in the back.

"What is with you?" Atsu shouted as Chaka attacked again, dropping low with a rushing attack.

Atsu jumped over the attempted throw and Chaka returned with an elbow smash, striking Atsu in the chest. Atsu grabbed his wrist, attempting to throw him and Chaka grabbed Atsu roughly by the hand, crushing it in a vise-like grip that brought him to his knees.

A malicious smile appeared on Chaka's face and his gray eyes glowed in blue-violet light as he glowered back at Atsu who shuddered in pain beside him.

"*I will get my revenge on you later, old man!*" Chaka hissed in a layered tone. "*You try to eradicate me and you will kill him. Remember, you are responsible for his life!*"

"You will pay for destroying his body," Atsu snarled back. "Why are you possessing him?"

"*This warrior has a great power I can manipulate to advance my plans.*" Chaka relent his grip and Atsu shoved him back.

"Don't even think of taking *Onikage*," Atsu growled. "You promised to return my sister's soul to me!"

"*You know where it is,*" Chaka snapped and kicked up the nearby black chokuto, grasping it in hand. "*Get it while you still can.*"

Atsu scrambled for the golden broadsword left behind and rushed up the steps, jumping over the littered bodies as he hurried back into the partially destroyed temple.

Chaka struggled to get through, fighting the pressure to see. He cried out and slipped to his knees, exhausted. "What are you going to do to me?" he wailed. "Who are you?"

"*I am called Tannozume,*" the voice of the crimson knight grumbled in Chaka's mind. "*You will follow my orders until I complete my objectives.*"

"I can't return home like this!" Chaka cried. "I would be a total failure!"

"*Then erase your shame.*"

Chaka stood and sheathed the bloodied cursed broadsword back in its scabbard. "*There is no way I am able to return to House Suzume,*" he mused in despair. "*The loss of face is too great...*" He looked out over the mound of corpses to the valley below. "*Until I cleanse myself of these sins, there is no use thinking about that.*"

"*Since you have free time now,*" said Tannozume, "*you can focus on a more important quest.*"

"The devil lord Ototanashi has been sealed away forever, more than a thousand cycles ago," complained Chaka. "There is no way he can return."

"*That is where you're wrong!*" Tannozume shouted. "*I left Makai to warn you cretins that he will break free from his thousand-cycle curse and return to Busshitsukai. He plans to slay the kamisama who fought against him and rule your realm, casting the world in eternal darkness and causing constant war and plague throughout the land!*"

Chaka scoffed. "A mere *akuma*, caring about this world, my world?" He let out a short laugh. "Why would you bother?" When Chaka received no answer, he picked up Atsu's broken naginata and started his trek back to the workshop in town.

Chaka walked all afternoon and late into the night, eventually returning to the converted farmhouse. Ascending the stoop, he knocked on the door.

Moments later, the entranceway opened, revealing Taiji who appeared sullen, wearing his hair pulled back in a single queue and dressed in a white kimono. Chaka handed over the broken naginata and Taiji gasped.

"He went back to get his sister and close the gate," Chaka said simply. "You were right."

Taiji took the weapon with shaking hands. "W-where will you go?" he stammered.

"I have other promises to keep." Chaka turned away and stiffened when he heard Taiji unleash his fan.

"I'm not letting you leave here until I hear from Atsuji," Taiji snarled.

"You said you wanted me gone before the cold sets in."

Taiji rapped Chaka on the shoulder and Chaka growled, turning to strike back, only to get struck in the face. Chaka staggered rearward and Taiji kicked him down the steps, forcing him crashing on the ground.

"Keep dreaming those foolish dreams and you'll only continue tainting everything you touch!" Taiji shrilled, pointing the closed fan at Chaka. "You'll only continue destroying without fail - no matter how many *akuma* you kill, no matter how many of your comrades die around you, you will never find peace!"

"I will keep trying," Chaka declared. "I will get stronger - my honor depends on it!"

"When you do, bring me back that devil's cursed blade and *Onikage* too!"

Chaka nodded. "I will," he promised.

"Leave here and do not darken my doorstep until you finish what you swore."

Chaka stood and dusted himself off. "Where is the nearest town?" he asked.

"Hanamura is two bells walk to the West and Kaedemachi is a bell's walk to the South. Where are you going?"

"I have to return to House Suzume."

"Chinokaigan is East of here."

"I don't wish to return there just yet," Chaka hedged. "I have something else to do before I go there…"

Taiji narrowed his eyes. "What is it exactly?"

"Have you heard anything about *Majin Tensei*?"

Taiji scoffed and waved Chaka away. "Why are you asking me? If you trained as *Senshuken*, then you would already understand that!"

"I skipped some of my studies to learn the art of warfare."

"Find a temple school and ask a monk. They can help you."

Before Chaka could ask where, Taiji stormed back indoors, slamming shut the door.

Chaka grunted and turned away, looking out over the fields. "*I have no other choice but to start walking,*" he mused. "*The closest village is Kaedemachi…*"

Chaka began his trek to the South, greatly ill at ease.

ELEVEN

Chaka walked the winding road through rocky hillsides and among high ridges that marked the course of the Dakusan River streaming below, its waters crashing around boulders and trees. Above him, the sun slowly rose, pushing away the dense antemeridian shadows enveloping the range's crevices and the dawn's light broke through the clouds, washing the sky in orange and peach hues.

Emerging from rough terrain, Chaka entered a modest village of small wooden houses peppered with maple trees that gave the town its name. The village, nestled near the base of the hill and surrounded by the river's boundary, rest under the shadow of a lone imposing yet run-down temple facing the cluster of houses near the riverbank, with a worn sign posted at the front gate.

Before the temple that overlooked the river surrounded by a high stone wall, towered the largest maple tree in the village. Its low hanging branches were bare from its yellowed leaves, having fallen from the autumnal winds. Further down the road, the other buildings that stood out was a modest inn, nearby teahouse and green grocer.

Chaka spotted a youngish man with tanned skin and graying reddish hair wearing dark brown robes with crests of white sparrows on the chest sitting on the worn steps of the temple, looking up at the early morning skies.

"Ho, *Souryo*," Chaka called as he walked up to the gate. "It's a bit chilly this morning, no?"

"How peaceful it is here," said the monk. "On such mornings as this, undisturbed by the noise of others living."

"What a cold thing to say!" Chaka cried, aghast.

"Of course you'd understand," replied the monk. "You stand there, reeking of guts and with the nerve to be offended!"

"I just want a bath and something to eat for right now," Chaka complained. "Then I can deal with your rudeness later!"

"Go wash in the river!" The monk stood and stormed back indoors.

Chaka huffed and made his way to the riverbank, untying his blades and propped them near a large boulder. After pulling out of his armor and undergarments, Chaka dipped a toe in the water and recoiled from its iciness. Holding his breath, he jumped in and surprised by its depth, let out a yelp once his body seized from the shock, forcing him to sink.

"*Are you trying to kill yourself?*" Tannozume's voice shouted in Chaka's head.

"*No!*" Chaka thought frantically. "*It never crossed my mind!*"

"*Where is your head, doing something as foolish as that!*"

Chaka saw red as his breath thinned and he tried to will his body to move, only to have his limbs refuse to respond. The fogginess began again and he fought to keep to the surface.

"Don't take over my body again!" Chaka yelled in his mind. *"I don't need your help!"*

"If you die, then we die!" Tannozume roared. *"I will use you as I see fit and if you keep trying to kill yourself, then your conscience will be no more!"*

Chaka found that he was able to move and shot for the surface. Cresting, he coughed and spat water, clinging to the edge of the riverbed, heaving and gulping for breath.

A sandaled foot stepped on his wet head and Chaka glared up, facing the monk standing over him. In his hand he held a heavy lance that glimmered in pale violet light.

"You're still filthy," said the monk and shoved Chaka back into the water with a firm push.

Splashing into the deep, Chaka quickly found footing and jumped to his feet. Growing enraged, he stormed out the water and sidestepped a lunge from the monk, whirling around him. The monk stepped in time, thrusting his glowing spear. Chaka swiftly backed away, dodging attacks aimed at his head and chest.

"Why are you attacking me?" Chaka yelped as he scrambled backwards from the cleric who kept advancing.

"You know the answer to that!" the monk snapped.

"What do you mean by that?"

"I know you didn't come here for spiritual guidance!"

"I did!"

"Reflect the error of your ways in Hell!"

Chaka leaned out of another attack and his back slammed against the maple tree. The monk jammed the blade into Chaka's shoulder, pinning him against the wood. Chaka cried out as fiery pain consumed his left arm, the prickly sensation quickly rising.

The monk kicked Chaka in the chest and Chaka grabbed his ankle with his right hand, twisting in an attempt to throw him off, only to get a reverse heel kick in the face. Chaka sagged against the wood, stunned.

With bleary eyes, he watched the monk turn away, approaching his armor left on the ground and picked up the cursed broadsword Onikage, then made his way inside the temple without a sound.

After several long moments, the monk returned with a kettle and cup, taking a seat beside the discarded armor and poured himself a cup of tea. He drank in the relative quiet of the morning, looking off into the middle distance.

After a long bout of silence, Chaka spoke up. "Care to share some tea with me?" he cracked. "It is cold after all." The monk grunted in response. "Why do this to me?" he protested. "I never attacked you, nor drew my blade!"

"I had to separate that cursed *chokuto* from you," the monk answered plainly and poured himself another serving after he finished his first. "Also, to quell that devil in your left arm."

"How could you could tell?" Chaka asked, surprised.

"I have a strong *Sensuosen* skill... I could tell half a *ri* up the road there."

"That's quite the feat!"

"How unlucky for you."

Chaka grunted. "Well, at least get me down from here!"

"Not likely."

"Damn you, old man!" Chaka screamed.

"If you struggle, you'll only bleed to death," the monk answered in a matter-of-fact tone. "So I insist you stay still and listen."

"Listen to what?" Chaka spat sourly.

"To the wind, to the river behind you, to the sound of nature all around."

Chaka blew a heavy sigh, rolling his eyes. "You must be mad," he muttered. "To think I could get any advice from you regarding *Majin Tensei*! I should've known that oily-haired dog was a liar!"

The monk raised an eyebrow. "*Majin Tensei*, you say?" he inquired.

Chaka narrowed his eyes, glaring back. "Yes," he said through gritted teeth. "I need to know all I can so I can rid this devil that's plaguing me."

"How did you get cursed in the first place?"

Chaka told his story and the monk nodded empathically while he sipped his tea. "I see," he said once Chaka finished. "You're an idiot."

"What?" Chaka shrilled. "How dare you–!"

The monk quickly rose to his feet and closed the gap between them, slugging Chaka with a fierce right hook to the face. Chaka's head snapped to the side and the monk threw another punch into his solar plexus, forcing Chaka coughing violently for breath.

"Stop your whining," the monk snapped. "I told you to listen!"

"Listen to what?" Chaka wheezed. "Your constant insults?"

"Hmph," the monk muttered. He left Chaka's side, taking up his kettle and cup.

Chaka found it increasingly harder to keep awake as his skin grew colder. He fought to keep his eyes open but the pain won out and he slipped into darkness.

Waking up some time later, Chaka found that he lay in a small room on a futon with a linen sheet covering his nude body. Sitting up, he glanced around, noticing a small writing desk across the room and an oil lantern placed aside near the edge, casting warm light.

Beside him lay a simple plain light brown lightly padded kimono folded near his pillow with a pair of leather sandals set on top and a small tray that held a bowl of rice gruel and cup of cold tea. Chaka noticed his shoulder was bandaged and an incantation in a language he couldn't read painted in burgundy henna drawn on his arm and left pectoral.

After downing his meal, Chaka grabbed the kimono and pulled into it then got to his feet. Leaving the sandals behind, he approached the door then slid it open, peering out into the hall. Finding no one posted outside, he walked down the corridor, looking for others.

Entering the atrium, Chaka spotted several bald monks in brown and yellow robes clustered about on cushions, reading books. He walked past them, heading for the veranda, where he noticed more monks in dark red robes sitting outside, drinking tea.

"Ho," Chaka greeted. "Have you seen that red-haired devil around?"

"What red-haired devil?" the monk closest to Chaka asked.

"Has having no hair robbed you of your senses?" Chaka snapped. "The one in dark brown, obviously!"

"Oh, you mean Hashira," replied another monk. "He's possibly in the garden."

"He could be in the fields," answered a third, "or maybe down river refilling the water jars."

"I thought he went to town to pick up some vegetables," retorted a fourth. "If you see him, make sure to tell him to get his eyes checked."

"Why?" Chaka spat.

"He keeps getting onions - it's bad during meditation sessions!"

Chaka ground his teeth and stormed out, hearing the monks laughing at his back. "Crazy old fools," he muttered.

Exiting outdoors, he spotted Hashira walking up the road with a basket of vegetables looped on his arm. Chaka picked up a rock near the steps and hurled it at him. The monk caught it with ease and cast it back, striking Chaka squarely in the head, knocking him down.

Chaka groaned, seeing stars. Hashira later approached, standing over him. "I see," he said simply. "You're not right-handed."

"What's that supposed to mean?" Chaka moaned.

The monk grunted and stepped over him, heading inside.

Chaka sat up, rubbing at his head, then scrambled to his feet and stormed the temple. "Wait, you!" he thundered after Hashira. "You will respect me!"

"I have no reason to," Hashira called over his shoulder. Chaka followed him into the kitchen where several other monks were busy cooking, talking amongst themselves.

"You obviously have the answers I'm looking for," Chaka retorted. "Why won't you tell me?"

"Until you're ready to listen, then I will." Hashira placed the basket of vegetables on the nearby counter. "Either go away or help cook lunch."

Chaka growled under his breath and snatched up a knife on the counter. "I don't care what I have to do to get you to talk, old man!" he bellowed. "If I have to slice you open, I will!"

"You won't do that," Hashira said calmly, then pushed past Chaka. "Since you're so eager to cut up something, go peel the *taro*."

Chaka let out a frustrated scream and lunged at Hashira. The monk turned out with a swift sidestep and grasped Chaka's wrist, flipping him overhead to the stone floor. Slamming the young man's body into the concrete, Hashira turned Chaka's wrist with a painful lock as he stepped on Chaka's chest, smiling down at him.

"This is a waste of your time," Hashira said brightly. "Please stop that." Releasing his grip, Hashira took the knife and set it aside, then left the room.

"Ho, you," called a monk to Chaka. "Go sweep the unused rooms and the stairs!"

"Why should I?" Chaka grumbled from his place on the floor.

"Unlike Hashira, we're very nice. You don't want whatever chores he has in mind!"

"What is he, some lecherous old man or something?"

The other monks burst out laughing and Chaka sat up, his face flushed scarlet.

"You're too old for us anyway," another monk replied. "You should be safe."

"You'd never know," teased a third. "Tastes change!"

Chaka stood, his face burning bright red as the monks fell into another round of laughter. He stomped for the corner, grabbing a broom and made his way to the rear entrance, sweeping the steps of dust and leaves.

"Ho, *Kengo*," a voice called to him. Chaka looked up, noticing Hashira sitting on the stone wall facing the river.

"Are you ready to talk to me?" Chaka grumbled.

"Are you ready to listen?" Chaka grunted and continued sweeping. Hashira leaned back on the wall's edge, placing his hands behind his head and folded his legs at the knee, sighing. "Beautiful day isn't it?" he said nonchalantly.

"I guess," Chaka muttered, making his way down the path.

"Haven't you ever gone on *Ko*?"

"I can't say I have."

"What are you saying, that you have no friends?"

"It's impossible for me to have friends."

"Why is that? You seem to be a likeable person, despite that temper."

"Have you gone senile?" Chaka spat, "I'm possessed, remember?"

"That's right."

After another long stretch of silence while sweeping the patio, Chaka spoke up. "What is with that cursed *chokuto*? I know it's not made of *Amahagane*, like my *Kagesureiyo*."

"You're right," answered Hashira, "it's not."

"What is it made of then?"

"I wouldn't know."

"Does it belong to a certain class?"

"*Takiletzachi*, I think."

"Isn't that the name of the hammer belonging to the blacksmith god, Shukenten?"

"Oh, you know your stories about the *kamisama*."

Chaka stopped his sweeping, glaring up at the monk who reclined on the wall. "Why are you wasting my time?" he thundered. "You know what I came here for!"

"I know, but do you?"

Chaka let out a roar and jumped, slamming the broom over the stone's ledge. Hashira immediately rolled to his feet when the wood cracked the surface and kicked the broom with the side of his foot as Chaka raised it again. Counter balancing with his other foot, Hashira tossed up the wood, catching it in hand and turned it around, chucking it at Chaka. The blunt end struck the young man in the chest and the force threw him back, sending him crashing into the stone.

Hashira jumped down with ease and landed softly on his feet over Chaka's downed form. "You're still not ready," he spat. The gong inside the temple rang and Hashira walked inside, leaving Chaka alone on the ground.

For the next several days, Chaka demanded answers from Hashira in regards to his request, only to get humiliated with a severe beating in some way every time. During the day, when not performing a chore ordered by the other monks, at night Chaka would retreat to his room unsuccessful yet again, with a small meal left for him on the tray at the desk.

The following morning, Chaka woke up gravely ill and hissed in pain when fierce burning agony coursed through his left arm and chest.

"What's going on?" he moaned and staggered to his feet. Leaving the room, Chaka found the assembled monks on the floor, deep in meditation instead of performing their usual housekeeping duties. He silently walked past them and headed for the great hall, only to get barred by a junior acolyte in a beige robe as he reached the door.

"You can't go out," said the acolyte. "Today is very unlucky."

"Bah," Chaka spat and pushed the junior monk aside. "There are no lucky and unlucky days!"

"If you were in training to be an *Onmyoji*, you'd know better!"

"I'm not," Chaka replied.

"Oh, are you searching for enlightenment so you can return to your path then?"

"In a way..." Chaka blew an annoyed sigh. "Are you letting me out, or what?"

"Say, you look ill," said the monk instead. "Did you eat onion and garlic soup?" Chaka shook his head. "Where are you going? There's no work for you today."

"Where is Hashira?" Chaka demanded.

"He's out doing purification rites. Maybe you should do the same."

"I'll consider it."

Unable to convince Chaka to stay indoors, the monk stepped aside and Chaka pushed open the worn wood. Exiting on the steps, Chaka clenched his teeth at the fierce cold wind blowing around him.

Glancing skyward, he noticed the skies overcast with low, hanging dark gray clouds. The burning in his arm worsened and he left the steps, heading around the side of the building.

"It's going to rain soon," Hashira called. Chaka turned, finding the monk standing under the large maple tree.

"So it is," Chaka called back.

"Now is the time to cut away all that distracts you," Hashira said seriously. "Put forth action and realize your ideas are nothing more than a dream."

"What are you trying to say?" When Hashira didn't answer, Chaka advanced, standing next to him. He looked in his line of sight, noting he stared at the craggy hills in the distance.

A rolling reverberation suddenly resonated around them and Chaka glanced skyward, searching for thunderheads. When the rumbling drone grew louder, Chaka looked around and tensed at the charge of five officers on horses, followed by a group of twenty soldiers running up the path, armed in bronze and white-gold breastplates, arm and shin guards.

"There he is!" the captain shouted. "It's Isawa Chaka! Take him!"

"What?" Chaka cried as the soldiers converged on temple grounds with their swords and lances drawn, surrounding him and blocking off any means of escape.

"Be careful, men," called the captain, "he's dangerous, even while unarmed! Don't underestimate him!"

"Then how are we supposed to take him in?" asked a junior officer.

"You're making a mistake!" Chaka yelped. He backed away into Hashira who stood calmly at the tree. "Please, do something!"

"Surely," Hashira answered and raised his hand.

A dozen arrows abruptly whistled past them and Chaka cried out when one struck him in the thigh, downing him. He broke off the missile and raced for the river behind them. Jumping the fence, he heard a loud explosion and a powerful, fierce fiery pain blasted in his back. Falling forward on his face, Chaka met darkness instantly.

TWELVE

When Chaka came to, he hissed from the pain blazing down his back and thigh. His foggy eyes took note of his surroundings, finding that part of his kimono torn and the remnants tied around his thigh and chest, keeping the wounds closed. He also noticed his wrists and ankles were bound, tied to a pair of posts carried by four soldiers who marched briskly down the road, counting their steps in encouragement.

Glancing around from his upside-down position, Chaka looked forward, sighting a group of eight lancers marching in the rear, with two deputies following close behind on their lightly-armored horses. To his left and right were the junior captains on unarmored horses and craning back his head, Chaka saw eight sword fighters marching in the front, with the division captain leading the way on his heavily armored warhorse.

"All this for one mere man?" Chaka thought incredulously as they reached the outskirts of Shinkunotani. *"When I see that dog Hashira, I'm sending him straight to Hell by my own hand!"*

From his inversed view, loomed Morikage Castle in the distance. The structure, crafted of dark stone and reinforced with heavy larch, was the largest building in the area, overlooking Shirosagi Port. Surrounding the castle were numerous temples dedicated the myriad of gods and goddesses in the area.

A row of guards blocked the wide bridge that led into the Northern Province owned by House Suzume, inspecting all passerby who approached. When the platoon sergeant showed his official seal, the guards let entry and the gang of soldiers marched across.

"Ho," called the gatekeeper as the group approached the second barrier of the inner compound. "State your business."

"I've brought the dangerous criminal Isawa," the division captain announced.

"How was that possible?" the gatekeeper scoffed. "From Uchitsune's runners, they claimed he'd easily slain a thousand men with only a measly sword!"

"He had to have help!" the sergeant said, rolling his eyes.

"He's even cut down Hisamasa and his horse at the same time," called a soldier from the rear.

"Bah, impossible!" spat the gatekeeper. "Hisamasa was as devilish as they come - he could smash boulders and trees with his bare hands; there's no way this yellow-haired sapling could even touch him!"

"Well, apparently they thought he's vicious enough to be executed."

"Executed?" Chaka squawked. "I'm not admitting to anything!" He shook against his restraints. "You try to kill me and I'll send you to Hell first so you can tell me how the weather is down there!"

"Shut it you!" snapped a junior captain. One swordsman closest to Chaka withdrew his scabbard, beaning him on the head with it. Chaka screamed and struggled harder, only to get struck again by two more soldiers.

"You keep up that racket and we'll slice you open!" snapped Chaka's handler.

"Why don't you?" Chaka shouted.

"We have orders to keep you alive enough until you're executed!"

"Come on then!"

The four soldiers holding Chaka set him down as a heap and struck him repeatedly with their scabbards. Chaka screamed curses, insults and threats at them as they continued whaling.

"That doesn't hurt!" Chaka chided. "You can only strike at branches! Corpses put up a better fight than you! Your wife has more strength in her arms than that! Your grandmother put more power in that blow when she beat you!"

When one enraged soldier withdrew his blade, the division captain whistled at them. "That's enough!" he spat. "Don't cut him up, neh?"

The soldiers grumbled as they put away their swords.

"My grandmother, heh!" the soldier over Chaka rumbled and gave him a swift kick. "You're lucky today, you worm!"

"What are your orders?" asked the gatekeeper, slightly amused.

"We're to leave him in the stockades until Lord Kuwanai and *Taishou* Setsuna return from finishing the current campaign," replied the division captain.

"And if he tries to escape?"

"As you see, we're only allowed to beat him, not kill him outright."

"What if he kills one of us?" the soldier from the rear piped up.

"Then you weren't strong enough to handle an ogre such as him!"

Some soldiers laughed and the gatekeeper waved a hand, signaling the lower-ranked guards to open the gate. The old iron portcullis creaked as the men wound the chains, raising it from its lowered position. The group of soldiers hoisted Chaka and marched through, carrying him to the inner keep.

Once dumped on the ground, the sergeant stepped off his horse and untied Chaka, then motioned two soldiers to follow him. The retainers kept their hands at ready to their swords while the captain led the way and Chaka said nothing, casting his sights at the ground as he hobbled along, keeping in step.

Walking toward a lavish garden dotted with many small soapstone statues of cranes, sparrows and dragonflies, they descended a limestone path leading to a pool of clear water that appeared glossy black on its surface. Chaka glanced down as they passed, noting black marble lining the bottom of the pool.

Prodded to continue moving forward, Chaka grunted and the group eventually reached a large beechwood shack at the end of the path, consisting of the bathhouse. A servant in dark brown trousers and pale beige jacket bowed to the captain on approach. "Ho, *Gunsou* Kiyotomo," he greeted politely.

"Get him cleaned up," instructed Kiyotomo. "If he as much sneezes, throw a brick at him."

"Hey!" Chaka snapped.

The soldier on Chaka's left withdrew his katana, striking him on the shoulder with the spine. Chaka cried out, crumpling to his knees.

"Only use the back of your blade if you absolutely must," Kiyotomo declared. "By orders of Lord Kuwanai."

The servant nodded and bowed again to the captain. Kiyotomo left his side and the soldiers followed, leaving Chaka behind. Chaka staggered to his feet and opened the bathhouse door when the servant made no motion to move.

Making his way inside, he paused short at a golden-haired woman with tanned skin and pale violet eyes wearing a plain blue and white kimono sitting on the bench across from the washing tub. Resting beside her was a small basket holding a few jars of herbs, strips of cloth, several needles and spools of thread. Propped against the wall behind her leaned a pair of swords, a wakizashi and matching tanto.

Folded on the other side of the bench was a plain white cotton kimono with brown bamboo as the running pattern, a pair of cotton socks and square wash cloth folded neatly into a pile, next a pair of straw sandals.

"Who are you?" Chaka asked.

"I'm Mitchikata Amaya," the woman answered. "I'm filling in for my father who is out on the current campaign."

"You can't be a doctor," Chaka said, mildly surprised.

"Oh?" Amaya chuckled. "Then you must not want that wound checked. If you wait for my father to arrive, you'd be a ghost by then."

"I didn't say I thought you were incompetent," Chaka fussed.

"I was told the monks at Shiromatsu Temple treated you, but at Lord Kuwanai's request, I have to make sure it's not infected."

"I'm fine," Chaka grumbled.

"I've seen many naked men before," Amaya said and grinned. "No need to feel embarrassed!"

"Please, get out." Chaka opened the door. "I don't need your help."

"I'll check later then?"

When Chaka said nothing else, Amaya grabbed her basket of supplies and left the room. Chaka shut the door after her and glanced back at the pair of swords she left behind.

Taking the short sword, Chaka crept to the door, thumbing back the blade from its scabbard. He pushed back the panel with his free hand and peered outside. Chaka noticed the servant pacing several feet away from the bathhouse, arms inside his padded robe. Gripping the sheath in a firm hand, Chaka nudged open the door then paused when he spotted an archer on patrol from the second story terrace.

"*I can't defeat them by brute force,*" Chaka thought and placed the sword back where he found it. "*I need time to think...*"

He stripped himself of what clothing remained, then approached the tub and put in a hand, finding the water extremely warm. Stepping in, Chaka groaned when he sat in the hot water, sinking into the depths until his head was underneath.

Later after getting dressed and hiding the dagger in his kimono's sleeve, Chaka was sent to the lower chambers, told by the guard accompanying him that it was rumored to be haunted by ghosts of bloodthirsty prisoners from ages past.

Chaka grew increasingly worried, only knowing how to defeat demons and not angry spirits. When another pair of guards appeared out in the corridor with thick wrist and ankle irons accompanied by heavy chains, Chaka immediately tensed, standing on the offensive.

"What's the meaning of this?" Chaka shouted.

"You're under arrest, remember?" Chaka's escort snapped.

"No prisoner is ever treated this well!" Chaka retorted.

"You're to be put in *agari-zashiki* until you confess to your crimes!"

"Forget it!"

Chaka threw a punch at the escort and grabbed him by the arm, throwing him forward against the guards holding the irons. The man bowled head over heels, crashing against the guards. Unleashing the dagger he had hidden, Chaka withdrew the blade, ducking under the attack of the other guards snapping the chain at him.

Turning out with a wild lash, he slashed open the neck of one retainer and cut into the arm of the second. Another guard came running at the sound of the scuffle and jumped over the tangled fray, jumping on Chaka's back. Chaka jammed his dagger into the man's arm that clamped around his neck and staggered back into the nearby wall, hurling forward.

Tossing the man off, Chaka stood, only to get a pair of leg and wrist irons pelted at him, bashing into his head and face. Chaka hit the ground, immediately seeing red.

"What a monster!" the retainer fussed as he kicked aside the dagger from Chaka's hand and jammed his knee into Chaka's chest, barring him from standing. "Hurry up and tie him down!"

"I'm not getting paid enough for this!" whined the servant as he scrambled for the chains.

"Damn dog sliced up my arm!" the second guard complained. "I don't know if I'll ever fight again!"

"Isn't that Michikata-sensei's *tanto*?" asked the servant.

"Make sure she's alive," ordered the warden over Chaka. "He probably killed her to get it!"

"After we tie this monster down, we will!"

"Mindless beast killed my friend Ikechi for no reason!" complained the first guard. "What a good man! Who's going to feed all those children of his?"

"How many he's got?" asked the fourth guard as he held down Chaka's arms.

"Six or seven..."

"He sure likes to keep busy, heh!" hooted the servant as he held down Chaka's legs.

"His wife will be upset for sure!"

"Oh? I heard after the last time he went to visit her, she wrote back she's got another one coming!"

"Maybe he ought to work the fields and care for them, eh?"

"Young dogs like this don't understand the meaning of responsibility!"

The servant and the injured retainer stayed behind over the body of the slain warden after the group clasped on the irons and threaded the chains. The remaining guards kept Chaka's arms pulled at his back and yanked him to his feet, dragging him down the corridor that lead to the lower stairwell.

Entering a dark, dank, musty room that had no light, Chaka was tossed in and immediately closed off from the outside. At first Chaka heard nothing, listening intently for sounds of other guards. He felt around in the pitch, trying to get a feel of the layout, only coming across a single worn bucket.

Once relegating himself to the corner, Chaka would at times change positions, either sitting with his arms around his knees or sitting against the wall while other times he sat on his knees with his hands on his thighs, staring into the darkness, even pacing at times to keep warm as the winds outside grew colder.

Chaka even relished the break in the monotony when the guards came, bringing a small tray holding a bowl of boiled noodles in a weak vegetable broth with a side of dried fish, switching out the former tray and taking the bucket in the rear of the room by replacing it with another one.

Chaka struggled with mentally keeping track of the days by counting which vegetable was used in the broth, the noodles used, or the dried fish he was given. Some days were the same, other days were different. As time went on, Chaka grew frustrated with the inconsistency, unable to remember what day it was. The demon inside also began to stir, grumbling curses.

"Oh, you finally awaken," Chaka spat sourly. "I know you're strong enough to break free once that incantation fades."

"*Chained by the ankles and wrists like an animal, you'll weaken before long,*" Tannozume snarled. "*There is no way you can withstand being in a dark hole such as this - you will break, spirit and all!*"

"Crickets like dark damp places," Chaka cracked. "It's only been twenty days... I think..."

"*Heh...*

Suddenly Chaka heard the door to the cell open and light seared through from the glow of a paper lantern. Chaka cried out, covering his face with his hands.

"He's prone to attacking," snapped the warden with the lamp. "Remember, the spine of your blades only!"

"If you're going to use your swords," Chaka vaunted as the retainers filtered in, "let me borrow one, eh? I promise your trip to Hell will be swift!"

"Shut it you!"

The guards snatched Chaka by the chains, pulling him out into the corridor. Realizing his wrists were before him, Chaka clasped his hands together and smashed a double-fisted punch into the lantern-wielding warden.

The others scrambled to withdraw their swords and Chaka swung the chain, knocking one blade out the hand of the fighter closest to him and snapping another in half against the one on his right. Chaka barreled through the remaining guards, snatching up the fallen katana along the way and hurried up the stairs.

Emerging at the top of the staircase, Chaka froze at the sight of a horde of police officers in padded coats armed with all manner of truncheons: staves, sai, jutte, tekkan, and tonfa.

Leading the group stood a middle-aged man with narrow gray eyes, short silver hair, graying short beard and mustache at the entrance. He wore a heavy bearskin cloak over a beaten brown and yellow-laced plate armor with a crest of a sparrow stamped on the breastplate.

"Father!" Chaka cried, startled.

THIRTEEN

Chaka glanced over his shoulder when he heard the guards coming up the stairs. The constabulary rushed forward at his momentary distraction and Chaka whirled around, making wild slashes at them.

Shattering his sword against an officer's sai, Chaka cried out when jammed in the neck, side and arm with jutte, the pressure points forcing his arm and leg numb. Left staggering, the enforcers easily took him down by overwhelming numbers and beat him with their batons and staffs.

Unable to resist when the guards wrestled him down to the ground and held his arms behind his back, Chaka screamed curses at them all. "I won't be satisfied with just killing you!" he bellowed. "I'll rip you apart and send you piece by piece to Hell! Let the demons gnaw on you for ages!"

"Shut your face, you loathsome degenerate!" snapped the middle-aged man once he approached. He delivered a forceful front kick at Chaka, snapping back his head.

"What shall we do next, Lord Kuwanai?" asked an officer.

"He's to be punished until he admits his crimes," Kuwanai answered. "Bind him and scourge him."

"How many strokes?"

"For all the men he's killed thus far."

The officer's eyes widened. "That's well over a thousand!" he yelped.

"Very well." Kuwanai stalked off indoors while the retainers dragged Chaka toward the courtyards.

Chaka grunted when thrown down to the dirt, and the guards tied his bound wrists and ankles against posts set in the ground, then sat on his arms and legs, preventing movement. Moments later, a police lieutenant brought out a case of bamboo canes while his commander held a scroll in hand.

"Ready," called the junior officer as he withdrew a rod.

The senior officer nodded and opened the scroll, reading aloud its contents. "*For acting as a lewd and sordid person, you must be taught to respect both the property and judgement of your superiors. To restore harmony and order, punishment is served until you confess your guilt. Such valid proof is then taken down in writing and sealed by you.*"

"I refuse to confess to something that was done in an altered state of mind," Chaka snapped. "I'm warning you, as the days go by, the devil inside me will only strengthen and your precious harmony will be the least of your worries!"

"If that is your answer, then for each name I read off this list, you shall get a strike," announced the official. "If after this punishment is complete and you still fail to confess, then you shall be punished more severely."

"It'll only prove insurmountable!" Chaka growled.

"Strip him," the senior officer commanded. Chaka struggled against his binds as his kimono was unlaced and pulled off his back. The second officer held his cane at ready and his commander nodded. "Nagamori, Terumasa, Shinnosuke, Kunimichi..."

Chaka ground his teeth, cringing in pain for each whack he received from the rattan.

When the afternoon descended to evening and a servant held a lantern for the officers to see more clearly once dusk approached, Chaka continued gaining whips to his profusely bleeding back. After the last name was read, the commanding officer frowned at Chaka who struggled to breathe. "What a monster!" he muttered. "Never once he passed out from the pain!"

"On the buttocks then, Sir?" asked the lieutenant.

"Strip him completely and let's start again. A thorough beating should be necessary enough." The senior officer waved to the servant. "Have a jar of water handy just in case."

"Hurry up and confess," a retainer sitting on Chaka's arm complained. "It's too cold to tolerate your foolishness!"

"Then I'll make you suffer more along with me," Chaka snarled. "I'm sure you have plenty of sins to freeze off!"

"Insolent dog!" spat the guard and bat Chaka on the back of the head.

The officers stripped the kimono completely off Chaka's body and the lieutenant enforcer restarted the whipping. Chaka let out a yelp in pain, struggling against those who held him down.

The evening turned to night and the commander blew a hard sigh when Chaka never once said anything.

"Quite stubborn, eh?" the officer grumbled. "Come now, men, pour the water on and let's try this one last time."

"Caning on wet skin!" the servant yelped, appalled. "Even the most stubborn prisoners confess at that point!"

"In this cold weather no less!" argued the lieutenant, dismayed.

"We'll see!" jeered the commanding officer.

"Any particular place?"

"Be random. He can't expect it coming."

Doused in water, Chaka screamed when struck on the shoulder, again on the thigh and anywhere else where his skin was exposed. Even after passing out from the pain and cold, he woke up sputtering when more icy water was thrown on and wailed when struck again.

Once the last of the caning was complete, the commanding officer blew a heavy disconcerted sigh. "Very well," he called. "Get him up and have him hug the stone."

"Five should make you confess!" snapped the lieutenant.

"He might have to go though ten," commented a third officer. "He's survived over three-thousand strikes!"

"Ten, heh!"

The guards untied Chaka's limp body and dragged him to the center of the courtyard where a platform of sharp three-cornered batons rest before a mid-sized wooden pillar. Forced on his knees, Chaka hissed in pain and offered no resistance when his arms were tied behind his back to the post.

Moments later, a group of four officers carried a heavy square stone slab from the nearby courtyard shed and dropped it on Chaka's thighs.

"Whew," one officer murmured. "I wouldn't be able to withstand one!"

"Be glad you're not a criminal in this lifetime, neh?" joked his partner. They laughed and Chaka glared at them both.

"If you think by some failing in a previous existence that I was not favored with the ability to be righteous," Chaka snarled, "then you are sadly mistaken!"

"Send for another," the senior officer called.

The team of officers left and returned with another slab, placing it atop the first one. Chaka grunted, but said nothing. After six slabs were placed on his thighs, Chaka shook in intensity, heaving for breath.

"Are you ready to confess?" demanded the commander. "It's late and I'd like to get some sleep."

"To Hell with you," Chaka rasped.

The senior officer stifled a yawn and waved at another group to bring out a slab.

Once the tenth one was placed, Chaka pressed his back against the post, wheezing for breath from the stone slabs weighing against his chest. "Is that the best you have?" he croaked.

The lieutenant grabbed Chaka by the hair, yanking forcefully. "Confess now!" he shouted. "This has gone on long enough!"

Chaka spat at the officer and grunted from a hard punch to the face.

"Let's call it a night," the commander called. "Let him reflect on his errors until the morning."

"About time!" a nearby guard grumbled. "I was starting to fall asleep standing up!"

The group left the courtyard and filtered inside the garden room on the other side. Once the door shut, Chaka groaned in pain.

"*How long are you going to continue this?*" he thought. "*If my body breaks, then you'll have no other place to be!*"

"*Pain will only make you stronger,*" Tannozume replied. The vermilion knight appeared sitting atop the stone slabs, holding onto his crimson sheathed katana. "*Your strength becomes my strength and mine, yours. Relish it, become one with it. You'll need it in the future!*"

"*You just enjoy watching me being tortured!*"

The red devil laughed in return. "*Maybe so,*" he retorted.

Chaka shuddered from the frigid winds blowing around him. After several hours, the winds increased their intensity, freezing his skin. The dark skies of late night slowly turned to dawn and then a cold hard rain fell.

"Damn you monsters!" Chaka screeched as icy rain pelted around him. "Get this thing off me!"

"*They won't come out until the rain passes,*" Tannozume answered.

"*How long will that be?*" Chaka thought frantically. "*I can't do this anymore... They won't believe me, despite my telling the truth!*"

"*Of course they cannot believe you,*" Tannozume spat. "*You, a killer of <u>akuma</u>, became possessed not by one, but by three!*"

"I need to understand this _Majin Tensei_ you've mentioned," Chaka insisted. "_I'll be willing to help if you just tell me what I'm involving myself in!_"

The crimson devil jumped off the platform and began pacing. "_As you know, it was Lady Oshiikaten who formed this world and appointed Lord Shinkunikkou and his wife, Lady Shidzuki to watch over the realm,_" he said. "_Yet Lady Oshiikaten's brother, jealous of her role, began stirring trouble and vowed to destroy her creation..._"

"I don't remember this story during training," Chaka murmured.

"_Ototanashi was his name and he came from the Void. His immense power overwhelmed the other kamisama and so Lord Shukenten, the strongest of all, joined the great war to end Ototanashi's foolishness,_" Tannozume went on. "_Lord Shukenten's Star Hammer shattered in the clash and fell here to your world. The great power destroyed your ancestors who couldn't handle the force of the kamui._"

"How is it that we can control it now?"

"_Lady Oshiikaten reformed anew with the ashes, granting your kind the ability to wield kamui against Ototanashi and the embodiment of his hatred - the akuma. Lord Shukenten revealed to your people a new way of fighting and eventually a way to combine that power into a deadly force._"

"So that's why the blacksmiths work in concert with Clan Champions and craft these devil-slaying tools... But why haven't these islands found peace in all this time?"

"_A thousand cycles ago, Lady Shidzuki was stolen away by Ototanashi and my former lord bound Lord Shinkunikkou to the Void, casting the world in darkness. Several legendary Senshuken who had_ *weapons fashioned from pieces of Lord Shukenten's Star Hammer, these shards you call <u>Amahagane</u>, rose up and challenged him, defeating him and returning light to the world.*"

"I was told he's only been bound for a thousand cycles," Chaka noted. "How is that so?"

"*The stars align and the seals that keep Ototanashi bound weaken, so he escapes to exact his vengeance. This time, he vowed to slaughter the sun lord Shinkuikkou, casting eternal night, since after each battle, he grows weaker and weaker.*"

"What of Lady Shidzuki then?" Chaka implored, intrigued.

"*I wouldn't know... I only know of my former master's plans.*"

"Is the reason you must use these *Takiletzachi* blades because the ones of *Amahagane* may hurt you?"

Tannozume vanished into mist and Chaka blew a short sigh, waiting in the rain.

Several hours passed and once the rains tapered, the police officers returned, with a servant holding an umbrella for the commanding officer.

"No," Chaka grumbled before the official could say anything.

"He didn't ask anything of you yet!" the lieutenant retorted.

"It's still no," Chaka growled, glaring back.

"Well, if that's your answer, you're to be punished again," the commander spat. "However, by the grace of Lord Kuwanai, he wishes you to be untied for recovery in the stockade no longer than a few days before starting again." He waved at his followers. "Unload the stone. Quickly now before it showers again."

A team of six men pulled off the water-soaked slabs, grunting with effort. After taking off the last one, the guards untied Chaka's binds and dragged him back to the dungeons. Tossed in the corner, the door slammed shut after them and Chaka immediately fainted on the floor.

FOURTEEN

Chaka slowly roused to the scent of garlic, onions, and sardines. He reached around in the dark, only to knock over the tray that held the bowl of soup and dried fish. Chaka cursed under his breath, feeling the floor for the fish.

Moments later, the door came open and Chaka glared up at Kuwanai wearing a heavy overcoat over his padded kimono standing at the entranceway.

"Enjoying the meal?" Kuwanai badgered.

"Your servants forgot to serve me tea," Chaka responded sourly and sat up on his knees. "What do you want from me?"

"Are you finished acting out?" Kuwanai snapped. "Your preposterousness has gone on for far too long!"

"I never amounted to much in your eyes anyway," Chaka spat.

"You were held in the keep for sixty-six days; any lesser man would have broken by now!"

"It seems I'm not any lesser man." Chaka smirked as Kuwanai clenched his hands at his sides and his face flushed scarlet in simmering fury. "Are you afraid the Isawa name would be sullied by someone known as a fearsome criminal?"

"I cannot have that," Kuwanai snarled. "What you have done is inexcusable!"

"We both know how horrible it would look upon you, Father!" Chaka bared his teeth. "Did you come down here to punish me yourself?"

"I'm warning you - you will be executed if you do not confess to your crimes." Kuwanai pushed back his overcoat and placed a hand to the hilt of the wakizashi he wore. "Out of those thousand you killed, you slaughtered a hundred of our own, *Ketsueki Kaiganjuu*."

Chaka's mouth dropped open in shock. "Is that what they're calling me now?" he yelped. "I'm telling you - I was cursed at the time; you *know* I'm not that strong on my own!" Chaka clenched his hands in his lap and hunched forward, growing tense. "I've only been in service to House Suzume for two cycles! What makes you think I've gained that sort of skill in a short amount of time?"

"You became *Fukutaichou* in that short span!" Kuwanai protested. "Don't lie to me!"

"Due to the power of the *Kagesureiyo,* I took a hundred heads belonging to captains, lieutenants, and generals!" Chaka complained. "I'm skilled fighting *akuma*, not men!"

"Then what is this talk about this 'Beast from the Blood Coast'? Own up to it and die or prove me wrong!"

Chaka shook in rage, growling. "You lost your right to penalize me as you see fit!" He got on his haunches. "You can't have me executed."

"Oh? How so?"

Chaka sprang to his feet and rushed forward with glowing hands. Kuwanai's eyes widened and he immediately grabbed Chaka's charged fist aimed for his face. Chaka reached over for his short sword at his back and Kuwanai grasped his wrist, struggling to hold him away. Taking a step rearwards, Kuwanai stooped down and hurled Chaka overhead, tossing him back into the room.

Chaka scrambled to his feet as Kuwanai withdrew his blade.

"*Inazuma Kougeki!*" Kuwanai thundered and made a swift stab at Chaka's chest as the young man lurched forward. Chaka abruptly collapsed on all fours, hacking up blood as Kuwanai sheathed his wakizashi.

"You'll regret that very decision just now!" Chaka wheezed.

"I doubt you can heal from a wound like that," Kuwanai grumbled. "I personally can heal with will alone! However, if you somehow sustain that injury, then I'll believe whatever you say."

"Even if I were possessed by *akuma*?" Kuwanai said nothing in return and Chaka chuckled. "You'll need to do much worse to me, old man!"

Kuwanai narrowed his eyes. "What a ludicrous thing to say!"

Chaka glanced up, his gray eyes glowing pale violet. "Let's have another go at this, eh?" He leapt to his feet and barreled forward. "*Inshotekina Sutoraiki!*" Chaka threw a charged punch as Kuwanai withdrew his wakizashi.

"*Hissatsu Hajiki!*" Kuwanai growled as he swiftly blocked Chaka's strike with his scabbard. The sheath shattered on impact and Kuwanai stepped forward, carving deep into

Chaka's chest with an upward thrust, then followed with a diagonal lash. Liquid crimson sprayed everywhere and Chaka's blood gurgled in his throat as he collapsed forward on the floor. "Is that not enough for you?" Kuwanai thundered as he flicked his wrist, flipping off the gore from his blade.

"*How could you tell?*" Tannozume growled through Chaka.

"I am a former *souhei*," Kuwanai answered. "I am telling you - you only have one chance to leave his body. Do so now if you wish to move on." When Tannozume said nothing else, Kuwanai left the room.

Tannozume appeared over Chaka's body and gave him a firm kick in the side.

"*Get up!*" the demon shouted.

"What is it?" Chaka moaned.

A servant arrived with a pair of retainers at the doorway and they paused, stunned at the blood and gore in the room.

"Is he even alive?" the servant asked.

"I'm still here, you bastards," Chaka mumbled from his place on the ground. "I don't go down that easily!"

"By orders of Lord Kuwanai," said the first guard, "you're to be trussed up until you confess!"

"Please just confess to your crimes," the second guard complained. "It's freezing out there and if you die, we'll be burdened with the paperwork!"

"Don't worry, I won't die." Chaka grunted when hoisted by the arms and dragged upstairs. "You'll see..."

Chaka said nothing when tied up like a lobster on the three-cornered platform against the post - his arms bound behind his back, his legs crossed with his ankles meeting his knees, and both legs fastened to his chest while connected with his wrists. Once the guards looped a weighted chain around Chaka's neck and attached it to the post, they sat on stools, looking pitifully at their prisoner. Chaka held his head down, sweating profusely despite the cold winds blowing around them.

"Such a wonderful bright day today is," said the first guard. "Wouldn't you prefer sitting in the garden room writing poetry about this lovely day than rotting over there?"

"The breeze is nice," Chaka cracked.

"You won't withstand more than a few bells," warned the second guard. "And with this chilly weather! Just admit defeat; we'll let you know when a bell's gone by."

"It's only a few bells," Chaka muttered. "I think I can withstand it."

"It's only a bit past the fourth hour," noted the first guard. "Look at you, shivering like a leaf in the wind! I'm sure some warm *shippoku* for lunch sounds good right now!"

"Once my skin turns white," Chaka grumbled, "you'll have to untie me."

"You're already pale as it is... Are you already near death?"

"Heh, maybe..."

"His skin is still red," said the second. "Once it goes from purple to dark green, we'll have nothing to worry about during that time."

"If you say so..."

Chaka said nothing else while the guards talked amongst each other about the weather and their families. He found it difficult to keep awake once the pain grew worse and his body increasingly numbed. After the first pair left for lunch and another pair of guards came out to take their place, one prodded Chaka in the chest with her staff.

"What is it?" Chaka grumbled.

"Good," she said, "you're not dead yet."

"Why is that a good thing?"

"Some *souryo* has been asking about you."

Chaka glared up, baring his teeth. "Is it that bastard Hashira?" he snarled.

"Oh, you know him!" The guard nodded to her partner and he ran off back indoors. "Look, *Kengo* Isawa, I don't know what it is you've committed, but obviously Lord Kuwanai's been generally merciful with you."

"Even after nearly cutting me open?" Chaka spat sourly. "I should thank him personally!"

"You're making our House look bad! Just admit what you did and pay for your sins in the appropriate manner!"

"It'd be a different story entirely if I were the son of a *daimyo*, now wouldn't it?"

The guardswoman blew a heavy sigh and sat on the stool before Chaka, resting her staff across her lap. "Why do you do this?" she groused. "Why must you disrupt the harmony here when you could be out there in service to the Empress?"

"You wouldn't understand."

The guard nodded. "I guess you're right," she murmured. "It's probably out of my realm of comprehension."

Moments later Hashira walked out into the courtyards followed by a retainer.

"This eggplant doesn't look dead," Hashira complained. "I thought you called me out here for last rites."

"Hey!" Chaka shouted, glaring up at the monk. "I'll show you dead in a moment - it'll be you!"

Hashira grinned. "Now, now, I know that devil's been stirring in you for some time now. Why hasn't it acted out I'm utterly surprised."

"He has other intentions."

"Oh?" Hashira laughed. "So that's why you're so full of life then, eh?"

"What did you think it was?" Chaka blustered. "Some false vitality from knowing I'll soon die?"

"If you truly are dying, then admit it."

"Never to you." Chaka looked away, staring off into the middle distance. Hashira stood offside, staring up at the clouds.

"It's going to rain soon," Hashira said after several long moments. "It may linger longer than the last time."

"If you sit out here, you'll surely freeze!" the guardswoman protested. "Please, just confess! Once you'll get cleaned up, I'll even pour *saké* for you."

"Heh, what a fine offer!" the nearby guardsman piped up. "I'll gladly take to that!"

Chaka said nothing else and Hashira returned indoors.

Afternoon turned to evening and the guards paced under lantern light, complaining about their work and the current campaign against the demons swarming the island. One guard left his post and peered over at Chaka.

"What's his skin color now?" one called.

"Dark green," he called back.

"Not white yet?"

"Not yet."

"Tough old dog, eh?"

"And to think he's only eighteen summers!"

"Eighteen!"

Chaka listlessly watched the patrol march about in an effort to keep warm, while some practiced cutting exercises and others sparred. After the last group left and another came to replace them, Chaka felt a firm prod at his back. He glanced up, spotting the crimson knight standing over him.

"*What do you want now?*" Chaka thought wearily. "*You could easily overtake them and escape!*"

"*That would ruin my plans,*" Tannozume answered. "*Hold out a bit longer...*"

"*What is it you have in mind?*"

Tannozume disappeared into mist when the guards approached, nudging him with their feet.

"Is he still breathing?" one asked.

"I think so..." said a second.

"His skin isn't white, so Death hasn't come."

"I wouldn't want him dying here. To think if that monster haunted us!"

"Let's just string him up and leave him hanging. We can lie and say his skin turned."

"How long should we leave him strung up?"

"Maybe a week."

"Knowing Lord Kuwanai, he'd probably ask for ten, maybe twenty days!"

"According to the *onmyoji*, she says it'll rain all week starting tomorrow!"

"That should suffice!"

"All right, so be it."

"Heads will roll if he finds out you've been this generous to me," Chaka muttered as the guards began undoing his ties.

"That monk paid us a *Ryo* to get you down," the guard behind Chaka whispered. "We're planning to give it to Ikechi's wife."

"Send her my regards, eh?"

"She'd rather have your head!"

Freeing Chaka's limbs, the guards bound his wrists at his back and threw the slack end up the post, catching it on the iron hook at the top. Looping it through an iron ring near the middle of the post, the retainers hoisted Chaka's body several feet from the ground.

"He needs to be higher than that," called a warden sitting on post near the courtyard steps. "Get more men to pull him!"

"Heave ho, men!" the others called and they struggled with dragging Chaka's body higher on the post.

Once the signal was given that he was high enough, the guards lashed the remaining rope tightly to the pole and made their way indoors for the night. Chaka shuddered in the cold as the winds picked up, beating around his body violently.

Following the harsh wind, a frigid downpour came in torrents and Chaka screamed, thrashing against his restraints. No one came out as the rains worsened and continued for what seemed like ages.

FIFTEEN

Chaka grew warm and sweat beaded on his brow and neck. Sensing a firm prod at his chest, he stirred, opening his eyes. Looking down, he spotted several guards with staves and in the center of the group stood Hashira, who wore a wide-brimmed straw hat, shading himself from the bright sun.

"A man can withstand a night of two of heavy rain, you know," Hashira called. "However, it's the sun that can be deadly."

"You beast, you monster, you cold-blooded fiend!" Chaka shrilled.

"Good, you're still with us." Hashira laughed. "How's the view up there?"

"Damn you, old man!" Chaka shrieked and thrashed about. "Once I get down from here, I'll take your head for humiliating me!"

"I'm surprised you've got any blood left in that empty head of yours," Hashira retorted. "The *onmyoji* says it'll rain for another week after later tonight. I doubt your body can withstand any more abuse. So, how about it?"

"I *will* kill you, never forget!"

"You'll have crows making a meal out of your eyes before long!"

"You're carrying this too far!"

"Oh, I am, eh? It's you and your stubborn pride!"

"Have a heart and just kill me, if that's what you intend on doing!"

"It's in my right to ridicule your misery while you hang up there half-dead."

"You call this punishment?" Chaka let out a short laugh. "I've dealt with much worse!"

"Well then, I don't have the means to deal with *onryo*." Hashira waved off Chaka. "Once you've suffered enough, I may change my mind." Hashira stalked off and Chaka screamed curses at his back as the other guards left with him.

By nightfall, the wind whistled loudly, forcing Chaka's body swinging from the force. Large raindrops fell and Chaka felt more chilled than before. After three days, the rains stopped, though low hanging clouds covered the skies.

"Chaka," a voice called to him. Chaka opened his eyes, surprised to see Kuwanai dressed in a heavily padded black kimono standing below with a servant by his side, holding a ladder.

"Poor boy doesn't have the strength to answer," murmured the servant.

"From what I hear, you certainly howl loudly for a man so close to death," Kuwanai vaunted.

"Maybe he's really *ujikaiju*," the servant replied. "Any other prisoner would've died from withstanding all that icy rain!"

"Do you think you can last another week up there?"

"He put his mind to withstand this long, Kuwanai-dono..."

Chaka shook himself violently, flinging his weight around though the thick rope that held him showed no signs of weakening. With his last bit of strength, he screamed.

"Once I get down from here, I'll go straight for your neck!" Chaka roared. "I'll tear you limb from limb!"

Kuwanai snorted and folded his arms across his chest. "Still have that fighting spirit, heh!" he drawled. "Is that a promise or a threat?"

"It's a promise!" Chaka bellowed.

"Then I'll wait. Chew through those ropes with your bare teeth if you can." Kuwanai sat on the nearby stool placed several feet from the post and looked up at Chaka struggling to get out of his restraints. The servant put aside the ladder and paced, saying nothing.

After several hours, the servant left Kuwanai's side and Kuwanai called again to Chaka. "Why do you keep acting out like that?" he snapped. "Stop making a fool of yourself - you're only getting nowhere with that noise. All you're doing is wearing yourself out."

"I'm no longer listening," Chaka said hoarsely.

"What good will that do you?" The servant returned moments later with a tray of soup and tea. "Smells good from down here," Kuwanai said as he placed the tray aside and held his bowl in hand. "How's your stomach? I'm sure it's empty."

Chaka said nothing as Kuwanai ate his soup in silence.

"I must say, all that strength you display would be put to better use working for the good of this country," remarked Kuwanai after finishing his meal. "Is it not better to meet your end on the field of battle and dying courageously than to meet your end here, strung up like a common criminal?" Setting the bowl aside, his servant immediately picked up the tray, waiting patiently for orders. "How dare you call yourself human?" Kuwanai shouted up at Chaka as he rose to his feet. "Your conduct until now gave no evidence that you were no more than a beast, with no respect for human life! Is that how you wish to be remembered? If you value your honor, then surrender and die with dignity." When Chaka gave no response, Kuwanai blew a hard sigh and turned away, storming back indoors.

"Wait," Chaka called weakly.

Kuwanai paused in step. "What do you want now?" he grumbled. "Have you finally come to your senses?"

"Don't tell me you're going to lecture me more."

"Think about it another night, then after you've decided, I'll cut off your head." Kuwanai continued his way for the garden room.

"No matter my answer, eh?" Chaka called after him. "I can't undo what I've done, you know!"

"I want you to be a better man," Kuwanai called over his shoulder. "Don't you realize how important that is?"

The door shut behind Kuwanai and the servant sighed, taking up the cup of tea left behind.

"What a waste," he muttered. Approaching the post where Chaka spent tied, the servant poured the liquid on the ground.

"Are you praying for rain?" Chaka spat.

"I'm praying for your safety," the servant replied. "All I can say is face Death bravely and quietly if you continue to fight."

"Why bother wasting your breath praying for me?"

"For the sake of your ancestors, at least have the decency to confess before going to Hell!"

"I'll think about it."

The servant marched back inside, the clatter of his sandals fading in the distance. Chaka looked up at the evening sky, noting the cluster of clouds.

"*Is Hell any colder than this?*" he wondered as the cool winds increased their intensity. "*And to think of the many sins I'll have to freeze off, heh!*"

After several more days, the cloudy skies cleared to a cold winter morning. Kuwanai and the monk Hashira ventured outdoors, followed by Kuwanai's servant and a pair of retainers. Clustered around the post, they looked up at Chaka's weather-beaten and limp body, swaying slightly in the breeze. A guard armed with a staff reached up, poking Chaka in the side.

"He's dead," the servant called back when Chaka made no response to move from repeated firm prods. "Look at him, thin as rails! Even his hair's gone pale!"

"That's too bad," Hashira murmured. "Stubborn until the end!"

"I'm not so sure," Kuwanai muttered. "Take him down and bring him inside, also dispatch Michikata-sensei right away."

"Yes, Sir!" the guards answered. The servant brought the ladder around and they hastily made their way up, immediately taking down Chaka's body.

Once the servants placed Chaka's body in an unused room, the doctor Amaya rushed in with a bag of tools. A servant lit an oil lamp for her as she went over every inch of Chaka's body, tallying his scars and inspecting his injuries. Opening his eyes with her fingers, she peered closely at them.

"He seems to be alive," Amaya called.

"Oh?" called Hashira from outside the door. "He never responded to anything we did."

"His eyes changed in the light," Amaya noted. "His spirit is near his body, but hasn't left yet."

"What shall I tell Lord Kuwanai then?"

"I'll keep close watch on him until he recovers. Now, just get me a futon and some blankets."

Hashira nodded and barked orders to the servants. Later they returned with another futon and several blankets and sheets. Amaya sat at Chaka's side, looking sadly down at him.

"What is it you're holding onto so?" she murmured. "Why not give it up and find peace?"

Over the next several hours, Amaya dipped a cloth in a bowl of water and placed it on Chaka's feverish forehead, changing it when it became warm. She tried feeding him broth and cold water and Chaka declined each time.

"But isn't your mouth dry?" Amaya pressed. "Aren't you hungry at all?" She heard a snort and glanced to Hashira sitting at the door, staff propped against his knee. "What do you want?"

"I'm just waiting for him to die," Hashira said smugly. "Someone's got to pray for that wretched soul of his!"

"Get out!"

"Fine by me, if you'd rather have him as a ghost to keep you company!"

"You–!" Amaya withdrew her dagger and tossed it at the monk. He immediately sidestepped the attack and the steel struck the wall. Chaka murmured under his breath and Amaya leaned over, straining to hear.

"What is he saying?" Hashira asked.

"It sounds like he's talking to someone," she answered.

"He's delirious, obviously!"

"All that time out there in the elements," Amaya grumbled. "No wonder you're sick! Your body can't take anymore abuse."

"Until I know whether his fever passes or he does," Hashira announced, "you'll have to be content in putting up with me."

"Fine," Amaya retorted, "but if you keep up with that nattering, you'll wake up without a voice!"

Six days passed and Chaka's fever subsided. He opened his eyes, glancing around the dimly lit room. Chaka first noticed Amaya lying on the floor across from him. He reached over, running a hand gently through her bronzed hair.

Sitting up on his elbows, he spotted Hashira sleeping in the corner with his legs crossed and his head against his chest, snoring softly. Beside him propped against the wall rest a simple walking staff.

Chaka sat up and reached over where a tray of cold soup and tea rest and he downed the tea, relieving his parched throat. Staggering to his feet, Chaka wrapped the sheets around his waist and shuffled over for the staff. Taking it, he leaned against it as he made his way for the door and slid it open.

Finding no one posted in the hall, Chaka silently made his way down the corridor. Noting the door to the garden room open, Chaka stepped inside, finding Kuwanai reclining on a low couch, gazing out the screened window of the winter courtyard, admiring the sunny morning view.

"Is that you, Chaka?" Kuwanai implored, not once turning around.

"It is," Chaka answered.

"Have you decided?"

"I have no feelings or awe for you," Chaka grumbled.

"Are you nonetheless filled with shame for having brought such dishonor to your ancestors and your family name?"

"I can't say that I have..." Chaka clenched his hands as he grew frustrated. "I knew you wouldn't understand! You think I must be mad to let some *akuma* take over my body - but at the time I had no choice!"

"Then what's keeping you from going to the temples?"

Chaka opened his mouth to answer, then shut it, realizing he had no ready answer. He slipped to his knees and knelt forward as his face burned in embarrassment.

"It's not beneath my dignity to toss you back in the room where the sun never shines," Kuwanai said sternly, "but however, you did confess, so I must castigate you accordingly."

"Whatever punishment you deem just," Chaka said weakly, "I'll accept it."

"Evidently, your schooling here was insufficient because as *Ichizoku Eiyu*, your will was too weak against the bargain that *akuma* made and you allowed yourself to get possessed."

"What do you suggest?"

"I suggest you travel to other Zhintai-ryu *dojo* and learn all you can. Don't return until you have *Seijuku Shita* from each one!"

"How many schools are there?"

"Seven on the mainland, but there are twenty-two total including the one you've trained in here."

Chaka lifted his head, eyes wide in shock. "A certificate of completion from each one!" he cried. "That'll take a lifetime!" When Kuwanai said nothing else, Chaka cleared his throat and bowed deeply to the floor. "Thank you Father," he murmured, "for being so generous."

Gathering the sheeting, Chaka held them with one hand while the other held fast to the staff and he exited the room. A servant stood outside the door with a fresh kimono, a pair of sandals and a set of towels in his arms. The servant bowed stiffly at Chaka and Chaka nodded back.

"Would Young Sir like a bath now?" the servant politely asked.

Glancing down the hall behind the servant, Chaka noticed Amaya talking to Hashira in hushed tones. He clenched his teeth, watching Hashira hand Amaya a decorated dagger. Suddenly flashing a grin to the servant, Chaka scooped up the garments from his arms.

"Sure," Chaka said brightly. "Have Michikata-sensei come too. I need to have this particular spot checked."

The servant nodded then left his side and Chaka headed in the opposite direction for the bathhouse, chuckling under his breath.

Relishing the hot water once he stepped in, Chaka dipped his head under the water, moaning in pleasure. Cresting, he spotted the doctor standing at the door with her arms folded across her chest.

"You need me for something?" she asked, slightly annoyed.

"Could you scrub my back, please?" Chaka asked, giving a gentle smile. "I'm not feeling all that well enough yet." Amaya raised an eyebrow and Chaka raised his hands in surrender. "Please?" he pleaded. "I'm too weak to do anything to you if that's what you're thinking."

Amaya blew a short sigh and approached the tub. Once she neared Chaka, he grabbed her sleeve and Amaya ducked down, yanking her arms out of her kimono. Spinning away as Chaka pulled the weapon, she withdrew her short sword as Chaka stood, gripping the dagger in hand.

"Why did you take my *tanto*?" Amaya demanded.

"You and that filthy no-good monk were planning something!" Chaka snapped. "I might as well put an end to it now!"

"You're mad!" Amaya shouted. "Kuwanai-dono should've just killed you right away; why he bothered to show you mercy, I have no idea!"

"All of you cretins are the same!" Chaka thundered. "Fine, be that way! You'll be the first one I'll kill in my present state of mind!"

"I know many ways to incapacitate a man," Amaya threatened as Chaka stepped out the tub.

"You should learn how to kill!"

Chaka advanced and Amaya swiftly turned away, stepping behind Chaka. Bashing the spine of the blade to Chaka's back, he faltered and she kicked him in the rear, sending him crashing forward. Chaka rolled to his feet and attacked again, only meeting nothing but air as he made vain attempts to swipe at her.

"*She's fast, I'll give her credit for that,*" Chaka thought as he missed his attack again and gained another strike to his arm, forcing it lame. "*Nary any strength at all - only going for pressure points to force me incapacitated! The good doctor has no chance against brute force!*"

Switching hands, Chaka made another failed strike and faltered when Amaya smashed the blade's spine against his leg. "*Inshotekina Sutoraiki!*" he growled and bit the tanto between his teeth, dropping low. Shouldering Amaya with a fierce tackle, the force threw her head over heels against the wall. Amaya coughed up blood and Chaka pounced, straddling atop her as he drew his dagger. "*Ataushinai Okyoda!*"

Amaya brought up her wakizashi to Chaka's neck as he jammed the slender blade into her chest. Amaya's hands fell limp once blood gushed from her heart cavity and the sword clattered to the floor beside her.

Chaka blew a hard sigh and wiped at his nicked skin with the back of his hand. "Too close!" he muttered.

Beside him, the fiend in red lamellar appeared, vermilion katana hoisted over his shoulder.

"*Did it ever occur to you to ask her what she had in mind?*" Tannozume asked. Chaka glared up at the demon who laughed when the young man had no ready answer. "*Now you have a mighty predicament on your hands - admit to killing her and face the death penalty or escape while you still can!"*

"She can't be that important!" Chaka snarled.

"She is - personal physician to the local <u>Daimyo</u> of this area!"

"I thought she worked for my father!"

"Her father does!"

"Damn it!"

Chaka immediately rinsed off the blood from his body and threw on his clothes. Taking Amaya's swords, he tied them on and burst out the bathhouse, racing for the back gate. A sudden whistle pierced the air and Chaka came to a stop near the rear garrison as a group of soldiers filed out with their swords ready in alarm.

"What's going on?" a soldier called.

"Stop him!" a retainer shouted as he ran up the path. "He killed Michikata-sensei!"

"I can maybe kill four of them in my current state," Chaka thought, withdrawing the wakizashi once the soldiers turned to him. *"I'm begging you, I need your help!"*

Tannozume appeared beside Chaka as the soldiers encircled him, blocking off all means of escape. *"Are you seriously considering my aid?"* the demon grumbled and withdrew his katana. *"Don't think of going back on your word like before, you impenitent recreant!"*

"Please, yes, I even swear my life to you!" Chaka thought frantically. *"Do it now!"*

"So be it!"

Chaka's arm burned as the devil pushed him to the rear and suddenly his vision flashed in blood-red, then his world blackened out completely.

PART TWO

THE ARRIVAL

SIXTEEN

35 Shigemoto (Cycle 2291)

Moon 9 (Insects Awaken) – 26th Day

It was an uncomfortably warm, humid, afternoon, with an overcast sky and high winds in the bay known as Midori Umiwan. Chaka leaned against the railing surrounding Kakita Kensukiru Shutoku, looking out at the white sands below.

In the far distance to the west, were the purple and black ridges known as Yugureyama and to the east, the large peak known as Kounnoyama surrounded by heavy murky fog. The blue-green waters from Kirinoumi, fed by the Kamigawa and Hoshinokawa rivers, wound through from the mountains and ended at the bay.

Below were the sandy foothills that surrounded the school at the bay that stretched from north to south, leading to the dirt paths toward the larger township of Heichimachi several miles away. The boardinghouse, a large two-storey building crafted of ebony with coral tiles on the roof, faced the academy down from the hill. Stone steps led up the path and a canopy of maple trees shadowed the courtyards.

The martial training hall was well renowned for its hard training regimen and preparation of entry into the Imperial Army. The school nestled into the cliffs facing the bay had a small class size; therefore its simple building had only three large rooms: one for records, another for sparring, the last for spear and sword fighting and the outdoor court for archery.

Chaka at first disliked what he saw when he visited the military institute the previous season, touring the grounds. Considered one of several elite schools on the island, the academy created Clan Champions and Imperial martial arts instructors. Chaka knew he could easily prevail, given his exceptional strength and ability, also having previous active duty in the Army.

Disturbed by the fact he somehow gained entry into the elite academy, Chaka failed to call to mind how he defeated the master instructor or the best students, since he considered the teachings there barbaric.

A sudden sinking feeling struck Chaka when he could not remember why he left the Army. It was hard work, but he enjoyed cheating death daily and risking his life constantly to protect his comrades so they could survive another day. Combating other men was easy, but demons were another matter...

The cool winds picked up Chaka's long ashen-blond hair, blowing the loose strands about his head. Looking down, he noticed he wore leather boots with simple broad leaf designs stitched on the sides. Chaka drew a blank in his mind where he purchased it, unable to recall if he got them - including the clasp-fly black slacks he wore - from the Trading House in town. He adjusted the baggy dark green pullover shirt that slipped off his shoulder, yet tight around his muscular arms.

"Why am I at this *shinan-jo*?" Chaka muttered, casting his gaze at the pale horned demon who sat nearby on the ground, enclosed by shadows.

"*You were running away, remember?*" answered the devil.

"Running from what?"

"*Only you know the answer to that!*"

Chaka grunted and folded his arms across his chest, glaring out at the beach below. "But why train at Kakita, Shiranosuke?" he complained. "I could have entered any other *dojo*..."

"*There is something here we need...*"

"What is it then?"

"*It will take time. Meanwhile, learn something useful.*"

"I have no reason to be here," Chaka said irritably.

Shiranosuke chuckled. "*Then leave,*" the demon said simply.

Chaka blew a heavy sigh as he ran his hands through his hair. "You monsters will be the end of me," he moaned and the devil snorted. Chaka relaxed his stance and leaned forward, resting his arms against the railing. The salt-tossed winds picked up and blew his long hair around his head, obscuring his view of the bay below. "I know there is no point of my leaving... your leader Tannozume will just take over my body again."

"*That's right,*" another voice growled behind Chaka. He stiffened when ghostly claws gripped his shoulder. "*Your body belongs to us, as we have agreed!*"

"This is sickening," Chaka spat. "I am a devil slayer and yet--!"

"*We do this to help you.*"

Chaka pulled away and whirled around, finding no one there. He narrowed his eyes and clenched his hands, growing incensed. *"Maddening, the whole lot!"* Chaka thought as Tannozume's hacking laughter resonated around him. *"There is no way to rid of them unless--!"*

"You'll do nothing of the sort!" Tannozume shouted. A phantom hand grabbed Chaka by the hair. Yanked rearward, Chaka cried out and threw a backhanded punch, only getting his fist caught in a viselike grip. He ground his teeth as the pressure increased. *"Now listen, my thrall, there is a savage beast who means to destroy us and with your <u>majutsu</u>, you can defeat him."*

"What if I refuse to accept?" Chaka hissed.

"Refuse and I take over your body again!"

"It will not be the first time!"

"You shall never find release, this I swear to you!"

The strong grip loosened and Chaka wrenched his hand away. Abruptly kicked in the back by a phantom foot, Chaka grunted, stumbling forward. His skin grew cold and his left arm began to burn. "Why are you now taking over?" he demanded.

"Pain is something you must get used to," replied Tannozume.

"I will fight you to my very last breath!"

"You came to us, or have you forgotten?"

Chaka let out a yell once searing pain shot through his left arm and dropped to his knees in shock. *"You fiends gave me nothing but trouble!"* he thought, gripping his arm. *"I should have known better than to trust you!"*

"Now I shall tell you only once..."

"I am no longer listening," Chaka snarled.

"*Your enchanted weaponry cannot defeat us!*" Tannozume thundered.

"Then I'll enlist a *souryo* for help!"

"*You are too far out of reach for a mere monk to be effective,*" the crimson devil snarled. "*We chose you as our vessel and you shall do as we command!*"

Blood seeped through his shirt and Chaka shoved up the sleeve, revealing three deep slender cuts. "I know if I dare dream of defeating you," he declared, "it will require me to sacrifice a lot to banish you *akuma!*"

"*I shall never let you go!*" Tannozume roared. "*Your conscience will be no more!*"

Chaka moaned in agony when the wounds in his arm deepened. He gripped his head, cringing in pain as the beach faded in dark light, outlining everything in shades of red and gray.

"*Why do you hesitate?*" another voice called to them.

Another shadowy form appeared before Chaka and he looked up, startled. "Akanasutsune!" he yelped. "What do you want?"

"*Get up!*" commanded the stout verdant-armored devil. "*The one that means us harm is coming and you are too weak right now to battle them!*"

"*So be it...*" Tannozume grumbled.

The world around Chaka returned to normal colors once the demons flashed out of sight. Chaka struggled to stand and grasped the railing, pulling himself up. Hearing footsteps, he turned about-face, only to find no one there.

"Damn it," Chaka hissed, clutching his hands. "I must find someone powerful enough to cleanse myself of this taint since I'm too weak to do it alone..."

Jumping the railing, Chaka dropped several feet below onto the white sands. He pulled out of shirt, tossing it aside on the ground and made his way toward the deep cobalt sea. Reaching the bay's edge, Chaka halted and looked ahead at the surf while the rolling waves from the tides licked at his boots.

"*Just step in and keep walking,*" he thought and pulled off his shoes. "*Go ahead and drown; free yourself of such misery!*" Dropping his boots behind him, a prickly sensation coursed through his arms and he glimpsed over his shoulder, spotting a man several years younger than he out on the railing. The red-haired young man wore a high-collared dark navy knee-length loose-fitting jacket that had slits on the sides, black wide-legged trousers and white socks with sandals. "*That unusually dressed man... would he be the one they fear?*"

Chaka turned back, returning for the academy. The red-headed stranger left the rails, making his way down the sandy path. Chaka waved and the young man returned the gesture. "*I have to find out who he is,*" he mused and the fiery tension in his left arm increased. "*It's obvious he has a lot of power -- they would rather destroy me and find another body to possess than to let me fight!*"

Noticing his control slipping, Chaka backed away then turned and broke into run, racing for the water. He slipped out of his slacks, tripping over his steps and threw them aside. Glancing over his shoulder again, Chaka saw the younger man standing near his discarded shirt, looking ahead at him. He saluted the stranger then dove into the sea. The cold water rushed over his head.

Jurou Seiki watched Chaka strip himself of all clothing and dive into the ocean depths. He felt unsettled as he picked up the discarded shirt and sauntered along the sands.

"That was a stupid thing to do," Jurou mused as he gathered the remaining clothing along the way. *"He's lucky he didn't have his <u>uchibukuro</u> on him."* His hands burned and he looked around, searching for the energy that disturbed him. *"I thought for sure I heard someone else with him, but they've vanished on me."*

Approaching the beachhead's edge, Jurou kicked aside the boots that lay near the shoreline and grunted when the seawater licked at his white sandals. He took a step back and waved at Chaka who swam with ease in the cold depths.

"Ho!" Jurou called.

Chaka ignored him, taking another dive in the dark waters. Jurou booted the shoes toward a nearby small boulder that jutted from the sands, made worn from the waters at high tide. He placed the boots nearby and took a seat on the rock, then folded the articles he held and placed them in his lap.

Jurou unhooked the collar of his coat and blew a short sigh as he wiped his forehead with the back of his hand, brushing back the sweaty locks that began stick. After watching Chaka's athletic form in the water, his thoughts returned to the notice he received last season that had him reluctantly arriving at the academy.

Jurou found it troubling to travel so far from the countryside, disrupting his training to become a teacher at his uncle's temple school and teach other monks how to combat demons. He hated the job but felt obligated since it was his family, after the same forces he swore to eradicate killed his parents.

Jurou cursed his uncle when forced against his will to venture out to Midori Umiwan, even arranging with the nearby school to continue his training there.

"Find enlightenment, he said," he grumbled. "Achieve *kensho*, he said." Jurou blew a hard sigh, rolling his eyes. "That's if I don't die after trying to exorcise this devil slayer I've been assigned to cleanse!"

Brewing over his predicament, Jurou wanted nothing to do with the people on the mainland, since his features from Hisuishima made him stand out. With his short, somewhat stocky athletic frame, long limbs, tanned skin and red hair, he contrasted immensely against the natives of Midorishima, who were tall and slender, olive-skinned and had dark hair.

Jurou wondered about Chaka who continued swimming in the bay, since he stood out significantly from the majority of Midorishima inhabitants. Chaka was a head taller than the natives with pale skin, thin crimson lips, light eyes, and fair wavy hair, also muscularly built with barrel chest and strong arms.

"*He looks almost like the demons that tend to attack the islands,*" Jurou mused. "*But he can't be a devil... saltwater destroys them outright!*"

Reaching inside his inner jacket pocket, he withdrew a sheet with details he needed about his mission. Unfolding the paper, Jurou reviewed the important information that had a sketch of Chaka's face and detail of the typical clothing he wore, as well as his vital statistics.

While reading and memorizing the data, Jurou hadn't noticed Chaka emerging from the freezing waters and approaching him.

"Ho," Chaka said, nudging Jurou with his foot.

Jurou glanced up and gasped in surprise, immediately recoiling at the sight of Chaka standing before him, dripping water. "What?" he cried, immediately crumpling the paper as Chaka wrung out his long hair with his hands.

"My articles," Chaka said, extending a hand.

"*So bold!*" Jurou thought, immediately stuffing the paper into his jacket pocket as Chaka nudged him again. "*He doesn't care that he stands naked in front of me!*"

"Well?" Chaka snapped.

"Right, that!" Jurou said and handed the clothes over. His face burned bright scarlet, watching Chaka soundlessly step into his pants.

"What is it you find so interesting about me?" Chaka wheedled.

Jurou stiffened and averted his gaze toward ground. "I'm sorry," he muttered. "I don't mean to stare."

Chaka grinned and perched down before him as he draped his shirt over his shoulder. "Do you find me handsome?"

Jurou's reddened face turned brighter. "W-what?" he sputtered. "What kind of question is that?"

"Do you ever go for a swim?" Chaka asked instead.

"It's too cold for that."

"Are you in training to become *Kensei*?"

"What?"

Chaka chuckled, standing. "Is that all you can say?"

"What?"

Chaka laughed and waved Jurou off. "*Itterasshai.*"

"What?" Jurou looked up, watching Chaka walk away. Realizing Chaka left his boots behind, Jurou took the shoes and scrambled to catch up. "Wait!" he called after Chaka and grabbed his arm.

Chaka suddenly stiffened and growled, swiftly turning around. "What do you want with me?" he snarled, grasping Jurou by the collar.

Jurou sucked in a weak breath when he noticed Chaka's pale blue-gray eyes growing dark. "You left your *ushinokawa*..." he said faintly.

Chaka tilted his head, seemingly misunderstanding and Jurou held up the worn leather boots. Chaka's eyes refocused and a warm smile appeared on his face as he released his grip. "Thank you!" he said brightly and took the shoes from Jurou. "I will need that." Tucking them under his arm, Chaka began walking ahead.

Jurou stayed behind, unwilling to follow and after several paces, Chaka paused, glancing back. Jurou swallowed hard, trying to find his voice. "What do you want?" he finally said.

Chaka waved at him to come over. Jurou cleared his throat and he raised an eyebrow, pointing to himself. "Who else?" Chaka replied, amused. Jurou sighed and marched up along his side, then matched his stride as they walked together. "Say, what are you called?"

"Ah, well..." Jurou stared off into the distance, uneasy in Chaka's presence while his hands continued burning in response. *"There's something off about him,"* he thought. *"Usually my hands hurt when there are <u>akuma</u> around, but I don't see any!"* Jurou gave Chaka a quizzical look and smiled nervously. *"Maybe he's been in contact with them lately...?"*

"Your name," Chaka pressed.

"Jurou," the younger man finally answered. "My name is Jurou Seiki."

"Seiki, eh?" Chaka smiled wryly. "What an odd name!"

"Oh, Seiki is my family name, not my given name!" Jurou clarified and Chaka laughed.

"Were you born here?"

"No, obviously... My parents are not from these islands." Jurou suddenly stiffened when he realized Chaka stood close nearby. Chaka bumped into him and took a step back. "Why do you stand so close to me?"

"This ear is bad," Chaka explained and tucked a wet strand of hair behind his ear.

"What about the other one?"

"I have to use it to listen out for certain things."

"Like what?"

"*Akuma*, perhaps."

Jurou decided not to press further. "I am foreign to this island," he said instead. "I live off the coast of Kitajima, far from here."

"You're a little dark to be from the North..."

"I work in a *Noson*."

Chaka nodded. "Makes sense," he murmured. "Will the other *Hyakusho* miss you if you're here?"

"The other farmers won't miss me too much," Jurou said vaguely. "Once I earn my certification, I can return to my farming village and become instructor there."

"That's fine. I don't hate you." Chaka gazed into the far distance. "Your surname sounds like it comes from the one of the seven islands, so you can't be entirely foreign."

"You can call me Sakuranbo if you want..."

"Is it because of your red hair?" Chaka looked down at Jurou, smiling warmly. "A fine name for a fine man, I'd say." Jurou blushed in return and looked away. Chaka then took his shirt he had over his shoulder and pulled into it. "Follow me, Saku; let us practice a bit before classes start."

"How did you know I attend the Kakita-ryu?" Jurou asked, following Chaka along the sands.

Chaka snorted. "Why else would you be here?"

"I guess you're right."

SEVENTEEN

Entering the Kakita Martial Academy's foyer, Jurou spotted other classmates sparring, practicing their blocks and mortal blows.

"What art do you practice?" Chaka inquired. "I'll get a *bokuto* or two from the back."

"I don't really have a particular style," Jurou answered.

Following Chaka to the weapons rack in the rear, he came to a pause when his hands burned strongly at the sight of the assistant instructor pacing outside the practice ring, shouting at the sparring students.

The teacher, with narrow amber eyes, short messy sandy hair and pale skin seemingly untouched by sunlight, wore black trousers, sandals and jacket with an orange trim. Strapped to his right hip was a decorated katana while on the other side was a holster for a dart gun.

"Come on!" the assistant teacher shouted. "You should have killed him by now!"

Jurou ran up to the group, watching a young woman with bobbed sandy hair and violet eyes wearing a dark green sparring uniform wielding two long swords. She held one before her as a shield and the other she held at ready against her opponent: a young man who wielded only a long spear. He crouched on bended knee, using the end of his lance as an aid to keep from hitting the floor.

"Sorry, *Sensei* Ikaruga," the students said gravely.

Ikaruga looked up and glared at Jurou. "You," he demanded, "What do you want?"

"I just wanted to meet the others," Jurou said apprehensively. "I'm new to this *dojo* and I thought..."

"We are not friendly here!" Ikaruga snapped, cutting him off. "We are at war; didn't you know that, Outlander?"

"Of course I know," Jurou spat back irritably. "Why else would I be here?"

Ikaruga put a hand to the hilt of his sword. "You must be mistaken to even think of training here, pathetic fool!"

Jurou clenched his hands. "Who are you calling pathetic, old man?" he shouted. "You devil, I should cut you where you stand for insulting me!"

"You would not be the first!"

"By Kairyushin--!"

Jurou advanced and Ikaruga swiftly unleashed his blade. Ikaruga lashed at Jurou with a flash cut and sheathed his sword with swift fluidity. Jurou staggered back, stunned.

"Any deeper," Ikaruga spat, "and you'd be dead!"

Jurou's eyes widened and he clutched his chest, feeling his slashed open coat and shirt. Growing pale, he pushed past the other students, racing for the lavatory.

Chaka watched Jurou flee to the washroom while the others students grew silent. "Good one, instructor," he called. "You may have frightened him; however, I am not afraid of you."

"Isawa," Ikaruga snarled. "I thought you were banned from attending!"

"I was given a second chance," Chaka said proudly. "I have worked my hardest to return here."

"Curse you, devil!"

"I should say the same about you." Chaka picked up a wooden practice sword from the rack and casually placed it over his shoulder. "Let us spar a bit and show these fools how to fight."

Ikaruga growled, narrowing his eyes at Chaka as he advanced. "You are not to be trusted," he snarled.

"Oh?" Chaka retorted. "What of you then?"

He charged, raising his sword high and Ikaruga drew back, unsheathing his blade. Chaka stopped short and tossed his sword at Ikaruga, smacking him in the head. Ikaruga fell back stunned and the wooden blade clattered to the floor behind him. Several students laughed nervously.

"Why you--!" Ikaruga shouted.

Chaka stepped on Ikaruga's sword hand before he could get up, smiling darkly down at him. "Who are you to question my motives?" he demanded. "Yield while you can to my awesome power before I destroy you!"

Ikaruga's amber eyes glowed dimly. "I will tend to you later, Isawa," he sneered.

Chaka snorted and relent his grip, then kicked up the fallen bokuto, catching it with ease. "You really should retire, old man," he said. "You will only look bad." Chaka turned to the class and tossed the practice blade to one student. She caught it, giving him a wary look.

Ikaruga sprang to his feet, snarling. "Those *akuma* you harbor," he spat, "they will only bring destruction to these lands!"

"Then defeat them if you so desire," Chaka answered smugly. Ikaruga bared his teeth, unable to speak. Chaka chortled and sauntered to the lavatory.

Kicking in the door, Chaka noticed the stall at the end closed. He approached the stall entrance and leaned against the wall, folding his arms across his chest. "Are you crying in there?" Chaka questioned.

Hearing no answer, he pushed against the door, revealing Jurou sitting on the floor with his head resting against the wall and his arms wrapped around his drawn knees.

"I'm fine," answered Jurou sullenly.

"Tell me something," Chaka said. "Your parents live in the boundaries of Kitajima, correct?"

"No longer," Jurou replied. "They were destroyed by invading *akuma* who destroyed all the coastal towns..."

"Eh? Demons, you say?" Chaka stood in the doorway of the stall, placing his arms against the frame. "Devils hadn't had interest in the North for almost twenty cycles!"

"They're killing everyone on the coast and making their way for the mountains. My uncle sent me here to become *Senshuken* so I can avenge their deaths."

"A lot to do on such short orders, eh?" Chaka murmured.

"Sure, that..."

"There is no bother in learning from Ikaruga," Chaka said smugly. "He is no real master."

Jurou glanced up at Chaka. "Are you telling me you've defeated him that easily?"

Chaka smirked. "I can easily be *Shihan-dai* if I wished."

Jurou looked away, blowing a short sigh. "If you say so..."

"What are you going to do?"

"What do you want me to do?" Jurou snapped. "I'm unfamiliar with this place and its customs; I just arrived several days ago."

"You know, I have been doing this for a long time." Chaka grinned. "Let me teach you what's needed to pass the test here."

"Do you have the time for that?"

"Oh, I have plenty of time." Jurou rose to his feet as Chaka entered and the door swung shut behind him. "I'll teach you what you need to know; I'll teach you everything."

Jurou gasped when Chaka's demeanor suddenly changed. "What do you wish to show me?" he asked nervously. Chaka grabbed him by the collar and bared his teeth. "Wait, what are you doing?" Jurou grasped at his wrist. "Don't strike me!" Chaka raised his free hand and Jurou took hold of Chaka's hair with his other hand, yanking hard. "Please answer!"

Chaka blinked slowly and his eyes refocused. "Eh?" he murmured.

"Are you all right?"

Letting go, Chaka's arms dropped to his side as a blank look appeared on his face. "Why do you not run away from my mere presence?" he muttered.

"I've been through a lot," Jurou answered softly. "Why, are you supposed to be scary?"

"How scary can I get is the question, Saku..."

Jurou cringed when Chaka gave a sardonic grin. "What do you mean by that?"

Chaka immediately grasped Jurou's hands, giving them a firm squeeze. "If I bared my soul to you," he uttered, "you would find that I am very easy to manipulate."

"What do you mean by that?"

The lavatory's door slammed open.

"Ho, where is Seiki?" a voice demanded. "*Sensei* Ishida is searching for him!"

Jurou pulled out of Chaka's grip and quickly stepped out, forcing the stall's door swinging shut behind him. He bumped into the young man who lost the duel earlier and paused, noticing the spear strapped across his back.

The young man stood a head taller than Jurou, with shaggy raven hair, tanned weathered skin and small, piercing charcoal eyes.

"What are you doing here?" Jurou asked.

"I sense something unpleasant," the young man murmured.

"I don't believe I know you," Jurou said quickly.

"I am Kaminaritou Rouru," the young man answered, "son of Norimono Fuukaze, who is the son of Umanou Hana, who is the son of the mighty Rouringukawa Roka!"

"So, I assume your family is full of fighters."

"No, those in my family who are not warriors are also farmers."

Jurou nodded. "I know farming is very hard work."

"These fighters are defenders of the mighty House Umaa and I have come to this hall to reinforce the training I've done at the Charger Society." Kaminaritou Rouru folded his arms across his chest. "This *dojo*, Kakita Kensukiru Shutoku, creates only the elite and I plan to become one of them!"

Jurou looked down at his feet as his face burned in discomfiture. "I'm not an elite warrior," he muttered. "Despite my training, I'm nothing more than a laughable excuse!"

Kaminaritou Rouru raised an eyebrow. "Then why are you here?"

"I have to defend my family's honor." Jurou sensed Chaka stirring behind him and looked up, facing Kaminaritou Rouru. "Demons have been attacking the coast and my uncle sent me here to train."

"What have you trained in from before?"

Jurou laughed nervously and waved him away. "It's nothing important."

"Is it a style from one of the seven islands?" Jurou shook his head. "I thought for sure you hailed from Seibushima." Kaminaritou Rouru gave the younger man a quizzical look. "Your features resemble such."

"I don't speak *Koukonen*, much less understand it," Jurou said quickly. "I come from Kitajima." He ran a clammy hand through his hair. "*What's with all these questions?*" he thought. "*Why is he so interested in me?*"

"*Koukonen*, eh?" Chaka answered from behind the stall. "Then by all appearances you're from the West, not the North!"

Kaminaritou Rouru glared at the door and growled under his breath.

"Please don't," Jurou said gently. "It really doesn't matter, please?"

"It matters," Kaminaritou Rouru grumbled.

"What matters where I come from?" Jurou gave a nervous smile. "What matters is my sword hand, true?"

"Of course."

Pushing past Kaminaritou Rouru, Jurou headed for the Kakita foyer. He spotted the main instructor in a deep green kimono with the name of the school on the left breast in lighter green sitting on the floor, holding a sword in a dark indigo scabbard broadside across his knees. His long black hair, pulled in a braid, graced over his shoulder and a single lock of hair hung in his face, the only thick strand stark white.

"I have summoned for a young man named Seiki Jurou," the man in green said. "Are you called by that name?"

"Yes." Jurou gave a short bow.

"I am Ishida Denzo, *Shihan* of the North Kakita-ryu. I have heard from others that you wish to become *Senshuken*. Is that true?"

"I'm no *Kengo* and I have no hope of attaining the title of *Kensei...*" Jurou murmured. Ishida said nothing and Jurou cleared his throat. "Yes," he said, wincing. "It is..." Jurou looked away as cold sweat broke out on his forehead. "*Well, partially true,*" he thought. "*I have no intention on being here.*"

"Your records indicate you have a residence in Kitajima. So why did you come here to the South Kakita-ryu?"

"*Akuma* slaughtered my family and my uncle thought it better to travel," Jurou answered. "He felt that if I went to school so close to home, I'd be unable to concentrate."

"Good enough." Ishida nodded. "What weapon do you wish to train with?"

Jurou shook his head. "Ah, the duelists from my hometown don't use traditional weapons," he explained. "They are mainly fishermen and farmers..."

"Oh?" Kaminaritou Rouru interjected. Jurou looked up and Kaminaritou Rouru gave a tight smile. "So you do understand."

"Er, yes," Jurou replied quickly. "We take whatever we can and turn them into weapons. Our true elite fighters have been conscripted into the Empire's army."

"Such a hardy individual," Ishida murmured. "Well, I wish for you to test your worth against my assistant."

"I test this worthless fool?" Ikaruga crowed from near the weapons rack and gave a curt laugh. "My skills are too much for this weakling before me!"

Jurou glared at Ikaruga. "I'm no weakling!" he snapped back. "You'll regret testing me, you devil!"

"Oh?" Ikaruga folded his hands across his chest and looked down at Jurou with disdain as Jurou stomped up to him. "Then why become ill over a mere shallow cut?"

"You caught me by surprise, is all!"

"I care not what grudge you have," Ishida grumbled. "You test him."

"He is not worth my time," Ikaruga growled and turned away. "I refuse."

"I've enough out of you, old man!" Jurou shouted, clenching his hands. "You keep insulting me and I'll cut out your tongue!"

"I don't believe you." Ikaruga pushed past Jurou and walked away. "I am finished with you."

"Don't turn your back on me!"

Jurou rushed forward and made a jumping front kick. Ikaruga immediately stepped out and grabbed Jurou by the ankle before he landed, slamming him down to the floor. Jurou grunted when the wind knocked out of him and his vision flashed red. The other students stared wide-eyed in stunned silence.

"What maneuver was that?" Chaka called, entering the foyer. "I've heard that you're a good fighter, but not good enough to slay *akuma*."

Jurou scrambled to his feet as Ikaruga turned around, growling under his breath at Chaka. "Where did you hear such a thing?" Jurou spat. "*I never told anyone about my past!*" he thought, horrified. "*Has he employed spies since he knows...?*"

Ikaruga grunted, unable to come up with a retort and Jurou froze, slightly startled.

Chaka pointed a thumb in their general direction. "We know of your condition, Master Ikaruga," he said coolly, "and we're not afraid of you."

"Do not enrage me!" Ikaruga snarled.

"Is that all you can say?"

"Chaka, what are you doing?" Jurou demanded, glaring at him. "Stay out of this!"

"If you truly know of my condition," Ikaruga shouted, "then you are well versed in what I can do in sheer anger!"

"I know well." Chaka approached the weapons rack, withdrawing a longbow and steel arrow.

"Chaka," Jurou yelled, "stop this madness right now!"

"He has plans to kill you," Chaka answered. "I need you alive."

"What for?" Jurou insisted.

"You'll see."

"I don't want to watch you get killed!"

"Who says I will die?"

"Please," Jurou protested, "don't fight over me!" He immediately blocked Chaka's path. "I'll just make this short and refuse to battle!"

Chaka shrugged. "Fine, but it makes no difference to me."

Jurou gestured toward the entrance. "I'll leave."

"Then leave," Chaka said coldly.

"You...!" Jurou backed away. "I don't know what to make of you."

"So don't."

Jurou raced outdoors and Chaka drew back the bow. "So now," he said, "try your sword against me!"

"You will not make that same mistake again," Ikaruga snarled. "I have heard of your exploits!"

"I'm sure everyone has," Chaka replied.

"I haven't," Kaminaritou Rouru growled and stormed up to Chaka, blocking his view. "Do tell us why you are truly here?"

"If you wish to know," Chaka declared, "I have my own reasons." He adjusted his aim. "Step aside, unless you wish to be my target as well."

"If you strike me," Kaminaritou Rouru sneered, "you dishonor your family's name!"

"Does it appear as if I give a care?" Chaka said smugly as Kaminaritou Rouru withdrew his spear and held it at ready.

"You will make a mistake," Kaminaritou Rouru warned. "You will open yourself to distraction and fail!"

"Oh?" Chaka set his sights on Kaminaritou Rouru. "Would you rather be my target instead?"

"I can sense that you are a threat to these lands."

"You are not strong enough to destroy me!" Chaka shouted. "None of you are!"

"Would you rather I show you my strength?" Kaminaritou Rouru thundered.

"Show me!"

Ikaruga turned to Ishida, who continued to sit silently on the floor as Kaminaritou Rouru circled Chaka, holding his spear at ready. Chaka followed him, aiming his arrow as he matched his stride. The senior instructor nodded and Ikaruga withdrew his katana, revealing a green steel blade.

"I shall!" Ikaruga bellowed and charged forward at Chaka. "*Shinzourippo*, commence!"

The blade glowed fierce gold and Chaka blocked Kaminaritou Rouru's attack with the bow, throwing him aside. He turned and Ikaruga plunged the glowing steel into his chest.

Chaka grunted, loosening his grip on the great bow and arrow then fell slack as his body drained of all color. Ikaruga kicked Chaka off his sword, sending him crashing to the floor. Kaminaritou Rouru jumped back once Chaka's head struck the ground near his foot.

"Your power seems to have failed you, *Sensei*," Kaminaritou Rouru murmured. "He is still alive."

"His chest should have caved in!" Ikaruga screamed. "I sensed no kind of willpower that could save him from my sweeping bolts of forces!" He stomped on Chaka's chest. "His heart should have been driven out of his body, instantly killing him!"

"He is strong," Ishida said calmly, "though he moves his mouth more than his body." The senior instructor rose to his feet with ease and tucked his sword into his belt. "Do not resort to decimating my students again."

"No one can survive such an obliterating maneuver!" Ikaruga roared and glared down at Chaka who stared up at the ceiling, agitated. He pointed his stained sword at Chaka's unmoving body. "Not even one who made a contract with *Akuma Jougi!*"

Kaminaritou Rouru backed away from the swordsman's glare, then sheathed his spear and exited the foyer.

"*He underestimates us,*" Tannozume snarled. "*Never forget; you are our slave, our conduit, and the more pain you endure, the stronger we become!*"

Chaka sighed heavily and closed his eyes. "*What is this power you posses?*" he thought. "*He barely missed my heart!*"

"*If you see such power,*" Tannozume snapped, "*you'll no longer live!*"

Chaka grit his teeth, growing aware of his mounting disconnectedness. "*I refuse to let you start the process again!*" He opened his eyes, facing a tall warrior outfitted in full crimson armor with a horned helmet and facemask that depicted a fanged demon standing over him. Chaka immediately sat up, clutching his hands that suddenly burned intensely. *"I swore to keep fighting!"*

"You seem to have forgotten that you wanted us here!"

Chaka leaned out of a grab and scrambled to his feet as the demon formed a phantom vermilion katana in its gloved hand. Chaka backed away when green light electrified the sword.

"Get away!" Chaka snarled.

"You are not strong enough to banish me, nor the rest of us," Tannozume hissed. *"You shall always be weak!"* The demon stepped forward with a swift drawing slash and vanished in a flash of light.

"Kengo Isawa!" Ishida called as Chaka staggered back, gripping his arm in agony. "What has come over you?"

Chaka grew apprehensive as the instructor approached with Ikaruga at his side. To his horror, he noticed the clawed wound on his arm reopening, oozing with deep red blood, turning almost black at Ikaruga's presence.

"If only you knew," Chaka said and pushed past them both, racing out of the foyer.

EIGHTEEN

Jurou ran up the boardinghouse walkway behind the academy where he rented a room. Clambering up the steps, he threw open the heavy weathered door and bumped into the young woman who battled Kaminaritou Rouru earlier.

Jurou gasped when he suddenly felt an invading force enter his head. Turning out, she grabbed for his arm, forcing him around to face her.

"Say," demanded the young woman, "where are you headed?"

"I'm in a hurry," Jurou said and pulled out from her grip. The eerie sensation rattled him and he shook his head.

"At least tell me your name!" Jurou gave his name and the young woman smiled brightly, holding out a hand. "I'm with the welcoming committee. My name's Kaemon Baiuko."

"Hello, Baiuko," Jurou said and shook her hand in return. The invading force returned stronger than before and he felt weak in the knees.

"There's no need to rush!" Baiuko complained.

"I just need to get out of here." Jurou let go and took a step back, taking in a shallow breath. *What is with this girl?* he thought. *It's like she can see right through me!*

"Where will you go?"

Jurou shrugged his shoulders. "As far away as possible to think," he answered nervously.

"About what?"

"Nosy girl, aren't you?"

"Don't be so rude!"

Jurou blew a hard sigh. "*Akuma* make me nervous, understand?" he said tersely. "I sense them here, but I don't see them. It's driving me mad."

Baiuko laughed. "Oh, don't use that excuse!" she teased.

Jurou frowned. "What are you talking about?" he snapped.

"I saw you staring at that man Isawa!" Jurou's face flushed scarlet. "Don't worry; he gets a lot of admirers."

Jurou nodded. "I have to admit, he is manly." He waved her away. "That however, has nothing to do with my interest in him."

"Let me warn you," Baiuko said in a low tone, "though he acts strange sometimes, he's actually a decent person from what I heard. He's *Ichizoku Eiyu* for House Suzume, slayer of a thousand devils!"

"Clan Champion, you say?" Jurou yelped, astonished. "Then why is he here? His skill surpasses us all if he's already attained that rank!"

"Perhaps he's intent on gaining the rank of *Kensei*?"

"Why are you here, then?" Jurou asked instead.

"I'm trying to strengthen my own battle prowess," answered Baiuko. "I come from a long line of defenders, just like my friend, Kaminaritou Rouru. I'm hoping to become the next *Senshuken* for House Umaa."

"Oh, so do you also hail where he comes from?"

Baiuko nodded again. "My society consists of mainly female warriors, called *Tatakai Shojou*, just like the legends tell of Lady Shidzuki..."

"You must be really fierce to become a defender, and a Battle Maiden at that!"

"I must." Baiuko clenched her hands. "I also combat the devils that have been terrorizing the coast. No one believes the greatness of my hometown, of our society, so I must prove that I can duel just as the rest!"

"I believe you can!" Jurou said, clasping his hands over hers. "You can, I know it!"

Baiuko pulled away. "If you believe in me, why not believe in yourself?"

"Where did you get that idea?"

"You're putting on a cheerful front," Baiuko accused. "Deep down you still hurt from the pain when demons murdered your family."

Jurou took a step back. "I'm not lacking courage!" he snapped. "You can't see into my soul!"

"I *do* have that skill - I saw it when I touched you."

Jurou clenched his hands and narrowed his eyes. "I should strike you for that," he growled.

"You're too softhearted for that," Baiuko retorted. "You've a kindness for women and children."

"Don't bother me," Jurou said, taking another step away. "You know nothing about me and only think you understand things about me!" He took off for the stairs.

"I can see a lot you know!" Baiuko called from below.

Jurou came to the top banister and leaned over. "You look in my soul again," he shouted, "and I'll put out your eye!"

"Liar!"

Jurou huffed and stormed for his room. After entry, he slammed shut his door and leaned against it. "That girl...!" Jurou grumbled. "Who does she think she is?"

Heading for his window, he opened the pane wide, admiring the view of the beach below. His gaze then fell on Chaka down in the courtyards with a weighted chain, whipping at the branches and striking the falling leaves with great accuracy.

"*What skill!*" Jurou thought. "*Such speed, his agility, his concentration...!*"

Chaka paused, letting several leaves flutter past him. He wrapped the chain around his shoulders and turned around, waving back. "Ho!" Chaka called.

Jurou immediately turned away from the window, ducking out of sight. Waiting for Chaka to leave, he slowly rose from his haunches and peeped out the window, spotting Chaka walking away from the courtyard. After his form faded from under the shadows of the canopy of trees, Jurou stood and leaned against the pane, blowing a heavy sigh.

"*I can't involve myself with him,*" he mused. "*He's going to be trouble...*" Moments later, Jurou heard a rap at the door. "Who's out there?" he called.

"Who else would it be, Saku?" Chaka's voice called from the other side. Jurou swallowed hard and approached the entranceway. Opening it partway, Chaka leaned against the frame, folding his arms across his chest. "I should punish you for spying," he teased, grinning.

"I wasn't spying," Jurou protested. "I just happened to see you, that's all!"

"Really, now?"

"What is it you want?"

"Is it not obvious?" Jurou stood there with a lost expression on his face and Chaka chuckled in return. "I want you."

"For what?" Jurou snapped.

"What are you going to do now that you have made a terrible impression to *Kenkyaku* Ishida?" Jurou turned away as his face flushed dark red. "You surely cannot show your face there again!"

"I guess I'll have to take you up on that offer," Jurou murmured.

"I guess you are right." Chaka pushed against the door. "Mind if I enter?"

"What do you plan to do to me?"

Chaka snorted. "Would you rather I do something to you?"

Jurou backed away as Chaka stepped in. "I'd rather you not."

"That's too bad, then..." Chaka glanced around the room. "It's modest," he said. "From all appearances, you have not been here long."

"Just a few days..."

"How could you afford the boardinghouse on a farmer's salary?"

"I have my means."

Chaka turned to Jurou, smiling crookedly. "Really now?" He put his hands on his hips as he studied Jurou closely. "I can harbor a guess..."

"It's not what you think, whatever it is."

"I have an idea..." Chaka's eyes grew blank as he approached and grabbed Jurou by the shirtfront.

"Please let me go," Jurou said sternly. "I don't have time for this."

"You can spare a moment, eh?"

Jurou put up a hand, pushing Chaka back by the chest. "Can we talk later?" he said in a terse tone. "I have other things to do."

"Maybe I can help?"

"I'm sorry, you can't help."

Chaka clamped his hands on Jurou's shoulders and Jurou grabbed for the chain draped around Chaka's neck. "Oh, want to see who's faster?" challenged Chaka.

"I don't like how you're testing me," Jurou snapped.

Chaka grinned darkly. "You are much too serious, Saku! Someone's obviously put you in a bad mood." He leaned over and Jurou stiffened as Chaka neared close to his neck. "What mood are you in?" Chaka murmured in Jurou's ear. Jurou let go of his hold, too stunned to protest and Chaka suddenly chortled, releasing his grip. "Did you seriously think I was going to bite you?" he teased, stepping away.

"I thought you might..."

"Kiss you then?"

"I–!" Jurou's face flushed bright scarlet and Chaka folded his arms across his chest, grinning wolfishly.

"Is someone causing you problems?"

"Oh, that girl Baiuko..."

Chaka's blue-gray eyes narrowed at the mere mention of her name. "You keep away from her," he said in a cold tone. "She's trouble." Jurou nodded. "Well, it seems I have overstayed my welcome." Chaka waved Jurou off and let himself out.

Once the door shut, Jurou staggered to his bed and slumped over on the edge, suddenly drained. *"He's so random!"* he thought as he laid back, staring at the ceiling. *"Yet I feel myself drawn to him..."* Jurou blew a hard sigh. *"I'm probably worrying about nothing."*

Chaka made his way down the stairs and wrapped the chain around his hand. Approaching Baiuko Kaemon's room entrance on the first floor, he knocked firmly on the door.

"Who is it?" Baiuko called from the other side. Chaka knocked again and the door came open, revealing the young woman with a towel about her head and around her waist. "Oh, it's you!" she said, mildly surprised.

"Yes, it's me," Chaka sneered.

Shouldering his way in, Baiuko screamed and ran to her desk. "What are you doing?" she shrieked, kicking up a nearby footstool. "Get out!" Catching it, she held it before her as a futile shield.

"You should stay out of my way," Chaka thundered.

Baiuko threw the stool at Chaka once he advanced and he caught it with ease. "Please, don't hurt me!" she begged.

Jumping out the way, Baiuko backed into the far end of her room as Chaka tossed the stool back. It crashed into the wall, splintering apart.

"I promise to do just that!" Chaka closed in, pressing her against the wall. "I'm stronger than you, so don't even think of fighting back."

Baiuko cringed when cornered, Chaka's tall hulking frame shadowing over her. "Please don't--!" Baiuko cried out once grabbed by the back of the neck and pulled forward. She kneed Chaka in the groin, the firm blow bringing him to his knees, stunned. Snapping her foot, she kicked Chaka in the face, tossing him back and he struck the floor hard. "You thought I'd be easy to pick on, you slime!" Baiuko shrieked, standing over him. "Well, think again!"

"Hush up!" Chaka roared and sprang to his feet. He threw a hard punch with his chain-covered fist and Baiuko swiftly sidestepped him, forcing Chaka's hand connecting into the nearby partition, blowing a hole in the wall.

Shoving Chaka back, Baiuko jumped on her desk, anticipating his next move. "Why are you attacking me?" she wailed. "Whatever have I done to you?"

"I sensed your presence on him," Chaka retorted. "You leave him be!"

"With that reason, maybe I should peek into your soul!"

"Don't you dare!" Chaka withdrew his hand stuck in the wall and charged again. Baiuko kicked at him once more and Chaka caught her foot. Giving a firm twist, Chaka flipped Baiuko over onto the floor face down. Baiuko kicked Chaka in the face with her free foot and turned onto her back as he staggered rearward, clutching a hand to his nose. "You witch!" Chaka growled. "You broke my nose!"

"Please stop attacking me!" Baiuko yelled.

Chaka wiped away the blood with the back of his uncovered hand and licked it. "Why should I?" He unlaced the chain around his hand as his pale blue-gray eyes turned blank. "Stop begging and scream for me!"

"No!"

Chaka lashed at Baiuko and she rolled out the way then jumped to her feet. He took a step forward and she backed away. "I suggest you run," Chaka snarled.

"Forget it!" Baiuko shouted. "You involved me and I will stop your plans - whatever they are!"

"Keep dreaming!" Chaka cracked the whip and Baiuko's head snapped back from the hit. She clutched her cheek, stunned when she found blood on her fingertips. "That was a light strike," Chaka vaunted. "If you really want to test me, just stand there and let me beat you!"

Baiuko's eyes widened and she took off for the door. Chaka immediately advanced, lashing her in the back with the chain.

Baiuko fell to her knees, crying out as the skin split open. "Stop, please!" she wailed and scrambled to her feet.

"I'll stop whenever I'm ready!" Chaka spat. "You started by meddling, so take your punishment!"

"Get out!" Baiuko shoved Chaka back, then ran around the room ducking and diving out of attacks as the young man gave chase.

Snapping the chain, Chaka caught Baiuko by the ankle and tripped her, drawing her over to him. Baiuko kicked him back and Chaka grabbed her leg, arresting movement. Baiuko then used her other leg to pin him and Chaka readjusted his grip. Giving a hard twist, he caused a sickening snap and Baiuko arched back, screaming in agony.

"Did that not feel good?" Chaka thundered. He leaned forward and put a hand to her throat as she grabbed his face. "What else should I target?" Baiuko dug her nails into Chaka's skin, gripping as hard as her strength allowed. Chaka knocked her hands away and tightened his hold around her throat, forcing her gasping weakly for breath. "Have you had enough?" Chaka bellowed. "Tell me!"

Baiuko made a weak grab for Chaka's face again, scratching at his skin. "Please," she wheezed. "No more..."

"I can't hear you!"

Baiuko's weakened hands fell at her sides, her face turning from bright red to pale scarlet. "Enough..." Chaka let go and Baiuko took in a large gasp of air before turning on her side, choking and coughing for breath. "I've had enough," she moaned. "You've gotten your way!"

"Tell me," Chaka commanded, "admit to me that you're not fit for fighting!" Baiuko shook her head. "Would you rather I break you even more?" Baiuko turned and Chaka grabbed her arm before she crawled away, yanking it out of socket. Baiuko let out another scream and he forced down, wrapping her arm behind her back. "Tell me, and I'll stop!"

"Never!" Baiuko screeched.

"You must enjoy it then, eh?" Chaka bent her fingers back, breaking them joint by joint. "Admit defeat, woman," Chaka shouted over her wrenching screams. "This is just one side of your body!" Baiuko's cries began to subside and Chaka leaned over, noting her blank expression as she became overwhelmed with the pain. *"That's enough for now,"* he thought and sighed heavily.

"Maybe she'll learn to keep to herself!" Tannozume grumbled.

Chaka grunted and hoisted Baiuko over his shoulder. *"She's just prone to getting her hands into things she shouldn't..."* Placing Baiuko in her bed, Chaka drew up the sheets, covering her. *"Is there a way to make her well since you've broken her already?"*

"I don't have that skill," Tannozume answered. *"But that boy you just met... you can always ask him."*

"How can you be so sure?" Chaka glanced up, spotting Jurou ducking out of sight from the door left ajar. *"If he has heard us, then so did everyone else on this floor!"*

"Only he was bold enough to come to the door!"

Chaka left Baiuko's bedside and strode over for the door. Throwing it open, he caught sight of Jurou at the staircase. "Wait," he called.

Jurou came to a pause. "Why should I?" he snapped in return.

"Are you going to face me?"

"And get beaten like you did that poor innocent girl?"

"All I did was taught her a lesson for you."

Jurou shook his head. "That was wrong."

"So teach me the right way to have handled it."

"I'm not your father."

Watching Jurou walk the rest of the way upstairs, Chaka grew incensed. "Have you anything else to say?" he called after

Jurou. "You monster, you fiend, you brute!" Chaka ran to the bottom of the staircase and looked up as Jurou ascended the steps on the second flight. "So I assume you refuse to punish me." Jurou entered his room and shut the door without a word. "Very well then - say nothing; be silent about this, see if I care! No one cares to know anyway!"

Turning around, Chaka sucked in a sharp breath when he felt steel pierce his back and shoulder. Reaching up, his fingers burned in response to touching the metal and he yanked out a large needle embedded in his skin. Suddenly growing weak, Chaka slipped to his knees as darkness came quickly.

Jurou exited his room and peered over the banister, finding Chaka unconscious. He cautiously descended the stairs and approached Chaka's downed body, perching at his side.

"*It's clear he's weak to Water jumon,*" Jurou thought and blew a sigh of relief. "*Thank Lord Kairyushin for such good fortune!*" Touching Chaka's hand, he let out a cry when Chaka grasped his hand, nearly breaking his fingers. "Let go!" Jurou cried. Chaka's eyes snapped open and Jurou gasped, finding his usual blue-gray eyes now violet. "Your eyes!"

Chaka bared his teeth at Jurou. "*We shall release you only once,*" he said in a layered tone.

"Who is in possession?" Jurou demanded. "I know that can't be you, Chaka!"

"*You caught us off guard this time...*" Chaka threw Jurou back against the wall. "*Next time, you will die for such infractions!*"

Jurou grunted, glaring at the possessed Chaka who stood with ease. "What are you planning?" Jurou demanded and clenched his hands that began to tremble. *"Keep composed,"* he thought. *"Don't let him see your fear!"*

"It is no business of yours!" Chaka snarled in his normal voice. He reached forward and Jurou grabbed his wrist with a glowing hand. Chaka yanked out of his grip and stormed away, heading outdoors.

Jurou clenched his teeth, growing incensed. *"Whatever is controlling him didn't want me to heal him,"* he thought. *"Maybe it's weak against Kairyushin's power!"* Jurou headed for Baiuko's room. *"I can't worry about him now..."*

NINETEEN

Later, Chaka awakened out on the beach when the sun's warm rays heated his skin. He sat up, refreshed, though he had no idea why. Rising to his feet, Chaka made his way back for the boardinghouse where he lived, intending to shower and change into a fresh set of clothes.

Slight pain coursed through his arm and Chaka gripped it with his right hand automatically as he continued along the beach. A familiar visitor appeared near the hill, watching him intently. Chaka released his grip and shoved his hands into his slacks pockets, hiding visible traces of pain.

"What happened to me last afternoon?" he thought. *"I have no memory..."*

"It's nothing for you to worry over," Tannozume growled.

Chaka shook his head, grimacing. *"You liar, I know something grave has happened!"* Pausing near the shore, he looked down at his reflection and noticed pale bloodstains on the arms of his pullover shirt. *"Blood has been washed out of this! Who have you slain?"*

"I murdered no one!"

"Then explain!"

"There is nothing to say!"

"Come here!" a voice called, breaking Chaka's thoughts.

Chaka tensed at the sound of chains rattling behind him. Turning around, a grappling hook ensnared his ankle, tripping him rearwards. He stumbled onto the sands and glared up at a slender middle-aged man standing over him wearing a loose-fitting brown and violet kimono and a large straw hat that shadowed his face, revealing only long white hair. In his gloved hands, he held a gleaming emerald boomerang.

"What do you want with me, old man?" Chaka demanded. "I have you know that I'm unarmed!"

"I want you to leave this place!" snapped the middle-aged man.

"Tell me who you are and I may consider it."

"I am Aida Ohara, priest of the nearby Kawaguchi Temple," said Chaka's opponent. "I have been granted power by Lord Kairyushin, protector of this area." Ohara held his boomerang at ready. "Now that you know who I am, do not force me to strike you again."

"Who summoned you?" Chaka snatched up the hook and chain as he scrambled to his feet. "My fight isn't with you, *Shisai*! I have done no wrong!"

"Perhaps, fair warrior, but it is that *akuma* Tannozume in which you harbor."

"*How dare you blame me?*" Tannozume screeched. "*You know nothing, foolish sorcerer!*"

"Wait!" Chaka cried as the cleric drew back with his boomerang that suddenly glowed in sapphire light.

"*Mizuokasuru!*" called Ohara. "Aim true at my target!" He hurled the weapon forward and Chaka ducked out of the boomerang's path, snapping the chain in return. Ohara sidestepped the attack as an eight-foot high wave abruptly surged from the sea, crashing into Chaka.

The aquatic force knocked Chaka down to his knees and he struck the sands, spitting water after the freezing rush washed over him. Ohara caught his boomerang as it circled back, seething when Chaka staggered to his feet.

"Are you mad?" Chaka screeched, clenching his hands. The marks on his left arm burned as Tannozume's rage intensified.

"You should have been obliterated!" Ohara shouted. "You are not immune to water!"

"I swim in the ocean every day!" Chaka spat. "Get away, old man!"

"I have not made a mistake; I shall remember this!" Withdrawing a talisman from his kimono's inner pocket, the cleric snapped his fingers and the paper burned in cobalt flame. In an instant, Ohara vanished in a flash of yellow smoke.

Chaka kicked up the hooked chain and wrapped it around his shoulders. Turning away, he bumped into Jurou. Jurou leaned back, mildly surprised when Chaka raised his hand.

"Please, don't strike me!" Jurou yelped. "I didn't mean to upset you."

"You startled me," Chaka stated. "I don't hate you." He shoved his hands into his pockets and started his way up the hill.

"You fought bravely," Jurou said, trailing behind Chaka. "I only sent the priest to check on you after finding you there hours before..."

"So was I out there for a while?"

"A long while."

"He caught me off guard," Chaka grumbled. "How else would I have reacted?"

"Why did he call you Tannozume?" Jurou asked instead. "Isn't that the name of a servant to the Devil Lord's general?" He chuckled. "If you're a demonic lieutenant, I'd be very surprised!"

Chaka glanced to Jurou who kept several paces behind. *"How would he know about you?"* he wondered. *"He doesn't appear to be a devil slayer!"* Chaka broke out in cold sweat when he heard no answer.

"Are you unwell?" Jurou pressed. Chaka grunted and looked ahead. "Maybe we should visit the temple soon," Jurou suggested. "At least get a blessing for your troubles."

"Why do you say that?"

"You seem to have this dark aura over you..."

"Thank you for you concern, but I doubt I will visit any time soon."

"Please don't be so sore about it!"

"I'm not." Approaching the path that led to the martial academy, Chaka turned, facing Jurou. "Do you not have classes today?"

Jurou came to a pause and stared ahead into the far distance. "Yes, but I'm not attending," he said sourly. "I don't see a real reason for me to be there."

"There must be a reason why you signed here."

"My uncle sent me here."

"That's all?"

"That's all."

Chaka puffed a sigh and ran a hand through his soaked hair. "If you don't like Ishida and Ikaruga, I understand."

"Oh, really?"

"If you like, I can teach you what you need to know."

"I'll think about it." Chaka touched Jurou by the arm to gain his attention. Jurou focused his gaze at him. "What is it?"

"I keep all that I promise," Chaka said seriously. "I swear with my life that I won't disappoint you."

"You swear with your life?" Jurou took his hand and squeezed firmly. "Swear to your *hogosha*."

Chaka looked down at Jurou, his pallid face becoming an emotionless mask. Jurou withdrew his hold at the sudden change and then continued his walk to the boardinghouse, leaving Chaka behind.

Jurou stood near his door, listening to Chaka's heavy footfalls as he made his way upstairs. He ducked out of his room and quickly made his way to the end of the corridor, catching sight of Chaka throwing around his belongings as he searched for an item of importance.

"Have you lost something?" Jurou asked once he entered the room.

Chaka grunted and sank onto the edge of his futon. "It's not that important," he muttered.

Jurou stayed near the door, watching Chaka kick off his boots. Chaka hunched forward, massaging his feet and Jurou clenched his teeth when he noticed Chaka's toes were previously broken, appearing scarred and knurled. "Did someone torture you?" he asked softly.

"It was ages ago," muttered Chaka, "I would rather not discuss it if you so mind."

"How long have you been living here?" Jurou asked instead.

"A little over than a season," Chaka answered, "though I have my own place in Shirubamachi." He crossed his legs and leaned forward, letting his loose ashen hair fall over his head.

"Why don't you stay in Shinkunotani and attend the school there?" Chaka shook his head, refusing to answer. "Will you be all right?"

When Chaka said nothing, Jurou watched him for a few moments in silence, unsure what to say. After making up his mind to leave, he turned to step out and Chaka put up a hand.

"Please stay," Chaka said softly.

Jurou glanced back at him, slightly intrigued. "Why don't you want me to leave?" Chaka shrugged. "What do you wish for me to do?" Chaka shook his head. "You ought to dry off and maybe we'll talk later."

"Tell me something..."

"What is it?"

"What is it about blood *akuma* like so much?"

"You already know."

"I really don't."

"You'll find out later if you come to class."

"Perhaps I should stay away."

"I suggest you should."

"Then shut the door."

Jurou stepped out and closed the door behind him. He leaned against it and clutched a hand to his chest, struggling to breathe.

Chaka lay back in his bed, facing Tannozume's shadowy form that hovered over him. "*I want to trust him,*" he thought. "*I want to be able to speak how I feel and share what I've been through...*"

"*Souryo and Souhei cannot be trusted,*" Tannozume grumbled. "*What makes you think he is any different?*"

"*What makes him so different?*" Chaka groaned and draped an arm over his eyes, blocking his view of the demon. "*I don't understand what draws me to him.*"

"*If it is not his looks, or his strength, then what is it?*"

"*His power perhaps?*"

Tannozume chortled. "*There is no point in you trusting others, even of such caliber!*" he growled. "*They all see you as some mindless object easily broken, to be used and thrown away however they wish!*"

"How dare you call me fragile?" Chaka thundered, immediately growing annoyed. "How can you say I can no longer place trust in anyone, even a weak acolyte such as him?"

"*He plans to destroy you... They all will!*"

Phantom claws grasped Chaka's shoulders and he winced. Removing his arm, he looked up, finding no one there. "You and your kind beleaguered me for many seasons," Chaka said evenly. "I can never trust your word, Tannozume!"

"*Consider my offer: you disregard me and you'll die, so let me stay and help you live.*"

"I'm unsure if I can…"

"*There is no point in knowing him.*" The devil released his hold. "*Speak to him even just one word of us and you'll suffer more than you already have!*"

Chaka moaned and gripped his hair. "Why do you continually plague me?"

"*Would you rather die?*"

"I already told you…"

"*You know there is no hope for your weak, tormented soul!*"

Chaka sat up as pain radiated down his back. "What shall I do then?" he inquired.

"*As if you have a choice in the matter!*"

Chaka left his bed and peeled out of his clothes, shucking them aside on the floor as he made his way to his private shower. Pulling the chain, the water came out as a blast. Chaka stood under the frigid cold and hissed in pain as his face stung when water struck it.

Clasping his hand over his cheek, the stinging pain worsened and Chaka left the shower, approaching the mirror on the adjacent wall. Pushing back his long hair, he stared back at a thin pale face with dark gray eyes, narrow nose and high cheekbones. Several long cuts lined the left side of his pallid face, starting from his forehead to his chin.

He growled and clenched his hands. "That witch marred my face!" Chaka sneered.

"*It makes you look more manly,*" Tannozume replied and cackled.

"What did you monsters do to me?"

"*Don't you remember?*"

Chaka let out a frustrated scream and bat at the air around him. "If you had flesh," he screeched, "I'd kill you right now!"

"*It gives you character,*" Tannozume jeered. "*This way you'd be less vain!*"

"My looks are all I have left!" Chaka kicked at the mirror, shattering it. "How can I make *okane* with this face now?"

"*There are other ways to obtain <u>okane</u>... As <u>watarikashi</u>, there's no need for a handsome face, just your sword arm.*"

"I am done with the mercenary life." Chaka returned to the shower, sulking underneath the stream. "You monsters enjoy ruining my life!"

"*Crying over looks not worth a couple of coin,*" grumbled the demon. "*Get over yourself!*"

"You enjoy torturing me, for you are happy when I am miserable!"

"*So what of it?*" Tannozume thundered. Struck in the back by phantom forces, Chaka cried out and dropped to his knees. He reached up for the chain with a weak hand once the water heat rapidly and his fingers met plate metal. Chaka looked up, his gaze falling onto a tall warrior standing before him outfitted in full crimson lamellar armor, wearing a horned helmet with a facemask that depicted a fanged demon. "*I have something for you to perform for me.*"

Chaka struggled to find his voice. "What would that be?"

"*Get stronger.*"

"No!"

Chaka quickly backed away once the water turned scalding and the crimson knight grabbed him by the hair, holding him in place.

"*Accept your fate, weak fool!*" Tannozume thundered over Chaka's scream as the burning water splashed on his skin. "*You've long relinquished your right to protest!*"

The crimson knight threw Chaka down on the floor and the young man crumpled at his feet, wheezing for breath. Tannozume withdrew his katana and Chaka squinted up at the demon, baring his teeth as he got up on bended knee. Tannozume beckoned Chaka to stand.

"Forget it!" Chaka shouted. "You might as well cut me down where I stand!"

The carmine devil took a step forward with a flash cut, splattering blood along the walls. Chaka slumped on his side, and Tannozume stood over him, pointing the bloodied blade at his throat.

"*Now for as long as you have that crescent mark on your back,*" Tannozume snarled and the eyes of the facemask glowed eerily in green light, "*you can never get far from my influence.*"

"Are you cursing me?" Chaka screeched.

"*Until the stars realign, you stay under my control!*"

"You--!"

Chaka sprang to his feet and the devil in red lamellar jammed his blade into Chaka's side, eviscerating him. Chaka fell forward without a sound, striking the tiles with a hard thud.

Jurou rummaged through his chest, withdrawing a set of wooden practice swords. Hoisting them over his shoulder, he headed for his door and stopped when a sudden weird chill coursed through him. Dropping what he held, Jurou immediately stood on the defensive, tense.

"*Something sinister is going on,*" he mused as he scanned the room for the source of his unease. Jurou felt a phantom touch on his shoulder and whirled around, finding no one there. He quickly put up a hand and made small motions as he murmured a prayer. "*Lord Kairyushin, wash away the darkness that may surround me.*"

Jurou clenched his teeth, unable to shake the disconcerting sensation that pressed against him. He blew a heavy sigh and picked up his fallen swords.

"I don't feel like investigating," Jurou grumbled. "I don't have time..." Opening the door, Jurou spotted Baiuko on the other side, ready to knock.

"Oh!" she said brightly. "I heard you were on this floor, so I just wanted to see about you."

"I'm fine," answered Jurou as he put on a fake smile, masking his anxiety.

"I see you're out to practice."

"Yes, I am."

"Would you spar with me?"

Jurou grinned. "Be careful or I might put out that eye."

Baiuko giggled. "I can see your moves before you make them!"

"Let's give it a try." Jurou shut his door and they both made their way downstairs.

"Saku," Chaka's voice called.

Jurou looked up, finding Chaka leaning forward against the banister in bare feet, his long ashen hair covering his face as he faced downward. He wore loose navy trousers and an untied black robe, revealing his broad pale chest and lean stomach.

"What is it?" Jurou asked. "I'm about to go out."

"Don't leave me alone again," Chaka murmured.

"Why, did something happen?"

"Let's go, Jurou!" Baiuko complained, pulling at Jurou's sleeve.

"Something happened," replied Chaka vaguely.

Jurou pushed Baiuko away. "I'll meet up," he said and waved her away. "Wait for me at the courtyards, please?" Baiuko huffed and snatched the practice equipment from his arms then stomped outdoors. Jurou stood near the wall. "Don't you have others that you are friendly with?" he called back.

Chaka shook his head. "They refuse to accept my friendship," he answered sullenly.

"What makes you think I would?"

"Because you're a nice and kind person," Chaka explained, "despite your initial cool front."

"Maybe I'd rather be alone." Jurou scoffed and crossed his arms. "What can two lonely people do?"

"Make good company."

Jurou left his place at the wall and waved a hand over his head, then made his way outside.

TWENTY

Meeting Baiuko at the courts near a row of stone benches, Jurou ducked a flying bokuto aimed at his head.

"What was that for?" he cried as it clattered near his feet.

"You're unworthy of such practice!" she said sourly. "You'd rather waste your breath on that difficult man!"

"I didn't see you exactly protesting," Jurou retorted and kicked up the wooden blade, capturing it easily.

"I know you're curious about him, but it's best to stay away!" Baiuko warned. "I've seen inside his heart. It's ugly and it'll only kill you!"

"Then that'll give me all the more reason to get closer to him."

"I'll beat you so badly; I'll turn you into a mere *onryo* haunting the halls of this *dojo*!"

"I promise to be gentle."

Baiuko's face became unreadable. "Then I'll go all out," she said darkly. "I've sparred against the best here, and Kaminaritou Rouru is the strongest student here, next to Master Ikaruga!"

"Don't change my mind!"

"Oh, you think I won't be enough of a workout for you?"

Baiuko charged forward and Jurou quickly ducked down with an underhanded diagonal slash. She blocked the blow, pushing back, immediately forcing him fighting on the defensive.

Jurou stepped out of her swift attacks, jumped on benches to evade her strikes and continually countered each hit she delivered, stunned at her speed as she kept his pace.

Kicking Baiuko back, Jurou sent her bowling head over heels on the ground. He slipped to one knee, panting hard for breath as she struck a bench.

Baiuko shook off her stun and immediately sprang to her feet then charged again. Jurou stepped back expecting an overhead slash, yet instead was checked in the chest with the bokuto's pommel.

The force sent Jurou sailing back against a nearby tree and Baiuko came at him with a forward thrust. Jurou immediately made a direct block, pushing against her.

"I thought you fought with two," he said through gritted teeth as she struggled against his strength.

"Of course," Baiuko answered, "but I have to train my weak shield hand if I lose my fighting hand in battle!"

"Damn, girl, you're strong!"

"Good!" Jurou pushed her away and Baiuko tapped him on the head. "That's *men!*" she crowed.

"You did something underhanded!" Jurou snapped.

"Your counters are too weak!"

"My defense is good enough!"

"Not when it leaves you open for a helmet-splitting attack!"

"Let's try that again."

Jurou pushed Baiuko by the chest with his shoulder and fought with blocking her fierce flurry of strikes as they went around the area. He turned and pulled back, finding to his dismay that instead of forcing Baiuko unbalanced, she only moved with him, keeping ahead by one step. Baiuko then struck Jurou's wrist and pushed him back with the spine of the blade to his throat.

"Your *kenno sukiru* are weak!" she spat. "You would've lost your hand and your head if this blade were live!"

"That's why I came here to practice my sword skill," Jurou said, smiling faintly. Baiuko backed down and picked up his fallen sword. "Where did you learn to fight like that?"

"I learned the *Garyuu* style at the Tamori-ryu on the mainland," Baiuko answered. "They're owned by House Tonbou..."

"The Tonbou Clan is full of strong fighters," Jurou said, nodding. "So how did you meet up with them if you're from House Umaa?"

"It's complicated," Baiuko said vaguely. She tossed him the practice sword and he caught it. "Care for another round?"

"I should get going," Jurou said. "I have class."

"Well, you shouldn't go in empty-handed!"

"What do you mean?"

"Go over there and look behind that bench."

Jurou sighed and looked around, his gaze falling on a worn flour sack he had not noticed before resting against a bench. Getting closer, he pulled up the bag and noticing its weight, opened it, revealing a pair of lacquered wooden batons with capped iron ends.

"Who would give me this?" he said, surprised. "I'm not strong enough to wield *tonfa*..."

"They arrived yesterday evening," Baiuko explained. "The courier stationed it outside my door, so that's why I was looking for you this morning."

"You didn't have to make excuses."

"You're the only person I thought of with the skill to use them."

Jurou snorted. "What made you think that?"

"I saw you had a coat with *Heiwa Shinkou* on the back and assumed you were *souryo*..." Jurou paled as Baiuko waved at him. "Let's have a go with it," she said seriously.

"Right now?" Jurou tossed Baiuko the other sword and she caught it.

"Yes, right now," Baiuko spat exasperatedly.

"Why are you so quick to test me?" Jurou grumbled. Dumping the sack over, he withdrew the batons and held them in his hands, performing several movements with them, studying their weight. "They seem balanced..."

Baiuko scoffed. "That can't be your ready stance!" she jeered.

"What's wrong with my ready stance?" Jurou retorted, glaring up at her.

"First, you're standing with your feet apart and your head turned towards the ground," Baiuko waved a dismissive hand at Jurou. "You're too flat on your feet to move out the way and you should look up at me to see whether I'm about to pull a trick!"

"I can hear just fine," Jurou snapped and waved the handle, moving the baton near his forearm. "I don't have to look; now let's get started."

"Fine, then!"

Jurou closed his eyes, waiting for Baiuko to move. He heard the blade hum as she brought it down and blocked with his left baton, bringing down his right to strike back.

Baiuko blocked and Jurou locked her hold then shifted his weight on his feet, pushing her rearward. Jurou turned out with an upper strike and rapped Baiuko in the face. She cried out, stunned.

Jurou kicked Baiuko away and opened his eyes, immediately ducking down from her overhead counter strike then tripped her with a low leg sweep that threw her onto her back.

Baiuko chucked her sword and Jurou crossed his tonfa, knocking it away as she scrambled to her feet. She charged forward and Jurou pushed the blade away, slamming the other baton into Baiuko's neck. She gagged and staggered rearward.

"You're tough," Baiuko moaned and slipped to her knees. She pitched her sword into the ground, leaning against it as she gasped for breath. "You had your eyes closed most of the time!"

"I can hear you," Jurou admitted, "even the breath of the swing."

"What if you're against someone swift as lightning?" Baiuko snapped back. "What if your opponent can strike once and make two cuts?"

"I'll get to it when I get to it."

"You might be dead before long!" Baiuko shook her head. "I heard of a fighter who can walk with the winds and fight in the shadows and no one's ever defeated them!"

"That's a legend, nothing more!"

"Are you partially blind?" Baiuko suddenly asked.

Jurou turned on his heel and waved her off. "I'll see you later," he grumbled.

"With the way you fight, it seems you can only see shadow and not fine details," Baiuko called after him.

Jurou walked way, ignoring her completely. Wood suddenly slammed into the back of his head and he grunted, coming to a full stop. "Damn it, girl!" he yowled, whirling around. "Stop throwing things at me!"

"Am I ugly or something?" Baiuko complained.

"What kind of question is that?" Jurou yelled.

"Your defense is fine, but since you're concentrating on listening to my movements and not watching them, it's making you slow!"

"Whatever!" Jurou stomped for the academy grounds. *"It's not that,"* he thought, stewing in annoyance. *"It's not that I don't see very well..."*

TWENTY-ONE

Walking up the Kakita Martial Academy's steps, Jurou pushed through the heavy doors and spotted two young men practicing near the entrance, with one who had a pair of wakizashi and the other a heavy spear.

"You're blocking the way," Jurou snapped.

"Excuse us, short stuff," retorted the spear fighter.

"Aren't you a little young to be attending here?" jeered the swordfighter. His sparring partner guffawed.

"I'm old enough," Jurou snarled.

"*Ja mata*," said the spear fighter and waved off his partner.

"*Sarabada!*" the swordfighter replied cheerfully, waving back.

Jurou grunted when checked and made his way to the practice ring, watching Ikaruga screaming at two fighters in cavalry attire delivering blows to each other in the isolated ring.

A fit young woman with bright green eyes and shoulder-length light red hair easily overwhelmed her opponent, a slim young man with messy short dark brown hair and bright brown eyes. The male cavalier, a powerhouse of nervous energy, was unable to keep his blows straight against his opponent and continued getting jarred with counter attacks.

"Move, curse you!" Ikaruga screamed. "You are the wind! You are the shadows!" The young man groaned when taken down with a blow to the head, stunning him. "You call that fighting? I can't believe you were in the Imperial Army!"

Jurou heard a laugh and turned, finding Kaminaritou Rouru and a young woman standing on the other side of the ring watching the fight. The woman of interest was tall and athletic, with pale brown eyes and cropped dark brown hair. She wore a form-fitting navy uniform, dark indigo boots and lightweight black leather gloves.

"Was she in the Imperial Special Services?" thought Jurou, stunned by the sight of her. *"Why would they come here to train?"*

"Come on, Toma Ittou!" the cavalry woman taunted. "You'll never hit me by standing still!"

"Stand still long enough and I'll do so!" Ittou snapped. He threw a powerful punch and she easily sidestepped him.

"You can't get a hit in with a swing like that!"

Ittou let out a shout and threw another punch. It finally connected, knocking her down. "Asano Tokiko is down for the count!" Ittou announced, pumping his fists.

"You got lucky," grumbled Tokiko, "that's all!" Ittou held out a hand for her to take.

"What is it that Master Ishida is always telling you?" the mysterious woman in navy called as Ittou pulled Tokiko to her feet. "He says to move your body instead of your mouth!"

"Gutless woman to the core!" Ikaruga jeered. "And that unstable creature behind you isn't worthy of such practice!" Tokiko glared at Ikaruga, her face flushing red in ire.

"No!" Ittou yelped when she bounded over the ring and jumped Ikaruga, slamming a heavy punch aside his head, causing him staggering back dazed. Ittou and the mysterious woman raced up to Ikaruga, grabbing for Tokiko to peel her off his back.

"Another word leaves your mouth," Tokiko screamed, "and I'll be there personally to shove it back in!" She bat Ikaruga again on the head. "I am the tiger of Kobarutoshi!"

"Enough, Tokiko!" Ittou cried, grabbing her arm. Tokiko punched him in the face and the force threw him to the ground.

The young woman grabbed Tokiko by the hair before she could react and flipped her over onto the floor. She swiftly kneed Tokiko in the chest and held a hand to her throat while her other hand grabbed her face, placing her thumb near her eye. Tokiko looked up, too shocked to fight back.

"Amazing!" Jurou said in awe as the young woman rose to her feet, flushing darkly.

"Sorry!" she said and laughed nervously as she held her hands behind her back. "Old habits die hard!"

Ittou approached, holding a hand to his nose. "Let's go, Tokiko," he grumbled in a muffled tone. "You're paying for my medical bills again!" Tokiko scrambled to her feet, frightened of the young woman who kowtowed deeply before her.

"I'm very sorry, Miss Tokiko," the woman said.

"Don't act like you're my friend!" Tokiko snapped and pushed past her.

"Wait for me!" Ittou called and hurried along Tokiko's side, escorting her out.

"Curse you!" Ikaruga growled after the two. "Never return here again!"

"We'll see you later, *Sensei*!" Ittou called over his shoulder. Tokiko kicked open the door and stormed down the steps.

Ikaruga spotted Jurou and placed a hand to the hilt of his katana. "Have you come to prove your worth?" he grumbled. "Or rather I humiliate you again? It's your choice."

Jurou grunted. "The *tonfa* are what I'm proficient with," he answered. "More or less..."

"So you say!" Jurou swallowed hard as Ikaruga stepped into the ring. "I've only time for one round. That should be enough to assess you."

Jurou sighed heavily and ducked into the ring, standing across from the instructor. "What are the conditions?" he asked and clenched his teeth when Kaminaritou Rouru approached the edge with the mysterious young woman. She smiled brightly at Jurou, her brown eyes fading as crescent lines on her face. Jurou nodded in her direction, giving a slight smile in return.

"After five strikes or one mortal blow, the round is considered over!"

"Oh, so you have little time for me?" Jurou groused, glaring back at Ikaruga. "How insulting!"

"Be brave," Kaminaritou Rouru said.

"I'm sure you can get him easily," said the mysterious young woman. "He's old you know and he's got a weak right."

Kaminaritou Rouru nudged her in the side. "Hush!" he scolded.

"The fight commences now!" Ikaruga withdrew his sword and Jurou swiftly blocked the attack, pushing back.

Turning out, Ikaruga came with a direct overhead thrust and Jurou ducked down, slamming one baton into the swordsman's knee, forcing him to falter. Ikaruga kicked Jurou back with his other foot and turned, bringing down his blade over Jurou's back.

Rolling out the way, Jurou struck Ikaruga's other foot with his free tonfa and Ikaruga kicked Jurou in the head, following through with a low stab. Jurou held his breath and deflected the blow, pushing back then sprang to his feet, continuously repelling the swordsman's swift attacks that came at him furiously hard and fast.

Striking for Ikaruga's neck, the swordsman staved off the attack with the katana's spine and pushed down, splitting the baton. The force of the blow sent Jurou to his knees, exhausted and panting for breath.

Ikaruga scoffed and calmly sheathed his sword. "Your blocks were ineffective," he said smugly.

"That was no test!" Jurou wheezed.

"If I continued my attack, you'd need a priest."

"How so?"

"You were holding back." Ikaruga punched Jurou in the chest and Jurou groaned, doubling over. "If you don't breathe, your attacks are weak!"

"That's enough," the young woman called, clenching her hands. "Stop picking on him!"

"I suggest you pick a new weapon of choice," Ikaruga growled. "The *tonfa* is a good weapon for those who fight unarmed - the strength is the base of power and that power is convened through it."

Jurou struggled to his knees. "What weapon do you suggest I take?" he asked faintly.

"For someone with your weakness and frailty, I suggest nothing!"

Jurou jumped to his feet, trembling in rage as he watched Ikaruga stomp out the ring. "Don't make fun of my short stature!" Jurou screamed after him and hurled his remaining baton at the instructor's head. Ikaruga quickly sidestepped the attack and calmly headed out the back door. Jurou leaned against the railing, seething.

"Don't worry," the young woman said as stepped up offside the ring. Jurou immediately calmed and smiled faintly as she returned with a gentle grin. "You're neither weak nor frail; I can see it!"

"Really, now?" Jurou spat sourly.

"Master Ikaruga wasn't being unusually hard on you," Kaminaritou Rouru interjected. "A simple defeat is all you've suffered."

"That and a blow to my honor," Jurou complained.

"That means you just need to build up and learn from your mistakes."

"I'm not ready to spar against you yet."

"Would you spar against me?" asked the young woman.

"You were in the Elite Forces," Jurou said and shook his head. "There's no way I can stand up to you."

"Even your best student here falls at my feet," she replied and chortled. Kaminaritou Rouru's face flushed dark red and he turned away.

"I assume that to be true by his reaction," Jurou said, watching him storm off outdoors.

"They always get that way." Jurou gave an abbreviated bow and gave his name. "Miyabi Nakiko," she returned. "But you can call me Ami if you like."

"What kind of pet name is 'Nectar'?" Jurou asked, grinning.

"Get close and you might just find out."

Jurou flushed scarlet. "Why are you so forward?" he inquired. "We're not close enough to be friends for me to call you Ami."

"I just like having many friends." Nakiko blushed slightly and looked down at the floor. "You know, with my former job, I was a scary woman..."

"I don't find you scary." Jurou chuckled. "Maybe we should team together and call ourselves *Daisho*."

Nakiko burst out laughing. "The long and short!" she crowed. "You're silly!"

Jurou relaxed in her presence and left the ring. "Care to walk with me?" he asked.

Nakiko fell in step along Jurou's side. "What about outside classes with Master Ikaruga?"

"I'm not in the mood for another round of ridicule." Nakiko nodded and they made their way for the foyer. "So, what style of fighting do you know?"

"It's called the *Shichi Nanatsu*," Nakiko answered. "I basically travel around to each Imperial Academy *dojo* on the islands and master each one."

"Why are you here at Kakita then?"

"This is the sixth before I move to the seventh."

"Are they learned in any particular order?"

"Not exactly, but some *senshi* state that there is a method in order to take less time in which to master it."

"How long have you been traveling?"

"Oh, only ten cycles."

Jurou paused in step, stunned. "You mean to tell me that you mastered five fighting arts in ten cycles?"

"There's this man I'm chasing after," Nakiko said. She paused at the door when she realized Jurou was several paces behind. "Why is that so unheard of?"

"I barely got down at least one fighting style in four seasons!"

"Well, this one I'm chasing, he mastered six styles in seven cycles." Nakiko punched a hand into her palm. "He's a terror and I want to kill him."

"Why do you want to kill him?"

"After he masters the style, he kills the teacher and the assistants, and all the best students."

Jurou gasped. "That's horrible!"

"That mad devilish beast slaughtered my father and gravely injured my uncle," Nakiko said seriously. "Before I can run his *dojo*, I first must put his soul at rest..."

"So you obtained permission for *kataki-uchi*?" Jurou asked and Nakiko nodded. "I see..." He waved her away. "Don't let me slow you down! I'm the worst student here and will only impair your skills!"

"Maybe it's fortunate that we met." Nakiko said once Jurou approached and she pet him on the head. "With my awesome skill, you'll improve greatly!"

"If you say so!"

Nakiko turned for the door and opened it, only to gasp and step back at Chaka who appeared disheveled on the other side. His long ashen hair hung as a frizzy mess around his shoulders and he wore an oversized shirt that hung loosely from his upper body, baggy slacks with a large belt slung low around his hips and worn leather boots on his feet.

"Hm?" Chaka murmured, glancing at Nakiko.

"What happened to you?" Jurou cried. "Did you duel someone?"

"Ah, Saku, I'm a born duelist!" Chaka held a hand against the doorframe and grinned at Nakiko. "Now who is this lovely creature?"

Nakiko took a step back, drawing her hands into fists. "I've seen you train at the Hokutou-ryu!" she cried, "and at least three others!" Chaka tilted his head, his expression becoming stony. "You're the Beast from the Blood Coast, Isawa Chaka!"

"Oh, I have an admirer!" Chaka reached out and Nakiko quickly put up an arm to deflect his hand. He then grasped her wrist and pulled her to him. "Is my appearance offensive, pretty lady?"

"Let go of me!" she growled.

"I don't hate you for it if you are offended." Chaka smirked. "I just fought someone who wanted to buy me."

Nakiko pulled out of his grip and pushed past him. "You're too ugly to even be bartered!" she snapped. "I've heard of your exploits. Tell me, why did you pick up the *manriki-gusari*?"

"What difference does it make?" Chaka said coolly as he put up his hands. "I come from a line of elite fishermen."

"That's a lie and you know it! I've never seen you use *chijiriki*!"

"Maybe I'm considering becoming *souhei*."

Nakiko scoffed. "That's an even bigger lie! You don't have the speed to use the *nage-gama*!"

"So what if I've trained at several *dojo*." Chaka shrugged his shoulders. "I'm no master." Glancing to Jurou, Chaka smiled warmly and pet him on the head. "How pleasant it is to see you again, Saku," he said brightly and walked inside, heading for the weapons rack at the rear of the room.

Jurou exited outside, watching Nakiko pace angrily. "What's your problem with him?" he asked.

"I know him from before," Nakiko grumbled. "I've seen him and I know he's from a wealthy family! He's something more than anyone would ever know!"

"He's not that legendary *senshi* you're chasing, is he?"

Nakiko came to a pause and threw up her hands. "Oh, what do I know!" she complained and looked up at the sky. "Lady Shidzuki, help me!"

"Why does he irritate you so much?"

Nakiko shook her head and waved a dismissive hand. "Forget it," she said. "The less you know about Chaka, the better I'd feel!"

"What do you know about him?"

"Why, what would you like to know?"

"I have to admit I am interested in him." Jurou's face flushed slightly. "I just met him yesterday and Baiuko told me he was very strong, having slain a thousand demons!"

"A thousand devils, you say?" Nakiko snorted. "I know he lives somewhere on these islands and in a major city either close to here or maybe a ferry away." Nakiko shrugged her shoulders. "If he's like what I've heard of his reputation, just stay away."

"Is there another reason on how he became known as 'The Beast from the Blood Coast'?"

"During the Winter Campaign seven cycles ago, he quickly worked his way up to a highly ranked officer, but apparently quit the army to travel."

"How old is he now?"

"No more than twenty-five summers, I believe."

"And what rank did he make?"

"*Fukutaichou.*"

Jurou paled, too stunned to speak. "*He made the rank of Lieutenant at eighteen summers!*" he thought. "*Either he's naturally skilled or...*"

"Well, let's find something you're good at," Nakiko called, breaking Jurou's thoughts. "I'll help you with it."

"That's fine," Jurou said and followed her back for the boardinghouse.

TWENTY-TWO

Chaka snatched up a heavy spear and stormed the sparring ring. Tannozume's shadowy form immediately appeared before him in response and Chaka held the spear at ready. "Come on!" he thundered, slicing at the demon.

Tannozume laughed, darting out the way. *"With those skills, you can never strike me!"* he crowed. *"Shiranosuke, Akanasutsune, deal with him."* The lithe horned devil and her stout companion appeared as Tannozume vanished.

"I will get you back for cutting me like that!" Chaka shouted and thrust the spear forward, striking at empty space when the demons swiftly darted out the way.

The devils proved too fast for Chaka as he sliced and pierced at nothing but air, eventually growing tired. Dropping the spear, Chaka leaned against the ropes, panting for breath. The fiends vanished once Kaminaritou Rouru entered the ring moments later.

"I had no idea you used the *yari*," Kaminaritou Rouru said, picking up the fallen weapon. "Did Ami speak truth?"

Chaka said nothing and jumped over the top rope. He made his way for the weapons rack and grabbed a weighted chain, then returned. Pushing up the sleeves of his shirt, Chaka wrapped the chain around his wrist, letting the remaining free slack along his side. "I ought to kill you," he said evenly as Kaminaritou Rouru practiced maneuvers alone in the sparring arena.

"I'll force your tongue from your throat for threatening me," Kaminaritou Rouru snapped, coming to a pause when Chaka stood behind him. "I've done no wrong to you!"

"Oh, so you call cutting me yesterday doing no wrong!"

"If you recall, I missed." Kaminaritou Rouru leaned against his spear.

"Then miss again."

"So you wish to practice with a flesh opponent?"

"What a fine offer!"

Kaminaritou Rouru turned around and took his place at the center of the sparring ring. He held the spear at ready, expecting an opening when Chaka entered and stood across from him.

"Very well," Kaminaritou Rouru snarled, "I can accommodate you." He beckoned to Chaka. "Let us begin."

Chaka held the chain taut, circling Kaminaritou Rouru. "Let me warn you that I am not in a viable mood today," he replied.

"It makes the fight all the more interesting."

Kaminaritou Rouru slammed the butt of the spear against Chaka's chest, pushing him back. He then turned and brought down the spearhead, slashing into Chaka's side.

Chaka immediately sidestepped the attack, whipping the chain forward. The chain wrapped around Kaminaritou Rouru's throat and Chaka kicked the spear aside when thrust at him. Pulling forward, Chaka forced Kaminaritou Rouru to the floor, sending him crashing on his side with a hard thud. Placing his boot-clad foot on his Kaminaritou Rouru's shoulder, Chaka yanked the chain, forcing his opponent looking up.

"Would you hate me if I snapped your neck?" Chaka teased darkly.

"All the more to haunt you," Kaminaritou Rouru growled, "since you do not have that skill!" Chaka frowned and slackened his grip. "We are not enemies, but if you wish to become mine, then I shall show no mercy."

"Then become it!"

Chaka withdrew the chain and kicked Kaminaritou Rouru away. Kaminaritou Rouru rolled back onto his feet and kicked up the spear that lay nearby. He easily sidestepped Chaka's numerous strikes and advanced under Chaka's guard, pressing forward with a deep thrust. Chaka staggered back, stunned as Kaminaritou Rouru leaned in, penetrating deeper into Chaka's chest. He growled, narrowing his eyes at Chaka who only laughed.

"You missed!" Chaka snarled and kicked Kaminaritou Rouru in the groin then shoved him aside. Kaminaritou Rouru stumbled rearward and dodged another strike with the chain, only getting tripped by the foot and thrown down on his back. "You'll regret crossing my path," Chaka growled and yanked out the spear and dropped it with a clatter.

Kaminaritou Rouru grabbed the spear as Chaka raised his foot to stomp on his chest. Kaminaritou Rouru pierced Chaka in the side and Chaka grunted, loosening his grip on the weighted chain. He sank to his knees as he grasped his side in agony.

"Quite a workout from the supposed 'Beast of the Blood Coast'," Kaminaritou Rouru said between hard pants for breath. "I know this isn't your true strength!" He turned the spear around and struck Chaka in the face with the blunt end, forcing him on his back. "I apologize in advance for this one."

Kaminaritou Rouru rose to his feet and lunged with an overhead forward pierce. Chaka immediately grabbed the blade with his hand before the tip met his throat. The steel sliced into his skin, causing rivulets of blood streaming down his arm.

"You don't want to see my true strength," Chaka declared. "What you saw was only a fraction!"

"Show me!"

"Why should I, you offensive dog?" Chaka pushed Kaminaritou Rouru away and scrambled to his feet, clutching his hands that flared in pale golden light. Kaminaritou Rouru advanced and Chaka thrust forward his bloodied glowing hand. Kaminaritou Rouru paused and Chaka grinned darkly.

"You use that *meisou* skill here," Kaminaritou Rouru spat, "and the *machikata* will be on your head!"

"Try *kirisute* against me without any witnesses and the *bugyo* will have your head as well!" Chaka retorted. "Come on!"

Kaminaritou Rouru grunted and withdrew his weapon. "You are not forgiven," he grumbled. "The next we meet, I will not be this kind!" He stormed away.

"Is he not from the temples?" Chaka thought as he lowered his hand, killing the light. *"Is that why you attacked?"* When Chaka received no answer, he blew a heavy sigh. *"How could I be wrong?"* More silence followed. *"You're looking for something else, are you?"*

"Your reasoning is correct," Tannozume grumbled. *"I will continue using you until I find it."*

"Once you find what you're looking for, will you release me then?"

"Perhaps."

"What are you saying?"

"You know what I am saying!" Tannozume laughed and Chaka cringed, growling under his breath.

Leaving sparring arena, Chaka headed for the lavatory and approached the faucet. Pumping the handle, cold water gushed through and he ran his hands in the stream then splashed water on his face. Looking up at his reflection in the mirror, Chaka hated what he saw.

"I don't know who I am anymore..." he moaned. Moments later, the doors kicked open and Ittou Toma entered, wheezing for breath. "What happened to you?" he asked.

"I should ask you the same," Ittou said. "You do realize you're bleeding, right?"

"It's only a flesh wound from fighting Kaminaritou Rouru..."

"At least it's nothing serious." Ittou grinned. "I lost against Tokiko again."

"Maybe you spar too often and you both know each other's maneuvers."

"Maybe you're right." Ittou entered a nearby stall and shut the door after him. "You leave the water running."

"I like the sound of water," Chaka answered. "My life is like the ocean in which surrounds Kakita."

"Is it calm and peaceful?" Ittou asked.

"No," Chaka murmured, looking wistfully at the water that ran down the drain, "but I wish." He blew a disconcerted sigh.

"So, is it turbulent and unforgiving?"

"Yes... just exactly."

"Hmm... well, I've suffered the same motions as the sea." The commode flushed and Ittou exited the stall, buttoning up his slacks. "Better suited for a rider, where I can escape the mindless activity of those bound to the earth by flying above them." He approached the sink near Chaka and washed his hands. "The rush of air is almost similar to the sound of water, but it is more like a whistle, not an exhaled breath."

"What a nice analogy."

"Well, I'm not much for thinking, for I do by action." Ittou dried his hands on the back of his slacks. "You should patch up that arm of yours, before it becomes infected."

"It's an old wound that opens every now and then," Chaka replied. "I'll be fine."

Ittou saluted Chaka then left the restrooms. Chaka ran his hands underneath the water and the clear liquid slowly turned muddy brown as it rushed through his fingers.

"*You must not make friends,*" Tannozume sneered. "*They will only get in the way!*"

"You're afraid that someone stronger may come along and banish you!" Chaka grumbled. "Including all the templars you've been avoiding!"

"*You had the power to do so once... but you threw it away.*"

"I was young and foolish when I made that mistake."

"*It is evident that even your <u>hogosha</u> have betrayed you!*" Tannozume laughed. "*Your holy power granted by them is corrupted by us, so what makes you think they'll listen to you now?*"

Chaka glared at his reflection and the mirror cracked from invisible forces, oozing blackish-red liquid from the fissures. "I accept your challenge," he snarled.

"Whom are you speaking to?" Kaminaritou Rouru's voice called.

Chaka turned, spotting the young man standing behind him. "Why are you here?" he snapped. "How long have you been standing there? You made no noise when you entered!"

"*Senshi* Toma asked me to check on you," Kaminaritou Rouru grumbled. "So, is everything all right in here?"

"Everything is fine," Chaka pushed him back by the chest. "You have your answer, so now take your leave!"

"Do you wish bad medicine upon yourself?"

Chaka shut off the water and pushed past the young man, making his way for the door. Kaminaritou Rouru strode over to Chaka and grabbed him by the arm.

Chaka shook out of Kaminaritou Rouru's grip. "I warn you," he said seriously, "you do not wish to get close to me."

"What are you saying?" Kaminaritou Rouru snapped, narrowing his eyes.

"I am tainted!" Kaminaritou Rouru's eyes widened and he took a step away. "I tell you now: get away before the taint reaches you and corrupt your soul as well!"

Kaminaritou Rouru clenched his hands. "Then why are you here?" he demanded. "You should go to the temples!"

"It is not as easy as you think."

"My shadow was stolen from me and I asked the *kamisama* for mercy," Kaminaritou Rouru declared. "They will bless you if you simply ask them!"

"Maybe the gods have nothing to do with me."

Kaminaritou Rouru tensed. "You will bring nothing but destruction on these lands," he growled.

"We'll see." The young man left and Chaka grunted when struck in the back by a phantom blade.

"*You shall speak no more!*" Tannozume roared. Chaka suddenly found it difficult to breathe and gripped his chest as his heart skipped a beat. "*Speak more of us and the end draws near!*"

"I promise!" Chaka wailed.

"*Liar!*"

Chaka cried out when struck over the head and his world dissolved away.

TWENTY-THREE

Jurou returned to his room later in the day, drained and devoid of energy. Nakiko followed him, bounding with restless vigor.

"Another round, please?" she pleaded.

"No, Nakiko!" Jurou protested and dropped onto his futon, kicking off his shoes. "Let me rest before you kill me!"

"We already covered the many weapons that you don't have a natural talent for!" Nakiko grinned fiercely. "There are many more we can discover!"

"We'll do more in the morning!" Jurou sighed heavily and lay back, draping an arm over his eyes. "I'm begging you, go away."

"I'll see you in the morning, then," Nakiko promised.

"Don't leave my door open," grumbled Jurou.

"Why not?" Jurou said nothing and she waved him off. "*Ogenki de!*" Letting herself out, Nakiko shut the door behind her and greeted other students in the hall as they returned from class.

A light knock resonated moments later and Jurou groaned, sitting up on his elbows. "I told you to come back in the morning!" he called. Another knock, harder than the last, rattled his door. "Who is it?"

"I bring greetings," a voice called from the other side.

Jurou huffed and left his bed, storming over to the door. Swinging it open, he grunted when struck hard in the face, corkscrewing him to the floor.

A strong hand grabbed Jurou by the arm before he could get up and twisted it behind his back as crushing weight descended on his shoulders, forcing him to the floor.

"Why are you doing this?" Jurou demanded and looked up from his place on the floor, finding a warrior wearing navy scale armor and another in white-gold chain mail standing at his doorway. Both wore horned helmets and facemasks that depicted demons, hiding their identity. "Who sent you?"

"Report us to the authorities," the warrior who held Jurou down grumbled from above, "and we will slaughter everyone here."

Jurou craned his neck and saw the warrior in violet-steeled plate armor withdraw a braided rope, calmly binding his wrists. "I promise I won't say anything to the *machi-bugyo*," Jurou pleaded. "Just tell me, why are you doing this?"

"We have orders."

"For what?"

"To kill you."

Jurou shouldered off his opponent and quickly sprang to his feet, kicking at the warrior in violet as he advanced.

"Tell me, who wants me dead?" Jurou yelled. "Who ordered this *ada-uchi* against me?" The amethystine warrior withdrew his broadsword and Jurou ducked out of a forward slash. Jurou backed away for his window when the three closed in. "At least give a dying man an answer!"

The warrior in damson armor rushed into Jurou, slamming his head against the windowsill. Jurou staggered forward and ducked out another swing, shouldering his opponent with a forceful check against the chest. He whirled around and released a swift side kick into the heliotrope-steeled fighter, only get his foot grabbed and thrown back against the wall.

Jurou's head snapped back from a hard punch to the face that sent him crashing through the opening and he watched in horror at the three assassins clustered near his window.

Suddenly he smashed into another person and Jurou gasped when he realized his body did not strike cobblestone. He heard a grunt and glanced up to see Chaka holding onto him with a nervous smile on his face.

"Fancy finding you here," teased Chaka. "It's not every day I catch men jumping from windows."

"How did you get here?" Jurou asked. Chaka set him down and Jurou slipped to his knees, suddenly growing weak.

"I just took a walk after a tough practice," Chaka replied and perched at Jurou's side on his haunches. "Thank your *hogosha* for leading me here."

"How did you know?"

"Know what?"

"Never mind," Jurou muttered and lowered his head, taking in a shallow breath.

"You really should be careful," Chaka said mildly. "The *kamisama* can't always keep us safe."

"I'll keep that in mind."

Chaka untied Jurou's hands and wrapped the rope around his shoulders. "What have you done to make you want to do such a thing?"

"What?" Jurou shook his head. "I wasn't trying to commit *munen-bara* or *funshi* or anything like that. I have no reason to do that."

"Would you rather I take your life?"

Jurou quickly looked up at Chaka who continued to smile. "*Is he joking or serious?*" he thought.

"Well...?" Chaka pressed.

"I can take care of it myself," Jurou said instead. "I really don't need a second."

"I don't want you die and suffer in *Jigoku* alone."

"What makes you think I'm going to have my soul burn?"

"If you get too close to me, it might just happen."

Jurou stood as Chaka rose from his crouched position. "Are you telling me," Jurou asked, "or are you warning me?"

"I'm telling you... if you stay with me, I'll drag you down into the deepest depths of The Darkness where it'll swallow you whole and never release you."

Jurou let out a nervous laugh. "Surely you jest!"

"Do you feel alone and cold inside every waking moment of your life?" Chaka asked instead.

"I really don't feel that way..."

"So why would you want to end your life?"

"I really wasn't trying to."

"You're a horrible liar, Saku." Jurou's face flushed and Chaka chuckled. "I might have to keep my eye on you."

"You don't have to do that." Jurou put up his hands. "I don't want you to promise your life to me or anything silly like that."

"Why not?"

"It'll only complicate things."

"Then why are you wasting your breath to me when it's clear you have other things to do?"

The flush on Jurou's face deepened. "I'd rather not return to my room alone right now," he murmured.

Chaka laughed and suddenly gasped as he doubled over. Jurou grabbed for him, only to get pushed away. "I'm fine," Chaka grumbled. "It's a flesh wound, nothing more!"

"Maybe you ought to see a healer for that."

"It's not the first time I've been cut on." Chaka stood upright and waved at Jurou to follow him. "Come, I'll protect you."

"I can't pay you if you're willing to be my bodyguard."

"I'll find other means."

"I can't accept your offer..."

"I'll sleep when you sleep and wake when you wake. I'll only stay by your side as much as possible. Is that all right with you?" Jurou paled, unable to say anything in response and Chaka chortled, running a hand through his hair. "It's agreed then!" he said brightly.

"But about your pay..." Jurou started.

"We'll discuss that another time."

At a loss for words, Jurou walked with Chaka back for the boardinghouse. He clenched his hands, growing ill at ease. "*My hands aren't burning,*" Jurou thought. "*They usually burn when I'm near him, but not today.*" He grit his teeth as they made their way upstairs. *"I don't understand..."* Chaka held out a hand to stop Jurou as they neared his room. "What is it?" he asked.

"What happened in here?" Chaka demanded.

"It's nothing important."

Chaka entered the room, looking around while Jurou stood at the door. "Did you steal something of worth?" Chaka asked, studying the nature of the overturned furniture and strewn objects.

"I wish," answered Jurou.

Chaka glanced back at Jurou. "Need a hand?"

"Sure."

After straightening the room, Jurou sat on the edge of his futon while Chaka took a seat on the floor, holding his knees.

"Would you tell me something?" Jurou asked.

"Anything, Saku," Chaka answered.

"How did you get known as 'The Beast from the Blood Coast'?"

Chaka's gray eyes turned distant. "I really don't like being called *Ketsueki Kaiganjuu*," he murmured. "It isn't who I am..."

"Then who are you?"

Chaka suddenly focused and smiled brightly. "Everyone knows of my hard work I've done for the Imperial Army," he nervously replied. "I'm loyal to the Empire and because of that, became a highly ranked officer." He shrugged his shoulders. "What else is there to know?"

Jurou furrowed his brow. "I wonder about that too, sometimes," he said. Chaka continued to smile and it unnerved

Jurou. "Why quit the army to travel?" he asked instead. "You know we have an eight-cycle contract after we are twenty summers."

"Oh, is there?"

Jurou gave Chaka a quizzical look. "How old are you?"

Chaka snorted. "How old do I appear?"

Jurou left his place on the bed and approached Chaka. Crouching down, he studied the young man closely. "You can't be no more than twenty-three summers, maybe twenty-five!"

Chaka chuckled. "You may not be able to see it, but I'm an old man in here."

"Oh?"

"Look, really look." Chaka grabbed Jurou by the sides of his head and Jurou gasped, shutting his eyes once pulled in. "Look into my eyes," Chaka ordered.

"I don't think I can," Jurou moaned.

"Come now, I won't bite."

"Promise?"

"Would you rather I did?" Jurou snapped open his eyes and stared back at cloudy gray flecked with gold. "What do you see?" Chaka murmured.

"I see someone in a lot of pain," Jurou said softly. Chaka released his hold and Jurou sat back on his knees in front of Chaka. "Will war do that?"

Chaka nodded. "When are you enlisting into the Imperial Army?" he asked instead.

"Next cycle."

"So you're only nineteen summers?"

"Twenty."

"Then why wait a cycle?"

Jurou looked down at the floor. "I buried my parents not too long ago," he said softly.

Chaka nodded empathically. "I see," he said gently.

"Is it true you were Lieutenant in the Imperial Army?" Jurou asked.

Chaka frowned and narrowed his eyes at Jurou. "Where did you hear that?" he said caustically.

"Rumors abound, you know." Jurou gave a faint smile and waved a dismissive hand. "People talk and I overhear things."

Chaka smirked. "Would you be surprised if I were?"

Jurou quirked an eyebrow. "It takes cycles to rise in rank, especially of that sort, true?"

Chaka frowned. "What made you think I'm not deserving of that rank?"

Jurou put up his hands. "I didn't say you're not. It's just..." He blew a sigh and shook his head.

"What is it you're trying to say?" Chaka pressed.

"I shouldn't let on how much I know about him," Jurou mused. *"If I get too personal, he'll find out and it'll be impossible to get answers from him by then..."*

"I did a lot I'd rather not explain," Chaka said vaguely when Jurou gave no answer. "The horrors of war are difficult to erase."

Jurou nodded. "It's getting pretty late," he murmured and stood. "We've wasted most of the afternoon and evening cleaning in here!"

"Why do you have so much?" Chaka inquired. "You said you only came here a few days ago."

"It's not important." Jurou waved Chaka away. "Thanks and please leave."

Chaka's face became unreadable. "No need to be rude," he snapped and unfolded from his position on the floor. "I know when I am no longer needed." Chaka rose to his feet and stormed away, slamming the door shut after him.

Jurou blew a sigh of relief and returned to his bed, falling back into it.

TWENTY-FOUR

Chaka stood outside Jurou's door, clutching his left arm that throbbed fiercely in pain. Shutting his eyes, he slid to the floor, besieged by the ache in his head.

"*We told you, I told you...*" Tannozume snarled. "*You are not here to make friends!*"

"*I know he's a danger to you,*" Chaka thought. "*Yet I cannot pull myself away...*"

"*Then why do you keep approaching him?*"

"*Because there's something about him other than your lust to kill him at the mere sight!*"

"*Leave him be if you know what's best for you!*"

"*Your telling me 'no' is only going to interest me further!*"

"*Then your disobedience to our orders shall have heavy consequences!*" Chaka sucked in a shallow breath when a clawed hand grabbed his ear and yanked him up. "*Already his life was threatened and it is better that he stays out of your reach!*"

"*If you gave those orders...!*" Chaka's eyes snapped open and the grip immediately released. Holding a hand to his ear that bled slightly, he glanced around, finding no one there. "*If he is powerful enough to be perceived as a threat, then I will get closer!*"

Chaka rubbed at his ear with his sleeve and walked to his room down the hall. Opening the door, he gave pause at once facing the tip of a vermilion katana at his throat. Chaka immediately held up his hands.

"I am injured and unarmed," he said quickly. "What is it you want?" Stabbed in the chest, Chaka grunted and suddenly an armored sandaled foot firmly kicked him off the stained blade, sending him crashing into the banister. He broke through the balustrade, plummeting two floors below.

Chaka groaned when he came to consciousness, cringing from the pain that radiated throughout his body. He looked up and around, finding his ankle and wrist chained to the stall in the lavatory and the rope he took from Jurou binding his legs.

"*How did I get here?*" Chaka thought, yanking against the chain hooked into the wall.

"*You have a choice,*" Tannozume grumbled from afar. "*Either leave him be or suffer!*"

Chaka looked up and around, finding nothing. "*I'd rather suffer if it means he's the source of your unease!*"

"*You wish to die over what you find?*" Tannozume thundered.

"*Ordinarily you carve through templars without a second thought, yet this one must be of importance, since you avoid him as if he's gotten the coughing disease!*" Chaka yanked harder against the chain that held him, growing agitated. "*I'm intrigued by your interest in him and if it means dying over it, so be it! I want to know why!*"

He stiffened, breaking out in cold sweat when a roar reverberated close by. Moments later, an intruder kicked in the lavatory's doors and stormed in, striking the walls and doors.

"*Are you in here?*" a dark sinister voice called. Chaka held his breath, cringing as the stranger kicked in the stall doors. He jumped, startled when his door banged in response from a strong jolt. "*I found you,*" the mysterious voice snarled on the other side. Chaka quickly leaned back as a tachi pierced the stall door, the tip of the blade barely meeting his face. "*Don't try to play dead. I can hear the fear in your heart... and it sounds delicious!*"

Chaka untied the rope fastened around his legs with his free hand as the warrior continued hammering into the door, splitting it. Chaka pulled the rope free in time once the door came down and he faced a fighter wearing a golden-red mask of a large-fanged demon.

"Who are you?" Chaka asked, noting the warrior's great armor consisted of lacquered red and black plates that had gold scrollwork detail on the edges. "I don't recognize the Clan in which you hail."

"*Find out in Hell!*"

Chaka yanked against the chain and leaned out of the overhead strike as the warrior in black and red hurled down his blade. Chaka quickly brought up his arm to deflect the blow and the steel cut through the chain.

Ducking out of a swing, Chaka tackled the fighter by the waist, throwing him down to the floor. The warrior dropped his sword from the resulting force and it clanged out of reach.

Struggling to throw Chaka, the fighter wrapped a foot around Chaka's leg, turning him over on his back. Chaka grabbed the facemask with his free hand as the warrior grabbed for his hamadashi hooked around his waist.

"Go on," Chaka hissed. "I'm not afraid to die, so do what you wish."

"*Let go,*" the warrior growled.

"If you're going to get rid of me, I'm dragging you with me to the underworld!"

"*I don't believe you!*"

"Do it and we'll find out then, eh?" The fighter struck Chaka in the chest with the dagger and Chaka coughed up blood. "You missed," he snarled, grinning darkly.

"*What?*"

Chaka threw a charged punch at the warrior's face, sending him sailing into the stall behind him. "I'll let you in on a secret," Chaka sneered. "My heart is on the wrong side, so using that maneuver will not work!" He yanked out the hamadashi embedded in his chest, threw it aside and reached for the tachi above him. "I will only let you try once." Chaka grabbed the blade and sliced at the chain entrapping his ankle.

The fighter shook off his stun and staggered to his feet. "*Mugen Houyou!*" the warrior shouted and two more shadowy armored copies appeared beside him from a flash of smoke. "*Konpekino Soujin!*" The two warriors withdrew matching long swords that glowed in azure light and the blade Chaka held gleamed in response.

Chaka stood, holding the glowing blade over his shoulder. "Let's go!" he declared. Both shadow knights charged forward and Chaka slashed at them, throwing them back with a blast of blue-violet light. "*Ataushinai Okyoda!*" he thundered, beheading the warrior on his left and sliced the other on his right in half with a fluid stroke. "*Seibatsu!*" Turning around, Chaka pushed forward with a thrust, only to strike at nothing but empty space.

Chaka felt a tap on his shoulder and turned around, still finding nothing. Turning back, he faced the warrior in the demon mask, holding the glowing black dagger.

"*Your holy power failed you, <u>Kenshi</u>,*" the warrior sneered, "*or should I say, <u>Katagimusha</u>?*"

"No one can block *genjutsu*," Chaka hissed, "not even *akuma* like you!"

"*You're not dealing with an ordinary devil!*" The fighter thrust the hamadashi as Chaka returned the blow, hacking down the warrior by the torso.

The dagger jammed into Chaka's forehead and he staggered back, stunned. Loosening his grip, the sword he held clattered away and he clutched his head as the world about him became shadowed in a deep shade of red.

Chaka screamed from the intense pain coursing through his body at once and slipped to his knees, struggling for breath. He fell forward on the floor, his body exhausted of all power.

"*Kouji,*" a voice called faintly. "*Kouji, do you hear me?*"

Chaka looked out from his place on the floor, staring at tiles that wavered and slowly shifted to bloodied tatami. "Eh?" he moaned.

"*Kouji...*"

"I hear you," Chaka answered faintly.

"*Kouji, they broke through the <u>hakudarani</u>...*"

"The *hakudarani*–!"

"*The <u>ruirinhou</u> wasn't strong enough...*"

Chaka tensed when he faced bloodied bearskin boots at his head, sensing weight on his back as the mysterious warrior stepped on him, barring movement.

"Go to hell without me," a familiar voice growled with contempt.

Chaka reached out and the shadows swallowed his world as he lost consciousness.

Jurou awakened with a start and sat up, heaving for breath. "*If only I could recall what that dream was about,*" he thought, groaning as he ran a hand through his sweat-drenched hair.

Getting out of bed, Jurou struck a match and lit his lantern near his bed, then pulled out of his clothes he left on the night before. Making his way for his bathroom, Jurou pulled the chain and cold water gushed from the showerhead. He stood under it, hoping the freezing rush would get him out of his daze.

The cold water suddenly turned warm and Jurou gasped, noticing shadows moving along the wall. Moments later, a knock resonated on his door.

"*Who would be up this late?*" Jurou wondered, growing annoyed when the knock came again, louder than before.

"Saku," a familiar voice called, "are you asleep?"

"What kind of question is that?" Jurou snapped and grunted, stepping out the stall as the knock turned persistent. He shut off the water and grabbed a robe he had hanging on a hook near the door, growing increasingly irritated as he pulled into it. Leaving the washroom, Jurou stomped for his room entrance. He swung open the door, finding Chaka dressed in a dark overcoat, trousers and leather boots standing on the other side. "What is it you want?" Jurou spat curtly. "You know it's not even daybreak yet!"

"I couldn't sleep," Chaka replied, "so I thought to ask you to accompany me on a walk tonight."

"But why me?"

"You know as they say, even a *kengo* can't fight in his sleep."

Jurou stood there dumbfounded as Chaka stepped past him. "*This is unusual,*" he thought, glancing over his shoulder at Chaka who paced the floor behind him. "*I wonder what he wants...*" Jurou shut the door and headed to his chest, withdrawing a change of clothes.

"No need for anything fancy," Chaka interjected. "Let's go."

"Is something on your mind?" Jurou asked, dressing in a simple kimono.

"Why do you ask?" Chaka murmured, coming to a pause. Jurou said nothing as he stepped into his sandals and waved at Chaka to follow. Chaka blew a short sigh and walked with him, heading downstairs. "Would you mind sparring with me?"

"Would that help you sleep?" Jurou grumbled.

"What a great idea, Saku!"

Exiting outdoors, Jurou followed Chaka down the stone steps, growing uneasy as they made their way across the courtyards. Glancing around, Jurou noticed the shadows shifting and moving around them.

"Should you be concerned if someone attacks you?" Jurou asked after several moments of silence. "If you're doing the *youjinbou* thing for a while, you should at least be armed."

Chaka snorted. "Oh, now you're concerned about my safety, eh?" He glanced at Jurou. "I can handle myself; however, you should be concerned about Death."

Jurou stopped short and Chaka laughed as he continued ahead. "What's that supposed to mean?" Jurou called after him. He growled under his breath and stomped after Chaka, following him toward the academy.

Reaching the outdoor court, a whistle pierced the air and Jurou immediately came to a stop when an arrow perforated the ground near his foot.

"Stop right there, Outlander," a voice called to Jurou from the darkness. "Step no further unless you want to go to the Underworld!"

"What is this about?" Jurou called back. "I'm not here to fight anyone and I've no reason to battle you, unless you were the attackers who tried to kill me earlier."

"This doesn't concern you, Outlander," the mysterious voice answered. "This is between us and the Beast of the Blood Coast!"

"What have you against him?"

When he received no answer, Jurou took off, searching for Chaka. Another whistle tore through the silence and an arrow struck his shoulder. Jurou yowled and stumbled forward to his knees, stunned.

Ahead, he spotted Chaka standing with his hands up in guard, surrounded by four masked swordsmen who had their blades drawn. Jurou noticed the fighters held all manner of field swords: tachi, odachi, nodachi, and jintachi. *"They came looking for a quick battle,"* he thought. *"There's no way Chaka can win with such a distance between them!"*

"Saku, stay out of the way," Chaka called, glaring at the swordfighters who closed in around him. "This is my fight!"

"What do they want with you?" Jurou shouted and broke the arrow stuck in his shoulder then scrambled to his feet.

"So, how much did they pay you?" Chaka snarled, withdrawing a weighted chain from inside his overcoat. "Twenty *Ryo*? Thirty?"

"What does it matter, Isawa?" one swordsman shouted. "You've a hundred *Ryo* on your head and we're here to collect it!"

"A hundred?" Jurou yelped, shocked. "What crime did you commit to have that much wanted on you?"

Chaka held one weight in his free hand and twirled the chain with the other. "Go ahead and give it your best," he growled. "You'll be dead before you can even count your pay!"

"Stay back if you know what's best for you," the archer called to Jurou before he could take a step, "unless you're that desperate to join your friend on the other side!"

"Watch closely Saku," Chaka said, "and I'll show you why I left the Imperial Army!"

Ducking out of a slash, Chaka snapped the chain at the odachi-wielding swordsman across from him, striking him in the neck, stunning him. Swinging the chain over his head, Chaka turned out of another thrust from the nodachi-wielding fighter behind him and launched the chain broadside, wrapping it around the swordsman's tachi on his right. Capturing it, Chaka gave a yank, pulling the long curved blade toward him.

Immediately blocking a strike from the jintachi on his left with the blade, the tachi shattered and Chaka kicked aside the fourth swordsman who aimed for his back. Turning, the jintachi-wielding fighter sliced off his comrade's arm with a fluid stroke.

Chaka ducked down from an overhead strike, grasping the fallen nodachi and cut the fighter across the chest. Dropping to his knee, Chaka slashed down into the odachi wielder aiming for his head, hacking him by the torso. Turning around again, Chaka rose and slammed his sword into the back of the remaining swordsman, dropping him into the ground.

"*His speed is incredible,*" Jurou thought, watching in awe as Chaka dropped the heavy field sword he held, pitching it into the ground and calmly picked up his chain, wrapping it around his wrist. "*I've never seen anyone move that fast and not get cut, even with four men against him!*"

"Ho, archer," Chaka called as he sauntered over near Jurou. "I know you're still here."

"What of it?" the archer called back from the shadows.

"If you were smart, you'd join your comrades in Hell!"

"What makes you think I'm willing to fight you?" the archer snapped. "It's obvious I didn't want to..."

"I will let you go and you can tell your friends about my awesome power."

"Sounds good."

Chaka released the chain and let out a shout, snapping the whip forward over Jurou's head.

Hearing a surprised cry, Jurou let out a yelp when a man in dark armor came crashing out of a tree near him, striking the ground. Chaka released the chain that held the archer's ankle and snatched up his wakizashi as the archer directed his short bow at him.

"Are you still trying to kill me?" Chaka asked, smirking as he backed away, hand to the hilt of the blade. "I already gave your chance to flee, so why don't you know your place and apologize?"

"I--!"

Chaka stepped out of three arrows released from the bow and unsheathed the short sword, then cut down three more as the archer shot another round. Racing up to the archer, Chaka hacked off his hand and the archer screamed, clutching his profusely bleeding wrist.

"Who sent you?" Chaka thundered. The archer crawled back and Chaka lopped off the fighter's foot, forcing the man screaming even louder.

"Chaka!" Jurou cried. Chaka glared up at Jurou and Jurou swallowed hard, taking a step away from the intense hateful stare glowering back at him. He struggled to find his voice. "Chaka, that's enough! Just take his head already!"

"These dogs deserve no mercy from me!" Chaka bellowed. He looked down at the squirming man who continued moaning in agony. "Tell me, why are you wasting my time, eh?" Chaka stomped on the man's shoulder and leaned in, baring his teeth. "Right now, you want to beg me to take your head, eh? Please end my misery, you cry! Make the pain stop, you cry!" Chaka let out a short laugh. "No!" he screamed. "I will take you apart piece by piece!"

Jurou suddenly found breathing difficult, watching Chaka cut into his hapless victim, awed and sickened at the same time. The man's screams chilled Jurou and he shuddered, unable to turn away.

"Piece by piece, I cut away," Chaka sang as he slashed into the man's extremities. "Piece by piece until none remains!" At last, he cut off the man's head and turned to Jurou who continued to stare wide-eyed and silent. "Well, why are you just standing there?" Chaka spat. "Are you going to punish me?"

"W-what do you want me to do?" Jurou sputtered. "Whatever issue you had with them... it's your concern, not mine."

"Collect their weapons and any *okane* they have," Chaka ordered.

"And then what?"

"Put it away for me."

Jurou watched Chaka stalk off, too stunned to protest. "*Is that it?*" he thought. "*Is this what he deals with all the time?*" Approaching the archer's body, Jurou blew a heavy sigh. "I'm sorry," he murmured. "I don't have any prayers for you... I guess I was in too much shock at his brutality."

"What are you doing?" Chaka called moments later. Jurou looked up, spotting the young man carrying several swords in his arms. "Take his gear and let's head back."

Jurou grunted and knelt down, grabbing for the bow then unstrapped the quiver, slinging them both over his shoulder. Digging through the dead man's pockets, he found a sheet of folded bloodied paper, also recovering a dagger and coin purse.

Tucking the paper and purse into his jacket, Jurou took the articles and made his way back for the boardinghouse, following Chaka upstairs to his room.

"Just set it aside there on the floor," Chaka ordered once Jurou entered the dark room.

"What about the *okane*?" Jurou asked and dumped the weaponry with the bundle of swords that remained at his feet.

"Keep it if you like."

Jurou scoffed. "You can't be serious!"

"With thirty *Ryo*, you can go two or three cycles without sleeping on the street."

"I'll donate it to the nearby temple instead," Jurou murmured.

"However you like."

Jurou frowned, watching Chaka standing at his bedroom window. "You never told me why you were attacked," he protested, "or why you're a wanted man. You should at least report the attack instead of running off into another *Han*!"

"If I told you," Chaka said coldly, "I would have to kill you."

"Surely you jest."

When Chaka said nothing else, Jurou left the room, shutting the door behind him.

Returning to his room down the hall, Jurou sat on the edge of his bed and pulled out the paper he took from the dead archer. Unfolding it, he found black ink smeared by drying blood.

"I can barely read this," Jurou grumbled and held up the paper to the light. He squinted, trying to make out the text against the blood. "Is this *Ryokutou* or *Teikoku*?" Jurou gasped when he came across a single phrase. "*Kanshi*?"

Hearing footsteps outside in the corridor, Jurou immediately blew out his lantern and sat in the darkness, listening to the footfalls come closer. He broke out in a cold sweat when a soft rap struck his door. Jurou sat extremely still, afraid to move and held his breath, waiting until the person on the other side gave up. When the footsteps faded, Jurou blew a heavy sigh and fell back in bed, overwhelmed by his thoughts.

"*What could Chaka be protesting against?*" he thought, "*and why were orders given to stop him, even using force to do so?*"

Unable to concentrate on anything else, Jurou disregarded patching up his shoulder and fell into a fitful sleep.

TWENTY-FIVE

Chaka looked out his window at the courtyard below, trying to ignore the increasing pain in his left arm that throbbed incessantly. He shifted his gaze toward the nighttime sky, watching the sparse clouds pass over the pale stars that dotted the heavens.

"This life is fleeting, just as those clouds," Chaka murmured, "As long as I have that warrant out for my arrest, *otokodate* and the like will continue to come for my head."

"*With a reputation such as yours in precedence,*" Tannozume's disembodied voice growled, "*it won't be long before he hears about it.*"

Chaka snorted. "He's too weak to stand against me," he protested. "I doubt he has the funds to even hire someone else to try their hand!"

"*Did you forget you gave him the thirty <u>Ryo</u> you recovered?*" Chaka grunted, bristling as Tannozume's hacking laughter filled the room. "*He'll soon devise a way to take your head as well!*"

"Not if I get him to cleanse me of this taint first!"

"*Your aura reeks of blood,*" Tannozume spat. "*You've long missed your chance at redemption!*"

Chaka turned away from the window, frowning at the sight of the bloodied weaponry lying on the floor near his door. "I can still seek redemption," he murmured. "There is a way to settle these sins."

"*The kamisama no longer listen to you. They want nothing to do with such a vile creature!*"

"We'll see about that."

Chaka grabbed his bed sheets and gathered the assorted weaponry, wrapping them inside. Hoisting them into his arms, he left his room and padded downstairs. Noticing light emanating from under Jurou's door, he knocked, waiting for an answer. The room immediately grew dark. Chaka sighed and left his doorway.

"*Where do you think you're going?*" Tannozume demanded as Chaka returned outdoors.

"The *machikata* will be swarming the place and asking questions if I don't report those bodies lying around out there," Chaka snapped. "These blades are useless to me and I have no need for them."

"*They won't believe you at all. You're a criminal, or have you forgotten?*"

"Surely they'll understand. I'm not even armed."

"*Armed or not, you are dangerous – even without my help!*"

After an hour's walk, Chaka entered through the city gates and blew a sigh of relief when he saw no one on post. Heading down the road, he spotted the town watchman with a paper lantern making his rounds and immediately grew tense.

"Ho," the guard called and Chaka came to a stop.

"*Konbancha,*" Chaka replied nervously.

"Lovely evening it is tonight, hey?"

"It sure is."

"What interesting toys you have there, *Kenshi*. Where are you headed?"

"I'm looking for the sword polisher... late delivery and all."

"Is that so?" The watchman gave Chaka a quizzical look. "Have a *tegata*?"

"It was stolen from me." Chaka shrugged. "As you can see, I have quite the parcel bandits want."

"Oh, so they stole your travel pass but not your gear." The guard snorted. "With the way you're stinking of guts, I'm sure it's not far from here."

Chaka gave an apprehensive smile. "I can't get paid if I don't deliver these by morning."

"Just one more question though... who do these fine blades belong to?"

"Eh?"

"Who sent you get them polished?" When Chaka gave no answer, the watchman smiled maliciously as he put his free hand to the hilt of his sword. "I figured as such. No one on the straight and narrow would carry such nice gear as that." He nodded to Chaka. "I'm bored tonight, so let's play a game."

Chaka raised an eyebrow. "Like what?"

"I'm known to be particularly skilled with the *uchigatana*. If you can make me drop this lantern, I won't report whatever crime you've obviously committed."

Chaka grinned. "I'm intrigued, *Bantaro*." A dark gleam suddenly appeared in his eyes. "If your boast about how your fencing one-handed must be legendary, then I want ten *Ryo* for the trouble you put me through once I win."

"What of the blades you carry?"

"Feel free to take them off my hands. I don't care for them."

The guard shook his head. "That's too easy," he said. "I want you to fight me without dropping that bundle. Good deal, no?"

Chaka ground his teeth, unable to respond.

The watchman withdrew his sword and dashed forward with a thrusting pierce. Chaka immediately sidestepped the attack and jumped back out of a swift slash.

"Impressive," said the guard, "I'd never thought for someone as tall and big as you are, you'd be quick on your feet."

Chaka dodged another stab and leaned out of a slice for his neck. He then ducked out of a swing and kicked the watchman back by the chest, sending him hurtling head over heels.

The guard rolled to his feet, keeping the lantern intact and sprang forward, smashing headfirst into Chaka. Chaka fell back as they both tumbled to the ground and the watchman stabbed Chaka in the thigh once he stat up.

Chaka used his free hand and grabbed the guard's wrist, prying off his grip. The watchman turned out, kicking Chaka back by the chest and whirled around once Chaka let go.

"Don't be surprised how difficult this is," the guard vaunted as Chaka struggled to stand, panting hard for breath. "You want to withdraw at least one to get me back, yes? I'm surprised you're able to keep up this far!"

"I'm no ordinary *kenshi*," Chaka growled. "You won't understand the path I chose."

"Oh, I see how tough you are... you must be used to this sort of thing."

"If you really knew who I was, you'd know this is almost a daily occurrence for me."

The watchman chortled. "With all those blades possible on you and can't even use one to stop my attack, you won't be able to dodge the next one."

"I'll say a prayer for you when you're dead, *Bantaro*!"

The guard thrust forward his blade, pointing it directly at Chaka. "Resign yourself to your fate and let the darkness swallow your soul!"

"Have at it!" Chaka thundered.

The watchman dashed forward and Chaka kicked high, easily missing his target as the man went around him. Chaka ducked down as the blade pierced the air where his head was less than a moment before and shifted momentum, rolling underneath the swing.

The guard returned with a heavy backhand, checking the pommel against Chaka's jaw as he stood. The force rent Chaka against the wall of the nearby building and the bundle slipped from his grip.

Chaka quickly kicked up the swords, capturing them before they struck the ground. He balanced the last one on the ridge of his foot as he leaned out of another stab at his face.

"Fancy footwork," the watchman admitted between hard pants of breath. "You are highly skilled... such talents shouldn't go to waste."

"Feel the weight of this blade scatter you to the wind!" Chaka answered and kicked up the sword, then followed with a reverse roundhouse, smashing his foot into the guard's arm. The slender sword escaped the watchman's grip and Chaka caught the blade before it hit the ground. The other sword crashed into the lamp, shattering it.

"You win," the guard groaned and grunted when Chaka stepped on his chest before he could get up.

"Why did you attack me?" Chaka demanded. "It's clear you don't want the bounty on my head, otherwise, you'd long call the *Bugyo* to collect!"

"I want to recruit your sword arm," the watchman said.

"Do you know who I am?" Chaka snarled.

"I saw your face on the wanted posters around town and know you have a lot of enemies, with your violent ways and all."

"Why not take the *okane*? Even the *Kagesureiyo* and the *Hitokiri* would fetch much more than the price on my head if you found them!"

"I care not for your crimes... it's nothing special at all. Hell, I only killed sixty in my lifetime and I'm older than you."

"What about this job you want to hire me for?"

Chaka heard a whistle and looked up, stunned as several police officers blocked off the alley entrance.

"There he is!" one officer shouted. "Torio's held here by that criminal!"

"Damn it," Chaka hissed and dropped the remaining blades he held on the ground. He held the guard's sword at ready, turning to his opponents.

"This here is a dead end," the head officer vaunted as he withdrew his baton. "Give up now and surrender to justice!"

"No need for you officers to tell me your names," Chaka declared. "Your lives will end in a few moments anyway."

The watchman behind Chaka scoffed. "By your stance," he retorted, "the *uchigatana* is not what you're proficient with."

"I won't defeat you all with just this one," Chaka snapped, glaring at Torio over his shoulder. "See if you can keep count!"

The officers charged Chaka and Chaka barreled through them, whipping his sword as he swiftly blocked their attacks. Kicking the head officer back, he used the second as a springboard and jumped over them, landing behind the group.

Chaka sliced through one arm of the third officer, and pierced the second in the chest, cutting him in half as he rent the blade through his sternum. He turned, hacking off the leg of the fourth officer as the leader sidestepped and cracked his baton into Chaka's face, sending him hurtling back. Chaka crashed onto the ground, seeing stars.

"This can't be the best you have!" the lead officer spat, standing over him.

"Saito, wait," Torio called and approached offside. "Why are you holding back?" he snapped as Chaka staggered to his feet.

"Because if I truly showed you," Chaka growled, "your very soul would regret it!" He held up the lightweight sword broadside, expecting their next move.

"Good form," Saito snapped, "but it won't save you from your trip across the river!"

The officer charged again and Chaka leaned out of another attack as a blade sprang from the edge of the baton. He turned around as Saito lunged again, dodging more wild slashes.

"Tsuihosuru!" Chaka called and jammed his glowing blade into the officer's groin with an underhanded swing, ripping upwards and cleanly slicing the man's head in half.

The officer's body fell on the ground, spraying blood everywhere. The remaining officers panicked as Chaka approached, grinning deviously.

"That's enough," Torio called. "They can't take any more shame."

"If you want to put them out their misery, go ahead." Chaka turned away. "I have elsewhere to be."

"Here." The watchman dug through his pockets and withdrew a small coin purse. He tossed it at Chaka's feet where it landed on the ground with a mild jangle. "Ten *Ryo*, as promised. Also, the sword polisher lives at Akagi Temple, just outside town."

"You never told me why you wanted my arm." Chaka kicked up the purse and pocketed it.

"I already have my answer."

"What about the *metsuke*?"

"Don't worry about it."

Chaka frowned as he approached and handed the blade back to Torio broadside by the handle. Torio took the sword and Chaka left his side, picking up the remainder of the fallen blades. He said nothing when Torio dispatched the two remaining police officers.

Leaving the alley, Chaka took the road leading out of town, heading for the temple.

Approaching the path, Chaka limped toward crumbling stone columns that led to the courtyard, holding the ramparts of the temple. Near the doors of the edifice hung a pair of lanterns with the name of the monastery painted on the front.

Chaka came to an immediate stop once he spotted a woman sitting on the wall's edge and his left arm burned. He noticed the woman wore a dark surcoat over lacquered leather armor, riding trousers, and lightweight bronze plate helmet.

"Ho," Chaka called.

"Are you just passing through?" the woman answered back.

"I'm looking for the *kenporissha*."

"You must be desperate for such work this late."

The woman jumped from the wall with a graceful leap, her clothing catching and fluttering in the wind. She landed smoothly and stood with ease, hand to the gilded hilt of her broad saber with nine rings set into the spine and the handle fashioned into a dragon's head with talons. Chaka grew tense, noticing her blade began glowing softly in aquamarine light.

"I have no need for them to be honest," Chaka replied nervously.

"You reek of blood... Are you giving up the blade and plan to join the monastery?"

"No."

"Seeking redemption then?"

"Possibly."

"I warn you, fair warrior, you might want to leave here while you can."

"Why is that?"

"This place is full of *akuma*."

Chaka chuckled. "I have dealt with devils before and I fear nothing anymore."

The woman nodded. "Is that the reason why I sense this evil aura about you?"

"Perhaps."

"If you are truly searching for a way to purge your sins... then I suggest you ask the *kamisama* for guidance."

"That glowing *choku segatana* suggests otherwise," Chaka noted.

"I doubt you will find any answers here." The swordswoman withdrew her cutlass that gleamed in blue light. "In fact, you should probably leave now, or I might be forced to kill you."

"So if that means I must fight you, then so be it." Chaka dropped the bundle he held. "What makes you think that blade will do anything to me?"

"Then you will have a large problem on your hands, *Kenshi* Isawa," said the swordswoman. "This *Takiletzachi* will prove it!"

"If you came for that bounty on my head, then join the line!" Chaka shouted. "I will take your soul!"

The swordswoman dashed forward and Chaka stepped out of a hard slash. Turning, the swordswoman struck Chaka in the arm with a swift blow, cutting into his skin.

Chaka grunted and staggered back, clutching his wound. He gasped when his power flashed and ground his teeth, wincing from the burning in his left arm intensifying as the devil inside roused.

"*That blade!*" Chaka thought as the swordswoman came at him again with a forceful strike. He staggered back once the scimitar jammed into his chest and his gray eyes blazed blue once his energy flared, unleashing golden flames from around his hands. Chaka bared his teeth, grabbing her wrist before she pulled away.

"*I have long waited for this night,*" Tannozume sneered through Chaka. Twisting her arm, she cried out when forced to her knees. "*Where did you get this Takiletzachi? Who crafted this?*" The woman said nothing, struggling underneath Tannozume's grip. "*There is more than just one, is there?*"

Tannozume lifted the woman off the ground and wrenched out the sword embedded in Chaka's chest. Throwing her to the ground, he raised the machete and cyan static charged between them as the swordswoman withdrew a glowing violet dagger. Chaka cried out and dropped the broad saber, collapsing to his knees.

"As long as you're cursed, you can't touch anything with *Amahagane,*" the swordswoman declared and stood unsteadily to her feet. "Your *kamui* will always stay weak."

"*Will it be enough?*" Chaka thought as the swordswoman approached, kicking him back on the ground. He looked up as she pointed the dagger at his throat.

"I don't want the bounty on your head," she said. "I was sent to cleanse your soul."

"Who sent you?" Chaka demanded.

The swordswoman kicked up the nearby falchion and grasped it firmly. "Defeat me and I will tell you," she challenged.

Chaka kicked her back and immediately jumped to his haunches, pushing back with flaring hands. "*Hanshaga Shokan!*" Chaka cried as his opponent came at him with an overhead swing. The blade passed through him and he grasped her wrist before she swung again, throwing her aside.

The swordswoman rolled with the throw and landed steadily on the ground as Chaka staggered to his feet. "Return to Hell, devil!" she bellowed and rushed Chaka again.

Chaka stood his ground, glaring at her as he clenched his intensely flaring hands.

"You're asking for death, woman!" Chaka shouted back.

The next blow Chaka failed to block, unable to stop the glowing dagger from crashing into his skull.

TWENTY-SIX

Chaka's eyes snapped open and he found himself staring up into swirling darkness. The shadows surrounding him slowly parted as he came to and Chaka sat up, finding that he was in a damp room that had stone floors and walls.

"*Am I back in the dungeons of Morikage?*" he wondered. Looking around, Chaka noticed dim light wafting in from the end of a long corridor where he sat. Nearby lay the glowing blue broad saber, stained with blood.

Pale golden light erupted from Chaka's hands and the pain in his arm seared. He stood unsteadily to his feet and kicked up the scimitar, capturing it in his free hand.

Chaka then started walking toward the end of the hall, drawn to an otherworldly force seemingly calling him. The closer he reached the end; Chaka grew tense the more he found bloodstains washed along the walls and floors.

Reaching the corridor's exit, Chaka came to a pause, finding the bodies of various monks littered around the room, all brutally hacked into with their remains and viscera splattered everywhere.

In the center of the room, a single stone stand burned brightly from mystic green flame; wedged in the stone, a heavy long field sword adorned with dark bell tassels hanging from the pommel, with a golden hilt and handle bound in dyed black and red leather. Chaka frowned when he noticed the stained sword owned an unnatural high mirror-polished sheen against the green steel.

Slowly making his way to the blade, Chaka grasped the handle and the golden light around his hands flashed, turning vermilion when he tried pulling the jintachi out the stone. The crimson knight appeared on the other side, armored hand also on the sword's handle.

"*Tell me now,*" Tannozume growled, "*or you may not be able to face me the next time we meet and live!*"

"I plan to destroy you, this you already know," Chaka snarled and let go, holding the machete at ready.

"*What brought on this renewed vigor?*" Tannozume jeered. "*Has getting struck in the head brought on temporary enlightenment?*"

"I know that holy power, the *kamui*, doesn't disturb you yet somehow these *Takiletzachi* blades strengthen you and blades crafted of *Amahagane* can silence you," Chaka admitted. "You made sure I was rid of both *Hitokiri* and *Kagesureiyo* by the time you wore me down!"

Cold emerald eyes glowed from behind the mask. "*One charmed blade will not be enough!*" roared the devil.

"I will find more, no matter how long it takes!"

The demon proved faster and withdrew the field sword from the enchanted boulder. Chaka stepped back as the devil ran at him full speed, blade raised high. Just as he brought down the sword, Chaka blocked the blow, struggling to push back. The falchion sparked brightly and the glowing sword flashed brilliantly in green.

"Heh," Chaka snarled. "You would have to do better than that to kill me, devil!" He let go and pushed back as the fiend flashed out of sight.

"*Gensho Satsu!*" Tannozume called. Chaka turned and stiffened when the green steel slammed through his back and his heart stopped beating. He looked down, finding the point of the blade protruding from his chest. Chaka coughed up blood as the sword wrenched free and Tannozume kicked him in the back of the head, forcing him to his knees. "*Water is stronger than Wind, or have you forgotten?*" Tannozume's voice growled as he stepped around Chaka. "*This wicked blade Tsukinoha is just the beginning! There is much to be done and you will be the one to do it for me.*"

"If you plan to kill me," Chaka rasped, "you had better hurry and do it quickly, before I kill you."

"*There is no need to kill you, for you are my thrall, remember?*" Tannozume cackled. "*I own your soul, your heart...*" He stood before Chaka and held out his free hand that glowed in dark amber light. A bloodied heart formed in his hand, beating weakly in his palm. "*Soon I shall devour your body and mind!*" The shadows wavered and two more devils in azure scale and green chain armor appeared beside Tannozume. "*Shiranosuke, Akanasutsune, hold him down!*"

"*Hageshii Arashi!*" Chaka thundered as the two demons approached. A circle of crimson light surrounded Chaka and flames abruptly exploded around him, covering the room with smoke.

The demons vanished as the walls and floor of the temple burned, also turning the littered corpses into ash. After the smoke began to clear, the vermilion knight stood in front of Chaka unharmed. The eyes of the facemask glowed bright green.

"*Was that supposed to kill me, feeble human?*" the devil thundered. "*If so, you disappoint me!*"

Chaka clenched his teeth and quickly dashed back as Tannozume reached forward for him. "*I knew the holy power had no effect,*" Chaka thought. "*I just need more time...!*"

"*Beg for mercy, miserable worm!*" Tannozume roared. "*You shall do as I desire!*"

"Never!" Chaka bellowed.

"*Then lie down and die!*"

Tannozume flashed out of sight before Chaka had a chance to counter. Chaka swung at air as the red-armored knight reappeared and disappeared like the flickering shadows of the flames that danced along the walls, hacking away at Chaka with swift speed.

Chaka dropped the cutlass with a clang and his bloodied body struck the ground as the devil reappeared over him, jintachi held high.

"*You shall not get in my way,*" Tannozume sneered. "*I control you, never forget!*"

Before the demon brought down the field sword, a steel arrow struck Tannozume in the wrist, forcing him dropping his weapon. Several more arrows struck the scarlet knight and he staggered rearward, stunned.

"Enough, devil!" a voice called from afar. Through the burning flames, Kaminaritou Rouru emerged armed with a glowing longbow. "Leave him be."

"*We will finish this fight later,*" Tannozume grumbled and disappeared.

Kaminaritou Rouru approached Chaka's downed form and nudged him with his foot.

"What do you want with me?" Chaka moaned. "I've had enough with everyone trying to kill me."

"I'm not trying to help you," Kaminaritou Rouru growled. "I simply came to investigate the killings around the area and it seems you are the cause!"

"Call a *shisai* then, will you?" Chaka struggled to sit up and Kaminaritou Rouru lent a hand. Chaka pushed him away. "Don't pray for my soul."

"Leave this place and never return," Kaminaritou Rouru snapped. "Do not darken Kakita's doors again."

"I need my certificate if I'm to pass my next Imperial exam!" Chaka complained. "I have obligations to keep..."

"There is nothing more to say."

Chaka stood unsteadily to his feet and kicked up the gleaming scimitar. Kaminaritou Rouru stiffened as Chaka swung the sword and pointed it at him. "I wouldn't bother tainting my blade on you," he said and gave a devious smile, "at least not now."

"Get out of here!" Kaminaritou Rouru sneered.

Chaka lowered his sword and picked up the dimly glowing field sword, hoisting it over his shoulder. "We'll have our battle some other time," he said and pushed past Kaminaritou Rouru, heading outdoors.

Jurou awakened with a gasp and sat up, wheezing for breath. He shuddered and held his head in his hands, moaning. *"What a strange destructive nightmare,"* Jurou thought wearily. *"Why would I dream about demons trying to kill me?"* He got out of bed and pulled out of his clothes, heading for his shower. *"Maybe I'm still nervous about that attack yesterday..."*

Pulling the chain, Jurou stood under the frigid water in the stall, trying to forget what he saw the night before. A firm knock scattered Jurou's thoughts, bringing him to the present.

"Saku," a familiar voice called, "are we up this morning?"

"I'm not decent!" Jurou yelped. He scrambled for something to cover himself as he heard his door open and grabbed a towel hanging behind his door. Jurou quickly wrapped it around his waist as Chaka poked his head in the washroom entrance.

"Oh," he said, smiling faintly. "I hadn't realized you were getting ready."

"What's the occasion?" Jurou asked tersely.

"Will you accompany me to the temples?"

"I thought we had classes today."

"Not today. Something about *akuma...*"

Jurou paled as Chaka left the doorway and stood outside it, waiting. *"Demons, again?"* he wondered as he set the towel aside on his sink and finished washing.

Jurou shut off the water and ran out into the bedroom, pausing at the sight of Chaka elaborately dressed. Chaka wore dark brown trousers, light tan leather sandals on his feet and an elaborate pale beige kimono with dark brown cranes etched on the sleeves and hem. Tied about his waist he wore a large brown sash that held a dimly glowing cutlass. Chaka moved about the room, swinging at an invisible foe.

"I'm sure that fine blade isn't for battle," Jurou said as he stepped around Chaka and approached his chest, pulling out a change of clothes.

"You're right, it's not," Chaka replied as he punched at the air. "We're going devil hunting."

"Why must we venture to the temples first?"

"In the case we get killed, our souls wouldn't be trapped here to wander the earth forever."

Jurou cracked a smile. "Are you saying that you're willing to get a blessing or two to keep from becoming a hanging ghost?"

Chaka grunted. "I'm just enchanting my weaponry, nothing more."

"Still don't have faith in the *kamisama*?"

"Not really."

"Why is that?"

"I'll tell you later."

Jurou hurried into trousers and a short jacket. "Do you have any weapons for me to use while we're out hunting?" he asked. "My tools haven't arrived yet."

"I'm sure I have something for you."

After pulling into socks and sandals, Jurou waved at Chaka. "Ready to go?" Chaka grunted and followed Jurou to the door.

Jurou paused in step when his hands burned at the sight of a green-steeled long field sword leaning against the wall nearby.

"Something the matter?" Chaka asked.

"I sense something unpleasant," Jurou murmured. "Where did this *jintachi* come from?"

"Oh, it's probably from yesterday, hence why we're heading to the temples."

"Did you pick this up last night?" Jurou crouched before the blade, studying intently. "I don't remember those assassins owning anything like this."

"I found it," Chaka replied vaguely.

Jurou shrugged and rose to his feet. "You can tell me about it later." Stepping out with Chaka following, Jurou tensed when Nakiko came up the stairs.

"Hey, Jurou!" Nakiko greeted, completely ignoring Chaka. "Ready for round two today?"

"Not today," Jurou said as he shut the door. "I'm going to the temples."

"Kaminaritou Rouru told me that *oni* attacked Akagi Temple," Nakiko replied, mildly surprised.

"Are you sure it wasn't *akuma*?"

"I didn't know you were a devil slayer!" Nakiko smiled brightly and poked Jurou in the chest. "You don't look the part."

Jurou's face flushed darkly. "I don't have to spend all my life in the temples to be good at what I do," he protested. "I can tell that nine-ring sword Chaka has is one of the finest blades made by the Imperial master smith Massai. It's made of a very fine and exceptional steel, durable and flexible, able to withstand the passage of a thousand cycles!"

"Oh, then I'm sure you name your weapons as well?"

"I don't," Chaka grumbled.

"I'm not old-fashioned," Jurou admitted. "But Massai is and named all the blades he created."

Chaka glanced at the flat of the falchion, noticing writing in the language he couldn't understand. Turning it over, he saw the name 'Massai' stamped near the hilt. "*Did Uncle Atsu create this?*" he wondered. "*This feels different from Onikage...*"

Nakiko giggled. "Are you trying to figure out the sword's name?" she teased Chaka.

"I can't read the inscription," Chaka muttered. "See?" He thrust the cutlass at Nakiko and she leaned back, glaring at him. Grasping his wrist, she turned the sword broadside and studied the engraving.

"Of course you can't read that," Nakiko chastised. "It's in *Koukonen*!"

"Why would he sign the name in a language no one can read?" Chaka complained.

"Let me try," Jurou insisted.

Chaka shook off Nakiko's grip and handed him the scimitar. Jurou stared intently at the sword as he ran his fingers over the caption, studying closely.

"Well?" Chaka asked in annoyance.

"It's name is *Tengoku Tejun*," Jurou said, handing the blade back to Chaka.

"Heavenly Steps, eh?" Chaka snorted. "I thought you couldn't read *Koukonen*, much less understand it!"

Jurou's face flushed and he waved a dismissive hand. "I studied a little," he said quickly. "But I can't speak the language."

"Are you going to combat them now?" Nakiko interjected, breaking the tension.

"No," Jurou answered, "we're heading to the temples first for a blessing. If it is an *oni*, then Chaka is better equipped than I am."

"Oh?" Chaka piped and grinned. "Thank you, perhaps..."

"Which temple?" Nakiko inquired, ignoring Chaka.

"Most likely Suijinja," Jurou answered.

"Is it the one that houses the Guardian of the Three Oceans?"

"If that's all there is." Jurou shrugged his shoulders. "My *hogosha* is Kairyushin and if I have to heal Chaka, then I'll need all the help I can get!"

"Enough clucking, ladies," griped Chaka. "Let us get this over with."

"Well then," Nakiko huffed. She bent over and kissed Jurou on the cheek. "For luck," she murmured.

Jurou stiffened, completely off guard as Nakiko walked away. He touched his cheek in awe. "*I didn't expect that!*" he thought.

Chaka grunted, rolling his eyes. Jurou glared back at him and Chaka stomped ahead, ignoring him completely.

Jurou and Chaka approached a small temple bordered by a large gate that led to an entrance with many stone steps. Chaka jogged up the stairs, approaching the ground level and Jurou followed, uneasy as they entered the lower level of the shrine. Around the corner, another stone staircase led to the second floor.

"Say, you look ill," Chaka noted, turning to Jurou who stood at the door. "Do you wish for me to fetch a healer?"

"I'm all right," Jurou lied. "Go on; I'll wait out here."

"Why don't you come with me?"

"I told you, I'm fine."

"There's no way that you are afraid of mere ghosts, *Satsugaisha*!" Chaka gave a wry smile. "Why, are you afraid those fallen warriors will seek you out and torture your soul because you have nothing to defend yourself with?"

"Stop teasing!" Jurou snapped. "I have my faith in Lord Kairyushin."

"We'll test that faith soon, eh?"

Jurou glanced at Chaka who entered the patio, searching for workers. "I wonder where all the monks have gone," Jurou said instead.

"Maybe they are at Akagi to purify the area."

"Right..."

Jurou left Chaka's side and approached a compact enclosed garden. He contemplated the simplistic beauty of the polished stones surrounding a slender shoot of bamboo next to a carefully trimmed red-leafed maple in the center. A slight ray of sunlight descended down from the small shaft in the ceiling, giving the plants an almost otherworldly glow. Sensing Chaka behind him, Jurou glanced in his direction, noticing the young man staring intensely.

"Do you need something?" Chaka inquired.

"Why are you looking at me like that?" Jurou asked.

"I'm just admiring you," Chaka replied.

"There isn't much to admire."

"You must stay in the sun often," Chaka noted.

"What do you mean?"

"You're so bronzed... You don't seem to be the type that works the fields, Saku!"

Jurou blushed. "I'm no farmer, if that's what you're getting."

"Oh, so you lied to me, telling me that you worked at a *Noson*, eh?" Jurou's face flushed darkly in response. "Then how did you get that way?"

"Hard work," Jurou replied vaguely.

Chaka grunted and folded his arms across his chest. "We're not going to find them by standing around," he muttered. "Let's go."

"Wait." Jurou approached Chaka and took his hand. Chaka stood there motionless as Jurou lifted his sleeve. "How can you be so pale if you were truly in the army?"

"The sun doesn't like me, I suppose," Chaka murmured.

"You're always swimming and working outdoors, aren't you?" Jurou ran his fingers up Chaka's muscular arms. "Is there something else?"

"What else?"

"I'm asking you."

"It's sad that the sun doesn't enjoy my presence. What brings color to you, runs at the mere sight of me." Jurou suddenly laughed. "Go; tell the sun to like me again! Maybe the mighty lord of the sun will listen to you!"

"I can't!" Jurou said between giggles. "What makes you think Lord Shinkunikkou will listen to me?"

"Give me good reason."

"I have none to offer!"

Chaka slipped out of Jurou's grasp and turned away. "I have a perfect reason," he said as he headed for the second flight of stairs. "The sun listens to no one. The only emotion it displays is its anger; its rage is enough to boil all the oceans depths!" They approached the balustrade and Chaka came to a sudden pause, gripping the rail tightly with his left hand.

"Are you in pain?" Jurou asked. Chaka grunted, gripping his side. He glanced up and then shut his eyes tightly, doubling over in agony. Jurou looked up in his line of sight, spotting dark brown and violet robes disappearing around the corner. He raced up the stairs, searching for the priest. "Why are you still here?" he called. "I thought you would be at Akagi Temple!"

"I have assistants to do my job for me," the cleric answered.

Jurou approached the second floor, finding a tall stone statue of a large winged warrior in the center of the open-air building, surrounded by small candles, bowls of water and sticks of burning incense.

The statue held a golden long sword in its raised hand and a brightly decorated belt of opal and pearl around its waist. The priest stood near the statue, holding his emerald boomerang at ready.

"Who do you think you are to let your assistants do all the work, Adia Ohara?" Jurou demanded. "I thought you worked at Kawaguchi Temple!"

"Someone has to come up with the protection talismans," Ohara retorted, "or have you forgotten about that?"

Jurou grunted. "There's no need to be blunt!"

"Besides, I was dispatched to help with preparations."

Jurou gave a short bow. "I didn't mean to be rude," he muttered. "However..."

"Why have you come here?" Ohara interjected. "I know you heathens are not in search of enlightenment!" He waved Jurou away. "Your mere presence desecrates this temple! I tell you now: leave!"

"I know I do not pray to this *kami*, but any blessing on our journey will help!" Jurou protested. "I asked him to accompany me!"

"No excuses," Ohara growled. "Leave or you will be thrown out!"

Unable to further reason with the cleric, Jurou retreated for the stairs and found Chaka gone. "*What kind of reaction is that?*" he thought, storming outside. "Chaka, where did you go?" Jurou called. "I'll create talismans and aid the monks at Akagi. If you wish to help, don't hesitate to appear." Blowing a heavy sigh, Jurou walked back for the boardinghouse.

TWENTY-SEVEN

Chaka stood underneath the stone staircase, watching Jurou walk away.

"*We'll deal with him later,*" Tannozume growled. "*You have more important matters to take care of!*"

"*Why are you here again?*" Chaka thought as he left his hiding place and ascended onto the second floor. "*What business do you have with that priest? You know he will not hesitate to strike me again!*"

"*No harm will come to you,*" Shiranosuke said softly.

"We'll see," Chaka grumbled. "I know how you *akuma* operate. You use my body, my voice to do all sorts of harm..."

"*It is for our master plan,*" Akanasutsune grumbled.

Ohara stood on guard once he spotted Chaka at the top of the stairs.

"Ho, *Shisai*," Chaka said and withdrew the machete he wore. "I came to return the favor you've shown me."

"I beat you once along the shore," Ohara snapped. "Turn away and walk right now; save yourself the humiliation!"

"Only because you caught me off guard." Chaka beckoned to the cleric. "Draw your blade and fight!"

"You smell foul, reeking of blood! It was you who killed those *souryo*, eh?" Ohara drew back and the emerald boomerang glowed dimly in response. "I will excise those demons for you."

Chaka shook his head. "Despite the trouble they cause, I need them."

"For what?"

"A reason I cannot tell you."

"With such power in which you possess, you can easily serve the monastery."

"I'm unable to fill that request."

Ohara threw the boomerang forward and Chaka quickly dashed ahead. The cleric dropped a talisman that flashed in violet flame and vanished in a puff of gray smoke as Chaka slashed down, hitting nothing but air. Chaka turned and the boomerang struck him in the head, throwing him onto the floor. Chaka sat up, growling as blood ran down his face.

Ohara reappeared before Chaka, catching the weapon. "Have you forgotten you are weak to Water *jumon*?" he retorted and stepped forward as Chaka crawled back. "This temple is surrounded by water."

"It should be weak," Chaka snapped, "since Earth absorbs Water!"

"Oh, so you know your correspondences." Chaka's back met the wall and the priest pressed his foot against his chest. "Then you know that blade you hold is of the Metal element, and it too contains Water."

"You're wrong," Chaka retorted. "It's Wind!" Glancing over the Ohara's shoulder, he noticed the golden long sword the statue held shimmering dimly. "*That tsurugi is of the Fire element,*" he thought. "*Why is it here?*"

"Let me free you of your burden." Chaka blocked Ohara's attack and slashed back, forcing him staggering rearward. Chaka pushed the cleric away and sprang to his feet, racing across the floor. "*Mizuokasuru!*"

Chaka ducked out of a blast of water and jumped onto the statue's base. The boomerang hurtled over, slicing into his sword hand and Chaka dropped the scimitar.

"*Ataushinai Okyoda!*" Chaka cried and quickly kicked up the blade, slamming the steel into Ohara as he came forward with a thrusting attack, slicing him in half. The priest's body sank to the floor and blood pooled on the stone tiles at Chaka's feet. "Not all warriors fight one-handed," Chaka snapped. "I am skilled in fighting with both, bothersome cretin!"

Dropping the falchion, Chaka snapped off the belt around the statue and wrapped it around his injured arm. Using the other end, Chaka looped it over the statue's outstretched arm and pulled it into place, hoisting himself up.

Grabbing for the blade, the tsurugi flared brightly in response and Chaka grit his teeth when the flames burned him. Letting go, the golden long sword struck the floor.

"This blade is also *Takiletzachi!*" Chaka murmured, surprised. "You're seeking these out... why?"

"*This mighty weapon, Taiyouno Tsubasa, will prove useful on my personal quest,*" Tannozume answered. "*That is all you need to know!*"

"I think I see your reasoning..." Chaka jumped down and approached the long sword that continued to burn. "The Sun Blade is of the Fire element, as you are. Then that means the others—!"

"Yes, the _Tsukinoha_ is of the Water element, as is Shiranosuke and the _Tengoku Tejun_ is of the Wind Element, as is Akanasutsune."

"There is more than you're telling me."

"_There is nothing else for you to know!_" Tannozume bellowed.

"If I'm going to be used as an instrument in handling these cursed blades, then I need to know!"

"_Who says you are going to use the Blade of the Sun?_" Chaka cried out when the wounds in his arm deepened. "_Without my knowledge, you have no way to use it effectively!_"

"You're not taking over my body again!" Chaka shouted. "Only once and it was under agreement when you forced me to fight House Suzume's _koyakunin!_"

"_You cannot control this destructive weapon's chaotic power!_"

"I care not what you do, but it will not involve me!"

"_Its power will devour you. Have you not learned your lesson after handling Onikage?_"

Unable to further protest, Chaka sighed heavily. "What do you have in mind?" he muttered.

Tannozume's overwhelming presence pushed Chaka back, leaving him only to watch as the devil took over his body. He picked up the golden long sword and the silver broad saber, sheathing them into his holster then stepped over the dead cleric, making his way outdoors.

Jurou hurried upstairs and paused when he found his door open. He cautiously approached the room and peered in, finding Ikaruga tearing through his belongings.

"What are you doing?" Jurou shouted. "Why are you bringing my room into utter destruction?"

"I sense evil in this room!" Ikaruga snapped.

"What are you looking for?"

"There is an evil force present, the same that comes from this *jintachi*!" Ikaruga tossed the green-steeled field sword towards Jurou and Jurou jumped back, letting it strike the floor.

"Chaka left that here," Jurou declared. "I know nothing about that!"

"Then let me find its source!" Ikaruga continued combing through various articles.

Jurou growled under his breath and stomped over to the blade, picking it up. He felt a firm hand on his shoulder and looked up, spotting a slender young man with shaggy brown hair and pale green eyes standing over him. The stranger wore an elaborate yellow kimono with orange fireflies as the running pattern and armed with a jade-handled daikatana sheathed in a hunter green scabbard strapped across his back.

"Don't strike him down," he said seriously.

"Who are you?" Jurou demanded, shaking him off.

"I am called Sanzuki."

Ikaruga froze at the sound of the young man's voice and quickly whirled around. "I don't need your help in this investigation," he said sourly.

"We must report about that stolen artifact," Sanzuki said calmly. "Get that *jintachi* and let us return with haste."

Ikaruga folded his arms across his chest, fuming. "Until we get a confession," he spat sourly, "I'm not dealing with the paperwork!"

"Don't fight in here!" Jurou snapped when Sanzuki clenched his hands that glowed dimly in golden light. "Please, take your matters and handle them outside!"

"Very well," said Sanzuki. He sauntered out into the hall and unsheathed his elongated field sword. "Let us battle."

Ikaruga growled, withdrawing his golden katana. "You wish for me to draw blood?" he snarled. "That is perfect by me!"

"Both of you, stand down!" Jurou shouted. "Why are you demons here causing me trouble?"

"We are investigating the murders as well," answered Sanzuki. "The priests did their blessings and the negative energies that are surrounding this *dojo* still have not dispersed."

"I want no part in this feud of yours!" Jurou withdrew the jintachi and Ikaruga growled, his amber eyes flashing orange. "Get out!"

"True, it is no concern of yours, *Satsugaisha*, however, you may be called to help us in the future."

"Who masters you?" Jurou demanded, glaring back.

"Montaro of Kanouana."

"Is it the same Kanouana on Enganokonbu?" Sanzuki nodded. "There is nothing but death out there!"

"How smart of you, *Satsugaisha*!" Sanzuki said brightly. "I'm surprised of your vast knowledge of the locations of all the *Akuma Nomon*!"

Jurou growled and slashed at Sanzuki then Ikaruga. Sanzuki sidestepped the attack and Ikaruga blocked and lashed back, throwing Jurou against the wall.

"Get out of here, both of you," Jurou shouted, "before I call down the might of Kairyushin and flush you both to the Bottomless Abyss!"

"Let's take our leave," Sanzuki grumbled as he sheathed the daikatana across his back. "There's nothing to find here." Sanzuki waved off Jurou and walked away.

"If I see you again," Ikaruga growled as he sheathed his katana, "be prepared to die!" He pushed past Jurou and stomped after Sanzuki.

Jurou stormed into his room and slammed shut the door. "Damn everything!" he screamed and jammed the jintachi into the wall.

Chaka headed up the path for the boardinghouse and paused in step when he spotted Ikaruga and Sanzuki exiting the academy grounds. Ikaruga came to a sudden stop and unsheathed his katana on sight at Chaka. Chaka withdrew the golden tsuruchi as Sanzuki approached calmly and stood several paces away.

"Why do you draw your weapon against me?" Sanzuki inquired innocently.

"Ask your guard dog why he has drawn his weapon against me," Chaka growled.

"Is he the one?" Sanzuki asked.

"I can smell the stink of his evil from here!" Ikaruga sneered. "It's the same as the blade we left behind!"

"I told you--!" Chaka started.

"Enough, devil," Sanzuki spat. "There is no need to say anything else."

Chaka took a step back, stunned. *"Tannozume, have you offended them somehow?"* he thought and swallowed hard when he gained no answer.

"Just admit to your crime and we will spare you suffering."

Chaka twirled the golden long sword around his body expertly with his hands then held the blade up high over his head as it flared in crimson flames. *"Kaminari Koshou!"* he shouted and charged at Ikaruga.

Ikaruga immediately ducked down and blocked over his head as Chaka slammed the blade with all his strength, pushing Ikaruga back on his feet several paces. Ikaruga grunted and struggled as his arms shook against Chaka bearing his weight. Shouldering Chaka rearward, Ikaruga kicked him in the side then spun away as Chaka turned with a counter attack.

Chaka immediately blocked behind him when Ikaruga sliced at his side, then rolled back on his feet once Ikaruga kicked at him in return. Falling back, Chaka withdrew the broad saber and chucked it at Ikaruga. Ikaruga ducked down with a forward pierce, slicing nothing but air as Chaka dashed around him.

Picking up the fallen falchion, Chaka dropped down to one knee when Ikaruga returned with a downward stroke, only to get struck with the edge of the tsurugi at his throat from beneath him and the cutlass pressed into his side. Ikaruga stopped short, eyes wide as Chaka panted heavily for breath.

"Enough practice, dog," Chaka snarled. "Don't shame yourself – give me everything you've got!"

"You bastard!" Ikaruga growled and slapped away the long sword with the butt of his katana.

Chaka jumped back, rolling out the way when Ikaruga slammed his sword down, aiming for his head. Chaka then bound to his feet, sidestepping Ikaruga who leapt over him.

Swinging back, Chaka struck air and turned, leaning out of a strike aimed for his neck. He thrust his scimitar down as Ikaruga's katana slashed for his feet and part of his blade shattered.

"You're fast," Chaka commented. "I'm impressed... I can give you that much."

"You think I will let you defeat me?" Ikaruga shouted. "I will never lose to you!"

"Then die!" Chaka brought up his machete with an underhanded swing as Ikaruga jumped back and jammed his katana forward, forcing Chaka still when the edge of the shattered blade nearly cut the tip of his ear.

"Go to Hell!" Ikaruga screamed.

"You first!"

"You dumb monkey," Sanzuki shouted as Ikaruga made a diagonal cut and Chaka moved with him, leaning out the way. "Don't give in to emotion; you'll only destroy yourself!"

"Listen to your master!" Chaka thundered and blocked a frontal strike, forcing Ikaruga's remaining blade breaking in half.

Pushing forward, Chaka jumped over Ikaruga as he made a mad lash for his throat and Ikaruga turned around, jamming the katana beneath him. Chaka flipped the broad saber under his back, locking the broken sword against his blade aimed for his side.

Bending down as he turned around, Ikaruga jumped above Chaka and made a savage swipe. Chaka shouldered the devil as he came up, sending Ikaruga bowling over onto the ground. Chaka growled, wiping away the shallow cut on his cheek with the back of his free hand.

"That's enough," Chaka snarled as Ikaruga heaved for breath on the ground, unable to move. "This game is over." Chaka sheathed the machete and kicked up the long sword, holding it over his shoulder. "I killed you twice over, old man. Admit defeat and save yourself the humiliation!"

Sanzuki scoffed and stepped forward. "Is that all you have?" he spat. "When did you take the time to learn fighting with two blades at once?"

Chaka faced Sanzuki, smiling darkly. "Oh, so you think you're enough of a challenge for me?" he vaunted. "I picked up a few things here and there on my travels."

"We'll see."

"Let's go!"

Sanzuki withdrew the jade-handled field sword strapped across his back and placed two slim fingers on the flat of the blade, forcing it glowing in soft beige light.

Ikaruga jumped to his feet, immediately sprinting toward Chaka and Chaka slashed back before he raised his katana.

Chaka kicked Ikaruga in the side, sending him head over heels and Sanzuki rushed forward, breaking Chaka's guard.

Ikaruga sprang to his feet once more and Chaka turned out, striking back with a forward thrust at Sanzuki. Sanzuki sidestepped the attack and Chaka made a sweeping stroke as he countered Ikaruga's pierce for his side.

"Don't even think of drawing your power!" Chaka screamed and stabbed Ikaruga in the chest then stomped him off with a hard forward kick.

"Project now!" Sanzuki shouted and the daikatana flashed in brilliant gold. "*Kuru Ichigeki!*" He struck down with a blast of force that hurtled Chaka back. "*Ryunosurou!*" Before Chaka could regain his balance, Sanzuki jammed the field sword into his chest, impaling him, then hurled the blade down, throwing him off. Chaka tumbled over onto the ground and Sanzuki made a running jump, wielding the sword high. "*Chimei!*" Green light surrounded the sword and Sanzuki drove the glowing steel with crushing force, smashing into Chaka's head and instantly knocked out his world.

"There's no point in going to Akagi," Jurou thought as he exited his room and hurried downstairs. *"There's a lot I need to take care of here..."* Leaving the boardinghouse, Jurou headed for the courtyard and spotted Nakiko practicing blows against Kaminaritou Rouru who seemed distracted. "Nakiko," Jurou called, "don't kill him!"

"Oh!" Nakiko exclaimed and withdrew her attack. Kaminaritou Rouru collapsed to one knee, gasping. Jurou ran up to them and stood offside. "We're just sparring, Jurou; it's nothing serious!"

"Even in pain," Kaminaritou Rouru replied, "there is a lesson to be learned."

"Why train so hard?" Jurou asked.

"You have to be able to withstand pain in battle." Nakiko lent a hand to her partner and he took it, getting helped on his feet. "I'm sure you knew that."

"I did," Jurou replied, flushing slightly.

"Do you wish to practice with me?" Nakiko inquired.

"It's fine, we don't have to continue today." Jurou waved her off. "I highly doubt I can find something to use."

Kaminaritou Rouru scoffed. "There must be something of worth," he spat. "There is no such thing as nothing to use! Even your body can be a weapon!"

Jurou blew a heavy sigh. "You're right," he acknowledged.

"We'll find something," Nakiko said in assurance. "There are many weapons and arts of fighting."

Kaminaritou Rouru waved to Nakiko. "Thank you for your time, Ami," he replied.

Nakiko laughed and her cheeks flushed scarlet as she waved back. "You're welcome anytime!" Kaminaritou Rouru walked away with a slight limp in his step.

"Have you heard of any word from *Kenkyaku* Ishida?" Jurou questioned.

"Nothing yet," Nakiko answered.

"So what do you think of what's happening around Kakita?"

"I'm surprised *oni* are on these lands. You'd think they'd long cease to exist, having been banished almost twenty cycles ago."

"What of the *akuma*? Apparently they haven't been fully banished like we thought."

"The gates were closed successfully, so I'm no longer concerned." Nakiko waved a dismissive hand. "If anything, it could've been someone testing their skill and murdered those monks and priests."

"Simply *tsuji-kiri*, you think?" Jurou scoffed. "If so, then why were *sohei* dispatched to investigate the area?"

"If devils were terrorizing the locals, wouldn't it seem strange that they are so close to the mainland?" Nakiko put her hands on her hips. "Historically they have always centered on the coast. Kakita is centered on a bay."

"That bay is fed by the ocean!" Jurou threw up his hands. "Demons can change, just like the stars!"

"It makes no sense." Nakiko shook her head. "Kakita trains fighters for the Imperial Army, nothing more."

"Unless they are targeting *Satsugaisha*..."

Nakiko gave Jurou a quizzical look. "What are you getting at?" she asked warily. "You are *Akumatokko*, right? Were you assigned to work at the Akagi Temple?"

"Never mind about me," Jurou said and waved her away. "Demons exist on these seven islands and always have, banished or not... All it takes is for someone with enough power to unseal the *Akuma Nomon* each of these islands holds."

"Well, it still sounds more like a bored *samurai* to me." Nakiko shrugged. "They're probably upset that the talisman the *souryo* gave them didn't work."

"Where do you hail from?" Jurou demanded.

"I come from Kaori, near Beidounei Gokaku." Nakiko turned away. "What does it matter to you?"

"That is on Kitajima!" Jurou pressed. "That is where I hail from as well!"

"So?" Nakiko waved Jurou away. "What does it mean?"

"If you had a childhood there, then you would have heard the stories and you would have learned the art of defense there!"

"I'm not a true resident." Nakiko walked away. "Maybe we spar another time."

Jurou ran after her. "Why do you hide your true identity?" he pleaded. "Why must you keep secrets from me?"

Nakiko pushed him away. "I hide them for various reasons," she answered curtly. "I'm sure you understand."

"Are you afraid that something terrible would happen?" Nakiko shook her head and continued up the walk to the boardinghouse. Jurou followed her. "Then why not acknowledge the seven *Akuma Nomon*?"

"Who would bother spending all that time and energy reopening them?" Nakiko spat back. They came to a pause at the entrance of the academy.

"Have I offended you somehow?" Jurou asked.

"Please leave me with my thoughts." Nakiko said flatly. Jurou touched her by the arm and she shook him away. "If you're so intent on finding these devils, then do your job!"

Jurou pulled away then stormed around the side of the building. *"I'm not going to find any answers here, being a stranger to this place,"* he thought. *"I might as well leave it to the professionals!"* Jurou walked down the sandy path toward the bay's shore.

TWENTY-EIGHT

Moon 10 (Grain Rain) - 1st Day

Chaka's eyes snapped open when he felt water on his face and groaned when he realized light rain showered over him. Jurou approached offside with an umbrella and Chaka shielded his eyes, squinting.

"Ho," he called. "Why do you stand in front of me?"

"Can't I check on you?" Jurou spat. "Besides, where did you get that sword from?"

"Eh?" Chaka glanced in the direction Jurou pointed and saw the golden long sword pitched into the sands nearby, several feet away.

"Why is it I always find you out here?" Jurou demanded. "How long have you been out here?"

"I don't recall..."

"Don't tell me you've been here all night and all morning too!"

"How long has it been raining?"

"Since the fifth hour!"

Chaka grunted and shut his eyes. "Let me drown," he moaned. "It's better this way."

"Don't act foolish," Jurou said and nudged Chaka with his foot. "Get up." Chaka blew a heavy sigh and sat up. "Come inside." Jurou held out a hand and let out a yelp when Chaka took it, pulling him down.

"You smell delicious," Chaka murmured as he embraced the young man tightly. "I could eat you."

Too stunned to say anything, Jurou dropped his umbrella and slugged the older man in the face. Chaka grunted and let go as Jurou scrambled to his feet.

"What was that for?" Chaka snapped and spat blood on the ground.

"You know!" Jurou shouted.

"Know what?" Chaka held his stinging jaw. "I didn't know you liked to play rough."

"Meet me in the courtyards," Jurou grumbled and picked up his umbrella.

"*What was that all about?*" Chaka wondered, watching Jurou storm away. Rising to his feet, he kicked up the tsurugi, caught it and hurried along the path. Entering the gardens, Chaka spotted Jurou sitting on a stone bench with his umbrella closed at his side. "Why are you letting yourself get rained on?" he called.

"I have my reasons," Jurou answered.

"Let's go inside." Chaka headed for the boardinghouse and paused in step when Jurou called after him.

"Did you kill those *souryo* there at Akagi Temple?" Jurou demanded. Chaka turned about-face, his expression grim. "If it were merely to test your strength, there are other ways to go about it."

"Where did you come up with that notion?" Chaka protested. "How dare you accuse me?"

Jurou narrowed his eyes. "I sense the *Tengoku Tejun* you have is the same as that *jintachi* and the *tsurugi* you've just acquired."

Chaka shrugged. "What about them?"

"I heard these artifacts were stolen."

Chaka scoffed. "How was I to know I received stolen property?"

"Why do you stink of blood then?"

Chaka smiled. "How else am I to respond when attacked?" he replied. "They came after me; I didn't instigate anything!"

"Is that the true story behind being 'The Beast of the Blood Coast'?"

"Possibly."

"Just admit to your crimes then and stop hiding behind your ready excuse of blaming demons."

Chaka tensed and pointed the long sword in Jurou's direction. "You know nothing about me," he snarled.

"You're nothing but a useless warrior, completely weak and frail."

"I'll show you weak and frail!" Chaka roared and charged.

Jurou immediately stood and jumped on the stone bench, ducking out of a hard slash. He unscrewed the umbrella's handle and countered Chaka's reverse thrust with the hidden kaiken, slicing his arm.

Chaka cried out and dropped what he held, clutching his wrist in agony. Jurou glimpsed at the dimly glowing dagger tinged in violet he held, then back at Chaka who doubled over, seething in pain.

"Where did you get that awful thing?" Chaka hissed.

"I borrowed it from Baiuko," Jurou said. "*Amahagane* shouldn't hurt you at all!"

"You thought I was some hired killer, a monster for the Imperial Army, eh?" Chaka let out a faint laugh. "I may be tall, strong and intimidating, but against *akuma*, I'm as fragile as they come!" Jurou shook his head, unable to respond. "I admit, I can never be like you," Chaka grumbled. "You're strong and tough in your heart. I'm merely strong and tough on the outside."

"Then maybe I should get rid of the demons that haunt you," Jurou said seriously.

Chaka tensed when Tannozume growled behind him. "If you did that," he said faintly, "you may regret it..."

"*That miserable worm!*" Tannozume snarled. "*Who does he think he is?*"

Chaka released his hold on his wrist and stood. Jurou tensed, noticing his vibrant blue-gray eyes turning blank and dull in his head.

"Oh," Jurou said, smirking, "did I offend you?"

"*I'm sure you'll keep your word,*" Tannozume snarled through Chaka. "*It won't be long before we control you as well.*"

"I have a stronger will than your current vessel." Jurou backed away as Chaka stepped forward. "Try as you might; you'll only fail in your attempt!"

"*Would you bet your life on that?*"

"Are you the true reason he's called 'The Beast of the Blood Coast'?"

"*Get closer and you'll find out.*"

Chaka unleashed the falchion and made a lunging stab at Jurou. Jurou quickly darted out the way, forcing the silver broad saber striking the tree.

Chaka gripped the handle with both hands and placed a foot to the bark, yanking at the stuck blade imbedded in the trunk. Jurou backed away when Chaka continued to struggle with all his might against the steel that refused to budge. He then took off running when the sword began glowing dimly.

"*What are you planning?*" Chaka thought as his hands flared in red light. "*What will you do to him?*"

"*Why should I tell you my plans?*" Tannozume answered. "*Just experience them as they happen!*"

"*What?*"

Chaka found it suddenly hard to breathe as he released the sword with ease. He turned and grunted when the green-steeled black and red-handled jintachi struck him in the chest.

Chaka staggered back from the force and hit the ground hard, gasping weakly for air. Jurou stood over him, heaving for breath.

"Tell me," Jurou commanded, "did you make a deal with them so you could kill people better?"

"What?" Chaka cried.

"Tell me!" Jurou shouted.

"You don't understand; I don't remember!"

Chaka screamed when Jurou ripped out the blade and struck him with swift accuracy, moving with each stab as he sliced at him repeatedly.

"What is there to understand?" Jurou yelled as he hacked at Chaka, enraged. "What is there to understand? I saw the aftermath! I saw it, I saw it all!" Chaka blocked Jurou's strike for his head with his cutlass and pushed away. Jurou came again and Chaka slashed back, slicing his shoulder. Jurou staggered rearward, gripping his cut shoulder and Chaka sat up, panting hard. "See there, even the demons protect you; you hardly bleed at all!"

"Listen to me," Chaka hissed. "Showcasing your strength in battle is all there is to life! Without it, you die, even when there are demons attacking the coast and all the other towns!" He struggled to his feet and pitched his blade into the ground, leaning against it. "I fought in that war to drive them back and close the gates. At the time, I was young and weak, just like you. They promised me..."

"What did they promise you?"

Chaka stiffened, sensing movement from behind. Taking his falchion, he staggered forward and made his way for the hidden canopy. Peering out into the clearing, Chaka spotted two members of the cavalry standing outside the boardinghouse under the eaves, conversing to Nakiko who stood on the steps, holding an umbrella.

"*Tokiko and Ittou*," he noted. "*What are they doing?*"

Nakiko suddenly froze and Ittou quickly put his hand to the hilt of his service saber as Tokiko immediately turned around and withdrew her weapon.

"Ho," Nakiko called. "What happened to you?" She left Tokiko's side and made her way over.

Chaka pointed his machete in her direction and Tokiko and Ittou stood ready to attack. "Stay back," he snarled.

"I'm coming for you," Nakiko called. "Do you want me to dispatch a healer?"

"No!" Chaka shouted. "Stay away, or they'll come for your soul as well!"

Nakiko paused. "My soul?" she asked, incredulous.

"Yes!"

"You're torn to pieces..."

"No matter, girl; just turn around and go away!"

Nakiko shook her head. "What shall I do?" she asked gently. "The sight of you makes me uncomfortable."

"Follow with what I say," Chaka said seriously. "Stay silent about this matter or I decimate you."

"Please, don't do that!" Nakiko said faintly. "Don't strike me!"

"Then leave!" She took a step back and Chaka stepped forward, pressing the steel against her throat. "Do you not understand my request?"

"I don't like this change in you."

"Leave!" Chaka roared.

Nakiko paled, then turned and ran to Tokiko. Chaka slammed the scimitar into the ground, clutching his head. He sucked in a shallow breath as the prickly agony he felt in his arm and hands spread to his face.

"*You are trying to break me!*" Chaka wailed in his mind. "*How much longer must I endure this?*"

"*We have plans,*" Tannozume answered, "*and you will be the one to execute them.*"

"*What happens if I fail?*"

"*Then you'll be nothing but a ghost with no purpose.*" Tannozume laughed darkly. "*So as you see, you cannot afford to lose this trial.*"

"*I don't want you to control me anymore.*"

"*Then would you rather we control him instead?*"

Chaka looked up, facing Jurou who stood across from him, watching him silently. "*What if I wish to control him?*" The pain lightened slightly.

"*You have no more control than we do!*" Tannozume let out a short, bitter laugh. "*Can you do that; is that what you want to do?*"

"*Try me.*"

"*Let go,*" Tannozume snapped. "*Why should you care?*"

"*I promised...*"

"*You promised nothing!*" Chaka cried out when struck in the back by a phantom blow and sank to his knees. "*Give up!*"

Sensing a shocking touch to his shoulder, Chaka gasped, hunching forward. "Please, don't!" he pleaded.

"I'm sorry!" Jurou murmured. "Please, forgive me!"

"I don't hate you," Chaka said softly.

Jurou knelt down beside him and placed a hand on his shoulder. "Are you afraid?" he asked. Chaka shook his head. "What do you need from me?"

"You just wouldn't know," Chaka muttered.

"I think I can help!" Jurou squeezed Chaka's shoulder. "I can try."

"A fine offer," Chaka said and sat up on his knees. He gave a bright smile and Jurou pulled away, apprehensive at the sudden change. "Take my blade and put this away for me. I'll return for it later."

"Where are you going?" Jurou stood as Chaka rose to his feet and slipped off his sword harness.

"I'm going for a swim to clear my mind." Chaka handed over the harness. "Take care of this." Jurou took the harness in hand, dumbfounded as Chaka left the canopy.

Jurou sheathed the silver broad saber and picked up the golden long sword left behind. Hoisting both and the black-handled field sword over his uninjured shoulder, he approached Nakiko standing with Ittou and Tokiko who appeared apprehensive.

"Do you want me to get you a healer?" Nakiko asked.

"It's not that serious," Jurou replied.

"What did you two talk about?"

Jurou shook his head. "I don't know if I'm strong enough to help him," he complained. "I only got lucky today..."

"Then don't deal with him anymore."

"I just can't give up on him. His soul needs to be cleansed."

"Are you willing to walk that path?" Nakiko touched Jurou on the arm. "I've seen my share of *Satsugaisha* become consumed by the very forces they swore to protect everyone from!"

"Do you think he was *Akumatokko* for the Imperial Army at one time?"

"I only heard stories... I know little about him actually."

"Will you help me?"

"I'll try my best, Jurou."

"Keep me from losing myself; I will need you to anchor me."

"I'll pull you out if you fall too deep." Jurou clasped her hand and Nakiko squeezed firmly. "So what will you do?" she asked.

"I have to figure out a way to get close to him..."

"I don't think he's had any lady friends."

Jurou let go and sighed heavily. "I'll think of something."

"Please, be careful."

"I'll try my best," Jurou murmured and left her side, returning for the boardinghouse.

Walking back for the hostel, Jurou grew preoccupied with numerous thoughts about how to handle Chaka's formidable nature. Making his way upstairs, he passed Baiuko and she came to a dead stop at the sight of him.

"What happened to you?" she cried.

"Your umbrella's in my room if you still need it," Jurou answered on passing. "Thanks for letting me borrow it."

"That's not what I meant!" Baiuko grabbed his sleeve before he walked away, stopping him. "Where did you get those blades from?" she demanded.

Jurou shook his head. "No matter; I'm putting them away."

"Twice your room has been gone through," Baiuko said. "I don't want anything important to get stolen." She led him to her door. "Store them here."

Jurou gave a faint smile. "I can't thank you enough!"

Entering Baiuko's modestly furnished room, he set the swords in her closet that had several sabers and staves leaning against the interior walls. After shutting the door, Baiuko blocked his path.

"If you were able to heal me from what he's done to me," she said softly, "why can't you heal him from what makes him that way?"

"My healing ability isn't that strong yet," Jurou murmured.

"You healed broken bones!" Baiuko protested. "What's the great difference between my illness and his?"

"A broken body is easier to fix than a broken spirit."

Baiuko stepped away, unsure what to say next and Jurou pushed past her, leaving her room.

Chaka stripped out his clothing and dove into the bay's aquatic depths.

"*Tonight is the final test*," Tannozume snarled. "*If you do not go through with it now, then you shall suffer for eternity!*"

"*Let me suffer*," Chaka thought. "*I've done enough of that...*"

"*You don't mean that!*"

Chaka let out a yelp once forces pulled his body under. He fought the shadowy demons holding him down and quickly broke the surface, gasping for breath.

"*Why is he here?*" Chaka wondered once he spotted Jurou approaching the shore, holding his discarded apparel in his arms. "*I thought I drove him away!*"

"*Stubborn fool won't leave you be...*"

"*Stay away!*" Chaka silently prayed as he trod water, watching Jurou take a seat on the wet sands, waiting.

"*Destroying him will be so easy...*"

"If you stay near me, you will die!"

Chaka swam for the shore, pushing away the deep until his feet met inclined sand. He rose out of the water, marching straight for Jurou. Jurou smiled nervously in return as Chaka stood before him. Chaka dug in his toes on the packed cold wet sands, trying to keep his balance.

"Did you gather your thoughts?" Jurou probed.

"Why did you not wrap your shoulder?" Chaka replied instead.

"It's not as bad as it looks."

"Do you swim?" Chaka asked and shuddered when the cool spring winds blew against his naked body, drawing the warmth out of his skin.

"Not in armor," Jurou replied impertinently. "How is your arm?"

"Do you know what Death looks like?" Chaka retorted. Jurou looked down at the garments he held, unable to answer. "Do you ever hear the wind speaking your name?"

"What kind of question is that?" Jurou answered.

"It talks freely, in hushed helpless tones, in angry screams, in a sad whispering." Chaka raised his arms. "It is speaking my name! How sad does it sound - the very *word* so full of emotion?" Chaka let out a short laugh. "My name, coming off my adored ocean... does it make you want to cry as well?" Jurou tightened his grip on the clothing and Chaka nudged him with his foot. "Does it make you want to cry in gratitude and apology?"

"I don't hear the ocean cry for me," Jurou said softly.

"Oh great ocean, I adore thee; I fear you; you master all," Chaka called. *"Petty beings such as we bow down to your might! Those fearful things, they know not what comes."* Jurou all of a sudden appeared disturbed and Chaka laughed. "Stand firm, Saku!" Chaka urged and prod him with his foot again.

Jurou looked ahead at the waves, watching the ripples form and fade away with every gust of wind. Chaka deeply inhaled the salty air and let out a heavy breath.

"Is this what you expected?" Jurou asked hesitantly.

"I don't feel well, Saku," Chaka muttered and reached down, grabbing for his trousers.

"Perhaps you ought to cut short your training," Jurou suggested as Chaka hastily dressed.

"Follow me Saku," Chaka abruptly said, throwing on his kimono. "I want to take you to Tatsumachi."

"Why do you wish to take me there?" Jurou asked.

"I wish to buy new clothes." Chaka held out a hand. "Come."

Jurou sighed and reached up a hand, having Chaka pull him effortlessly to his feet. "Should we wait a bit?" Jurou inquired as he slipped out of Chaka's grasp. "It's still raining and besides, we haven't time to know each other well."

"Perhaps we should wait," Chaka parroted. "Do you think so?" Jurou nodded. "Ha." Chaka poked a finger into Jurou's chest. "Do you really think so?" He poked Jurou again. "Right, you have nothing to worry about, right?"

"If you say so," Jurou answered and winced when poked once more.

Chaka grinned, shaking his head. "I'll go alone, then," he said.

"Very well."

Chaka stepped into his sandals and walked down the sands alone, heading up the hill.

TWENTY-NINE

Jurou let out an anxious breath, watching Chaka walk away. *"How does he know the protection prayer to Lord Kairyushin?"* he wondered. *"If this is his way of asking me to help him, then to drive out those monsters, I need to get closer..."* Leaving the beachhead, Jurou raced the hill, heading for the boardinghouse. *"Hopefully he will tell me his true reason for letting himself become possessed in the first place."* Hurrying up the steps, Jurou paused in the hall when he noticed his door ajar.

"Who's in there?" he called and threw open the door. Jurou took in a weak breath when he found Nakiko sitting on his futon. "What are you doing here?" Jurou demanded. "I thought you were going out to practice with Tokiko!"

"I wanted to spar with you," she answered. "Do you wish to practice now?"

"In the rain?"

Nakiko shrugged her shoulders. "Why not?"

Jurou gave a faint smile. "Sure." Nakiko stood and Jurou blocked her path to the door. "Is there another reason you're here?"

"What do you mean?"

"I mean..." Jurou put up a hand and shook his head before she could reply. "Never mind, you don't have to answer." He stepped aside, letting Nakiko out and shut the door after her.

"Tape your hands," Nakiko called over her shoulder as she headed downstairs. "I won't be easy on you."

"That's all right, I don't mind," Jurou answered, following behind her. "I need the work."

"You need to get tougher if you're that bad in handling weapons," Nakiko reprimanded. "I thought your skill in *Taijutsu* would be better than what it is now."

"Hence my coming here for more practice," Jurou said sheepishly.

Exiting outdoors, Jurou took off his short jacket and placed it aside on a nearby bench. Nakiko's face flushed slightly as she held up her hands in guard.

"Ready?" Nakiko called.

"Just come at me," Jurou answered.

"If that's your ready stance," protested Nakiko, "then you're just looking to get killed!"

"Don't worry about my stance." Jurou waved to Nakiko. "Come at me like you mean it!"

Nakiko charged and dropped low with an elbow feint, then followed with a reverse leg sweep, throwing Jurou back on the ground. He rolled with the fall and sprang up, pushing Nakiko by the waist.

Ducking down to his knee, Jurou leaned away from a front kick and threw a heel palm strike at Nakiko's calf, forcing her to falter. Shouldering Nakiko in her chest, Jurou came down hard with an elbow smash over her back, sending the young woman flat on the ground. Jurou flipped to his feet, panting for breath as Nakiko shook off her stun and sat up on her knees.

"Impressive," Nakiko said breathlessly. "You're fast."

"I have to be," Jurou simply said.

"Now let's get serious!"

"What?" Jurou cried. "Don't tell me you were holding back!"

"If you thought that was my best," Nakiko declared, "then you better take notes after I'm through with you!"

Jurou immediately stood on the defensive when Nakiko rose to her feet and furiously attacked.

The sparring match carried late into the afternoon and after the skies waned, shifting to early evening, Jurou gave in to exhaustion, unable to counter. He took a hard hit to the back and collapsed on his knees, wheezing for breath.

"You didn't have to be so rough," Jurou moaned.

"The whole point of this match is to toughen you up!" Nakiko said brightly.

"Are you sure you're not making *mochi*?"

Nakiko laughed. "This must be a good day for you!"

"Not so much," Jurou spat sourly. "Why do you say that?"

"You didn't pass out!" Jurou grimaced and Nakiko held out a hand. Taking it, she pulled him to his feet. "Come, I'll help you upstairs."

"It seems like a long way from here." Nakiko put an arm around his shoulders and Jurou leaned against her as she aided him inside the boardinghouse. "I'm happy you helped me pass the day, nonetheless."

"Will I see you tomorrow afternoon?"

"Yes, you'll see me."

"Will you be able to handle it?"

"I hope so..."

After getting upstairs, Nakiko assisted Jurou into his futon and he groaned once he laid back.

"Are you sure you'll be up for tomorrow?" Nakiko asked.

"A cold shower will take the pain away," Jurou replied.

Nakiko smiled tersely and touched him on the shoulder. "I can go easy on you if you like..."

"No, don't change."

"Good, that's what I want to hear!" Nakiko pat Jurou on the head and left.

Once she shut the door, Jurou put an arm over his eyes and blew a heavy sigh. "Lord Kairyushin, help me!" he muttered. Jurou grunted and turned over on his side, throwing the sheets over his head. "*She's out to kill me,*" he mused. "*If that's the skill she's learned in the Elite Forces, then what am I doing here?*" Suddenly his hands burned intensely and Jurou sat up on his elbows, stunned. "Leave here," he called. "There's nothing you want with me, demon."

"*You should have put up a ward, boy,*" a dark voice hissed back. "*All Devil Slayers know this!*"

"This is the first time I had to do it full time," Jurou cracked. "Cut me some slack, will you?" He tensed when a chilly presence entered the room and shadows moved along the wall.

"*You don't even have your enchanted weaponry...*" Jurou clenched his teeth and winced as phantom hands grabbed him by his injured shoulder. "*A true devil hunter never leaves his tools behind!*"

"They were delayed," Jurou snapped. "It couldn't be helped!"

"We will have to punish you..."

"For what?"

"For stealing!"

"What?" Jurou grunted when a heavy fist slammed into his face, knocking him out onto the floor. He scrambled back onto his feet, drawing sapphire light in his hands. *"Tamashibai!"* Jurou thrust forward a hand, releasing silver darts. The shadows split and separated from where the quills struck the floor, transforming into spikes. The inky lances slammed Jurou against the wall before vanishing and Jurou fell to his knees, moaning in pain.

"With such weak skill, you stand no chance!"

"I'm strong enough!" Jurou hissed.

"We'll see about that!"

A sudden bang thundered outside his door as the shadows formed into a warrior in black plate armor. Other shapeless beings appeared beside the demon with glowing yellow eyes.

"Jurou!" a voice called from the other side.

"Don't come in here!" Jurou shouted back and shoved past the shadowy intruder as it withdrew its sword. The devil swung its phantom blade, cutting his arm. Jurou growled in pain, grasping the steel that came for him again with a bloodied hand. *"Osoroshii Shiroe!"* The sword the demon held suddenly disintegrated into particles of light.

"Curse you!" the shadowy fighter roared and kicked Jurou aside. *"Attack him!"* The other minor demons rushed Jurou and their leader faded out of sight.

"*Shinseina Jouki!*" Jurou yelled as the phantoms closed in around him. A sudden blast of force tore into the group, turning the shades into ash on contact. Jurou moaned, collapsing to the floor from the drain.

Moments later, his door was broken into and a small lamp brightened the corner of the room. Jurou looked up, spotting Nakiko holding a paper lantern while behind her stood Kaminaritou Rouru with Chaka out of breath and soaking wet, standing nearby in front of the broken door armed with a war hammer.

"Jurou!" Nakiko cried. "Are you all right?" She rushed in and knelt beside Jurou as he struggled to sit up. Setting the lantern beside him, she took Jurou gently by his uninjured arm, pulling him to his knees. "I heard you scream," she murmured. "I'm glad you're not dead..."

"Seiki looks fine, Ami," Kaminaritou Rouru snapped, rolling his eyes. "He fended off whoever it was."

"It's clear they nearly overpowered him," Nakiko snapped back, glaring at him. "If assassins are trying to get rid of him, we should at least try to lend a hand!"

"Do you think it was *akuma*?" Chaka asked. "They've been unusually active lately..."

"Why are they attacking you?" Nakiko demanded. Jurou glanced at Chaka who looked away, appearing uninterested. Nakiko touched Jurou on the shoulder and he turned to face her, smiling faintly.

"I'm fine," Jurou replied. "Please don't worry."

"He is not ill or seriously injured," Kaminaritou Rouru grumbled. "He looks healthy."

"You don't have to get involved in my problems," Jurou said softly to Nakiko and took her hand, squeezing gently. "I heal quickly."

"Is it related to your family?" Nakiko asked.

Jurou tensed. "Who told you?" he demanded.

"Baiuko did, why...?"

Jurou pushed her away and hastily stood, his face shadowed by anger. "Please leave," he snapped.

Nakiko withdrew, appearing hurt. "I'm sorry to have upset you, Jurou!" she cried.

"All of you," Jurou exploded, "get out!"

Nakiko picked up her lamp as she rose to her feet, her face becoming stony. "If you didn't want our help," she said coldly, "don't make such horrible noise next time."

"See, Ami, he is fine!" Kaminaritou Rouru groused. "Let us retire for the evening!" He stormed away.

Nakiko blew a hard sigh. "We won't spar tomorrow afternoon if you don't feel up to it," she said icily and left the room.

Chaka stood in Jurou's doorway and his shadow covered the floor, seemingly leading to the open window. Jurou glanced warily over to him and Chaka appeared smug.

"Why are you still here?" Jurou spat. "I told you to leave!"

"I wish to keep watch for you," Chaka replied, grinning broadly. "Is that all right?"

"Don't bother me." Jurou stomped over to his futon and sat on the edge.

"Are you worried about that Baiuko talking too much?" Chaka left the hammer at the door and entered the room. "I heard about your family," he said, perching across from Jurou, "and I truly understand. *Akuma* decimated my family as well."

"I thought you came from a wealthy family!"

Chaka grinned. "That was before I became suicidal and entered the army." He grabbed Jurou by the foot, pulling him toward him. Jurou grunted when he struck his back and pushed Chaka away. He sat up across from Chaka and winced as Chaka ran a cool hand through his shaggy hair. "So you see, we have something in common, Saku!"

"I'll be fine," Jurou said, shoving him away. "I really don't need you here."

"Do you wish for me to guard your room?"

"You really don't have to do that." Jurou put up his hands. "I doubt it will happen again."

"Those monsters won't stop until they get what they want." Chaka rose to his feet and lent a hand, pulling Jurou up. "Rest and heal yourself and I'll stake out a place near the door."

"Just for tonight," Jurou conceded. "This doesn't mean you can stay for good, understand?" Chaka chortled and headed for the door as Jurou gathered his sheeting.

"I will listen to you whenever you want to talk."

"Aren't you going to dry off first?"

"In a bit."

Jurou lay back in bed, staring up at the ceiling as Chaka took a seat at the door, sitting stiffly on his knees. Jurou turned on his side away from Chaka.

"Sitting on your knees like that will destroy them when you're older," Jurou murmured.

"Oh, I don't see myself getting old," quipped Chaka. "Nothing to worry over; I'm used to it." He grunted. "How can you tell?"

"I heard the way you move and your breath when you sat down," Jurou answered. "You cross your ankles behind you, which is unusual."

"You have keen hearing."

"It's not that great."

Chaka continued watching as Jurou's breathing eventually turned even and heavier once he fell into slumber.

THIRTY

Chaka later rose to his feet and clenched his teeth when his skin grew cold. *"I know you are planning something,"* he thought. *"Otherwise you have no reason to take over my body..."*

"What shall we do with such a predicament?" Tannozume asked once Chaka approached the bed and looked down at Jurou. *"Do you have any suggestions?"*

"I'm unsure..."

"Good, therefore you have no protests."

Chaka sat on the edge of the bed, running his hands over the linen. *"What do you want with him?"*

"The same reason you want with him." Chaka quickly pulled away as faint pain bit at his hands, traveling up his arms. *"Control..."*

"No, only a dishonorable piece of trash will take over when one is weak."

"He turned his back to you!"

"I don't trust you!"

"Then do something."

Chaka leaned over to Jurou's ear. "I wish not to hurt you," he whispered, "but if you get close to me, you will regret it."

"That's enough," Tannozume growled.

"*He's not a part of your game,*" Chaka thought. "*If you destroy him...*"

"*But I wish to...*"

Chaka clenched his hands. "*I refuse to go along with this.*"

"*Your body is mine to use at will!*" Tannozume thundered. "*I can destroy whoever I want and there is nothing you can do to change that fact!*"

"*There is and he's the one to do so!*"

"*So I must destroy him, just as all the others!*"

Chaka's eyes turned blank and he crawled over on top of Jurou, straddling him by the knees. He placed his hands above Jurou's head as Jurou turned on his back.

Jurou's eyes snapped open and he gasped, staring up at Chaka who grinned fiercely down at him.

"What are you doing?" Jurou cried.

"*Nothing, yet,*" Chaka answered in a layered tone.

Jurou kneed Chaka in the groin and flipped him onto the floor. Chaka smashed his head against the nearby chest and growled in pain.

"What is with you?" Jurou shrilled, glaring down at Chaka as he sat up on his elbows. "You are trying my patience!"

"That is a good question," Chaka grumbled and gripped his left wrist that began to bleed.

"Why are you holding your arm like that?" Jurou demanded. "I didn't scratch you!"

"It's an old wound, nothing more."

"I thought you were here to protect me!" Jurou complained. "You were trying to hurt me!"

"Why would I wish harm to you, Saku?" Chaka smirked. "You are much too handsome to mar like that. Such beautiful skin as yours..."

"You...!"

Jurou jumped out of bed, throwing a snapping front kick at Chaka. Chaka grabbed Jurou's foot and flipped him back on the floor, then pounced atop Jurou's body, trapping the young man beneath his weight.

"What about me?" Chaka teased, grinning devilishly. "You want to get close to me, eh?"

"Get off me!"

"We can wrestle all night if you like."

"If you do violence against me..."

"I would not dream of assaulting you!" Jurou threw a punch and Chaka caught it, slamming his wrist on the floor. "I would hold you I have you know..."

"I don't want to be held!"

"Then what are you doing?" Jurou raised his other hand and Chaka grabbed for his wrist, swiftly clamping it onto the floor. "Forget it, Saku. You are too weak from all those injuries."

"Is this really you?" Jurou asked as Chaka leaned in.

"Do you hate me?" Chaka murmured. "I don't hate you, but I know someone who does..."

"Do you want me to hate you?" Jurou responded.

Chaka drew closer. "It'll make it easier," he whispered in Jurou's ear.

"Chaka..." Jurou mewed.

"Hm?" Chaka withdrew, looking down at Jurou wolfishly.

"Closer," Jurou said softly. "I need to tell you something."

"Tell me right now," Chaka snarled.

"The walls are too thin for that."

"Oh?"

"Please..."

Chaka bared his teeth. "Don't beg," he derided. "It hurts to see you do that."

Jurou shut his eyes, blowing a hard sigh. "Please, don't do this to me," he pleaded. "Stop teasing me and just listen to what I want to tell you."

Chaka grunted. "Fine," he grumbled.

Jurou opened his eyes as Chaka leaned forward.

"*Osorenoutorinozoku*," Jurou hissed and blew in his ear. Chaka suddenly stiffened and the blank look in his eyes slowly cleared. "Chaka...?"

Chaka gasped and the color drained from his face. He let go, abruptly scrambling to his feet. "I have done nothing!" Chaka cried as Jurou sat up. "Nothing wrong I did, I swear!"

"Chaka, wait!" Chaka ran out the room and froze in the corridor when he stood in front of the knight in crimson lamellar.

"*You useless, spineless piece of trash!*" Tannozume screeched. "*Keep resisting and I will do more than possess you outright!*"

"I will destroy you!" Chaka snarled and backed away as the red-armored devil put a hand to the hilt of his scabbard and unhooked his katana. "By Lord Shinkunikkou's might, I will send you to Hell!"

"*I prefer this vessel!*" Tannozume thundered. "*Fail us again and never will you own the power of choice!*" Chaka turned out of a forward thrust and slipped to his knees when slashed in the back with a counterblow. The crimson knight grabbed Chaka's hair, yanking back his head as he placed the edge of the blade under his chin. *"Or would you rather lose your head and become a restless spirit?"*

Unable to come up with an answer, Tannozume jammed the sword's pommel aside Chaka's temple. The young man slumped forward exhausted as the darkness took over his entire being.

Jurou stood under the frigid blast of water in his shower and shuddered in fear despite the cold, unable to concentrate on anything else but Chaka.

"If I don't find out which demon it is," he mused, *"it'll take over him completely and he'll hurt others, maybe even kill!"*

Thunder rumbled softly from outside, taking him out of his thoughts. Jurou pulled the chain and stepped out, dripping water onto the floor as he made his way for the window. Gripping the pane, he leaned forward, taking in a deep breath of cool salty air as the high winds blew in.

More thunder boomed and lightning crashed across the sky as a shower of rain pelted down, throwing small pieces of hail that clattered against the academy's roof and on the courtyard pavement below.

Amid the flashing lightning, Jurou caught sight of a human figure below, fighting the shadows. He moved quickly just as the lightning, his movements highlighted by each brief flash.

"Ho," Jurou called, "why are you practicing in the rain?" Another figure departed from the canopy, sneaking behind the practicing warrior. Jurou gasped when the secondary fighter unsheathed a saber. "Watch out!" he shouted.

The warrior raised his saber, taking a leap and the other fighter turned out of a deadly slash aimed at his back as he withdrew his own blade. The swordfighter plunged his katana into his opponent's chest, also losing his head to the saber fighter's swift stroke.

Jurou backed away from the window in stunned silence. Growing immediately ill, he rushed into the washroom and vomited into the commode.

"It's not my place to know why he was killed," Jurou thought as he gripped the commode's lid with weak hands. *"But I can't have his spirit come and haunt me."*

Jurou got to his feet and turned on the tap at his face bowl, splashing his face with cold water. He then cupped some with his hands, taking a gulp to swish and spat out.

Shutting off the water, Jurou left for his chests, taking out a simple kimono and a heavy poncho. Throwing them on his slim frame, he stepped into a pair of sandals and left his room, hurrying down the hall.

Exiting onto the boardinghouse steps, Jurou found Chaka standing in the rain over the headless body of the fighter. In his hands, he held a dark decorated scabbard and the bloodied katana. Draped over his shoulder was Jurou's discarded jacket from earlier.

"What are you doing out here?" Jurou asked. "Come in or you'll catch your death!"

"I was on my way to return your *haori*," Chaka murmured, "and this happens..."

"You didn't have to do that; I could've gotten it in the morning!"

"I was too late…"

"There was nothing you could have done."

"They left another elaborate blade behind…"

"What do you mean?"

"What do I mean?" Chaka let out a short laugh. "Even I misunderstand!"

Jurou grunted and turned to the headless fighter. "*Spirits of purification, created from Order and Chaos, with all the respect from the depth of our hearts we ask that they hear us,*" he said solemnly. "*Mighty Oshiikaten, giver and taker of life, guardian of souls, please hear our intent with sharpened ears, together with Spirits of the Sky and the Land. Take away the negativity, disasters, and sins and purify all things. Lead not his soul to Ruin, but to everlasting peace.*"

Chaka appeared uncomfortable as the body of the headless fighter began glowing dimly in pale violet light. He clenched his teeth and took a step back as the soul of the fighter left the top of his removed head and floated up near Chaka.

Chaka stiffened as the spirit withdrew his phantom blade and made a swipe at him before vanishing into particles of white light.

Jurou held out a hand to Chaka. "Do you wish to come inside?" he asked. "You'll catch an illness if you stay here any longer!"

Chaka's gray eyes grew blank in his head and he looked far into the middle distance. "No, I enjoy the rain," he answered mechanically. "The lightning… it empowers me."

Jurou sighed in defeat. "Well, if you wish..." He turned on his heel.

"Saku?"

Jurou paused in step. "Yes?"

"If I ever desire a warm and dry bed, is it all right if I sleep in yours?"

"As long as my door is open."

"Is that a promise?"

"I promise." Jurou turned and touched Chaka by the arm. Chaka made no movement to acknowledge him. "Are you sure you don't want to come inside?"

"I am sure."

Jurou left Chaka's side and cringed when he heard haunting laughter at his back. Thunder crashed louder around them and he took off indoors, escaping the worsening storm.

THIRTY-ONE

Moon 10 – 2nd Day

Chaka opened his eyes, finding himself in his bed without clothing. He sat up, rubbing his eyes and squinted from the dim rays of early morning sunshine filtering through his window.

Getting to his feet, Chaka stumbled over a cold object and looked down, finding an intricately carved saber at his feet that had a gilded hilt, bound leather and cloth handle with lavender feathers protruding from the end.

"Where did this come from?" he wondered, picking it up. Chaka suddenly grew nauseated at the encrusted blood staining the handle and the edge of the dimly glowing blade. *"These stains are fresh; someone must have died last night and I was there again!"* He dropped the saber to the floor with a clang. *"Am I walking in my sleep and slaying these people?"*

Stomping for his washroom, Chaka stood in the stall and pulled the chain, clenching his teeth as the cold water he expected to gush from the shower head turned scalding hot. Chaka ran his hands through his hair and ground his teeth when he noticed old blood washing down the drain.

"Chaka?" a familiar voice called from his room.

"I'm washing," he called back. "Come later."

"I'll wait."

"*Why would Saku wait for me?*" Chaka mused and finished scrubbing at his body.

After washing his hair, he pulled the chain and stepped out. Grabbing for a nearby towel that hung on the rack, Chaka wrapped it around his waist then approached the sink and glared at his pale reflection as he squeezed out the excess water from his hair, despising what he saw staring back at him.

"You devil," he snarled. "How I hate you..."

"*Until you let your hatred manifest,*" Tannozume grumbled, "*I believe nothing that leaves your face!*"

Turning away, Chaka padded into his bedroom and spotted Jurou sitting on the edge of his futon with his legs crossed. He rested his elbow on his knee, holding his chin in his free hand.

"Saku," Chaka exclaimed, "what a surprise to find you here!" The younger man looked up, smiling faintly. "Do you need anything?"

"Ah..." Jurou straightened up and uncrossed his legs as he rested his hands on his knees, blushing. "I came for my jacket..."

"Oh, it's yours then, eh?" Chaka grinned. "I hoped for a pretty girl coming by to claim it." Jurou suddenly laughed. "What is it?" Chaka complained as he gripped the towel tighter around his waist.

"What woman you know wears a marine jacket like that," Jurou crowed, "especially with the name 'Shinjin' written across the back?" Chaka said nothing, running a hand through his wet tresses and Jurou held a hand to his mouth. "Are you disturbed?" he said softly. "I'm sorry; I didn't mean to offend you... I just thought what you said was comical."

"No, no, it's not that," Chaka murmured. "Shinjin, eh?" He sighed. "I just..." Chaka unexpectedly smiled brightly at Jurou. "So, aside from that, what else have you come for?"

"Classes were canceled again today," Jurou answered tentatively. "Another body was found on campus and now there's a full investigation."

"Are the *machikata* involved?"

"The *onmyoji* are looking into it first, to see if has any supernatural origin."

"How serious..." Chaka left Jurou's side and approached his chest, searching for clothing.

"Where did you get that ugly scar on your back?" Jurou asked.

"From the war, Saku."

"The others too?"

"What kind of question is that?" Dropping the towel, Chaka took out a pair of slim-fitting trousers and pulled into it.

"I wonder why the *akuma* are so set on destroying our world," Jurou murmured as Chaka withdrew a blue outer jacket with white cranes as the running pattern and slipped it over his broad shoulders then tied it shut around his slender waist. "I don't understand how they're escaping if the gates were closed for a thousand cycles!"

"Because the stars are shifting alignment," Chaka interjected. "There needs to be a new sealant on the *Akuma Nomon*."

"I don't know of any *onmyoji* strong enough to travel to each island and close each one."

"I'm sure all the best senior *Ichizoku Eiyu* will be vying for that position."

"Are you?"

"Me?" Chaka laughed and waved Jurou away. "Don't insult me; I'm the worst there is."

Jurou gave Chaka a quizzical look. "I thought..."

"No, I'm not, otherwise I wouldn't have the condition I have now, eh?" Chaka turned to Jurou who lay back in his bed with his hands on his chest, staring up at the ceiling. "What of you?"

"*Senshuken*," Jurou answered. "However, I don't feel deserving of that title."

"Oh?"

"My skills weren't good enough to save them..."

"Avenge their deaths by trying harder!" Chaka said cheerfully. "No need to be burdened with guilt. Turn that into strength!"

Jurou scoffed and sat up on his elbows. "Maybe you ought to take your own advice!" he spat.

"In which House do you hail?" Chaka probed.

"A very minor one," Jurou replied cryptically and lay back once more. "Don't try changing the conversation."

"I don't understand why they do the things they do," Chaka admitted. "However, those fiends don't need reason - they just act upon it. It is a primal urge, something that cannot be rid of easily." He approached the futon, looking over Jurou. "It must be fed or their souls are forever trapped wanting." Chaka nudged Jurou with his foot. "Do you understand what I am saying, Saku?"

"I guess."

"Let us go to Kakita for practice; I can help you with your forms."

Jurou sat up on his elbows, raising an eyebrow at Chaka. "Didn't you just hear me?" he snapped. "Classes are closed today."

"Then let us practice nonetheless." Chaka grinned devilishly. "We can use some equipment that is normally off-limits!"

"Don't cause trouble here!"

"Oh, did you not hear?" Chaka jumped on the bed and Jurou let out a cry as the older man stood over him. "I caused so much trouble for the Asahina-ryu that they expelled me."

"How horrible!"

"Oh, I passed the exam in the case you are wondering," Chaka declared. "I have mastered all styles..."

"I've only mastered one!"

"What is that?" Chaka stepped off the bed and headed for the door. "Show me."

"Are you serious?"

"Grab the blades I asked you to keep for me."

Jurou slipped off the futon and hurried out the room, rushing downstairs. "*What is the meaning of his mood this time?*" he thought as he knocked on Baiuko's door.

The door opened moments later, revealing Baiuko in a beige bathrobe with pink clover flowers as the running pattern. "What's wrong?" she asked.

Jurou pushed his way indoors and headed for her closet. "Chaka asked me to duel him," he said as he flung open the door and pulled out the black and gold swords.

"What for?" Baiuko said incredulously.

"I'm not certain, but I know for sure that fiend inside probably wants to test me."

"Please get rid of it."

"I'll try my best." Jurou exited her room and found Chaka standing near the boardinghouse exit. "What are you thinking about?" he called.

"Eh?" Chaka turned to Jurou and smiled faintly then waved at him to follow.

Pushing the doors open wide, Chaka stomped off on grounds, heading across the way for the academy. Jurou huffed and tied on both swords, then hurried after Chaka, following closely behind.

Chaka entered the training hall and made a direct line for the weapons rack in the rear. Jurou approached the sparring ring once the older man returned with a heavy spear. His gray eyes were blank and Jurou withdrew the weighty golden long sword.

"Let me use a weapon I'm more familiar with," Jurou protested. "The *tsurugi* is more suitable for you because of your strong arms!"

"You need to cross-train," Chaka snapped. "Now, attack me!" He rushed forward with a driving thrust and Jurou jumped over the attack, quickly dodging and sidestepping the blows. Eventually tiring out from swinging forcefully at air, Chaka leaned against the lance, panting hard while Jurou stood across from him against the sparring ring's ropes, heaving for breath. "Fight me back!" Chaka shouted.

"Not when you're like that!" Jurou snapped.

"Then I will have to hurt you." Chaka withdrew his spear and held it at ready. "Here is a tip: I cannot strike what does not lie still."

Jurou backed away and put up his guard as Chaka let out a war cry and advanced, slashing the lance. Chaka broke through Jurou's counterattack and Jurou jumped aside, blocking the next strike. Cold sweat beaded on Jurou's forehead and neck when the spearhead barely missed piercing his face in return.

Pulling back, Jurou scrambled to his feet, diving out the way when the spear came down again. Chaka thrust forward the blade, locking the edge of the lance against Jurou's sword and struggled against him, straining to bring his weapon down with all his might.

Jurou pulled back, causing Chaka stumbling forward. Turning, Jurou slashed back, cutting into Chaka's side when the older man failed to block. Chaka grunted and slammed the spear into the floor as he fell to his knees, wheezing in agony.

"Well done," Ikaruga's voice called. Chaka relent his stance, quickly rising to his feet and yanked up the lance. He placed it over his shoulder and turned away from Jurou as the swordsman approached the ring. Jurou leaned against the ropes, gasping weakly. "But you had many chances to defeat him!" Ikaruga pointed a thumb in Chaka's direction. "It is true that he cannot strike what moves." Ikaruga then pointed his thumb Jurou's way. "You need to face your target, foolish boy!

If you do not survey what comes, then you are merely asking to die!"

"Will it matter?" Jurou snapped.

"It does for honor!" Ikaruga responded.

"You honor-bound fool!" Jurou roared, growing irate. "Is that all there is?" Ikaruga growled and Jurou held up the golden long sword. "Come at me if you think I'm wrong!" he bellowed. "You can't do it!"

"The next time we meet," Ikaruga snarled.

"Why are you here?"

"You two shouldn't be here." Ikaruga stormed for the rear courts. "You two had better be gone when I return!" he called over his shoulder.

Jurou let out an exasperated sigh and lowered the tsurugi, then sheathed it back into its harness.

"Honor, eh?" Chaka muttered. "I'm afraid I'm all out of that..." He groaned and dropped his spear with a loud clatter.

Jurou glanced over at Chaka, noticing he clutched his left arm. "What's with you, Chaka?" he queried. Chaka said nothing and exited the ring, heading for the lavatory. Jurou jumped over the ropes, following at his heels. Opening the lavatory door, he found Chaka washing down his left arm furiously. "Chaka!" Chaka's upper body became tense and he let out a cry, gripping the face bowl with both hands as he struggled to breathe. "Chaka..." Jurou entered and approached from behind, placing a gentle a hand against Chaka's back. "Chaka, please tell me what's wrong," he pleaded. "Are you ill?"

Jurou withdrew when Chaka suddenly straightened his stance, clenching his hands at is side.

"If you heal me," Chaka snarled, "I will kill you."

"You honestly don't mean that!"

"I mean it!"

"Face me and say it!"

Chaka turned to Jurou and he tilted his head, smiling broadly. Jurou swallowed hard and stepped away when he noticed that his blank eyes changed color, turning blue-gray.

"I will tear you limb from limb," Chaka said darkly. "Your soft flesh between my fingers will be like--!"

Jurou backed out the door, bumping into Kaminaritou Rouru.

"Ho, why are you pale?" Kaminaritou Rouru asked when Jurou whirled around. "You are not ill are you?" He put up his hands. "Stand away, for you are not getting sick on my shoes!"

"I'm fine!" Jurou protested. "I'm just worried about Chaka; he doesn't seem altogether well."

"Then ask him if he is." Kaminaritou Rouru pushed Jurou aside. "Please do not block the door. I've come to seek relief!" He entered the restrooms and Jurou waited several moments before opening the doors again, finding Chaka leaning against the sink, his arms folded across his body.

"Do you need something, Saku?" Chaka asked, gazing at him.

"Not really..." Jurou answered.

Chaka stared off into the middle distance, making no reaction when a commode flushed and Kaminaritou Rouru exited a stall.

Approaching a sink, Kaminaritou Rouru washed his hands and glanced at Chaka. "I have you know," he said coolly, "that Shinjukaigan is hosting the annual skill contests."

"So?" Chaka snapped. "Is that the reason you came searching for me?" He scoffed. "Otherwise, there is no reason for you to be here."

"The same applies to you."

"I won't accommodate you."

"If you wish to place first for a change..."

"You do it for honor," Chaka replied icily. "I have my own reasons for participating."

"Heh!" Kaminaritou Rouru shut off the tap and shook his hands. "Then show me your reason."

"Not likely, you barbarian."

"Tch." Kaminaritou Rouru left the lavatory, pushing past Jurou.

Jurou walked in. "Why not enter those contests?" he asked. "If you're so skilled as you were from the army, then you could easily open your own *dojo* or if you're really exceptional, teach at an Imperial academy!"

"That was my father's dream," Chaka grumbled. "I have no part of that."

"Then why did you learn all those arts in such a short amount of time?" Chaka turned his gaze to Jurou. "Did you have something to prove?"

"Do you think you can enter those contests?" Chaka insisted.

"What makes you think I have that kind of skill?" Jurou shrugged his shoulders. "If you feel I can then I feel I can."

"Do you think you can best the likes of Kaminaritou Rouru in a contest of skill?"

"Not anyone like him!" Jurou held up his hands. "He's ruthless; he'd slaughter me with his eyes closed!"

"What about me?" Chaka gave a wry smile. "Can you defeat me in combat?"

"You're very strong..." Jurou laughed nervously. "All I have is speed."

"It took me many seasons of hard training to get like this," Chaka admitted. "I wasn't always like this..."

Jurou let out a short laugh. "I don't believe you," he exclaimed. Chaka's cheeks flushed scarlet and he turned away, facing the mirror. Jurou gasped, putting a hand over his mouth. "You're serious!"

"Perfection is unattainable," Chaka said evenly. "We can never be perfect. No matter how hard we strive for it..."

"But isn't that the goal?" Jurou argued. "Isn't that the whole point of living, dying, and trying again until we can free ourselves from that endless course?"

"Look at me," Chaka snarled. Jurou laughed nervously, running his hand through his hair. "No, look!" Jurou clenched his teeth when Chaka leaned over the sink, clenching his fists and his forehead touched the tiled wall. "This is what happens when you try to be taintless. You'll only get corrupted."

Jurou ran a nervous hand through his hair again. "How can you live with yourself, knowing that?" Chaka said nothing. "Well, I'm seeing Nakiko." Jurou left the lavatory, heading back for the boardinghouse.

Growing frustrated at Jurou's words, Chaka gripped his head, unable to get the echo out of his mind.

"Hush up!" he screamed and struck the mirror with a swift punch, shattering it on contact. "Look at you," Chaka said to his pale fractured reflection in the remainder of the glass. "How can you continue living like this?"

Jurou crossed the courtyards and spotted Nakiko coming up the path in her training uniform. He greeted her as she waved to him.

"How are you?" Nakiko called. "Are you feeling well today?"

"Have you heard about the skill contests on Shinjukaigan?" Jurou inquired.

"That's news to me!"

"It seems Chaka's entered many times before, also Kaminaritou Rouru."

"I'll look into it." Nakiko walked toward the path leading to the school and Jurou grabbed her gently by the arm. "What is it?"

"Classes are canceled today."

"Oh?"

"Another mysterious death."

"I see..." Nakiko blew a hard sigh and put her hands on her hips. "Well, who will be my sparring partner today?"

"I guess I can."

Nakiko grinned. "Are you ready to vomit out your guts?"

Jurou put up his hands. "No!" he cried.

"Then how are you going into the Imperial Army next cycle? They train harder than I do!"

"Kairyushin, have mercy!"

"Take all you can get," Nakiko crowed, "because the enemy surely won't show you any!"

Jurou let out a terrified yelp when Nakiko lurched after him. He jumped out of her reach and she laughed.

"You're going to kill me!" Jurou wailed.

"If I do, I'll just have you resurrected so I can beat on you some more!"

Jurou took off running and Nakiko giggled, chasing after him in the courtyards.

THIRTY-TWO

Chaka left the lavatory, catching sight of Jurou sparring against Nakiko in the empty room near the foyer. Nakiko glanced Chaka's way, getting struck from an errant blow.

"Oh!" Jurou yelped in surprise, turning to see her line of sight.

Chaka put up his hands. "I hope I haven't distracted you, Saku," he said mildly.

"We're just having a friendly bout," Nakiko replied. "I don't have time for you today."

Chaka grinned darkly. "Oh, afraid to lose to my might, eh?" he teased. "Let's have a go at it!"

Chaka crossed the floor and Nakiko tensed, putting up her hands in guard. Jurou immediately stood before Nakiko, blocking Chaka's path. "Check yourself, please," he pleaded apprehensively. "Tomorrow Kakita is closed for cleaning, so do you still want to practice with me?"

"I'm busy tomorrow, Jurou," Nakiko answered, glaring at Chaka. "You'll have to find someone else."

"I will still practice with you, Saku," Chaka answered mechanically as he tensed and clenched his hands at his sides.

Nakiko blew a hard sigh and turned on her heel to walk away. Chaka grabbed her by the arm and she immediately socked him in the chest in return. Chaka staggered back, stunned and Nakiko recoiled from pressure.

"Don't tell me that's your best!" Chaka retorted.

"You won't be standing for long," Nakiko snarled, narrowing her eyes. "You disgusting monster!"

"You're not the most powerful *sentouki* I've ever faced," Chaka spat. "You'll never match my strength!"

"You will stand before me and tremble!"

"I'm sure you'll enjoy that," Chaka replied. "But that day will never come." He chuckled as Nakiko's face reddened in rage and then left for the rear exit, kicking in the door.

"Wait!" Jurou called after Chaka and ran to catch up.

Chaka stepped onto the outdoor court and sat on the tiles, letting his long legs stick out as blew a heavy sigh and leaned back, resting his head against the stone exterior wall.

"This is exhausting," he murmured and Jurou exited moments later, standing offside near him.

"Chaka," Jurou said gently, "are you all right?"

"Does it matter to you whether or not I am ill?" Chaka grumbled.

"Yes, it does." Jurou perched before Chaka, mildly concerned. "I care very much."

"Stop, for I don't need your care." Chaka waved him away. "You just wish to kill me as well."

"If it's about the devil slayer ability..." Jurou smiled weakly. "I'm actually quite bad at it."

"I am not assured."

"You're the only friend I have," Jurou pleaded.

"I just met you, Saku."

"It's better to have friends, isn't it?"

"Well, it is better than enemies."

"So, will you be my friend?"

Chaka snorted. "You have Nakiko," he persisted. "She is friendly to you."

"Only when sparring," Jurou retorted and rolled his eyes. "I think you're willing to listen to me. You won't chide me when I say foolish things, will you?"

"You hadn't said anything foolish yet." Chaka glanced up at Jurou. "I make terrible friendly material, Saku," he said seriously. "Go and find someone your age. I am much too old for you."

"There is no one here..."

"Kaminaritou Rouru and Baiuko are about your age. Go talk with them."

"I'm not interested in the same things that they are." Jurou shook his head. "They have a history and I'd be nothing more than an outsider."

Chaka lowered his head and folded his arms across his chest, pouting. "Why me, Saku," he complained. "Why me, of all the people you know?"

"I find you interesting; is that so bad?"

Chaka glanced up, startled. "You find me interesting?"

"Yes, I find genuine interest in you."

"So you are not out to kill me?"

Jurou rolled his eyes skyward before setting his sights on Chaka and smiled gently. "What makes you think I have a chance of killing you?" he said brightly. "You're much more skilled and stronger than I am; it'll take seasons before I catch up to you!"

"You have speed, remember?" Chaka said grimly. "There is no way I can stop that; I'm much too slow on the field of battle."

"Then let's spar and share techniques." Jurou put out a hand. "You teach me how to become strong in body and use many weapons in which you're skilled and I'll teach you how to become fast. Is that a deal?"

"I don't hate you," Chaka said calmly. He reluctantly put out a hand.

Jurou grasped it and pumped firmly. "Good," he said happily. "This warms my heart."

"Would you be upset that you may be hated for dealing with the likes of me?"

"Why should I care?" Jurou let go and rose to his feet. "Have you thought about entering the Silver Conference on Shinjukaigan?"

Chaka grunted. "I've no intention of speaking to Master Ishida about it," he grumbled.

"Then will you train me so I can enter this cycle? You know the Imperial Army selects the winners of the contests as junior officers." Jurou let out a weak laugh. "With my skill, I'd probably lose right away and get stuck as *ashigaru*!"

"You'd be resorted to looting your armor and weaponry on the field of battle; that is if you don't die first, lowly foot soldier." Chaka chortled. "All right then, I'll help you train, but it is only because you asked me nicely."

"I'll stop by your room tomorrow!" Jurou waved off Chaka and left the courtyard in brighter spirits.

Chaka moaned and leaned back as he shut his eyes. "Lord Shinkunikkou," he murmured, "I know you are watching with your all-seeing eye. You know what he is getting himself into and you know I do not have the will to stop it." He blew a disconcerted sigh. "Please, strike me down right now!"

When he received no answer, Chaka groaned and opened his eyes then slowly rose upright. He pulled out of the sleeves of his overcoat, tucking them about his waist and shuffled over to weapons rack.

Withdrawing a long bow and several arrows, Chaka sensed a presence behind him and turned, finding a pale-skinned middle-aged fighter with square jaw, deep blue-green eyes, shoulder-length shaggy silver hair and a thin mustache standing across from him.

The man wore a lacquered blood-red breastplate with black and gold ties, vermilion bracers with golden spiked gauntlets that had four tapered talons curving forward from the wrists. On his lower body, he wore crimson and black plate thigh protectors, shin guards, and armored boots. Harnessed about his waist he wore a double-edged katana in a vermilion scabbard. A stiff breeze blew against them, scattering granules of sand around them.

"How much longer are you going to stay, Tannozume?" Chaka spat.

"*I control you,*" sneered the devil, "*never forget!*"

"After you complete your objective," Chaka retorted, "will you release me then?" When the demon said nothing, he swallowed hard and loaded his bow. "Then what of Akanasutsune and Shiranosuke?"

The armored knight narrowed his soulless marine eyes and bared his teeth. "*Are you calling me weak?*" Tannozume shrilled.

Chaka grunted when fierce pain burned intensely in his left arm. "I never said that at all!" he protested.

"*I shall show you weakness!*" Chaka released his arrow and the devil withdrew his blade, swiftly knocking away the projectiles. Rushing forward, Tannozume cut through Chaka's weak block, slicing the bow in half and stabbed Chaka in the guts. Chaka hacked up blood as his senses snapped and his world thrust into hazy shades of red and gray. "*They now have a new assignment, since you keep resisting my orders...*" Tannozume released his hold and Chaka dropped to his knees, gripping his profusely bleeding side.

"Why are you targeting him?" he moaned. "Whatever has he done to you?"

"*He has the power to destroy us...*"

"Of course he does; he's trained in the very same skills I have!"

"*Or rather, you used to have!*" Tannozume chortled. "*You refused to do your part and I realize I cannot trust you at all!*"

"No, please, I beg of you!" Chaka cried as the demon raised his blade.

"*I dare you to keep resisting!*" Chaka sprang to his feet, shoving Tannozume aside and sidestepped the savage blow aimed for his head. "*The kamisama will never hear your cry!*" the red-armored fiend shouted. "*You are so far away that you are nothing more than a meaningless leaf in the wind!*"

Chaka stepped under Tannozume's attack and threw a punch with a charged hand, instantly breaking it when he clipped the demon's jaw. "You got what you wanted!" Chaka screamed. "Let me go!"

The fiend in red lamellar laughed darkly, pushing Chaka aside. "*I own you forever, or have you forgotten?*" he snarled. "*For the rest of your days, your body, your soul, your mind belongs to me!*" Tannozume's eyes flashed in cold emerald light. "*I shall use you however I see fit! Also, if you refuse and fight me, know this: this is a battle you will not win!*"

"I will fight you to my very last breath," Chaka hissed. "I *will* destroy you!"

"*We'll see, false Slayer!*"

Devilish laughter filled Chaka's mind as the crimson knight vanished into mist. Chaka grit his teeth, trying to absorb the pain as he doubled over. "I will stop you!" he seethed. "Mark my words!"

"I don't see how you two can stand this uncomfortable humidity!" a familiar voice complained.

Chaka looked up as the rear gate opened and Sanzuki entered with Ikaruga and a tall slender man with long white hair, armed with a wakizashi constructed of shiny crystalline steel harnessed about his waist. The man wore a black cloak over an indigo kimono, a breastplate of bone and silver chain and calf-high leather boots.

"There he is, Master," Sanzuki announced.

"Who are you?" Chaka demanded, straightening his stance. "Have you come to kill me as well?"

"I am Ujiie Montaro," answered the mysterious man, "and the time isn't right to kill you yet, *Kenshi*."

"What?" Chaka clenched his right hand that glimmered dimly in golden light and the swordsman put a hand to the hilt of his blade.

"Don't think of attacking unless you don't mind losing your head."

"He's obviously stronger than me," Chaka mused. *"His mere presence silenced Tannozume!"* He drew a shallow breath. "Why are you here?" Chaka asked tentatively.

"My servants alerted me about three *Takiletzachi* blades possessed by you," Montaro answered. "I came for them."

"You can't have them yet."

"What reason would that be?"

"I know of mystic alignments that have begun to become disturbed and I'm trying to prevent a horrible cosmic event."

"You alone cannot stop *Majin Tensei*!"

"And you think you can?" Chaka stepped forward and threw a charged punch at Montaro who blocked with the flat of his sword, but made no effort to strike back. "Get out of here, old man!"

"You shall atone for your sins with your blood!" Montaro snarled.

"To Hell with you!"

Chaka grabbed for Montaro's arm, only to get shoved back with a palm strike against his chest, hurtling him head over heels. Rolling to his feet, Chaka stood as Montaro immediately vanished in a flash of white light. Chaka staggered back when he received a cut to the side and slipped to his knees as

Montaro reappeared behind him instantly, grabbing him by his hair and yanking violently back.

"Listen carefully," sneered the sorcerer, glaring down with glowing yellow eyes. "This is only a warning!" Montaro threw Chaka aside and stormed away, vanishing into dark mist.

"You can't order me to back down!" Chaka shouted. "This isn't the last of me!"

"Shut your face before I take out your tongue!" Ikaruga retorted.

"Have you forgotten the beating I gave you the last time?" Sanzuki replied smugly. "You're weak without that devil to aid you, *Satsugaisha!*"

"Why are you pestering me?" Chaka snarled and scrambled to his feet. "Must I remind you how foolish you are in combating me again?"

"I am making sure all corrupt devils return to where they belong and you do not belong here!"

"Silence," Chaka thundered and stepped forward as golden flames erupted from his hands, traveling up his arms. "Say no more!"

"*You're fighting a battle you cannot win!*" Tannozume screeched. "*My true power is not measured by raw energy!*"

"You have no power to defeat me!" Sanzuki said darkly. "That's why you hide behind that *akutenshi!*"

"*How dare you think your petty <u>majutsu</u> can harm me - try your <u>genjutsu</u> once and you shall suffer my devastating effects!*"

"Return to *Makai* where you belong!"

"*You first!*"

Both Sanzuki and Ikaruga advanced and Chaka thrust forward his charged hands.

"*Raida Shinden!*" Chaka called and a volt of violet lightning burst forth. The two demon servants instantly vanished in a flash of dark smoke.

"*Weakling!*" Tannozume spat. "*What a waste of my time!*"

Overwhelmed and exhausted, Chaka clutched his sides as he collapsed forward on his knees and fell face down into the stone. "I don't know how much longer I can endure this," he moaned. "The pain is unbearable!"

"*Are you doubting my strength?*" Tannozume growled. Chaka cried out when fierce agonizing irritation clouded his mind and a low drone buzzed in his ears. He gripped his head, struggling to see as the demon pushed his way through. "*Let me show you and erase those doubts from your mind!*"

Too weak to fight back, Chaka lost consciousness.

CONTINUED IN

VOLUME 2

(contains chapters 33-70)

CONTINUED IN VOLUME TWO:

DEMONIC AWAKENING

When the very forces Chaka Isawa trained to destroy slowly consume him, the master swordsman cuts a path of destruction, leaving behind corpses wherever he happens to be.

Controlling such fearsome power tests the strength of the warrior monk Jurou Seiki, who is under orders to kill the man known simply as 'The Beast'. His task, to destroy the sinister force influencing Chaka proves difficult, as his life is under threat as well!

Cast of Characters

MAIN CHARACTERS
(names are given name/family name format)

Chaka Isawa – an accomplished *kengo* (master swordsman) and skilled with the *yari* (spear) and *kusari* (chain); he has mastered 6 fighting styles in 7 years. Chaka is also known as the 'Beast of the Blood Coast' after becoming *fukutaichou* (lieutenant) in a short a mount of time in the Imperial Army and defeating several master swordsmen at various schools.

Jurou Seiki – After his parents were killed by demons, Jurou gets sent by his uncle to train at a different martial school and improve his skills at being *souhei* (warrior monk). He meets Chaka there and takes the task to exorcise his demons.

Nakiko Miyabi - a fierce *kenshi* (fencer) from Kaori in Beidounei Gokaku and formerly of the Imperial Army's Elite Forces (Special Forces division); Aspiring to master the *Shichi Nanatsu* (Quality Seven) she has trained in 5 fighting styles over 10 years and knows of devil slaying. Very little else is known about her and it is unknown if she's able to use enchanted weaponry or has any Slayer abilities.

MINOR CHARACTERS

Kaminaritou Rouru – a *mahoubujin* (warrior mystic) and fellow student at the Kakita Martial Academy's Southern Division, also friends with Baiuko; he is skilled in spear fighting, archery, and horseback riding.

Baiuko Kaemon – a fellow student at the Kakita Martial Academy's Southern Division; fights with two swords, *Soutou* style (one sword used for offense, other defense). She has the ability to see a person's true nature by touching them.

Ittou Toma – a member of the cavalry, called *Usegi* (rabbit) by his peers in the army because of his speed.

Tokiko Asano – a female cavalier and ghost slayer from Kobarutoshi, called *Tora* (tiger) by her peers in the army because of her headstrong nature and fierceness.

DEMONS

Tannozume – a swordfighter skilled with the *katana* and *kusari*, wears crimson lamellar armor; currently in possession of Chaka's body. Aligned with Fire Element.

Shiranosuke – a lancer skilled with the *naginata* and *nagamaki*, wears azure scale armor; currently in possession of Chaka's body. Aligned with Water Element.

Akanasutsune – an archer skilled with the *daikyu* (great longbow), wears verdant chain armor; currently in possession of Chaka's body. Aligned with Wind Element.

Ikaruga – a *tanuki* (raccoon dog) skilled with the *katana*, also an assistant teacher at the Kakita Martial Academy's Southern Division.

Sanzuki – an illusionist and master of Ikaruga; controls a jade-handled magic *daikatana* (field sword) that shifts elements.

OTHER CHARACTERS

Atsuji Massai - a retired *onmyouji* (exorcist) from Matsumura of Izumimori Temple. Skilled in *renkinjutsu* (alchemy) and fights with a *naginata*.

Taiji Yoshiru - Atsu's 'wife', a skilled sword dancer from Seibushima. Skilled with *chisagatana* and *gunsen* (heavy war fan).

Hashira - a tactless *souryo* (monk) of Shiromatsu Temple, knowledgeable in Midorishima lore.

Montaro Ujiie – a skilled *mahoutsukai* (sorcerer) and devil summoner, also knowledgeable about battle magic.

Denzo Ishida– a skilled *kenkyaku* (master swordsman) who instructs at Kakita Martial Academy's Southern Division. Mainly delegates teaching to his assistants.

The terms used in the *Devil Hunter Isawa* universe
(based on the Japanese language):

Ada-uchi – 'to track down and kill one's enemy'; an act of
private vengeance (such as to avenge the death of a family,
clan member, or master), similar to duels of honor. Such
revenge was legally acceptable under two conditions: 1) one
performed the vengeance in the prefecture where it took
place (because each prefecture was controlled by a different
daimyo, so this was rather like fleeing across state lines) and
2) one informed the authorities in advance of carrying out
the vengeance, if approved by the *bugyojo* and registered
with the *hantei-jo*.

Agari-zashiki - a special cell for imprisoning high-ranked
soldiers.

Akuma – a type of devil, usually male, who devours human
spirits. Their enemies are *shisai* (priests), *souryo* (monks),
and other exorcists trained to banish them. Those who
specifically hunt them are called *akumatokko* (devil slayers).

Akutenshi - 'shadow fairy'; corrupted chaotic guardian
spirits, opposite *shugotenshi*.

Amahagane – 'star crystal'; mystical shards from the
shattered Star Hammer of Shukenten, the god of smithery.
These stones give the owner a god-like power called *kamui*
and tend to glow in violet light.

Ashigaru – 'light feet'; Peasant troops recruited into a *daimyo's* service, lower ranked infantry. An *ashigaru* was normally a peasant who worked in his home village when not on his lord's campaigns and often fought with little or no armor, footwear or weaponry until they could be looted from the enemy. Sometimes armed with only a breastplate, helmet and short sword if the *daimyo* was wealthy enough to provide basic armaments.

Ataushinai Okyoda – 'smite'; Chaka's *reiken* skill used to rend limbs or behead easily with a single stroke.

Banshi - 'duty officer'; low-ranking police officials who manned checkpoints along the major byways.

Bantaro – night watchman, town gatekeeper.

Bokuto (also Bokken) – a hard wooden sword used for training, usually the size and shape of a *katana* (long sword), but sometimes shaped like other swords, such as the *wakizashi* (short sword) and *tanto* (dagger); differs from **shinai**, a sword made of flexible bamboo used for practice and competition in *Kendo,* representing a *katana.* Also differs from a **suburito**, a thick heavy *bokken* used for cutting exercises.

Bugyo - a position combining the functions of mayor and town police chief. The *bugyo* was in charge of administration, maintaining the peace, and enforcing the law.

Bugyojo – police precinct station; the *bugyo* was a high-ranked samurai charged with keeping the peace with the help of others under his command and volunteer posse members.

Busshitsukai - the material world.

Chijiriki - a heavy spear with a length of chain attached on the end, used to harpoon sea creatures such as whales. Also effective as a weapon in skilled hands.

Chimei – 'deathblow'; Sanzuki's *reiatsu* skill, a super stabbity/slicer-dicer technique. If done incorrectly, he could break his blade!

Chinokaigan - 'Blood Coast'; an area of Minamijima in the territory of House Suzaku, House Suzume, House Kuren and House Tonbou. So named after the bloody battle during the time of the closure of the gates, many soldiers lost their lives to the demonic forces there.

Chisagatana - a protosword, longer than a *wakizashi* yet shorter than a *katana*. Can be used with one or two hands.

Chonin – 'townsman'; a social class consisting of mainly merchants, craftsmen and other artisans. In times of unrest, they hire the protective services of *otokodate*.

Daigo (also Daigo-tettei) – 'great realization'; the final absolute enlightenment. Contrasting to the initial glimpse, or *kensho*, *daigo* is attained when one has risen above the discrimination between delusion and enlightenment.

Daimyo – lords or barons of provincial feudal domains known as Han. Ones of lesser prestige are known as *Shomyo*.

Daisho – 'the long and short'; the samurai's *katana* and *wakizashi*.

Dojo – a hall for martial arts training, also a training center for swordsmanship.

Enma - the god of judgment in Hell, lording over 7 officers who guard the 7 levels. In the *Devil Hunter Isawa* universe, he is called *Akuma Jougi* (Devil King).

Fukutaichou – 'lieutenant'; a rank in the Imperial Army, under *Taichou* (Captain) and over *Gunsou* (Sergeant).

Funshi – committing suicide stemming from hatred.

Ganbare - 'press on!' or 'hang in there!'

Genjutsu – 'sorcery', 'illusion'; the use of applied *mahou* (magic).

Gensho Satsu – 'extreme heat diminisher'; Tannozume's *reiatsu* skill, used to drain *ki* of the opponent and transfer power to increase his own.

Goshi – 'country samurai', 'samurai of the land', 'samurai of the soil'; low-ranking *samurai* who lived in the countryside, also farmers who were formerly landed gentry. Also known as *jizamurai*.

Gunsou – 'sergeant'; a rank in the Imperial Army, under *Fukutaichou* (Lieutenant).

Hageshii Arashi – 'fiery storm'; Chaka's *meisou* skill under the Fire element, used to drive back and burn the opponent with a burst of flame.

Hakukishinoheiya - 'Plains of the Ivory Shore'; the rugged hillsides that surround near Chinokaigan (Crimson Coast).

Hamadashi - dagger with a small guard, relative to *tanto* (dagger with a large guard).

Hanshaga Shokan – 'reflection summon'; Chaka's *meisou* skill under the Thunder element, used to reflect or negate attacks from enchanted weaponry.

Hantei-jo – an official ruling of the court.

Heishi - soldier

Hissatsu Hajiki- 'deadly play'; Kuwanai's *reiken* skill that can cut through any material (flesh, metal, stone) with a single stoke.

Hitokiri– 'man slayer', 'assassin', 'murderer'; a black *uchigatana* (lightweight one-handed long sword) with bronze accents and hilt shaped into a crane, also comes with an ornate brown and gold scabbard. Originally belonged to Chaka Isawa who gained it after earning the rank of Lieutenant in the Imperial Army.

Hogosha - 'guardian', 'protector', 'patron'; used in reference to one's patron deity.

Hoshinokawa – 'River of Stars'; one of two main rivers on Okinashima that wind through its mountainous terrain. Bits of *Amahagane* from Kounnoyama are commonly found in the water.

Hyakusho - farmer, villager, cultivator, also *Nomin*.

Ichizoku Eiyu - 'clan champion'; A master fighter skilled in various forms of combat and sorcery, able to use both *Takiletzachi* and *Amahagane* armaments. Higher ranked than *Senshuken*.

Inazuma Kougeki - 'lightning attack'; Kuwanai's *reiken* skill that can pierce through any material (flesh, metal, stone) without shattering the blade.

Inshotekina Sutoraiki - 'impressive strike'; Chaka's *reiken* skill used to shatter armaments or equipment with a single blow.

Itterasshai – 'please go and come back', 'have a good time', 'see you later'; said when sending someone off from the home or some other place where they will be returning to at a later time. Often said together with *Kiotsukete* (take care).

Ja mata - 'see you!' or 'laters!'; an informal parting (see *Itterasshai*).

Jigoku – 'hell'; one of seven levels of the underworld lorded over by *Enma*, the god of judgment. After a soul works off their sins, they reincarnate.

Jintachi - long katana with a blade about 27 to 32 inches in length.

Jisatsu – suicide.

Jutte - a blunt hooked truncheon from 12 to 24 inches in length used by police officers; also used as a badge and represented someone on official business. All law officers carried one. The jutte was used to strike into weak parts of the body or large muscle groups, press into pressure points, or hook onto parts of clothing to easily aid in diffusing opponents.

Kagesureiyo – 'shadow slayer'; a golden *tachi* (field sword) with an ivory handle shaped into a dragon's head with a pair of star rubies embedded in the hilt. Originally belonged to Chaka Isawa who earned it after becoming Clan Champion for House Suzume.

Kaiken - a long, straight-edged double-bladed dagger used in self defense.

Kairyushin – 'great sea dragon'; Jurou's protector god, the lord of the sea in the *Devil Hunter Isawa* universe.

Kamigawa – 'Spirit River'; one of two main rivers on Okinashima that wind through its mountainous terrain.

Kaminari Koshou – 'thundering breakdown'; Tannozume's *reiken* skill: a throwing attack with the sword.

Kanpai – 'dry glass'; a toast (in which a drink is taken as an expression of honor or goodwill). Similar to 'bottoms up!'

Kanshi – committing suicide as a form of protest against a master's unfair treatment or to force an official to reconsider a certain decision.

Kataki-uchi – 'institutionalized revenge'; the official vendetta that became a ritual with minutely organized norms and procedures. The warrior whose master had been, or considered himself, a victim of any type of offense, ranging from procedural slight to an attempted assassination or attempted murder, assumed obligation of avenging his master even it took years to accomplish. When complete, the head of the enemy was placed at the master's feet or if the master was dead, upon his tomb.

Kengo – 'master swordsman'; *Kengo* usually went on a *musha shugyo* (warrior pilgrimage) to improve their skills.

Kenno Sukiru (also Kensukiru Shutoku) – 'sword skill', 'sword skill mastery'; the art of mastering all there can be done with a sword.

Kensei – 'weapons master', 'master swordsman'; in *Kendo*, it means 'sword saint' and is a rank rarely given, usually to the most highly skilled. Can also mean 'legendary swordsman'.

Kenshi – 'extraordinary warrior', 'swordsman or swordswoman', 'swordsman', 'fencer'; a common title given to swordfighters that have decent skills and can survive campaigns in the Imperial Army. Also known as *kenkyaku*.

Kensho – 'seeing one's nature'; an initial insight or awakening, catching on to an idea to one's place in life. It takes further training to deepen this insight and learn to express it in daily life. It is the first step to achieving *daigo*.

Ki – 'life force'; psychic power that can be used to enhance fighting techniques and produce supernatural effects.

Kirinoumi – 'Sea of Mists'; the ocean that surrounds Midorishima.

Kirisute (also Kirisute Gomen) – 'authorization to cut and leave the body of the victim'; permission to kill someone of a lower class to protect one's honor for perceived affronts or compromised their honor.

Ko - friends getting together to take in the sights or visit temples.

Koku – equivalent to feeding a man for a year, equaling 5 bushels of rice, 1 *koku* could be farmed on 280 square yards of land (whereas an acre had 2000 *koku* and a 2 acres yielded 8000 *koku*). A *cho* (about 3 acres) yielded 9000 *koku* and was what most *samurai* aspired (if not vying to become *daimyo*). A decent *samurai* was paid a stipend of 100 *koku*.

Konbancha - 'good evening!'

Konpekino Soujin – 'azure twin blade'; the shadow warrior's *reiatsu* skill, used to drain the *ki* of the opponent in battle.

Konzetsu Suru - 'exterminate'; Tannozume's *reiken* skill used to instantly kill an opponent with a single stroke. Used as a desperation attack since it drains a lot of energy.

Koukonen – a dialect in the *Devil Hunter Isawa* universe spoken by people off Seibushima. It is difficult to understand by Midorishima mainlanders.

Kounnoyama – 'Mountain of Fortune'; a large mountain with impact craters in the sides surrounded by fog on the mainland, rumored to have *Amahagane* jealously guarded by vengeful ghosts embedded in the stones.

Koyakunin - castle guards

Kuru Ichigeki – 'black one shot'; Sanzuki's *reiatsu* skill used as a concussive force that pushes back his opponent.

Machi-bugyo – 'town magistrate'; A judge over a jurisdiction who is also a part of the supreme court of justice (*hyojosho*).

Machikata – town police officers.

Mahou – magic.

Mahoubujin - 'mystic warrior', 'battle mage'; a fighter who uses *ki*-based attacks.

Mahoukenshutu – 'magic detection'; Jurou's *reiatsu* skill used to detect *ki* of another person up to 60 feet away, also used to sense if a person is possessed by a negative entity.

Mahoutsukai – 'mystic practitioner ', 'magician', 'spell caster'; a person who uses *ki* for other means, usually by casting *jumon* (spells) or performing *saishiki* (rituals).

Majutsu – sorcery, arcane power, magical art.

Makai - the demonic world.

Manriki-gusari - a weighted whipping chain.

Meikai – The netherworld, one of the seven levels of the underworld where ghosts and other wandering souls reside before judgement. Also referred to as Oblivion in the *Devil Hunter Isawa* universe.

Meisou – 'meditation'; a *ki*-based attack.

Metsuke – 'censor' or 'inspector'; a post combining the functions of chief intelligence officer and chief of police.

Midorishima - 'Emerald Islands'; The country where the adventures of *Devil Hunter Isawa* takes place. It consists of seven islands: Kitajima (Northern Island), Seibushima (Western Island), Minamijima (South Island), Okinashima (Great Island), Hisuishima (Jade Island), Kurisutarujima (Crystal Island), and Onikisujima (Onyx Island).

Mizuokasuru – 'water animation'; Ohara Adia of Kawaguchi Temple's *reiatsu* skill for his mystic boomerang, controls Water.

Mochi - cake made by pounding rice into a mushy paste.

Mon - A unit of money which was silver coin with a square hole in the center that equaled rice for a month (around 67 *Zeni*).

Montsuki Haori – a long jacket worn over a kimono. Usually has one, three, or five family coat of arms on the back.

Mugen Houyou – 'illusion of vapor and shadow'; the shadow warrior's *reiatsu* skill, summoning two more fighters to help him in battle.

Munen-bara – committing suicide stemming from rage.

Nage-gama - a javelin with a short sickle-shaped blade set at right angles on one side and a long length of chain attached on the end.

Naginata – a pole arm with a curved blade-edge similar to a *katana*, used by foot soldiers. A longer variant used by calvary members is called a *nagamaki*.

Ningenkai - the world of humans.

Nodachi - a field sword with a blade length of 35 to 40 inches.

Noson – farming village.

Ochazuke - a rice soup crafted with a green tea base, flavored with various vegetables.

Odachi - a long heavy katana with a blade length between 32 to 38 inches.

Ogenki de – 'stay healthy'; a very polite way of saying 'see you later!'

Okaeri nasai - 'welcome home!', 'welcome back!'; a greeting in response to *Tadaima* (I'm home!)

Okane - money

Oni – a type of ogre that eats human flesh; their enemies are *samurai* who hunt them. They differ from *akuma*.

Onikage - 'ogre's shadow'; a *chokuto* (straight-edged broadsword) crafted of black steel with a navy scabbard, A *Takiletzachi* blade under the Shadow element, rumored to have a blood curse.

Onmyouji – a *Shinto* priest skilled in exorcising spirits, driving away demons, fortune telling, and communicating with the *kamisama* (deities) and *kami* (nature spirits). In the *Devil Hunter Isawa* universe, it is the highest rank an exorcist can obtain.

Onna-girai - 'woman haters'; a term for men with an aggressive distaste of women in all social contexts. Also a pun for men who preferred male sexual partners.

Osanojin – rain god in the *Devil Hunter Isawa* universe.

Oshiikaten – the creator goddess and goddess of death in the *Devil Hunter Isawa* universe.

Osorenoutorinozoku – 'remove fear'; Jurou's *reiatsu* skill used to remove negative energy temporarily from a person or object. It is unable to weaken demons.

Osoroshii Shiroe - 'horrid wilting'; Jurou's *meisou* skill under the Water element used to destroy targets to ash up to 30 feet away.

Otokodate - a society of fighters not belonging to the military class, composed of armed commoners with martial skill and sometimes *ronin* (masterless *samurai*) to defend against bandits and abusive *samurai*. At times hired out as *watarikashi* (mercenary fighters) during times of war.

Raida Shinden – 'violet lightning flash'; Chaka's *meisou* skill under the Thunder element used to summon chain lightning.

Reiatsu – 'spirit pressure'; *ki*-based skills used to enhance the senses or weapon attacks.

Reikai - the world of spirits.

Reiken – 'spirit sword'; a *ki*-based weapon attack, mainly used with bladed weapons.

Renkinjutsu - 'alchemy', a type of advanced applied *mahou* (magic) used by *onmyouji* in the *Devil Hunter Isawa* universe.

Ri - A unit of linear measure equal to 2.445 miles, similar to Li in the Chinese system of measurement, equal to 2.440 miles.

Ryo – a unit of gold currency, worth about 4,000 Mon.

Ryokutou – the old language spoken/written in the *Devil Hunter Isawa* universe. Everyone speaks a modern version of it, called *Teikoku* (Imperial).

Ryu – a sword school.

Ryunosurou – 'dragon's throw'; Sanzuki's *reiatsu* skill, used to throw the opponent with the sword. If done incorrectly he could break his blade!

Sai - a blunt truncheon with two curved forked prongs used by police officers, used for trapping and blocking attacks.

Saké – a generic term for alcohol, not necessarily for rice wine (see **Seishu**). When served hot, it is called *Atsukan*.

Samurai – 'one who serves'; a member of the warrior class, a warrior in *daimyo's* service. The status of *samurai* was somewhat fluid, and within the grasp of those born in the lesser classes-especially in times of war. Many *samurai* worked alongside the peasantry until they were called to service. All men who carried arms were considered *samurai* (of varying ranks) and made to live in the castle town of their *daimyo*.

Sarabada – 'farewell!'; a formal parting, similar to the polite *Sayonara* (Goodbye!).

Satori – 'enlightenment'; where *kensho* is a glimpse of seeing one's true nature, *satori* is a deeper spiritual experience when one fully realizes and accepts their nature and makes use of it in daily living. It is the second step to achieving *daigo*.

Satsugaisha – 'slayer'; a rank to a general exorcist who destroys demons, ghosts, and *oni*. Limited to using armaments crafted from *Amahagane*.

Seibatsu – 'conquest', 'subjugation', 'overcoming'; Chaka's *reiken* attack that can cut through stone.

Seijuku Shita - 'exit exam'; a certificate of completion from a *dojo*.

Sekisho - 'checkpoints', 'barriers'; Garrisons with special inspectors (see **Banshi**) were placed at blockades located along the main roads and byways linking the various domains (*han*), regulating travel. The central government restricted travel and all travelers had to submit paperwork in order to gain clearance (*sekisho-fuda*, see **Tegata**) at official checkpoints on the roads in and out of the capital city.

Senshi – an ordinary fighter, warrior, or solider.

Senshuken - 'champion'; A fighter skilled in combating demons by using *kamui*. Limited to using armaments crafted from *Amahagane*.

Sensuosen – 'sense taint'; Chaka's *reiatsu* skill used to detect demonic and other negative energy up to 60 feet away.

Sentouki - fighter

Shidzuki - moon goddess in the *Devil Hunter Isawa* universe.

Shihan – a respected official instructor of the sword.

Shihan-dai – 'senior instructor'; in a sword school, swordsmen skilled enough to teach the school's technique in place of the head of the school.

Shinan-jo – a training center for swordsmanship.

Shinatsuhiko – wind god in the *Devil Hunter Isawa* universe.

Shinigami – 'gods of death'; In the *Devil Hunter Isawa* universe, they are soul reapers, taking spirits to the underworld.

Shinkunikkou - sun god in the *Devil Hunter Isawa* universe, also Chaka's protector god.

Shinseina Jouki – 'holy steam'; Jurou's *meisou* skill under the Wind element used to banish lesser demons by destroying their energy and weaken the power of stronger devils.

Shinto – 'the way of the gods'; an earth-based religion honoring nature spirits and gods as well as family ancestors.

Shinzourippo – 'heart ripper'; Ikaruga's *reiatsu* skill, a super-stabbity technique. If done incorrectly, he could break his blade!

Shippoku - a boiled noodle dish made with *soba* (buckwheat noodles), with an assortment of vegetables, such as spinach, *shiitake* and *shimeji* (mushrooms), bamboo shoots, green onions, *kamaboko* (minced fish patty), and *satoimo* (Taro potato).

Shiratachi - a long heavy katana with a blade about 65 to 70 inches in length.

Shiro Morikage (also Morikage-jo) – 'Castle Morikage' (also 'Morikage Castle'); based in Minamijima, a castle complex owned by House Suzume in the township of Shinkunotani (Crimson Valley), rumored to harbor ghosts of former prisoners and demons in the dungeons.

Shisseki - 'rebuke'; Tannozume's *reiken* skill used to unleash fissures in the ground and throw the opponent with force.

Shitsurei Shimasu - 'please pardon the intrusion'; similar to 'excuse me' for anything from entering someone's office to walking out of a classroom.

Shochu – an alcoholic beverage distilled from barley, sweet potatoes, or rice, sometimes produced from other ingredients such as brown sugar, buckwheat or chestnut with 25 percent alcohol content. *Shochu* is weaker than whisky or vodka, but is stronger than wine and *seishu*.

Shugotenshi - 'guardian fairy'; lawful honorable guardian spirits.

Shukenten – blacksmith god in the *Devil Hunter Isawa* universe; uses a hammer crafted of *Amahagane*, the Star Crystal. When Shukenten fought the devil god Ototanashi, the hammer shattered, scattering the Star Crystal to earth.

Souhei – 'priest soldiers', 'armed priests'; commonly known as warrior monks, but could also be non-ordained warriors recruited by the temples. The warrior monks were the armed warriors that acted as military muscle for the temples. *Souhei* were used as an important political force as destabilizing elements against the courts, as their support was often sought after in times of war. In the *Devil Hunter Isawa* universe, they are mainly exorcists who fight on the field of battle against demonic armies.

Tachi - long katana with a blade about 24 to 30 inches in length.

Tachisaru - 'leave'; Tannozume's *reiken* skill, an enhanced piercing attack that can punch through the thickest armor.

Taichou - 'captain'; a rank in the Imperial Army, over *Fukutaichou* (Lieutenant) and under *Taishou* (General). Called *Bansho* by title.

Taijutsu - 'body technique' or 'body skill'; a blanket term for any combat skill, technique or martial art using body movements, mainly used in an empty-hand combat skill or system. Can include elements of *Jujutsu* (focus on grappling and striking), *Judo* (focus on throwing and grappling), *Aikido* (focus on throwing and joint locks) or *Karate* and *Kenpo* (focus on striking).

Taishou - 'general'; a rank in the Imperial Army, over *Taichou* (Captain).

Taiyouno Tsubasa – 'sun blade'; A *tsurugi* (straight dual-blade edged broad long sword) crafted of gold steel with a crimson scabbard. A *Takiletzachi* blade under the Fire element.

Takiletzachi – alchemic weaponry produced by the mysterious alchemist Inochi Massai named after Shukenten's Star Hammer. The weapons glow in mysterious blue light.

Tamashibai – 'soul bind'; Jurou's *meisou* skill under the Wind element used to destroy negative energy whether in a person or object, however it doesn't kill demons. It commonly manifests as silver darts or needles.

Tegata – travel passes issued by the government to allow travelers to pass through checkpoints (*sekisho*) along major byways.

Teikoku – the modern dialect spoken/written in the *Devil Hunter Isawa* universe. It is based off the old dialect, *Ryokutou* (Emeraline).

Tekkan - an iron truncheon used by police officers, resembles a blunt *wakizashi* (short sword) or *hachiwari* (helmet buster).

Tengoku Tejun - 'heavenly steps'; a silver-plated *choku segatana* (straight back sword with a broad curved edge, similar to a scimitar, falchion or machete) that has 9 rings embedded in the spine, gilded handle fashioned into a dragon's head and ivory talons on the hilt. A *Takiletzachi* blade under the Wind element.

Tonfa - a hardwood truncheon with a handle third of the way down the shaft used by police officers. It's used the same way as nightsticks by modern officers to beat unruly criminals. Also used as a defensive martial weapon.

Tsuihosuru – 'banish'; Chaka's *reiken* skill used to cut through a body with a single stroke.

Tsuji-kiri – 'to cut down at a corner'; anonymous killers, assassins or obsessed swordsmen who would attack people randomly on the street or challenge passing *samurai* to combat as a way of testing their own skill.

Tsukinoha – 'moon blade'; A *jintachi* (heavy long field sword) crafted of green steel with a black scabbard. A *Takiletzachi* blade under the Water element.

Uchibukuro - coin purse.

Ujikaiju - water monster.

Watarikashi – mercenary fighter.

Yaketsuku Yunahikari - 'searing light'; Chaka's *meisou* skill under the Thunder element used to destroy lesser demons, up to a radius of 100 feet .

Yari – a spear.

Yarikihei - spearman, lancer.

Yomi - the world of darkness, where the dead go to dwell and rot indefinitely. Once one has eaten at the hearth of *Yomi* it is impossible to return to the land of the living.

Youjinbou – a bodyguard.

Yugureyama – 'Twilight Mountains'; a range of purple-black mountains on the western side of Okinashima.

Yukinogami – snow goddess in the *Devil Hunter Isawa* universe.

Zeni – A unit of money; appears as a small round copper coin with a square hole in the middle. One *Zeni* equaled one meal of rice or one cup of tea.

Timekeeping

In the *Devil Hunter Isawa* universe, the inhabitants of Midorishima follow a 13 month solar-lunar-galactic calendar. Lunar calendars are focused solely on the cycle of the Moon, which has 2 main cycles: the synodical cycle, from new moon to new moon, is 29.5 days (what most lunar calendars are based on), and the sidereal cycle, the measure taken from where the moon appears at the same place in the sky, is 27.33 days.

A 13-Moon Calendar is the logical and natural way to count the 365-day year cycle. Instead of 12 months which are 28, 29, 30, or 31 days long, the year is instead measured into 13 months, each one an even 28 days. 13 moons of 28 days each gives 364 days - plus 1 'day out of time', a day of celebration and forgiveness, to acknowledge the passing year and welcome in the new year.

Unlike the 12-month calendar which corresponds to no natural cycles, the thirteen moon calendar is a 'solar-lunar calendar' because 365 days is the measure of the Earth going around the Sun (solar) and 28 days is the average measure of the Moon's synodic and sidereal cycles (lunar).

Every year cycle begins not as January 1st, but instead with July 26th as Day 1 of Moon 1. The correlate dates are fixed - for example, 'January 1st' will always correspond to the 20th day of the 6th moon. Hence when age is referred to, it is counted as 'summers', since the new year begins a month after the summer solstice.

Since neither of these cycles serve to accurately measure the 365-day solar cycle, (a year of 12 synodic revolutions is only 354 days) the number 28 is used as an average of the 2 main lunar cycles. 13 months of 28 days each = 364 days, plus 1 day out of time, = 365 days. In this way, the 13 'Moons' of the calendar do not begin in line with the new moon, as standard lunar calendars do, but the use of the 28-day cycle synchronizes with the moon's revolutions.

In addition to a 13-month calendar, time in the *Devil Hunter Isawa* universe follows a temporal hour system - six daytime units from local sunrise to local sunset, and six night time units from sunset to sunrise - giving an uneven time schedule. As such, time varied with the seasons with the daylight hours longer in summer and shorter in winter, while the opposite at night.

The six hours were numbered from 9 to 4, which counted backwards from noon until midnight. The hour numbers 1 through 3 were not used for religious reasons, because these numbers of strokes were used by the local priests to call to prayer. The count ran backwards because the burning of incense used to count down the time. Dawn and dusk were therefore both marked as the sixth hour in the timekeeping system.

In addition to the numbered temporal hours, each hour was assigned a sign from the zodiac. Starting at dawn, the six daytime hours were:

6. HARE (4.45a)

5. DRAGON

4. SERPENT

9. HORSE (noon)

8. RAM (3p)

7. MONKEY

From dusk, the six nighttime hours were:

6. SPARROW (6.30p)

5. DOG

4. BOAR

9. TORTOISE (midnight)

8. OX (2a)

7. TIGER

www.ingramcontent.com/pod-product-compliance
Lightning Source LLC
Chambersburg PA
CBHW070758180626
46818CB00001B/6